"Bet you'd like some lemonade," he said. "It's really good. I made it myself."

She watched him as he placed the tray on a small table.

He took a tissue from the box and dabbed at her tears. Black streaks came away.

She cringed when he took the knife from the table. "Don't worry," he said. "I ain't gonna hurt you none. Just wanna make a little hole in the tape so you can have some lemonade. That's all. Okay?"

She nodded.

He placed his hand behind her head to steady it and raised the point of the knife to the duct tape covering her mouth, piercing it just slightly. "Okay?"

She nodded again.

He put the knife away and poured the glasses of lemonade, putting a straw in hers. He poked the straw through the hole in the tape, wiggling it around until she could drink.

"More?"

She shook her head.

He pulled the straw from her mouth and took the glass away. He was smiling when he turned back to her. "Don't worry," he said, "I ain't gonna hurt you none if you're nice."

She wanted to scream, but she could only moan helplessly and shake her head as he reached for her . . .

GARY AMO

COME DARKNESS

PINNACLE BOOKS
WINDSOR PUBLISHING CORP.

For Joan,
who has read every word—good and bad.

PINNACLE BOOKS are published by

Windsor Publishing Corp.
475 Park Avenue South
New York, NY 10016

First Printing: November, 1993

Printed in the United States of America

Prologue

After the argument, Billie Rae Scott danced with the big truck driver in the smoke-filled juke joint, rubbing her breasts against his chest as she chewed on his ear. "Hank, baby," she whispered. She called almost everyone Hank when she was drinking. Hank had been the second of her three husbands. Worthless pricks, all of 'em. But at least Hank loved her before the big nigger cut him so bad that he bled to death in the East Texas jailhouse. Hank hated niggers. It musta pissed him off something bad to let one kill him like that. Billie Rae liked to think Hank died whispering her name. Probably he said something like, *Oh, fuck*. Hank always was a little slow figuring things out.

It was godawful hot in the juke joint. Ceiling fans beat futilely at the muggy air, while the third-rate local trio competed with shouted conversations and drunken arguments, wailing one song after another, alternating between George Strait and Garth Brooks and Willie Nelson, even throwing in an old Hank Williams song on occasion.

The truck driver had his hands on her ass now, pulling her close to him, almost lifting her off the floor. She rubbed against the bulge in his faded jeans. He groaned. "Oh, baby, let's you and me go out to my truck."

"I ain't doing it in no truck. I'm a lady, Hank, and this lady wants a shot and another beer." Billie Rae broke away and pushed through the crowded dance floor and back to the booth, knowing old Hank would follow, helplessly. They always did. Wiggle a pretty little ass at a man and he lost all his sense. And Billie Rae knew all about that. She had been wiggling her ass since she was thirteen and in the eighth grade for the second or third time. They always sniffed right along behind.

Except for Drew.

The waitress waved acknowledgment as Billie held up her empty beer bottle. The truck driver slipped into the booth, pinning her in the corner, kissing her while he pawed at her breasts. Billie responded, feeling the tingle spread through her nipples. God *damn,* they were sensitive, always getting her in trouble.

"Can I interrupt y'all long enough to get paid for these drinks?" the waitress asked.

"Aw, shit, honey," the truck driver drawled. "Cain't you see we're busy."

"Me too, hon—me too." She grinned at Billie. "Watch yourself with this one. Thinks he's the only white boy around with a ten-inch dick. Or so he says, anyway."

"I swear, Linda, you're gonna be begging for it again one of these days soon." He fumbled for a bill and dropped it on the wet tray.

"Not me, hon, but thanks. Y'all have fun now, hear?"

Billie tossed the shot back, grimacing before tilting the beer bottle to drink thirstily. "God, it's hot in here."

"Ain't too hot for a little loving. Where you want to go?"

"No place right now. Plenty of time."

"I'm ready right now. Let's get out of here."

"No." Billie drank the rest of the beer and put it down with a crash. "Let me out."

"Aw, honey, don't be like that. I was just kidding around with Linda. Don't mean nothing. Where you going now?"

"Find my boyfriend." Drew was nice. She always remembered his name, even after six or eight bottles of beer, even when she was mad at him.

"You prick-teasing bitch."

"Take your fucking hands off me." The nickel-plated revolver was shiny in her hand, reflecting the swirling multicolored lights flashing through the bar.

"Aw, shit," he complained, sliding backward out of the booth.

Billie kept the gun on him until she was standing. Then she put it back in her purse. "Don't fuck with me."

"Ain't worth it. You ain't the only woman in this place."

"That's right. You just keep remembering that and I won't have to shoot your dick off." Billie turned and pushed her way to the door.

Outside, Billy Rae fumbled in her purse, bringing out a crumpled cigarette package. She lit the cigarette clumsily and stood in the parking lot, slapping at mosquitoes and trying to chase the sudden dizziness away. Shouldn't had that last shot, she thought. The cigarette tasted awful. She let it drop to the ground and stumbled coming down the steps of the juke joint. Oh, shit, I'm gonna pass out. Billie Rae made it to her car and leaned against it, trying to catch a tepid breeze off the river, anything to cool her sweaty face, make the nausea go away.

The hot Mississippi night was filled with noise, the screech of crickets and cicadas, the mournful hoot of an owl, a car passing by on the road to the river, the din of the music from the bar, cries and laughter.

Drew, honey, where are you?

He came out of the shadows.

Billie Rae stepped forward, swaying, waiting for him to take her in his arms. "Drew, honey, I knew you'd wait." He came closer. Billie squinted drunkenly. "You're not Drew. Where's Drew?"

The stranger hit her and the night went silent for Billie Rae Scott.

He didn't know it would be so hard to tie the limp and unconscious woman to the frame used to stretch and dry deerskins. He could not hold her dead weight high enough to secure the rope to the corner of the wooden square. Finally he dumped her body on the ground and tied her ankles tightly together. That way, if she regained consciousness before he was ready, she wouldn't be able to run. He smiled, pleased with his plan.

He gently pushed the frame over, lowering it to the ground over the woman. Now he was able to tie the ropes around her wrists and pull them above her head, securing each to a corner of the wooden frame.

He grunted as he lifted the frame again and pushed. Her body slumped against him and he nearly dropped everything. But he finally walked the frame high enough to set it on its supports again. She groaned as her arms took the weight of her body, but she did not wake up.

He stepped back to admire the woman. He thought she looked real pretty hanging there in the clearing outside the empty hunting cabin. When she opened those big round eyes she would look just like a doe. The moon was up now and he could see her features clearly, even imagine the lips that were hidden by the duct tape plastered across her mouth. It was too bad he wouldn't be able to hear her cries when it was time. She groaned again. It was time to finish, before she woke up.

He went back to work, untying the knot that fastened her ankles together. He unwound the rope and used it to stretch her legs apart, tying each ankle to the bottom corners of the frame. She wasn't wearing any stockings. He put his hand beneath her dress, feeling the smooth softness of her thighs and the dampness between her legs. Oh, it was so wonderful.

He took the knife and cut the dress away, ripping at the reluctant cloth. The panties were easier, but when he slipped the point of the knife between the cups of her brassiere, he nicked her flesh, drawing blood. He thought he was going to faint when the white breasts burst from their covering. It had been so long since he'd seen a woman's breasts, except for his sister's when he'd peeked through her bedroom window to watch her undress, and in the magazines and videos he kept hidden away. It wasn't the same.

He groaned as he suckled one nipple and then the other. He put his face between the woman's breasts and tasted the specks of blood from the little cut. He hadn't meant to cut her, not yet. He hoped it wouldn't spoil the signature.

He had to be careful now, though. He couldn't let this whorish daughter of Satan tempt him. He had to save himself for the other one, the woman he loved. She would be here soon now, and it would be different then. She would love him the way he loved her. He reached out and touched the soft breasts again, pretending they belonged to another.

Billie Rae regained consciousness slowly. Her arms ached. Her jaw was sore where Drew had hit her. Why? No . . . not Drew. Someone else . . . a stranger. Her nipples were swollen, responding to caresses. Not caresses—bites. Someone was biting her nipples. She opened her eyes and tried to scream, but the scream wouldn't come.

Billie tossed her head frantically from side to side, seeing the ropes that dug painfully into her wrists. Her struggles made the wooden frame shudder.

He looked up at her and smiled.

Oh, God, no, Billie pleaded silently.

He smiled again.

No!

Part I

One

Kathryn Anne Gallagher waited in her office for ten o'clock and the second day of the trial, remembering the argument of the night before. Normally, Kate would already have gone down to the courtroom, to ensure her witnesses were present and prepared, to drink coffee and spend a few minutes bantering with the bailiffs, the clerk, and the other attorneys. That was what conscientious deputy district attorneys for the County of Los Angeles did, and Kate was a conscientious DDA, one of the best, a rising star and marked for continued promotion. She glanced down at the open file on her desk, but she could not concentrate on it. She expected to rest the People's case this morning, or at least, shortly after lunch, but she could not focus on the case. Not this morning . . . not yet.

"Damn," she said for the seventh or eighth time since arriving at her office.

Harry had presented her with a florist's box containing a single long-stemmed rose and a small blue velvet box. The box embraced a beautiful engagement ring. Kate looked up, shocked, as she heard him say, "Kate, I love you. Will you marry me?"

The words still rang in her ears. Stunned, Kate stammered, refused. "I can't, Harry. Someday, perhaps, but not now. I'm not ready for marriage again yet."

They had argued then.

God damn it, how can you argue over a proposal? Kate asked herself, replaying the argument in her mind—again. You love him, don't you? Yes, Kate answered her own question—at least, I think I do.

Kate cried. Harry argued convincingly. Kate argued back, fuming for a time, crying a second time. Chastened, Harry asked, Why? You love me, don't you? he said, knowing the answer.

Finally, they fell into each other's arms and made love on the living room floor, but it wasn't the same as before. Kate faked her pleasure, positive that he had not suspected.

But as beautiful as it was, she wouldn't accept the ring.

Kate glanced at her watch. It was time. She gathered her papers and files and started for the courtroom, trying to forget Harry and the argument for the moment. It was time to send one of the bad guys to jail.

Everyone called him Dr. Death.

He slipped into the courtroom and sat in the front row to watch impassively as Kate questioned the older woman sitting on the witness stand.

Kate glanced at him briefly, acknowledging his presence. He was the only person in the spectator area behind the rail. She turned back to her witness and forgot he was there.

"Mrs. Harris," Kate said, "on the day in question, what time did you leave the shopping center?"

"It was shortly after lunch," Mrs. Harris answered nervously, twisting the strap of her purse around her fingers, "about one-thirty. I remember because Virginia had an appointment at one, so we had to cut our lunch short."

"Who is Virginia?" Kate asked, smiling reassuringly at her witness.

"Virginia Powers. We have lunch every week."

"But she was not with you at the time."

"No. I stopped to browse through a couple of stores. I didn't take long—not more than thirty minutes. So it was right about one-thirty when I started back to my car."

"And where was your car located?"

"Near the supermarket."

"Tell us what happened as you approached your car."

"I was walking toward it when a small car pulled up and stopped. A young man leaned out the window and asked if I could tell him how to get to Pacific Coast Highway. I started to tell him, he seemed so polite . . ."

"What happened then?"

"He grabbed my purse and started to drive off."

"Did you resist?"

"I screamed. I was so shocked."

"Did you hold on to the purse?"

"Yes. He dragged me until I finally let go."

"He used his car to drag you until you finally released the purse?"

"Objection," the public defender cried, "leading the witness."

"I'll rephrase the question, Your Honor," Kate said.

"That's exactly what happened," Mrs. Harris said. "He used his car to drag me along the pavement until I had to let go."

Kate shrugged, smiling helplessly at the jury while the public defender shook his head angrily. In the courtroom, Kate Gallagher was a striking woman, calm and professional as she addressed juries in an opening or closing statement, took prosecution witnesses deftly through their testimony, or dispelled reasonable doubts when she cross-examined defense witnesses. Today she wore a trim dark blue skirt and matching jacket with a red blouse. A white silk scarf was tied around her neck. For the last year, Kate had let her dark hair grow out for Harry, and now it flowed to her shoulders and swirled around her head when she turned quickly to make a point to judge, jury, or witness.

Concentrate, God damn it.

"Would you be able to identify the man who took your purse?"

"Yes."

"Is he in the courtroom today?"

"Yes. He's sitting right there. He's the one wearing the brown sport jacket." Mrs. Harris pointed to the defendant seated next to his young attorney.

"I have no further questions." Kate went to the prosecutor's table, smiling at Dr. Death before she sat down.

Kate didn't mind the presence of the head deputy district attorney. She was one of the few deputy DAs in the South Bay office who wasn't intimidated by Dr. Death. But she always felt a chill in his presence. Tall, lanky, even gaunt, he resembled a dark, cadaverous Ichabod Crane as he went from courtroom to courtroom, observing his attorneys in action as they conducted preliminary hearings, argued bail hearings, prosecuted the cases where the bad guys wanted to jerk the system around and wouldn't take the easy way out and cop a plea to save everyone the time and energy and money.

Like today. The perp was a small-time loser with a rap sheet that went on for pages, a dismal record of arrests, dismissals, and a couple of convictions. He was classed as a career criminal—Kate's assignment in the South Bay branch—but he was a pathetic excuse for a career criminal. Kate shook her head as she listened to the public defender attempt to shake Mrs. Harris's identification, but Mrs. Harris persisted stolidly. Your client is going away, Kate thought. Kate wanted to send him to hard time at the relatively new high-security prison at Pelican Bay in the furthest reaches of Northern California. Let him languish in the Security Housing Unit there. The people who served their time in SHU got out and spread the word on the streets.

"Hey, man," they said, "you don't want to go to Pelican Bay, man. No fucking way."

They said there were only three ways to get out of Pelican Bay's SHU—parole, die, or debrief. But there was little likelihood of parole at Pelican Bay. Once there, you served hard time to the very last day of your sentence. That left death or debriefing, and if you debriefed—snitched on everyone you knew—you might die anyway when you were returned to a mainline correctional unit. If you didn't snitch, you sat in a silent never-ending solitary confinement until the mind threatened to snap. It was hard time all the way.

Kate glanced at the smirking defendant and didn't care if he went to Pelican Bay. He deserved it, she told herself. It'll stop him from preying on other helpless women like Mrs. Harris. Hurting them. He should have let his attorney plead. There was no way he was going to beat the case, not with a positive ID from three of his victims. A few years in Pelican Bay will teach him the error of his ways.

Christ, I've gotten hard, Kate told herself, turning back to the cross examination. That's what happens when you spend ten, twelve, fifteen hours a day in the furtherance of justice.

The public defender gave up finally, unable to cast doubt in the jury's mind about the victim's identification of his client.

"We'll take a short recess before calling your next witness, Mrs. Gallagher."

Kate nodded in agreement and turned to Dr. Death, who pushed through the rail nodding politely at the judge and the bailiff.

Dr. Death—his real name was Philip Moore—came by the nickname not because of his resemblance to a corpse, although that helped, but rather because of his uncanny ability to obtain convictions in cases involving special circumstances, cases in which there were only two possible penalties—life in prison without the possibility of parole, or death. Kate knew of at least fourteen men and one woman who awaited their dates with the gas chamber because of Moore's efforts. That was the reason for the chills each time Kate saw Dr. Death. Fifteen people sat on death row, waiting for their death warrants to be signed because of Dr. Death's efforts. Kate had never prosecuted a death penalty case. She had no qualms about sending criminals to jail, but she didn't know if she could harden herself enough to live with the thought that she had sent someone to the gas chamber.

Kate had followed Dr. Death's prosecution of the woman when she was still working in the Mainline downtown at the Criminal Courts Building. At the time Moore sent Regina Wilcox to death row, she was still only nineteen, pretty and virginal in appearance. Betting odds in the office had been heavily against Moore's obtaining the death penalty for Regina, especially when she wept before judge and jury, pleading for mercy, begging to be forgiven for the two brutal murders. Office wags had predicted life without parole for Regina Wilcox during the penalty phase of the trial, but Dr. Death had immunized the jurors too well and they'd returned the death penalty without hesitation.

"How'd I do, boss?" Kate asked.

"You were fine, Kate, but that's not why I'm here." He hesitated. "Your mother called."

The smile froze on her face. "What's wrong?" she asked, suddenly frightened. "Who died?" That was the only reason her mother would call her at work—if someone in the family had died.

"I'm sorry. I'm clumsy at this," Moore said apologetically. "It's nothing like that."

"What, then?"

"Your mother was very upset. It seems your brother has been arrested for murder."

"What?" Kate was incredulous. "Drew?"

Moore nodded. "Let's go into the judge's chambers. You

can call home from there. Margie's calling for flight schedules."

"Thank you," Kate said automatically. Her mind was numb.

The public defender watched them going to chambers and started to follow. Dr. Death turned and stared him down. "This is personal business," he said coldly, "nothing to do with your client."

"How do I know that?"

"Don't fuck with me, little man."

"Jesus Christ," the public defender said, but he sat down again next to his client.

The line was busy. God damn it. Kate suddenly wanted a cigarette. She didn't smoke anymore, but crisis always brought on that old craving. It had happened each time her former husband had announced he was having another affair. It came over her during the divorce, when she was studying for final exams in college and law school and taking her bar exams in California and again in Mississippi, just in case she ever wanted to go home again, or the night before a big closing argument, or when one of the girls was sick.

There was a framed photograph of the judge and his family on the desk, all smiling for the camera. He curled his arm around his wife's shoulders protectively. Two teenaged children—boy and girl—grinned self-consciously. They were a solid family, safe, without cares and worries that day, immune from the problems of society.

Twenty-four hours ago, Kate's own life had been untroubled, until the argument with Harry, until Dr. Death approached her.

Kate tried her mother's number again.

Still busy.

She heard Moore and the judge talking softly outside.

Murder? It couldn't be. Not her older brother. There was some mistake; there had to be a mistake. Drew was kind and gentle. He wasn't a killer.

The telephone in her mother's living room rang finally.

"Mama?"

"Oh, honey, thank God you called."

"Mama, what's happened?"

"Drew's in jail."

"I know that, Mama. Tell me what happened."

"It was that woman. I don't want to speak ill of the dead, but I knew that woman was trouble the first time Drew brought her home. Oh, Lord, honey . . ."

"Mama," Kate interrupted harshly. "What woman? What happened?"

"Don't yell at me, Kathryn Anne, I'm so upset."

Kate sighed. "I'm sorry, Mama, but please, tell me what's going on."

"Some boys found her out to Drew's hunting cabin. Dead. Cut up something awful. They say Drew done it."

"Who, Mama? Who's dead?"

"That Billie Rae Scott. I told Drew she was trouble from the very first I laid eyes on her. White trash from East Texas. I told Drew that." She started crying.

"Mama, you've got to calm down. Tell me what happened."

"I don't know. Drew wouldn't see me. Sent a guard out to say you was the only person he would talk to. You've got to come home, Kate—you've just got to. I don't know what to do. I told him she was trouble, but he wouldn't listen. You know how he is sometimes."

Oh, yes, Kate thought. I know just how he is, and he wouldn't kill anyone, especially not a girlfriend, not someone he cared about. "Tell him not to talk to anyone until I get there. If he won't see you, use a guard to send him the message."

"All right, honey, I'll do that. When will you be here?"

"I don't know," Kate replied. "Someone's checking flight schedules for me right now. I'll let you know."

"All right, honey."

"Don't worry, Mama. This is all some kind of big mistake. Everything will work out."

"Oh, praise the Lord, honey. I just knew you'd know what to do."

"Bye, Mama, I'll talk to you later, as soon as I have a reservation."

Kate stared at the telephone. There was no use in disturbing her mother further, plaguing her with questions she couldn't answer. But a hundred questions raced through Kate's prosecutor's mind—evidence, motive, opportunity, alibi. Who was Billie Rae Scott? Who'd killed her? Why? How? Where was Drew? Why didn't he have an alibi? Jesus. Not Drew. It couldn't be true.

In the anteroom, Moore and the judge were still talking in low tones, unwilling to disturb her privacy. Jesus, they must wonder what kind of family I've got. She got up and joined them. "He didn't do it," she announced. "I know he wouldn't do something like that."

"Of course not, Kate," Moore said. He put his arm around her shoulder. "Anything you need, Kate . . ."

"Thanks, Phil. I have to go home."

"Naturally. Let's go see what Margie has from the airlines."

"I'll grant a continuance, of course, Kate," the judge said.

"That won't be necessary," Moore said. "I'll finish the case. Kate can give me her notes."

"The public defender will cry foul."

"From what I've seen, that's about the only defense he has for the perp."

"Thanks, Phil, Your Honor." Kate paused. "God, there's so much to do."

"Get it done, Kate."

* * *

There was a flight out of Los Angeles International Airport that night to New York with an intermediate stop in St. Louis. With a two-hour layover there, Kate could be on an early flight to Memphis, rent a car, and be home by nine-thirty or ten. There were late afternoon flights that would get her to the Delta that night, but there was so much to do before leaving—brief Phil on everything that was pending for the next few days, go home and pack, call Christopher and make arrangements for him to take Melissa for a few days. Thank God, Allison was in her first year at UCLA and living in a dorm, reading, studying, working too hard, as usual. It was one less child to worry about.

Kate gave Margie a credit card and asked her to make the reservation for the late flight. There was nothing to be gained by getting home in the middle of the night, nothing she could do to reassure her mother until she knew the facts of the case against Drew. *Christ, what can I do even then? Oh, Drew, what did you get into?*

Kate drove home, wheeling the little convertible through the clogged streets as the remnants of Southern California's defense and aerospace industry let out for the day. No matter how many people were laid off because of government cutbacks, the traffic never seemed to get any better, the air remained dirty, and there was a seething tension in the hot air, a threat of random street violence always lurking just beneath the surface, simmering, waiting to erupt. The only growth industry in Southern California seemed to be the mushrooming numbers of the homeless who stood holding crudely lettered cardboard signs on too many street corners. HOMELESS. WILL WORK FOR FOOD. Or VIETNAM VET—WILL WORK. DO ANYTHING. GOD BLESS! Like millions of others in the City of Angels,

Kate shut her eyes to the pain and wondered what had happened. How had they managed to destroy paradise? And now this. Drew, Drew, Drew. What happened? God damn it, there were too many questions and too few answers.

Kate pulled the car into the garage, put the top up, swung the heavy briefcase from the passenger seat, pulled the garage door down, and locked it.

The house was quiet, lonely. Mycroft crept out of his latest hiding place to greet her, rubbing against her legs, purring. Kate leaned over and scratched his ears for a moment. Then she went to the telephone.

"Christopher, it's Kate." She was nervous with him, as usual. Her life was still intertwined with his, even after all these years. And there were years to go yet until both girls finished college. That was the agreement, the price he paid for all his affairs, was still paying. "I have to go to Mississippi. Will you take Melissa for a few days?"

"What's wrong, Kate? Is everyone all right?" That was so typical of Chris. He still cared about her family. Kate was the only one he couldn't get along with. I never should have married him, Kate thought for the thousandth, the millionth time.

"Drew's been arrested for murder."

"What? I don't believe it. What happened?"

"I don't know what happened yet," Kate said. That would become her refrain for the afternoon.

She called Harry next. "I don't know what happened," she replied again.

"I'll be right over," he said.

She reached Allison in her dorm at UCLA. "I don't know," she repeated, sighing.

Harry—dear, sweet, Harry—was there before Melissa got home from summer school. She was grateful for his embrace and his silence. Why won't you marry him?

When Melissa bounced through the door, Kate repeated the familiar phrase, "I don't know. I'll give you a call as soon as

I know what really happened. Meanwhile, just stay with your dad and make sure Mycroft gets fed." The cat was hunched in the middle of her suitcase, watching the activity with interest. Anytime a suitcase came out, Mycroft perched in it, afraid he was going to be left behind. Kate shooed him out for the third time.

"Don't worry, Mom, you'll get Uncle Drew off," Melissa said, before disappearing into her room to pack up the latest hard rock CDs for the stay at her father's home. "You're a great lawyer."

"That's what Allison said, too."

"The girls are right," Harry replied. "You *are* a great lawyer."

"I'm a prosecutor, for God's sake, not a defense attorney. Beside, I can't defend Drew. It wouldn't be right."

"Why not?"

"He's my brother, for one thing. I wouldn't be objective. I'm not up on Mississippi criminal law, for another thing. I only took the bar down there in case I ever wanted to go home."

"He couldn't get a better lawyer."

"Oh, hell, I don't know. I just can't do it. I don't know what to do except go home and see how I can help."

"What time's your flight?"

"Eleven."

"Finish packing and then try and take a nap. You've got plenty of time. I'll take you to the airport."

"I can take the shuttle. There's no need for you to take me."

"I'd like to."

Kate smiled wearily. "Thanks. I'd like that. I'm sorry I snapped at you."

Harry shrugged. "You didn't snap. This has got to be more than a little upsetting."

Kate shook her head. "I just can't believe it. I see families of criminals every day. I suppose none of them believes that a relative of theirs can do anything wrong. None of them wants to believe it, either."

"You're going to get down there and find out this is just some big mistake."

"God, I hope so."

"You'll see."

Kate tried to smile at Harry with an assurance she didn't feel. Something bad is happening, Kate thought. Something very bad is happening.

Two

For Kathryn Anne Gallagher, traveling was something reserved for melancholy occasions—the sorrow of funerals, severe illnesses of distant relatives, departures of loved ones to a distant place. Even modern airports always reminded her of tears, cheap suitcases, and grease-stained paper bags filled with sandwiches for a journey. For Kate, the gleaming terminal at LAX was just as lonely and mournful as the bus stations of her youth in Mississippi when relatives had gathered at the old Greyhound or Continental depots to send an uncle or cousin or brother off to Detroit to seek work in the automobile plants and escape from the mind-numbing poverty of the Delta. She remembered hiding behind her mother as the men talked quietly among themselves and the women clung to them, listening to the hopeful and optimistic conversations and the promises to send money orders home as soon as a job was found on the assembly lines. She remembered the smell of cheap aftershave lotion and the rough scratch of their whiskers as they lifted her up for a goodbye kiss. She remembered the sadness that lingered for days after one of the solemn leave-takings.

"It's funny," Kate said.

"What is?" Harry asked. He reached across the cocktail table and took her hand.

"I like to travel, but I always find it so depressing. When I was a little girl, we could hear the train whistles late at night. I wanted to go places, but . . ." Her voice trailed off as she watched a young Marine wander slowly down the long empty aisle between departure gates. A single silver medal gleamed on the breast of the forest-green blouse. His hair had barely begun to grow out again after release from boot camp. Kate turned back to Harry and smiled weakly. "And now this. There's never anything but trouble at the end of the line."

The compartment was half-empty and Kate was thankful to be alone in her row of seats with no one to intrude upon her gloomy thoughts.

The aircraft roared into the night sky over the Pacific before turning back to the continent in a steep, climbing turn. Kate looked down at the glittering metropolis. Headlights flowed along the freeways like glowing waters rushing swiftly on their journey to the sea. Kate wondered which tiny pinprick of light belonged to Harry's car. He had held her at the gate in a tight embrace, kissing her passionately, releasing her only at the last moment to present her boarding pass to the stewardess. It was as though he wanted to impart his strength to her. Now the smell of his cologne lingered in her nostrils, tantalizing her with memories of the evening after Melissa had left for her father's home.

They had gone to bed then only to nap for an hour, carefully setting the alarm although Kate felt too keyed up to sleep. And when he put his hand on her breast as he always did before they slept, Kate turned to him, feeling a swell of desire as they kissed, suddenly wanting him desperately. She arched her back as he slipped the thin straps of her nightgown from her shoulders, lifting her naked breasts to him, moaning softly as he teased her nipples with soft kisses. He loved her breasts and she offered them willingly, allowing him all the time he might want for his caresses, his kisses—and her pleasure. But tonight, there was no waiting. Impatient for release from the day's tension and family worries, Kate rolled on top of him and took him deep into her, riding his body until he cried out and pulled her down, kissing her frantically while she crushed her breasts against his chest until they both screamed at their abrupt explosions.

Afterward, they held each other tightly, but the agony of learning of her brother's arrest had not disappeared. The pain remained, along with new feelings of guilt. And I acted like such a whore, too, she thought. Drew's in jail, and I'm playing bimbo.

Harry had masked his disappointment at her refusal of marriage, pretended that nothing had happened, and sought only to please her, to offer reassurance on her brother's plight. You're such a bitch. Marry the man. He loves you.

"Would you like something to drink?" a smiling flight attendant asked.

The young man startled Kate. The drink cart was at the front of the cabin. She blushed. She had been wishing Harry was still inside her and her nipples were pressing against her brassiere. Was the attendant staring at her breasts? Could he see her nipples standing out? She pulled her jacket tight.

"Are you cold, ma'am?" he asked. "I could get you a blanket."

"No, maybe later," Kate said, flustered. "I'd like a glass of chardonnay, though." She'd already had one glass at the airport with Harry. If sex hadn't worked, perhaps alcohol would. A good Southern drink. "No, I'd like bourbon on the rocks," Kate said. "A double."

When he returned with her drink, the attendant brought a blanket, placing it on the empty seat beside her. "Just in case you'd like it," he said.

"Thanks."

She leaned her head against the cold pane of the window

and sipped the bourbon. It tasted harsh on her tongue. She didn't drink much, a glass of wine with Harry, a drink or two at an office gathering or a party, more during her brief abortive affair with Rainey. Christ, I'm thinking of sex a lot. How did Rainey get into this? At least I like sex again. Until last night. But tonight was all right again. Rainey did that. We were good for each other at the time. An impotent cop and a frigid deputy district attorney. We helped each other back.

Conrad Rainey, a Los Angeles Police Department detective, now retired. They had met when he was one of the investigating officers on a brutal rape case Kate prosecuted two years ago.

Poor Valerie Rush. After taking turns with her, the assailants had left her for dead. But Valerie didn't die. Her life was destroyed, but she didn't die. The case dragged on for months with the perps jerking the system around, brutalizing Valerie more and more as she was forced to confront them in court during the prelim and again when the case finally came to trial.

There had been a mistrial when a single woman juror had refused to believe that Valerie had not brought it on herself. But the bad guys were in jail now. They were going to be there for a long time. On her desk in the office, Kate had a date written down on a piece of paper. She would carry it with her each time she was transferred. January 6, 2005—that was the date Nelson and Thompson would have their first parole hearing. Kate planned to be there. She planned to keep them in jail the rest of their lives.

We were all their victims. Valerie would never get over it. Her memories of that terrible night when Nelson and Thompson had so callously shattered her life would never leave her. They were burned into Valerie's soul.

But Valerie wasn't the only victim. In the end, they got all of us—me, Rainey, his partner Sandie Harrison, even George Devers. George, a legend in the criminal justice system, had defended Nelson until his client had attacked Kate in the deserted parking lot one night shortly before the trial. Devers had come to her then and said he was disqualifying himself from Nelson's defense. "I'd rather prosecute the bastard," he told her.

Even Harry had been victimized when Kate had broken off their relationship, traumatized by too many years of prosecuting sexual offenses, unable to stand his touch any longer. It had taken months before she could see him again.

In between, there had been Rainey. They had come together as two tormented individuals who'd slowly found solace and comfort, each in the arms of the other.

The airplane was over the desert now, a vast black emptiness below that was broken by only an occasional light, stretching to the ends of the world.

The bourbon made her lightheaded. She put the rest of the drink aside and spread the blanket around her, burrowing beneath its warmth, a cocoon within a cocoon, hurtling through the cold night, wondering what to expect when she got home. She was flying into the unknown.

Kate slept fitfully, restlessly, disturbed by the dreams. "Kathyrn Anne. Where are you? Kathryn Anne! Where are you? If you don't come home right now, I'll give you away to the Voodoo Lady, you hear?" She hid in the closet. The Voodoo Lady was a witch. She stuck pins in naughty little girls and they got sick and died. But the mean witch couldn't find her in the closet. It was dark there. Safe.

"The Voodoo Lady can see in the dark, Kathryn Anne. The Voodoo Lady can always find a little girl who's been bad."

I'm good, she pleaded. I'm always good.

But she wasn't. She didn't like Sunday school. They made you memorize verses from the Bible: *and God saw that the wickedness of man was great in the earth and that every imagination of the thoughts of his heart was only evil continually and it repented the Lord that He had made man on the earth and it grieved Him at His heart and the Lord said I will destroy man whom I have created from the face of the earth both man and beast and the creeping things and the fowls of the air for it repenteth me that I have made them . . .*

Lacey memorized more verses than any of them, but she cheated and lied and didn't *really* memorize any of the verses, but they gave her the yellow ribbon anyway, even though it was all lies. Lacey's a liar Lacey's a liar Lacey's a liar yellow ribbon liar yellow ribbon liar . . .

Voodoo Lady go away, come again some other day, they chanted.

The old witch cackled through toothless gums as she approached with the tiny pin sharp and shining and gleaming in the wrinkled, drooping flesh of her hand. The pin grew longer. Kate watched as the Voodoo Lady plunged the pin deep into her brother's heart. Kate wanted to scream, flee, but the evil held her motionless. The crone was coming to her now with pins in both hands growing longer and longer. The bile rose in Kate's throat as the pins pressed against her eyes.

Jesus! Save me! I'll be good!

The cackle grew louder, filling Kate's ears with a terrible din.

I didn't let him touch me. I didn't. I didn't!

The pins pierced deep into her eyes.

Kate awakened with a start, sweating and disoriented, wondering where she was. The cabin was dark. Behind her somewhere, two of the flight attendants laughed. A few rows away, a fat man snored loudly. Kate threw off the suffocating blanket. The bourbon coated her tongue and mouth with a bad taste.

Everything had been fine until Dr. Death had walked into the courtroom that morning. That's not true. It wasn't fine, but it was bearable, at least. Things would have worked out with Harry. But this? Oh, Drew, what happened?

Like millions of other people, Kate read her horoscope

each morning, a brief legacy from the time spent with Rainey. Her birthday was January 15—Capricorn. That morning, it told her to avoid horseback riding and camping trips. And there would be a reunion with a long-lost relative. Drew wasn't lost. Her mother wasn't lost.

God, we're all lost.

Drew, what did you do?

What did I do? What put my life so off course again?

Kate released her seatbelt and struggled into the aisle. The flight attendants smiled at her before she closed the bathroom door behind her.

The cold water on her face helped. The brown paper towel was rough against her face. Kate dropped the towel into the toilet and flushed it. The water swirled angrily as it was sucked into the void by the rushing air.

The aircraft droned through the night.

As Kate stepped off the commuter flight at the Memphis airport, she half-expected to see Drew's smiling face in the mix of people waiting at the gate. Drew was always there when she came home to visit, laughing, hugging the girls, teasing them about the latest in California teenage fashions. Now he was in jail. It had to be some horrendous nightmare from which she would soon awaken. It just had to be. Drew was not a killer.

It was a lonely walk to the car rental counters with the weight of her carryall heavy upon her shoulder. She had never made the walk alone before, not in the twenty years since moving to California with Christopher, not since Melissa and Allison were born, not ever. But then, she had never come home when her brother was charged with murder.

With the air conditioner turned high in the rental car, Kate headed south, having to pay attention to streets and roads. Drew always did that, too. The last time she'd been home with the girls—two years ago, or three—Drew had detoured, taking Melissa and Allison down Elvis Presley Boulevard, past the shrine of Graceland. It had been a happier trip then. Or had it?

Kate had taken time off after the first trial of Valerie Rush's assailants. It was an emotional time. Breaking it off with Harry. Unable to maintain the prosecutor's necessary detachment, she had become too involved with Valerie and her case, wanting more than anything to set things right, and being unable to do more than ensure that the bad guys went to jail.

Kate turned the radio on to drown out the roaring air conditioner. "And now the weather report for the Memphis area. It's going to be another hot and muggy day, Kelly. Temperatures are expected to hit the ninety-degree mark again, with late afternoon thunderstorms predicted. There may be tornado warnings later in the day."

That's not surprising. At least the Delta weather is predictable, Kate thought, as she passed the WELCOME TO MISSISSIPPI sign.

"In other news," the woman named Kelly said, "the so-called Delta Ripper, Drew Anderson, the Mississippi doctor charged in the brutal torture-murder of Billie Rae Scott, will be arraigned today. Scott's body was found two days ago near the Mississippi River, outside a hunting cabin belonging to the accused. According to authorities, the thirty-eight-year-old Scott was Anderson's girlfriend."

Damn it.

Kate pressed the accelerator. There would be no time to go to her mother's first to shower and change. She had to get to the courthouse and see Drew before the arraignment.

Kate called her mother from a pay phone in the courthouse lobby. "I'm here, Mama, but I didn't have time to come home first. They're arraigning Drew this morning."

"What's that mean, honey?"

"They're simply stating what they believe to be true. It's the formal accusation and the filing of charges against Drew."

"But he didn't do it."

"I know that, Mama. It's just a formality at this point. I have to go. There's a lot to do. I'll be home as soon as I can. Don't worry."

"I'm awful glad you're here. Thank the Lord. Everything will be all right now. You just tell 'em they made a mistake."

"All right, Mama." Kate hung up wishing she could share her mother's simple belief that everything was all right now. It wasn't right; it wasn't right at all.

The headline screamed at her: *DELTA RIPPER TO BE ARRAIGNED TODAY.*

Kate dropped a quarter in the machine and quickly scanned the story. Some enterprising reporter had made a connection with Jack the Ripper and filled the story with allusions to London's East End before the turn of the century. God damn the media, anyway. They always had to sensationalize a story, come up with some lurid angle to sell papers. "A modern Jack the Ripper," Kate read, "prowled the Mississippi Delta night, killing a young woman with precise surgical strokes, just like the storied mass murderer of old. But unlike the investigators of the original Jack the Ripper, whose identity was never discovered, authorities acted quickly in the case of the Delta Ripper, arresting Drew Anderson, a prominent local physician, for the latest copycat killing in imitation of the storied Jack." Kate folded the newspaper and tucked it under her arm.

The holding tank off the courtroom was vastly different from Division 30, the Central Felony Arraignment Court in Los Angeles. The holding tank there was always crowded with defendants awaiting their first appearance in the long process of the criminal justice system. They were the latest catch in the never-ending battle against society's transgressors—murderers, burglars, thieves, rapists, gang members, armed robbers, felony drunk drivers, and the occasional drive-by shooter who was identified and apprehended. But no matter how many were swept off the streets, the holding tank was always crammed again the next morning.

"Hello, Drew."

"Hello, Kate."

Her brother was the only person in the cell. Kate waited until the bailiff left them alone. He locked the door as he left.

When she worked downtown in Los Angeles, Kate had seen the criminal attorneys and public defenders lined against the bars of the cell talking to their clients, using bent knees as support for their legal tablets as they hurriedly scribbled the pertinent facts—and lies—of the case. Often, it was their first encounter with their clients.

"What happened, Drew?"

"I didn't do it, Kate. I swear."

"Just tell me what happened."

"I was with Billie Rae that night. We met for a drink in a juke joint out near the river. She wanted to dance. I said it was too hot to dance and she got mad. Billie Rae had a temper when she didn't get her way. We argued. She said she didn't need me. I left. That's the last I saw of her. Then the deputies showed up at the office the next afternoon. That's all I know, for God's sake."

"Did anybody see you after you left?"

"I went straight home."

"No stops for gas, another drink, talk to a neighbor, anything?"

"I went home and went to bed. Got up the next morning and went to the office as usual. That's it."

"How was she killed, Drew?"

"You know they found her at my hunting cabin?"

Kate nodded. "I heard it on the radio, driving in."

"She was cut up pretty bad, Kate, just like a doctor would do. Whoever did it used my hunting knife. My fingerprints are all over it."

"Christ."

"I want you to defend me, Kate. You're the only one I trust."

"Drew, I can't do that. You need a good criminal lawyer."

"You're a criminal lawyer."

"I'm a prosecutor," Kate said. "In Los Angeles. I can't defend you in Mississippi."

"Why not? You passed the bar down here. You're a Mississippi lawyer, too."

"I have to work, Drew. What about the girls? Everything?"

"We'll work it out. I'd rather have you as a part-time lawyer than any of the people around here. I trust you, Kate. You're my little sister."

Kate was silent, staring into Drew's eyes, seeing the unspoken plea. "I have to see the judge," she said.

"Will you do it, Kate? Please?"

"I don't know." She went to the door and knocked. The bailiff opened it. Kate turned back. "Why wouldn't you see Mama?"

"I didn't want her to see me like this," he answered. "I didn't want you to see me like this."

Kate saw Judge Harlan P. Girardeau in his chambers. Girardeau was a big, hulking man in his early sixties. From the framed pictures and the Rebel flag on the wall, Kate knew he had played football at Ole Miss sometime way back. He looked like he could still go out and bang a few heads around. When he stood up to shake her hand, Kate saw the .38 revolver holstered on his hip.

Girardeau acknowledged her glance. "We've had a few incidents around here. Seems like folks don't care much for judges when the verdict ain't to their liking. I figure me and Mr. Smith and Mr. Wesson can keep order in my courtroom."

"I understand, Your Honor," Kate said. "I've had occasion to carry a pistol myself." Rainey had given it to her. Although she no longer carried it, she still kept it hidden in a desk drawer in her office.

"Did you, now?"

"Yes, sir."

"And did you have occasion to use it?"

"Yes, sir, I did." Kate shivered slightly, remembering how close she'd come to pulling the trigger when Nelson had attacked her in the parking lot.

"Well, that's a story I'd like to hear sometime. Perhaps over a drink."

"Perhaps." Christ, is he hitting on me? Already?

"Time was, Miss Gallagher," Girardeau said in a thick good-old-boy accent, "I would have had to recuse myself from a case like this. Time was, your brother probably would have been my doctor, and I'd have had a big conflict of interest. But this is a big place now. Lots of doctors. Lots of lawyers, too. Oh, I know there's nothing against someone defending a relative in our code of ethics, but don't you think you might be a little too close to this case? If it was me, I think I'd advise my brother to get someone else, a lawyer who doesn't have any emotional involvement in the case. You ought to think about that, young lady."

"I haven't had time to think about it, Your Honor," Kate replied. "I flew all night and just arrived this morning. I'm going to talk to Drew about this, of course, but for the moment, he wants me to represent him in the matter before your court."

"Well, I reckon it won't do no harm for the arraignment. But you think about what I said, hear?"

"Yes, sir, I will." Kate brought back a little of her own accent. "Yes, sir, I surely will."

"Have you met our head prosecutor?"

"Not yet, Your Honor."

"You will. He's going to prosecute the case himself. It's an election year, you know. Very ambitious young man. Wants to go on to Jackson and then Washington. He's gonna enjoy a real high profile case like this." He paused for a moment, looking at Kate with a mixture of pity and contempt in his gray eyes. He turned to shout at his clerk. "Miss Maisie!"

Kate had a doll in her childhood, a ragged filthy thing she'd found on her way home from school one day. After her mother helped repair the forlorn little thing, transforming it into a pretty and petite doll once again, Kate had named it Miss Martha.

The homely and grizzled woman who stuck her head in chambers was no Miss Martha. "Yes, sir, Your Honor?"

"Go on out and see if the right honorable district attorney has graced us with his presence as yet. If he's here, ask the right honorable young man to step in for a moment."

"He's right here, Judge," Maisie said, stepping aside to allow the tall, immaculately dressed black man to enter chambers.

"Mr. Cowles," the judge said, "this is Ms. Kate Gallagher. Our district attorney, ma'am, Wilson Cowles."

Kate rose and extended her hand. "It's nice to meet you," she said. "I'm Drew Anderson's sister."

"It's a pleasure to meet you," Cowles said. "But I wish it were under better circumstances."

"Ms. Gallagher's a colleague of yours, Mr. Cowles, a deputy district attorney out in Los Angeles. But for the moment, she's going to represent her brother, although I've counseled her against it."

"You're a member of the Mississippi bar?"

Kate nodded. "I took it in case I wanted to come home someday. I didn't expect to use it."

"Well," Girardeau interrupted, "let's go on out and get this arraignment over and done with."

"How did the woman die?" Kate asked.

"Billie Rae Scott was gutted like a deer," Wilson Cowles said. "It was very precisely done."

Three

He licked his lips nervously when she entered the courtroom. Except for the hair, she looked just as he remembered her—soft, beautiful, vulnerable. He was pleased she'd let her hair grow out. The last time he'd seen her, the hair had been cut short. It made her look hard, like his sister. She was more feminine now. As she crossed the courtroom, he imagined what she would look like naked, coming to him, eager to be in his arms, desperate for his touch. He longed to caress her breasts. He could see her breasts move beneath the white blouse and the jacket. Big, soft white breasts, and she would cradle his head tenderly as he suckled at their dark tips. She wouldn't talk dirty, not like the last one, begging him to do bad things. She couldn't talk because of the tape he plastered over her filthy mouth, but he knew what she was saying. He listened to her thoughts and heard what she was begging him to do. Not like Kathryn Anne, who would love him. Oh, Kathryn Anne, I love you . . . I've always loved you. I don't want you to leave me again. That's bad. If you leave me this time, you must be punished. You have to stay with me forever now.

Kate followed the judge and the prosecutor into a courtroom crowded with spectators. She was surprised by the number of people. Her work was usually done in anonymity, observed only by a few relatives of the accused, other attorneys, the court watchers who found the real-life dramas of the courtroom more absorbing than the daytime soap operas on television. Of course, there were the occasional trials when juries were actually impaneled, but they were rare. The criminal courts were overcrowded and, more often than not, defendants would plead out, prosecutor and defender reaching amiable agreements. If every criminal case went to trial the system would halt as abruptly as an aircraft crashing to earth. But Kate realized that she should not have been shocked by the number of spectators. For her small hometown, this was a high-profile case. Dr. Drew Anderson was well known locally. The sordid killing would provide endless hours of high excitement and suspense.

Kate had been in perhaps two dozen or more different courtrooms during her career, and they were no longer mysterious and alien places, populated by initiates in baffling customs that she would never learn. Since joining the district attorney's office and her first assignment at the Santa Monica branch, Kate had grown accustomed to the intricate rituals of criminal law, the unfolding dramas of the courtroom, and the strange ceremonies involved with the pursuit of justice. She had honed her skills during the two years in Central Courts—the Mainline of the DA's office—and again with the new assignment in the South Bay branch office. Kate Gallagher was a good trial attorney and marked for advancement by her superiors as an excellent prosecutor. One day, she might be a head deputy DA herself, in charge of her own branch or special prosecution division.

Here, it was so different, yet so familiar. With the bench, the jury box, the witness box, the clerk's desk piled high with papers, a chair and smaller desk for the stenographer, tables for the prosecution and the defense—it could have been one of her own assigned courtrooms in the South Bay. The flag of the United States of America was in its proper place behind the bench, but it was flanked by the Mississippi flag, with its insert of the Confederate battle flag, that incongruous reminder of another time.

Kate automatically started for the prosecution table, the one closest to the jury box. She deviated quickly to the defense table, hoping that Girardeau and Cowles didn't notice. She carried only her purse. At home, she would be burdened with armloads of papers, case files, motions, legal opinions, precedents. It was all wrong. She was again a stranger in her own world. Christ, I don't even know the facts of the case, except that a woman was gutted like a deer and they think Drew did it.

Behind her, the people in the audience murmured. A young news starlet with long blond hair stood at the back of the courtroom with her cameraman. They were probably from one of the Memphis stations. Kate assumed at least some of the others were also from the media. The rest would be the curious, eager to follow the drama of a prominent local man accused of murdering his girlfriend.

Wilson Cowles approached Kate with a thick file. "I brought these for the defense attorney. It's the complete file so far. As anything else comes in, I'll make sure you have it all under the appropriate rules of discovery."

Kate smiled gratefully. "Thank you, Mr. Cowles."

He nodded. "I'd have provided them sooner, except that your brother refused to talk with us, retain an attorney, or allow the court to appoint an attorney."

"I know. Thanks again." Kate turned to the file, leafing through it quickly. The complaint was there, along with the police reports, the witnesses who testified that Drew and Billie Rae Scott argued violently at the bar, and the results of the autopsy. Kate cringed at the photographs of the body. Her stomach turned as she leafed through the photos. Billie Rae Scott had been tied, arms and legs spread-eagled, to a frame used for stretching animal skins. Oh, dear Jesus. Drew couldn't have done that. Not Drew . . . not my brother. Kate closed the file quickly, but the images of Billie Rae Scott's mutilated body stayed with her.

The bailiff escorted Drew to her side. His face was drawn and haggard. He sat down beside her, sighing heavily.

Kate took his hand and squeezed it, smiling at him with an assurance she did not feel.

"What do I have to do, Kate?"

"Just remember two words when the time comes: not guilty, period. Okay?"

Drew nodded.

"There will be no cameras or recordings in my courtroom," Girardeau announced from the bench.

There was a collective groan from the reporters.

"And there will be no complaining, or I will clear the room."

The ritual began when the case was called.

"Are the People represented?"

"Wilson Cowles for the People of Mississippi, Your Honor."

"Kathryn Anne Gallagher for the defense, Your Honor."

The complaint was read to the assemblage by the clerk. "To wit, on or about the sixteenth day of July, the accused, Drew Anderson, with malice aforethought, did . . ."

"The defendant will rise."

Kate and Drew stood.

"How do you plead to the charges against you?" Girardeau asked.

"Not guilty."

"The clerk will note that the defendant has entered a plea of not guilty to all specifications. The preliminary hearing will be held on, mm . . ." The judge leafed through a calendar. "The preliminary hearing is set for August fifteenth at

10 A.M. in this courtroom. The defendant will be held in custody in lieu of $200,000 bail."

Kate was surprised. She had expected to argue for bail.

"Your Honor," Wilson Cowles said, rising quickly, "the people oppose bail in a capital case."

"I reckon the defendant will not flee this jurisdiction. He's lived here all his life. His business is here. Call the next case."

"Can you make bond?" Kate asked.

"They'll take the house and office building as collateral?"

"Yes."

Drew nodded. "I can make it."

"You'll be out shortly, then," Kate said. "I'll wait and make sure everything goes properly."

Again, the bailiff escorted Drew out of the courtroom.

Kate gathered her purse and the file.

Wilson Cowles held the gate open for her. "A black man would not have received bail in a case like this," he said.

So nothing had changed. The myth of the New South was nothing more than a fantasy. The old hatreds remained, simmering beneath a glossy veneer.

"I'm sorry," Kate said.

Cowles nodded and followed her to the door.

Half-a-dozen reporters clamored for Kate's attention in the corridor outside the courtroom.

"When were you retained by the defendant?"

"What's your line of defense going to be?"

"What is your comment on the Jack the Ripper similarities?"

"Is Anderson going to post bail?"

"What law firm are you with?"

For the reporters, all young and eager, it was a major story, one that would swell their clip files, perhaps allowing them to make the big jump to a large city daily. The television reporter hung back, allowing the local print reporters to shout their questions, as though her status on television made her aloof to shouted questions. A Los Angeles TV reporter would have screamed right along with the best of them.

Kate, suddenly hot and flushed, leaned against the wall, feeling trapped by the insistent shouts and circling predators. "I have no comment at this time," she said.

"When will you have a comment?"

"No comment," Kate repeated. She pushed through the crowd and into the ladies rest room. As the door shut behind her, the reporters turned to Wilson Cowles, who waited patiently for their attention.

Kate wet a paper towel. The tepid water felt cool and refreshing against her face. When she opened her eyes, she saw the television reporter looking at her in the mirror.

"Are you all right?" she asked.

"Tired," Kate replied. "I flew all night to get here."

"I'm Carole Vaughn?" She spoke with a soft southern lilt, raising a question at the end of her sentences. "Carole, with an E?"

"I still have no comment."

"That's all right. I just wanted to see if you were all right. You didn't look very good out there. I mean, well, I didn't mean it the way it sounded. Just that you looked ill."

"I know what you meant," Kate said. "I appreciate it."

"Are you related to Mr. Anderson?"

"What makes you ask that?" There had been no mention of their relationship in open court.

"There's a family resemblance."

"Drew's my older brother."

"I thought so. And you're here to defend him?"

"I don't know. That hasn't been decided yet."

"But you represented him today?"

"Where are you from, Carole with an E?"

"Vicksburg, originally. Then Oxford. Now Memphis."

"Are you one of those Mississippi beauty queens?"

Carole blushed. "No. I'm not so pretty as that."

"But you're Southern, and you know what it means when there's family trouble. You drop everything and come do what you can?"

Carole nodded.

"That's why I'm here," Kate said. "Family trouble. I'm going to do what I can to help. And all that's pretty long for a no-comment."

"I wasn't asking on the record, although I suppose that's not what a good reporter would do."

"You can use it if you like," Kate said. "Thanks for asking after me."

"Are you all right? I mean, really all right?"

"Hot, tired, worried about my brother, but I'm all right."

"Where are you from? You said you flew all night?"

"Los Angeles. I'm a deputy district attorney."

"That's a great angle for my story, but I'm sorry about your brother. I don't think he did it."

"Thank you," Kate said. "He didn't do it."

"You take care, then?"

"You, too, Carole."

The reporters were still waiting when Kate and Drew hurried to her rental car. Drew turned his face away from Carole Vaughn's cameraman as he ran to the car.

"Drive around for a while," Drew said. "In case they try to follow us."

Kate glanced in the rearview mirror. "There's no one behind us."

"Drive around anyway. I'm not ready to face Mama yet."

"You better tell me about it."

"I don't know anything," Drew said, his voice choking.

Kate looked over at him. Tears rolled down his cheeks.

"She didn't deserve that," he said. "I liked her a lot . . . maybe even loved her."

"Maybe?"

"We had fun together most of the time, but . . . well, she had a hard life . . . sometimes . . ." His voice trailed off.

"Drew, I know you're upset and hurting, but you have to talk to me."

"God damn it, I don't know anything."

"Then I might as well get on the next plane. I can't help you."

"Kate, I didn't do it."

"I know that, but who did? Who hates you that much?"

"Couldn't it just be a random killing? Some crazy who she picked up in the bar?"

"Drew, she was killed at your hunting cabin. With your knife. It's circumstantial evidence, I know, but it doesn't sound random to me."

"Let's go to my place," Drew said, "get a beer. There's something I'd better show you."

"What about Mama?"

"We'll call her from there."

The white antebellum mansion stood alone on a secluded estate surrounded by thick dark oak trees casting a shadowy shroud over the yard and house. The gleaming coats of paint on the walls and the four tall pillars did not, could not, allay the aura of darkness that enveloped the old house.

Drew waited for Kate to drive through and then closed the gate behind the car, walking up the gravel drive after her.

The old childhood fears returned each time Kate approached her brother's house. She pulled the car around the circular drive, pointing it back at the gate as though poising for a quick flight from some unknown terror. "It still looks haunted to me," Kate said, when Drew reached the car. "I've never liked it here."

"Nobody left to haunt it," Drew said. "Except me."

The people around town still referred to it as the old Randall place. The house dated back to before the Civil War, a relic that had been built by one of the town's founders, Derek Randall, and had passed through successive generations of Randalls until Kate and Drew were children, when a mentally deficient nephew had killed the spinster aunt who cared for him. For three days after the murder, the nephew had smeared his own feces on the walls before finally killing himself.

The old Randall place stood abandoned for years then, an object of mystery and darkness for the children of the town, including Kate and Drew, who climbed over the fence on cold Halloween nights to creep through the trees with hearts chilled by apprehension. It was a brave soul who dared to climb the creaking steps to the massive door and rattle the chains that precluded entry.

"I still don't know how you can live here," Kate said.

Drew had purchased the mansion years ago, stripping the interior walls, restoring it slowly, room by room, project by project—paint one year, a new roof the next, new plumbing in another year. "Privacy," he said. "Nobody wants to come up here. They think it's still haunted. Like you."

That's better, Kate thought. That's a glimmer of the old Drew and the puckish sense of humor he'd possessed in better times. "I still remember the time we came up here and you put that cold slab of raw liver on my neck."

"I thought you were going to raise the whole town. Can you still scream that loud?"

"If I have to, I suppose."

Inside, Drew said, "I'll be right back. Why don't you fix us a drink? I want Scotch—a stiff one."

"I thought you wanted a beer."

"I changed my mind." He ran up the stairs.

As Kate poured his drink, she heard his footsteps through the ceiling. The house was thin and frail, like an old man creaking through his last years. She went to the refrigerator and took a beer for herself, pouring it into a water glass.

Drew returned and solemnly exchanged a plain white envelope for his drink.

"What's this?" Kate asked, looking at the meticulously exact address and postage stamp applied exactly square to the corners. There was no return address.

"Open it."

Kate took a sheet of rough notebook paper from the envelope and unfolded it. Block letters had been glued to the paper in straight, measured lines.

TELL YOUR SISTER TO COME HOME. OR ELSE. I LOVE HER.

Their mother rushed out of the house when Kate parked on the quiet residential street. "Praise the Lord, you're home. You're both home." She embraced Kate and then Drew, and then Kate a second time, finally ushering them into the house, shooing them along like naughty children. She was oblivious to the parted curtains as her neighbors peered out at the reunion.

Margaret Anderson hovered around her two oldest children, fearing perhaps that if she closed her eyes for even a moment they would disappear, the one back to Los Angeles, the other to a jail cell. The two of them were a continuing source of mystery and pride for her. She wondered how they'd been able to break the mold of poverty and hard, backbreaking work into which they'd been born, Drew working his way through college and going on to attend medical school at the University of Tennessee, and Kate, an honors graduate from Delta State, managing, after her divorce, to raise two girls and become a lawyer at the same time. Betsy, her youngest daughter, was the only one of her children Margaret Anderson understood. Betsy had married young, right out of high school, and had followed the traditional pattern of childbearing and homemaking known to her mother. Of Drew and Kate, she could only say, 'My, my, my, they sure can get up to the dickens sometimes."

Margaret Anderson now resorted to her own customary form of denial. Her solution for any of the travails life presented was to feed everyone within hailing distance. She fed colds and fevers, joy and sorrow, tragedy and triumph, arrest and release, all with the same determined resolution.

While she piled food on the kitchen table—ham, fried chicken, potato salad, cole slaw, greens, black-eyed peas—Kate showered and changed clothes, emerging to sit at the table, but the overnight flight, the tension of the courtroom, and Drew's precarious position were catching up with her. And there was the anonymous note . . . where had that come from? Who loved her? How could an anonymous note sent months ago have anything to do with Billie Rae and Drew? God, what a mess.

"Mother, Kate's going to stay with me this trip."

After showing her the note, Drew had insisted that Kate stay at his house. "Who knows what kind of crazy is out there," Drew reasoned. "And we can't tell Mother. It'd just make her more upset than she already is."

"You should have told me about this," Kate said.

"I thought it was just some crank note. Besides, you were out there in California."

"But now I'm here."

"That's why I want you to stay with me this time. Mother will get over it."

The announcement angered Margaret, though. "I expected her to stay here," she said. "I haven't seen her for so long."

"Drew and I have a lot of work to do, Mama."

"I suppose that's true."

"I'll make it up to you. There'll be time for us to get together."

Margaret complained when Drew and Kate only picked at their food. "I just don't now what's going to happen if you don't eat right."

"I'm too tired to eat, Mama."

"I expect so, but Drew, he don't have no excuse."

"I'm just not hungry, Mother. I have a lot on my mind."

"I told you that woman was no good."

"Don't start on that."

"It's not Drew's fault, Mama."

"Well, I sure would like to know whose fault it *is.*"

"It was the killer's fault," Drew said, "pure and simple."

"We better go, Mama. I want to take a nap."

"Sure, honey, you do that. I know you're tired."

"Let me clear up."

"I'll do that, Kate. You just come back for dinner, hear?"

"We will, Mama."

"Who invited him?"

"Aw, Mother, don't be like that." Drew leaned over and kissed her cheek.

"I'm just so riled up about all this, I don't know what to do."

"I know, Mother, I know."

"It'll be all right, Mama."

"If you say so. Go on now, get out of here and let me get my work done."

The rest of the day blurred. Kate took a sluggish nap and awakened reluctantly, feeling drugged. She took another shower before returning with Drew to have dinner with her mother. The meal was just as elaborate as lunch, but conversation was halting and stilted. None of them wanted or dared to mention the reason they were together again.

They left early. Drew dropped Kate at his house, saying, "I have some business to take care of. I may be late, so lock the doors."

Alone, Kate watched the evening news as Carole Vaughn did her standup in front of the county courthouse. "In a new and paradoxical development today, Kathryn Anne Gallagher, the sister of Drew Anderson, who is charged with the murder of Billie Rae Scott, arrived from Los Angeles to represent Anderson at his arraignment. In an exclusive interview, Gallagher, ironically a deputy district attorney in Los Angeles, California, said . . ."

God, if I could only be so young, pretty, and enthusiastic as Carole, Kate thought.

"In other news tonight . . ."

Kate switched off the television and went outside into the hot night. She sat in the porch swing and rocked gently back and forth, listening to the incessant chirp of crickets. Moths fluttered around the porch light. Kate slapped at a mosquito and then another. Still, she did not want to go in. If I close my eyes, I could be a little girl again, out playing in the hot Delta night with Betsy while Mama shouts for us to come in. Kate closed her eyes, but no miraculous transformation occurred. She remained an outsider, a deputy district attorney from Los Angeles, here to help her brother, who was accused of murder.

"Damn it," Kate said. She stood abruptly and went into the house to call Harry. Behind her, the empty swing rocked back and forth.

He watched the swing until it stopped, imagining all the while he was sitting there with her, kissing her, touching her breasts, feeling the wet between her legs as she breathed heavily in his ear, whispering, *yes yes yes oh yes.* He didn't move until a light came on in an upstairs bedroom on the side of the house. Then he crept quietly through the darkness and the trees until he could see her shadowy form pass by the curtained window. *Yes yes yes oh yes yes.*

Her bedroom was barren and unoccupied, one of those rooms kept neat and clean for the occasional visiting relative, but otherwise showing no sign of a personality. It had none of the touches that make a room, however small, a home, a place where a warm, breathing individual lived, thought, cried, made love, dreamed of a bright future. It had all the coldness of a jail cell. Its only decoration was the sheet of notebook paper Kate had propped up on the dresser.

TELL YOUR SISTER TO COME HOME. OR ELSE. I LOVE HER.

Drew said it had come months ago. Some crank . . . nothing to worry about. Maybe it wasn't intended for Kate. Maybe it was for Betsy, who lived outside town to the south, toward Jackson and Vicksburg. Except . . .

TELL YOUR SISTER TO COME HOME.

And here I am, Kate thought; here I am. But where's Drew? Why hasn't Drew come home?

She undressed and got into bed, pulling the telephone into her lap. She dialed Harry's number, and while she waited for him to answer, she stared at the note.

"Hello."

"Hi, darling, I love you," Kate said. Oh, yes, I do. She turned the light out and let Harry's deep voice enter her soul.

Outside, in the hot Delta night, he watched as the light in her bedroom went out. He pretended he was with her in the darkness, her naked body open and vulnerable to his touch as he pressed her to the bed, squeezing her titties harder and harder as she begged for more. Her mouth would be warm when her soft lips closed around him and she would moan with pleasure when he finally entered her and their sweaty bodies became one. *Yes yes yes oh yes* . . . He ached with his desire for her and cried out in the night. Soon. Soon now she would belong to him. And so long as she pleased him, he would allow her to live.

Four

For a time, twenty-five years were erased and a lifetime of pain and failure disappeared magically. It seemed as though nothing had changed. Out on the highway, the drive-in restaurant served the same wonderful chili dogs and french fries. The drive-in movie still showed three features nightly. Closer in, the Kroger supermarket was in the same place. The banks, the drugstore, the funeral home were all familiar landmarks. The drugstore did have a new coat of paint, the only visible testimony to the passage of time.

At the high school, Kate pulled over and stopped, watching summer school students enter the campus grounds listlessly. Kate closed her eyes and she was seventeen again, a senior in high school and the yearbook editor, already making plans for college, applying for the scholarships that would enable her to attend. She thought of her boyfriend, Tommy Harper, dead for so many years now, another of her classmates who'd fallen victim to high speed and alcohol, crashing his truck into a tree late one Saturday night. Kate's mother had sent the obituary. Oh, Tommy, what would have happened if I'd married you? Would you be alive now? Would I be alive?

She watched as a black student carried books for a pretty blond girl. They were laughing together. That wouldn't have been possible when Kate went to school there. Then, it was still segregated, seemed it would always be segregated. The South, her Mississippi, had changed, at least outwardly. Beneath the surface, however, the old hatreds still seethed, festering sores waiting to erupt in the poisons of enmity and prejudice. A black man would not have received bail, Wilson Cowles had said. The two students parted at a fork in the walkway. The blond girl took her books, glanced around, and then gave her friend a quick kiss before dashing off to her class. Kate watched as the young man ambled off in another direction, looking back after the girl, waving once, before he disappeared among the trees.

Kate wondered if they were lovers, too, meeting furtively in out-of-the-way places where they would not be seen together. Mississippi was still no place for racially mixed couples, certainly not kids their age. Again she thought of Tommy. He'd been her first real boyfriend, the first to touch her breasts after a football game when he'd scored the winning touchdown, the first to kiss her naked breasts after a Christmas party their senior year, finally becoming her first lover, parting her legs on that summer graduation night. Tommy, what happened? We loved each other. But then he joined the Marines and she went off to college and they drifted apart and into the arms of others.

Kate shook her head. Twenty-five years had passed all too swiftly. She would never be seventeen again. She was no longer that bright-eyed young woman filled with optimism.

Kate started the car and drove away, leaving her youthful spirit to wander among the trees of the high school campus, perhaps to meet Tommy there again.

The courthouse stood as it had for years. The Confederate memorial, a statue of a young soldier staring into eternity, still graced the center of the walkway.

It's impossible, Kate thought, as she passed the memorial

and started up the courthouse steps. There's so much to do, and no time to do it. Not if it was to be done right, and it had to be right. This was not some sleazebag murderer. Her brother was accused. Despite all her arguments, Drew still insisted that she act in his defense. "We're family, Kate. That's what family means. I want someone I can trust."

"I can't prepare a defense from California."

"It'll work. I want the best. And that's you, Kate."

Oh, shit.

So much to accomplish—ask Cowles for the list of witnesses omitted from the materials he'd provided, visit the scene, find an attorney to assist with the case.

At least Drew had agreed to hiring co-counsel, someone familiar with the latest in Mississippi criminal law, someone to develop potential lines of defense, answer the unasked questions, interview witnesses, be a local presence.

Kate found the frosted glass door marked ENTER. The receptionist told her that Cowles was in a meeting, but that it would be over soon, if she cared to wait. "Thank you," Kate said.

The office wasn't much different from her own office or any of the branch offices at home. Kate sat in an old wooden chair and listened to the familiar litany as two detectives presented their case to an assistant DA. One of the detectives glanced over at Kate, looking her up and down before turning away. Kate saw the admiration in his eyes. He would probably start a conversation, given the chance. Cops and prosecutors naturally gravitated to each other. She had dated enough cops in her time. And Rainey. Dear old Rainey.

But for the deep drawl in their voices, the conversation might have taken place in Los Angeles County rather than the Mississippi Delta. The attorney agreed finally that they had enough evidence to file charges in a series of residential burglaries that had taken place over the last two months. The perp, a longtime suspect in the case, had been caught with stolen items in the trunk of his car. The cops had used out-of-date registration as probable cause for the stop. Dumb, Kate thought.

"He's free now," the receptionist said. "It's the first office through the double doors." The receptionist pushed a button beneath her desk and a buzzer sounded. Kate pushed through the now unlocked doors, leaving a disappointed detective in her wake.

Wilson Cowles, dapper in a gray three-piece suit, white shirt, and red tie, was standing in the doorway of his small office. "Good morning, counselor," he said. "You're out and about early."

"Good morning," Kate said, smiling and offering her hand. "I have quite a lot to do."

"I can imagine," Cowles said, shaking her hand briefly. "How can I be of assistance?" He guided her into the office. "Would you like some coffee?"

"That would be nice," Kate said.

"How do you take it?"

"Black."

"Just like me."

"I didn't mean . . ." Kate felt a blush start in her cheeks.

"I didn't, either. I meant, I take my coffee black." He took the telephone and dialed a two-number extension. "Lori, would you bring in two black coffees, please?" When he replaced the receiver, Cowles turned back to Kate. "Do you get home often?" he asked.

"Every two or three years, I guess. Not that often."

"Things change. You must find everything vastly different."

"That's funny. Driving into town this morning, I was thinking how much everything was the same. Nothing seems to have changed since I was here last."

"At first glance, perhaps, but nothing ever remains the

same. Children are born, grow up. People move away. Some die."

"Like Billie Rae Scott?"

He nodded gravely. "Like Billie Rae Scott."

"My brother didn't do it."

"You're going to have a chance to prove that in court."

"I will."

There was light rap on the door.

"Come in, Lori."

"You sure y'all wouldn't like anything else? We have some nice muffins that Jack brought in."

"Ms. Gallagher?"

"Please, call me Kate." She smiled at Lori, another Southern mother in the making. Food cured everything. "The coffee's fine."

"Nothing for me, Lori. Thank you." Cowles sipped at his coffee. "I called your boss in Los Angeles."

"Checking up on me?"

"Of course. Aren't you going to do the same with me?"

Kate smiled. "Of course," she said.

"He spoke very highly of you. He said you're a kick-ass prosecutor."

"I am."

"Well, I'm not going to let you kick my ass. Count on it," Cowles said. "Now, how can I help you?"

"I'd like the list of witnesses. It wasn't in the folder."

"I have it right here." He passed another folder to Kate.

"Thank you. I also want someone to act as co-counsel. I thought you'd be able to make a recommendation or two."

"That's a little unusual. Coming to the prosecution for a defense recommendation."

"Who would know the defense lawyers better? I want someone good."

"I'm supposed to put criminals in jail, not help them get off."

"Your job is to see justice is done. That's what a district attorney does."

"That's the ideal, perhaps. But you're a prosecutor, too. We both know that our job is to put criminals in jail so the fine, upstanding people of our society can sleep at night without worrying about some crazy nigger taking a razor to them."

"There's no call for you to talk that way, not with me," Kate said. "It's the third time you've made reference to color."

"Once, it was unintentional. You misunderstood."

"Did I?"

"Yes."

Kate didn't believe him. Nothing was unintentional, not between black and white in Mississippi. Not yet. Perhaps the children of some future generations might learn to live without prejudice if their parents finally refused to perpetuate the old hatreds. But not yet. Not in Mississippi. Hell, why should it be any different from Los Angeles? That supposedly "enlightened" Southern California society was a cesspool of racial enmity. White, black, Asian, Hispanic—all locked together in a grotesque dance of fear and suspicion that had culminated in riots and would again if something wasn't done soon.

For Kathryn Anne Gallagher and Wilson Cowles, the old barriers remained. Two centuries of hate and fear and mistrust could not be erased by a few strokes of a judicial pen, no matter how high the court, no matter how lofty the intent.

Kate glanced at the degrees from Mississippi State and Ole Miss displayed on the wall. Wilson Cowles, and others like him, black men and women, might graduate from the universities, might be elected to public office in the New South, but the Old South lurked in the darkness.

Kate rose. "Thank you for your help, Mr. Cowles."

"Please wait a moment, Ms. Gallagher. Tell me what you're looking for in a defense attorney."

"Thank you," Kate said. "I'd like someone . . ."

The cop was waiting on the courthouse steps when Kate left the building. He threw his cigarette down and stepped on it as Kate approached. "You're Kate Anderson," he said.

"I used to be. It's Gallagher now."

"I thought I recognized you. We went to school together. I'm Cory Martin."

Kate didn't recognize him. "I'm sorry . . ."

"Actually, I went to school more with your sister, Betsy. We were freshmen when you were a senior. My sister, Harriet, was in your class."

"I remember Harriet. I saw her a few years ago at a class reunion. Is she still teaching down in Jackson?"

"Sure is." Martin paused, looking out to the street where his partner was standing next to the unmarked police car that never fooled anyone. "I'm sorry about your trouble," Martin said, turning back to Kate. "I don't think he did it."

"I appreciate that, but do you have any evidence?"

"Naw, nothing like that. I just don't think he did it. Everybody knew about Billie Rae."

"What about her?"

"Her family ain't no good, and she wasn't much better. Don't know why your brother took up with her, anyway."

"You knew?"

"Hell, everybody did. You can't keep a secret in a small town like this."

"I suppose not."

"Say, Kate, it's good seeing you. I'd like to see you again. Maybe we could get together for coffee and a piece of pie."

"Thank you for asking, Cory, but I'm really busy. I've just got so much to do." In the office, Martin had been unable to disguise his admiration for her. Now he was unable to hide his disappointment. Kate felt sorry for him and added, "Perhaps another time, though."

He brightened immediately. "I'd like that, Kate. You take care, hear?"

"You, too, Cory."

"I'll call you."

"Do that, Cory, and tell Harriet I said hello when you see her."

Tracie Sanders matched the profile Kate had described for Cowles. She was young and hungry, bright and articulate, hard-working and energetic, and a confident, experienced criminal defense attorney. Tracie had spent two years working as a public defender before opening her own very small, very spartan office. "She's good," Cowles had told Kate. "And she's going to be very good."

Kate agreed with Cowles's assessment after talking with Tracie for fifteen minutes. What Cowles hadn't revealed was that Tracie Saunders had once been a finalist in the Miss Mississippi beauty pageant, one of those achingly beautiful young women who emerged from the state all blond hair and slim figure and long legs and possessing the delicate features and full lips that would drive men to distraction and madness. Kate could not imagine what the young woman who'd won the pageant must look like. Kate felt drab in Tracie's presence, but the young woman seemed unaware of her beauty, even downplaying her appearance by applying makeup sparingly, wearing her long hair in a severe bun, using glasses instead of contact lenses, and dressing in a plain business suit.

"I'll have to thank Mr. Cowles for the referral," Tracie said.

"He spoke highly of you."

"His prosecutors have learned not to take me for granted."

"Why criminal defense?" Kate asked.

"Someone has to defend people in trouble."

"That's it? Idealism?"

Tracie hesitated. She turned and looked at an *Arizona Highways* calendar and its photograph of a stark desert mountain. It was the only decoration in the room. Tracie turned back. "When I was in the pageant," she said, "they wanted some publicity photos. You know, beauty queen goes to law school, that sort of nonsense. Well, anyway, they shot photos in this empty courtroom. They had me stand at the prosecution table and it didn't feel right. I made them take the photos while I was at the defense table. I felt comfortable there, as though I was out of place on the other side of the courtroom. It was just a feeling I had, that I was supposed to be there. Now, it sounds pretty silly even to me."

"I would never discount a feeling like that," Kate said. "I have a friend back in Los Angeles—Nelson Rainey. He retired from LAPD and opened a New Age bookstore, if you can imagine that. It was just a feeling he had. I guess we all meet our destinies in strange ways."

"There's something else," Tracie said. "You should know this before you hire me. It might make a difference for you. My brother's one of those crazy survivalists, running around the backwoods waiting for Armageddon, preaching Christianity and white supremacy. That's another reason I do what I do. A lot of my work is for poor black people. It drives my brother nuts. He hates me. Calls me a traitor to the white race. I'll understand if you don't want to hire me."

"I'm not sure this case will make him any crazier, but we could try," Kate said smiling.

"Thank you."

"You're hired, then. What do you know about the situation with *my* crazy brother?"

"I've read about the case, of course, but I don't know anything else," Tracie said.

"We're together on that," Kate replied. "All I know is that Billie Rae Scott was brutally murdered after a number of witnesses testified that my brother and the victim had a violent argument in a bar. He denies killing her, but has no alibi."

"And the woman was murdered at his hunting cabin with a knife belonging to him."

Kate nodded. "He says he loved her. I believe him."

"Then someone else killed her." Tracie smiled. "I suppose we'd better find him."

"Or her."

Tracie raised her eyebrows. "A jealous lover?"

"I don't know why I said that. It's not the kind of murder a woman commits. It just popped out."

"I was thinking of a man, someone who wanted Billie Rae for himself and got carried away."

"Why wouldn't he kill Drew, then?"

"I don't know," Tracie said. "Yet."

"Ready to go to work?"

"I have a court appearance at two. I'm free before and after."

"Let's get this file copied for you. Then we can start by making a list of possible motives. I think we need to find out all we can about Billie Rae. If we can figure out why someone wanted Billie Rae dead, maybe we can put some names to the motives."

The air hung thick and stale around the cabin, as though the natural process had been unable to cleanse the stench of fear and violent death. Flies still buzzed around a dark spot on the ground beneath the rough wooden frame where Billie Rae Scott had been tied to wait out the remaining minutes and hours of her life. During hunting season, it was used to stretch and dry deerskins. Kate didn't know why Drew still kept it outside the cabin, anyway. His idea of hunting was to tramp around in the woods, carrying a rifle, all the while making enough noise to scare away any animals he might have to shoot. Probably the frame was there when he acquired the cabin, the legacy of a boyhood friend who needed money in a hurry and sold the place to Drew.

But a less squeamish hunter had converted the frame, using it to spread-eagle a woman. The photographs provided by Wilson Cowles had been graphic, detailing Billie Rae's agony as she hung on her perverted cross, her struggle to free herself as she fought the ropes digging deep into her wrists and ankles. The photos clearly showed the blood that had streamed from beneath the ropes on her wrists and the tiny square carved in the flesh between her breasts. Dear Jesus . . . how long had he made her suffer?

The flies swarmed angrily when Kate approached the killing frame, still seeing the pale naked body slumped in death. Kate forced herself to touch the frame. She wanted to be able to describe for a jury what it must have been like for Billie Rae Scott . . . no. That's the prosecutor's job. I'm defending this time. Oh, Christ, this is so confusing.

In her own professional world, Kate always began a personal preparation for trial by visiting the scene of whatever violent crime had been committed—murder, rape, spousal or child abuse. Such visits set the scene firmly in her mind, and her detailed notes provided grim memories months later when a case was in trial. With the photographs of Billie Rae's body and the horror of the scene in mind, Kate would have no trouble remembering. When it was all over, the difficulty would be to forget.

Kate turned away from the frame. The woods surrounding the small cabin were quiet. She had disturbed the natural order just as surely as the killer had that grim night. She felt a thousand pairs of wild eyes watching and waiting to see what the intruder would do. Through the thick foliage, Kate could catch glimpses of the lake, and above, the thick, sullen black clouds gathering for an afternoon thunderstorm. Kate saw a streak of lightning flash in the distance. A long time later, she heard the muted clap of thunder. The placid lake would churn violently when the storm broke.

Kate stood at the door of the cabin, the silence growing and enveloping her. She began to wish that she had not come out here alone, had waited for Tracie to finish her appearance in court. She reached out slowly and pushed the door open. "You won't need the keys," Drew had said. "Whoever did it broke in. Cops think I did it to throw them off. Jesus, how God damned stupid do they think I am?" The old wood creaked under her feet as she entered the cabin.

It was a mess. The cops had searched it thoroughly, not bothering to replace anything. Pots and pans were thrown haphazardly on the counter next to the sink. The blankets on the bunkbeds were strewn on the floor. Cushions in the ragged chairs had been pulled out and now lay where they had fallen. A low coffee table, scarred by cigarette butts and stained by beer cans, was covered with old copies of *Playboy* and *Penthouse,* each with the centerfold pulled open. Kate could hear the coarse comments of the cops amusing themselves. "Boy, I'd sure like to make her squeal. Man, look at the tits on that one. Oh, baby, come to Papa." Kate closed each of the magazines carefully, as though protecting the modesty of the young women.

Kate heard another faint dull boom of thunder. The storm was still far away, across the river in Arkansas, but it was coming. Bad luck. There had been no rain for a week. No mud for a vehicle or shoes to leave tracks in. The killer had everything going in his favor. Kate closed her eyes and tried to imagine the killer and his movements that night.

According to the police reports, Billie Rae Scott had been last seen leaving the nightclub. Her car was still there in the morning. She had left with someone willingly, or someone had waited for her in the parking lot, forcing her into his own vehicle. What? A car? Pickup? Van?

Did Billie Rae know her killer?

"She was strong. Would fight like a wildcat, sometimes," Drew said.

Why did she acquiesce that night? It would not have been an easy task to tie a struggling woman to that drying frame. Unconscious, then?

God damn it. There were so many questions and no answers. The police had followed the path of least resistance. Drew and Billie Rae argued in front of witnesses. Angry, violent words had been exchanged.

"Aw, it didn't mean anything," Drew told her. "Billie was like that. She'd fight like crazy, and then come back the next day like nothing happened."

Least resistance. Motive was provided by angry rage. Opportunity came when Drew waited for Billie Rae in the parking lot, enticed her into his car, took her to the cabin, tied her to the frame, and cut her guts out with his hunting knife, later covering his tracks by faking the break into his own cabin.

Circumstantial, but a jury might believe it.

Kate went back outside and stood in front of the frame.

It was big. Billie Rae had hung high above her killer, looking down at him, gagged with tape, able to plead for mercy only with her eyes. Just like in the photos. Except that those eyes were lifeless. That night, Billie's eyes must have been bright and flashing with fear and terror and the awful knowledge of what her killer was going to do.

Kate stepped closer to the frame, looking up at how high Billie had been tied. It had taken a big man to reach her with the knife. What was the angle? How tall was Drew? Not that big, taller than Kate, but only of average size for a man. Could Drew have made the killing stroke? It was something. It might cast doubt in a juror's mind. Reasonable doubt in one juror's mind . . . that was all that was necessary. Did the autopsy report even describe an angle? Kate couldn't remember. The file was on the front seat of the car. Kate turned to go for it.

And screamed.

She frightened the old man almost as much as he'd frightened her. He fell back, dropping his fishing pole and a metal pail.

"Oh, lordy," he cried. "Didn't mean no harm, missy. No, sir, no harm."

"Oh, Jesus," Kate cried, her heart beating. "You scared me."

"Didn't mean to. No, ma'am. Sure didn't mean to. Old Abe's just going down to the lake. Catch me a fish for my dinner."

"I'm sorry," Kate said. "I didn't hear you."

"Shoulda sung out," the old man mumbled in a thick backwoods accent. "Let you know Abe was a'comin'. Wouldn't hurt you, though. Just be on my way. Catch a fish for dinner." He stooped to pick up his pole.

"Wait," Kate said. She bent and picked up his pail, holding it out to him. He was an old black man, maybe ninety, maybe more. He had a little nap of white hair fringing his wrinkled scalp and grizzled white whiskers on his cheeks. "I'm Kate Gallagher," she said, extending her hand.

The old man wiped his hand on faded jeans that hung loose on his tiny, aged frame. With his other hand, he removed an old slouch hat and held it at his side respectfully. "Pleased to meetcha, ma'am. Everybody calls me Ole Abe. Got another name, but don't rightly 'member it no more."

"Well, Mr. Abe, I'm pleased to meet you. I'm sorry I screamed that way."

"Ole Abe, he don't bother nobody. Yassum. Better that way. Go to bed early and say my prayers. Thas what I do."

"What are you doing out here all by yourself?"

"Just be, thas all. Live down the road. White folks don't mind none. Show 'em where the deers been. Thas all."

"Did you hear anything strange three or four nights ago?"

"Heard Ole Mistuh Death walking."

"Death?"

"Ole Mistuh Death hisself. The woods go all quiet when he's out walking, tormentin' folks. He's out ever' night."

"Have you ever seen Mr. Death? Can you describe him?"

The old man frowned, nodding. "No offense, missy, but ole Mistuh Death, he's white. God is black, a course, but ole Death, he's white as you are. Thas his punishment for being evil like he is."

"I suspect you're right," Kate said. "I do believe you're right."

"Come in a car that night. Thought it was strange. Mistuh Death don't usually ride in no car."

"You heard a car?"

"Yassum."

"Did you see it?"

"Ole Abe was praying. Didn't wanna see no Mistuh Death that night. No, ma'am."

"Did you hear anything else?"

"Just ole Mistuh Death in his chariot."

Five

He followed the whore out to the River Inn, driving past when she pulled into the parking lot. He went on a ways before turning around and coming back to park behind the trees. He could see her sitting there, still wearing the white scarf around her hair.

He didn't know why they called it the River Inn when it wasn't an inn, nothing but a juke joint where people gathered to drink, dance, swear, fornicate—to sin in a multitude of ways, to mock the laws of God. He had saved one woman from lust. Three, if you counted the others. He would save more.

She had looked real peaceful, lying there on the table. He had fixed her up nice, too, making her look as though she was going to church on a bright, warm Sunday morning. Put a real dress on her, in place of that slut's dress she was wearing that night. Prayed for her the whole time he was fixing her up, just like he prayed for her that night. Told her to pray, too, but he couldn't tell if she did or not with the tape across her mouth like that. Told her to pray, though. Wasn't his fault if she didn't.

The whore should pray, too, instead of sitting there in the little red car with the top down, using the rearview mirror to put Satan's makeup on her lips like that, getting ready to entice some man into the flames of hell. It wasn't right for Willie's sister to act like that. Willie called her a whore, too, always taking up for the niggers and the poor white trash like she did, keeping them out of Parchman when they deserved punishment for their transgressions. Now, she would lead Kathryn Anne into sin, too. He'd seen them together that afternoon, coming out of the whore's office across from the courthouse. He waited to see what the whore would do instead of going after Kathryn Anne, and when she came out of the courthouse an hour later, he followed as she drove out of town, her white scarf flying in the wind.

He looked at her through the binoculars and could see the slashes of red on her lips. Willie was right: she acted like a whore. Willie said it wouldn't surprise him none if she slept with niggers, too. They ought to take her out one night and teach her a lesson. Willie wouldn't want to kill her, not his own sister, but maybe they ought to take her out one night and string her up, beat some sense into her with a horsewhip. That's what they used to do if a white woman started doing wrong.

Maybe Willie wouldn't want to hurt his sister, either. He said he hated her, but she was family, and people were funny about family sometimes. It wasn't like that with his own sister. Maybe he should do it to her. Then she wouldn't pick on him all the time like she did. No; he couldn't do that to Sally. He had to be nice to her so she would invite Kathryn Anne over to dinner one night. He wanted to show Kathryn Anne his stamp collection. He had to be nice to Sally, for a while longer, anyway. Had to do it just right, too, real casual-like. Say, I saw your friend Kathryn Anne downtown. Must be home visiting her folks. No, that wasn't right. Sally would know she was home because of the trouble her brother was in. Just say, I saw your friend Kathryn Anne. Let Sally think it was her idea to invite her over. Then I can invite her into my room and show her the stamps and she'll lean over and I can feel her titties all soft and nice and she'll rub against me and say how much she's missed me all these years and come back and live with me and we'll throw Sally out and stay in the house together all the time.

He was still thinking about touching Kathryn Anne's breasts when she pulled in and parked next to the whore. Kathryn Anne and the whore both got out of their cars and stood together, talking for a few minutes. Then, his Kathryn Anne helped the whore put the top up on her convertible. They turned toward the entrance and the flashing neon lights of sin.

Kathryn Anne, don't go in there with that whore. Please, Kathryn Anne, don't be like her. Don't make me hurt you, too.

Six

Images of death danced through Kate's mind as she drove away from the cabin, the air conditioner turned high, pumping the chill air of the grave into the car. In the rearview mirror she saw the old man standing forlornly in the clearing in front of the cabin, fishing pole in one hand, pail in the other, waiting for death. The old man heard Mr. Death in the woods that night and reminded Kate of Philip Moore, Dr. Death and his victims who sat on death row in San Quentin, awaiting their appointment in Samarra. The epigraph was from John O'Hara's novel. Kate had read it years ago, in college. How did it go? *What are you doing here? Death asked. I have an appointment with you in Samarra.* That can't be right, Kate thought . . . I'll have to look it up.

On the seat beside her, the pages in the case folder riffled in the stream of cold air from the air conditioner, as though life still flickered in the black-and-white images of Billie Rae's body, as though she struggled to return from the underworld. Kate turned the vent aside and the pages within the folder quivered one last time and then lay still. Kate shuddered, and not entirely from the cold air streaming over her.

Still thinking about old Mr. Death in his chariot, Kate nearly passed the River Inn. She had never been in the River Inn, although it had been there for as long as she could remember, a gathering place for wild young women and even wilder men seeking excitement, and for couples bored with the hard existence of life in the Delta. It had a long history of fights, knifings, even an occasional shooting. In the old days, anyone under the legal drinking age would be served at the River Inn. In an even more distant time, legend had it that the River Inn was a whorehouse, but the old aluminum trailers that had been parked in the back were long gone. As Kate braked hard, she wondered if the newest generation of River Inn pleasure seekers worried about AIDS.

When she parked next to the little red sports car, Tracie waved and smiled.

"I have one of those," Kate said. "Same color and everything, but how do you stand the humidity with the top down?"

"Drive fast, I guess, but I'm going to have to put the top up now. It looks like a bad storm is coming."

"There was a lot of lightning and thunder over on the Arkansas side of the river. It'll be here soon."

Kate went around to the passenger side of Tracie's car and helped lift the top up and over. She reached in and snapped the handle down to hold the top in place. Opening the door, she rolled up the window.

"Thanks," Tracie said. "Did you find anything out at the cabin?"

"Not really." Kate told her about the old man. "He'd make a great witness if I could get him to remember something and if I could get Cowles to promise not to cross-examine." Kate shook her head. "Can you imagine him on the stand? And what time did old Mr. Death drive past your humble home?"

"Too bad."

"Yeah," Kate said, smiling ruefully. "Well, let's go in and see what we can dig out of the poor sinners of the River Inn."

Kate and Tracie stood just inside the door, letting their eyes adjust to the dim light. The place smelled of stale smoke, beer, and loneliness. The lament for a lost love that played on the jukebox did nothing to dispel the friendless atmosphere. There were a couple of solitary drinkers seated at the bar, staring at their reflections in a long mirror. The barman washed glasses slowly, whistling along with the mournful song. The tables around the small dance floor and the booths that lined the walls were empty. A waitress stood at the far end of the bar, leafing through a magazine. She looked up hopefully when Kate and Tracie entered. The men seated at the bar turned to stare at Tracie.

"Let's take a table," Kate said.

"You don't want to belly up to the bar with the real men?" Tracie asked, smiling at Kate.

"Later, when the action starts."

"This place could use some action."

The River Inn was depressing. Kate wondered why Drew and Billie Rae would meet there. She thought again about Tommy Harper and wondered what might have happened between them in marriage, if the River Inn or another of the countless places just like it would now constitute an important part of their lives. Hey, Kate, let's go on down to the River Inn and dance.

"What can I get y'all?" the waitress drawled.

"Tracie?"

"I'm a good Southern gal. Beer for me."

Kate nodded. "Make it two, please."

"Coming right up."

"Is this place as wild as it used to be?" Kate asked.

"If you mean are there fights and an occasional murder, the answer is yes."

"Some things never change."

"You gals want to run a tab, or what?" the waitress asked.

"Sure," Kate said, distracted, glancing down at a note in

her hand. Kate looked up at the waitress. "We're looking for Linda Russell. Will she be working tonight?"

"That's me," the waitress said, her eyes widening. "Oh, lordy, what did I do now?"

"Nothing," Kate said quickly. "I understand the police talked with you about the man who's accused of murdering his girlfriend."

"Yeah, they sure did."

"Well, we're representing Drew Anderson. We're his attorneys. We'd like to ask you a few questions, too. Will that be all right?"

"Sure, I guess so. I like Drew. He's always nice to me, not like some of the jerks you meet in here, but let me go tell Jack first so he don't think I'm loafing with the customers. Do y'all want to talk with him, too? He was here that night."

"Yes, we'd like that very much."

"I'll tell him."

When she was gone, Tracie raised her beer bottle to Kate. "Welcome home, and here's to our success."

Kate clinked her bottle against Tracie's. "To home, and success," she said.

Linda Russell returned carrying a coffee cup and pulled a chair up to the table. "Jack don't mind talking to you," Linda said, "specially since it's so slow right now. Are you really lawyers? No kidding?"

Kate nodded. "We're really lawyers. Drew's also my brother."

"Oh, shit," Linda said. "I bet you feel real bad about what happened."

"We don't think Drew did it," Kate said.

"I don't, either," Linda said. "Like I said, Drew's always nice, too nice to do something terrible like that."

"The police report said you heard them arguing."

"Everybody did. Billie Rae was real loud. She was saying

things to him that he didn't deserve—mean things. I think she wanted to hurt him real bad."

"Do you know what started it?"

"The usual stuff, I suppose," Linda said. "She was already drinking pretty heavy when he got here. Kinda primed, you know."

"They didn't come together?" With two versions of the same story already from the police and Drew, Kate didn't expect great variations, but on occasion the unexpected happened. Preparation was the only way to win in court. Whether you were appearing for the prosecution or for the defense, you had to get into the facts of the case, poke and pry around, worry things about. Look for the discrepancies that inevitably appeared.

"Billie Rae, she'd been here for an hour, kinda steaming, you know? I guess maybe your brother was late, and that kinda pissed Billie Rae off. She was already making eyes at Ronny."

"Ronny is the truck driver?" Kate already knew the answer.

"Yeah. The bastard . . . that thing of his is like a snake, you know? Always looking for someplace warm."

"Does he usually find it?"

"I reckon he does. But not that night, not with Billie Rae. She got pissed at him. Pulled a gun on him."

"What?" That wasn't in the police report.

"Sure, pulled a little ole gun on him. One of them shiny ones."

"Nickel-plated?"

"Yeah. That's it. Nickel-plated."

"You didn't tell the police that."

"Sure I did."

Kate turned to Tracie. "Was it in the police report?"

Tracie shook her head. "No mention of a gun."

"What did Ronny do after Billie Rae pulled the gun on him?"

"Nothing. Went back to drinking. Kinda sobered him up, I reckon."

"How long did he stay here?"

Linda hesitated. "Closing time."

"Did he leave with anyone?"

Again, Linda hesitated. "Yeah, he did."

"Do you know her name?"

"It was me," Linda said. Even in the dim light of the bar, they could see the blush spread through Linda's cheeks. "Ronny's my guy. He gets likkered up sometimes and tries to play around a bit, but he's always real sorry later. I sure made him beg for it that night."

Scratch Ronny as a suspect, Kate thought. "Can you remember anything else that might help us?" she asked. "Forget about the argument between Drew and Billie Rae, forget about her and Ronny for the moment. Was there anything else unusual about that night? Did anyone else in the bar seem interested in Billie Rae, talk to her, dance with her, anything like that?"

"No, not really. They just had this argument, and then your brother stormed out of here. He was real mad at her. I could tell. She just finished her drink, calm as can be, and moved right up to Ronny and started rubbing against him. She was like that sometimes. I don't mean to talk bad about the dead, you know, but Billie Rae, well, she was real crazy sometimes."

"Did she come here before? I mean alone, or with someone other than my brother."

"Sure, lots of times."

"Can you give us their names?"

"Gee, I don't wanna get nobody in trouble."

"We just want to talk to them, see if they can help us."

"I guess it'll be all right."

Tracie wrote down the names as Linda recited them. The waitress was able to provide details about several of the men, but for the rest . . . "I'll spend some time with the telephone book," Tracie said.

The door opened and two more men walked in. "Whew!" one of them shouted. "Big storm coming, Jack. Better start pouring us some weatherproofing."

"I guess I'd better get back to work," Linda said.

"Thanks for your help," Kate said.

Tracie handed Linda her card. "If you think of anything else or hear of anything that might help us, give me a call."

"What's this E-S-Q mean?" Linda asked, spelling it out.

"It's just a fancy way of saying I'm a lawyer."

"Oh. Well, I hope you find the guy who did it. Billie Rae was a little crazy, but she didn't deserve nothing like that."

Jack the bartender added little to what Linda had told them. He'd heard some of the argument, but so had everyone in the bar. "I was pretty busy," he said. "Lot of people in here that night. Always pretty crowded, good times and bad. People drink to celebrate when the money's coming in easy, and they drink to forget when times get hard. Seems like they always got money for a few beers."

"Did you see Billie Rae pull a gun on Ronny?"

"Is that what happened? Thought he looked a mite pale when he came back to the bar. Figured Linda might shoot him, but she's a forgiving woman, I reckon."

"So you didn't see a gun?"

"Naw, nothing like that."

"Thanks for your help."

"Linda has my card," Tracie said. "If you remember anything else, I'd appreciate it if you called."

"Sure. Be happy to, but like I said, I was pretty busy."

"How much do we owe you?" Kate asked.

"Those two fellas at the bar would like to buy you ladies a drink."

Kate smiled. "Thank them, but we have to be going."

"They're gonna be real disappointed."

"Believe me," Tracie said, "so are we."

"That'll cheer them up."

"It better, because that's all they're going to get."

"Y'all come back, hear? I'll buy you a drink myself."

"Now, we might take you up on that sometime."

"It'd be my pleasure."

Outside, the early evening had turned dark and angry. Rain poured down, lightning flashed, peals of thunder rocked the heavens. The two women stood under the overhang and glumly looked out at the rain.

"There goes our hair," Tracie said.

"Would you like to meet your client?"

"I guess I should."

"Come to dinner at my mother's."

"I don't want to impose."

"You won't."

"If you're sure . . ."

"Positive," Kate said. "Follow me. I'll take it easy in this weather."

Neither Kate nor Tracie noticed the headlights that suddenly flashed on in the rain behind them.

Margaret Anderson greeted Tracie effusively, pretending everything was normal. "You just make yourself at home, hear? Drew, you get Tracie something to drink. What would you like, dear? Iced tea? Or would you rather have some of that Scotch Drew keeps hidden away where he thinks I won't find it?"

"Iced tea is fine, Mrs. Anderson."

"I'll get it, Mama."

"It's no bother, Kate. You three just go on and sit down. I know you got things to talk about." Margaret went off into the kitchen, quickly returning with a pitcher of tea and glasses for Kate and Tracie. "You want some tea, Drew?"

"No, I'm going to have Scotch."

"Well, dinner'll be ready in just a little bit. Pork chops and scalloped potatoes. I hope you like pork chops, Tracie."

"I do indeed, Mrs. Anderson."

"Well, I'll call you."

Drew took the bottle of Scotch from a hallway closet. "Sure you won't join me, Tracie, Kate?"

"Tea's fine, Drew."

"Are you related to Willie Sanders?" Drew asked.

"Unfortunately," Tracie replied. "Do you know him?"

"I've seen him around, and a few of the boys he runs with. They have some strange ideas."

"I told Kate about Willie this morning," Tracie said. "If my brother's a problem for you, I'll certainly withdraw."

Drew shook his head. "I was just wondering if you were related. It's not a problem." He turned to Kate abruptly. "Did you go out to the cabin?"

"I talked to an old black man. Says he heard Mr. Death in his chariot that night."

"Old Abe? He always hears things in the night, but he's harmless. A lot of the boys throw a little work his way, especially during hunting season. If you hire Abe as a guide, you almost always get your buck."

"Are you an avid hunter?" Tracie asked.

Drew shook his head. "I don't like hunting much, killing things. I just like to go out there and sit around. I like the smell of the woods. Used to, anyway. Reckon I'll sell the place off now."

"Did you take Billie Rae to the cabin?"

"A few times. She didn't like it much out there."

"Did you know Billie Rae carried a gun?" Kate knew she

sounded like a prosecutor, accusing Drew of withholding facts that might be important.

"Sure."

"You didn't tell me."

"I didn't think of it."

"But you knew she carried one?"

"She always had it with her. Let fly at the drive-in one night. She didn't like the movie we were watching."

"Drew, God damn it, why didn't you tell me that? You've got to talk to me, to us, tell us everything. The gun wasn't mentioned in the police reports. It wasn't found afterward."

"The killer took it. So what does that tell us?"

Kate shook her head in exasperation. "I'm going to see if Mama needs some help. You tell him, Tracie."

"It indicates Billie Rae knew her killer. She wasn't hesitant to use a gun, apparently. She pulled it on the man who tried to pick her up after you left the River Inn. You say she fired it at a movie screen. It would seem that whoever met her after she left the bar didn't appear to be a threat to her."

"There could be a hundred explanations for that. He came up on her from behind. She passed out. Anything."

Kate returned from the kitchen. "Or she knew the killer," Kate said, "and didn't feel threatened by him. We've got to start somewhere. I mean it, Drew. You've got to talk to us or we can't help you."

"She had a mole on her right breast. Called it her devil's mark. Does that help?"

"I don't know," Kate said solemnly. "Yet."

"Jesus, you're serious about all this."

"I have to be, Drew. Otherwise, we may have an appointment in Samarra."

"What?"

Kate shook her head. "It's nothing. Just something I remember reading in college."

* * *

After dinner, Kate made her mother go into the living room and sit with Drew while she and Tracie cleared the table and started on the dishes. Kate washed, thinking she would get her mother a dishwasher for Christmas whether she wanted one or not, although she knew her mother would resist, just as she'd refused to get an answering machine or a microwave or a VCR for her television, although each of her three children nagged her constantly about the convenience and luxury of such appliances. Kate handed a plate to Tracie and asked, "Well, what do you think?"

"Drew is going to have a hard time of it. He's confused and caught up in something he doesn't understand and doesn't know how to solve. He's going to find out who his friends are, that's for sure."

"I don't believe his receptionist quit just like that. She's been with him for years."

"It's a small town," Tracie said bitterly. "There are a lot of mean-spirited people in a small town like this, always willing to believe the worst about someone, even without a shred of proof. At least, Drew has his family. He's lucky to have a sister like you. I wish I had a brother like him."

"Has it been hard for you, Tracie?"

"Oh, it's not so bad. I don't have many friends here because of Willie. People are afraid of him. He's been arrested for murder, but they couldn't prove it. It's just a matter of time, though. He'll do something that he can't lie his way out of. I find it just a little ironic that I'm defending your brother from a murder charge and when my brother was arrested, I wanted to prosecute."

Standing at the kitchen sink and washing the dishes in the familiar rite of her childhood, Kate looked out into the darkness of the backyard. The rain had stopped, but flashes of lightning still lit the yard. Suddenly, Kate reached across and flipped the switch for the back porch light.

"What is it?" Tracie asked.

"I thought I saw someone out there." Kate went to the door and opened it.

Tracie followed, still absently drying the plate in her hands. "Where?" she asked.

"Over by the hedge, but I don't see anything now," Kate said.

They stood on the porch for a moment. "Probably just shadows," Tracie said.

"Probably," Kate agreed. "God, it's muggy. I'd forgotten what it's like around here during the summer."

When they were back in the kitchen, Kate said, "Since I've been yelling at Drew for full disclosure, there's something I'd better let you know about."

"What's that?"

Kate told Tracie about the note sent to Drew.

"If it weren't for the 'or else' part, you might have a secret admirer."

"It's probably nothing. Some crank."

"Do you think it's connected?"

"I don't see how it could be. Drew got the note months ago."

"It's certainly strange."

"Everything's been strange since Dr. Death walked into my courtroom."

"Dr. Death?"

"My boss back home. He's sent a lot of people to death row."

"That's not very pleasant to live with. Have you ever tried a death penalty case?"

"Not yet."

"We're lucky that Cowles's case is circumstantial, or this would be a death penalty case."

"In California, Drew wouldn't get bail if, quote, the proof was evident or the presumption thereof great, unquote, in a special circumstances case."

"What are you girls talking about?" Margaret asked, bustling into her kitchen. "I wish you'd let me help."

"We're almost done, Mama. You just go in and talk to Drew."

"That boy! He hasn't said a word the whole time I've been in there."

"He's got a lot on his mind, Mama."

"And I suppose I don't? I just can't take much more of this worry."

"Everything will be fine, Mrs. Anderson," Tracie said.

"I know you're right, honey, but I just can't help it. I never thought anything like this could ever happen to us."

"Drew didn't think so, either," Kate said.

The telephone rang. "Hello?" Margaret Anderson answered. "Well, I declare, Sally Roberts . . . I appreciate that, Sally, I truly do . . . Yes, she's right here. Kate, it's Sally Roberts calling for you."

"Sally, how are you?"

"Jimmy told me you were in town. I suppose I should have guessed, what with all the trouble Drew's having. I think it's a damned shame how anybody could think Drew would do anything like that. It just doesn't make any sense."

"I know. We're all sick about it."

"Well, you tell Drew we're all praying for him."

"I will, Sally. Thank you. He'll appreciate it."

"I know you're busy and all, but I'd love to see you before you go back. Do you think we could get together sometime? Come over here for dinner. Jimmy'd like to see you, too, I know."

"How is Jimmy?"

"Same old Jimmy. All he cares about is that old stamp collection of his. He's still working at the mortuary. I think being around death all the time has made him even slower than he was."

"Well, tell him I said hello."

"He's out right now, but I'll do that, Kate."

"And let me give you a call about dinner. I just don't know right now. I'd love to see you. Can I give you a buzz tomorrow, maybe?"

"Sure, Kate, you just let me know." Sally paused. "Just so long as it's before I go to Europe."

"You're not," Kate said. Sally had talked about going to Europe for as long as Kate could remember.

"Yep. I'm finally going to do it."

"Good for you. I'm really glad to hear it. I think that's great."

"Me, too. I can hardly believe it myself. Well, you give me a call now and take care, hear?"

"I will, Sally. You too."

"That was nice of Sally to call," Margaret said, when Kate had replaced the phone. "She always asks about you whenever I run into her at the market. But that brother she has is a strange one."

"Jimmy's all right, Mama. I like him. He's just a little slow, that's all. But he's harmless."

Seven

Death invaded Kate's dreams, stalking her through a dark forest where the skeletal fingers of trees pulled and tore at her clothing until she ran naked, heavy breasts bobbing painfully as she sought to escape the clutching fingers that now ripped at her flesh like the talons of a great bird of prey. Crude wooden signs were nailed to trunks of trees, each with a single word and an arrow painted in blood still wet and dripping.

Samarra.

Kate ran, twisting and turning away from one arrow's direction only to confront another sign and another blood-streaked arrow. Behind her, Death glided silently and patiently through the darkness. She could not escape.

Kate burst into a clearing and saw the scaffold waiting to embrace her. She fell sobbing to the ground and slithered away on her back as the shrouded figure approached. Long black snakes wrapped themselves around her wrists, their mouths wide, venomous fangs dripping blood . . . her blood. The snakes pulled her arms widespread above her head and dragged her to the wooden frame. Her heels left streaks in the dirt as she was drawn to the scaffold and hoisted aloft, the snakes binding her bloodied wrists to the wooden posts.

Kate hung helplessly from outstretched arms and watched Death's grim approach. She wanted to plead, cry out, tell

Death that it was a mistake, but thick, rough tape plastered her mouth.

The cowled shroud parted and Kate looked down at Billie Rae Scott's lifeless eyes and the thick worms writhing out of the bloody slit in her belly. The silent scream echoed through her mind.

No!

The hands of Death were cold on her breasts, suffocating her. She couldn't breathe. The fingers of Death ripped the tape from her mouth.

Kate sat up in bed and screamed, gasping for breath. A cat squalled in answer. The weight was gone from her chest. Sweat pasted the nightgown to her flesh. Heart pounding, Kate turned the bedside lamp on.

A black cat sat at the foot of the bed, contemplating her with large yellow eyes.

"Jesus, you scared me. Where did you come from?"

The cat—more of a kitten really, it wasn't very big—stretched and approached Kate timidly, mewing softly. Kate stroked its fur, feeling a purr begin. Kate sighed and got out of bed. After putting a robe over her damp nightgown, Kate carried the cat downstairs and poured milk in a saucer, watching as the cat lapped greedily.

A window was propped open six inches, a gap large enough for the cat to enter the house. There's the explanation, Kate thought. There's an explanation for everything . . . even death and nightmares.

Tracie was late, so Kate left her car parked in front of the office and walked the two blocks to the public library, where she quickly found a battered and dusty copy of John O'Hara's *Appointment in Samarra* on a bottom shelf. When she'd talked with Harry before going to bed, she'd asked him about the epigraph for the novel, but he couldn't remember how it went, either. She had called both of the girls, too, but neither Allison nor Melissa had read it. Perhaps no one read O'Hara anymore. That was a shame, Kate thought. It'd be a good Christmas present for both Allison and Melissa.

The book in her hands now was the same old Modern Library edition she'd read in college. Kate carried it to a reading table and opened it to the title page. She was surprised to find that O'Hara had taken his title from a play by W. Somerset Maugham. The epigraph was headed "DEATH SPEAKS." Kate read:

> There was a merchant in Baghdad who sent his servant to market to buy provisions and in a little while the servant came back, white and trembling, and said, Master, just now when I was in the market-place I was jostled by a woman in the crowd and when I turned I saw it was Death that jostled me. She looked at me and made a threatening gesture; now, lend me your horse, and I will ride away from this city and avoid my fate. I will go to Samarra and there Death will not find me. The merchant lent him his horse, and the servant mounted it, and he dug his spurs in its flanks and as fast as the horse could gallop he went. Then the merchant went down to the market-place and he saw me standing in the crowd and he came to me and said, Why did you make a threatening gesture to my servant when you saw him this morning? That was not a threatening gesture, I said, it was only a start of surprise. I was astonished to see him in Baghdad, for I had an appointment with him tonight in Samarra.

So, Kate thought, Death is a woman, just like my nightmare last night. She leafed idly through the book and read passages at random.

Kate closed the novel. Did Billie Rae believe in God or a

rabbit's foot or her gun? They had all failed her finally, leaving her alone to keep her appointment with death in an isolated clearing. If Billie Rae had not argued with Drew, or if Billie Rae had stayed with Ronny, or if Billie Rae . . .

Or what?

Kate left the book on the table. On a whim, she went to the library's computerized catalog and typed in S=JACK THE RIPPER. A number of entries appeared on the screen. With the catalog number in mind, she went to the stacks.

Every book on Jack the Ripper was checked out.

Kate went to the librarian's desk. "I was looking for material on Jack the Ripper," Kate said.

The librarian, an attractive woman in her late thirties, frowned. "Everybody's suddenly interested in the subject since that horrible murder. That young reporter was the first—he checked everything out. Since then, a number of people have asked for them. A morbid curiosity, I suppose. Even our district attorney, Mr. Cowles, came in yesterday. I did have one book on the reference shelf . . ."

"Did?"

"Well, I let Mr. Cowles have it, seeing how he was so interested and it was official. Technically, I suppose, I shouldn't have done it, since reference materials are supposed to be noncirculating. I let him have it on a seven-day loan only, though. He'll return it next week. You could use it then."

Kate shook her head. "Thanks, anyway."

Walking back to Tracie's office, Kate felt people watching her from inside the stores or turning to look back at her as she passed by. She felt like the strange kid in a new classroom with everyone staring, appraising her shoes, her dress, even the way she combed her hair, whispering about her, laughing cruelly as they made instant judgments, determining her future for all time without hesitation. Kate had heard those whispers in too many classrooms as a child and remembered the long-ago pain. She could imagine what they said now in the ebb and flow of smalltown gossip.

"She's that Anderson girl—Drew's sister. The man who killed that girl out near the river? I hear she's a lawyer now. Out in California someplace. Come back home to get her brother off. Well, doesn't she just look full of herself? Walking down the street like she owned it. Wonder where she got that dress? She got divorced, didn't she? Heard she had a couple of kids. Well, she oughta be home taking care of them, then—that's what I think."

I don't care what you think.

But the murmurs—real and imaginary—followed Kate.

Tracie's car was in front of the office now, parked next to the rental car. The top was down and the red paint gleamed in the morning heat.

"Good morning," Kate said.

Tracie gave Kate a Polaroid photograph with a trembling hand. "I found this when I went out this morning. That's why I was late."

Kate looked at the photo. It was Tracie's little sports car. A single word was scrawled in white on the windshield: WHORE.

"Soap?"

Tracie nodded. "I took the picture . . . I don't know why."

Kate looked at the photo again. The car was parked on what appeared to be a quiet residential street. "Did you report it? Ask neighbors if they saw or heard anything?"

Tracie shook her head. "I was too embarrassed. I had to scrub like everything to get it off. I feel like it's still there for everyone to see and laugh at."

"Has anything like this ever happened before?" Kate asked.

TELL YOUR SISTER TO COME HOME.

OR ELSE.

I LOVE HER.

"No," Tracie said. "I keep pretty much to myself."

"No old boyfriends who might want to hurt you? Anything like that?"

Tracie turned away and stared at the *Arizona Highways* wall calendar. The month had been moved forward to August, even though it was only mid-July. The calendar photograph had been taken at sunset. The rippled clouds above the desert floor had turned dark red, as though the heavens were bleeding. A lone saguaro cactus stood in the foreground.

When Tracie turned back, Kate saw the loneliness in the glistening tears. She wanted to take Tracie in her arms, comfort her, tell her that everything would be all right. It would be a lie, though. It was never all right. "Next year in the promised land . . ." It was always next year that things would be better. Kate had heard it all her life.

"You must know what it's like, Kate. The people I meet . . . The cops ask me out and sometimes I go, but they just want to see how fast they can get my clothes off, get me into bed with them. Or worse, in the back seat of a car. The other lawyers aren't much better, and most of them are married. It's a dead end here."

She's so beautiful and so filled with hurt, Kate thought. "Do you know a cop named Cory Martin?" she asked.

"He's one of the married ones," Tracie replied. "He's been after me to go out with him. Why?"

"Just curious. He asked me out the day I got here. Pie and coffee."

"And the back seat of his county car."

"I figured as much."

"I'm not a whore, Kate. I'm not."

"I know, Tracie, I know."

The young woman turned to the calendar again. "Sometimes I think I'd like to go there, lose myself in the desert. Have you ever been to Arizona?"

"Once. On vacation." Harry had seduced Kate in the hot, bubbling waters of a hotel Jacuzzi late at night, kissing her passionately as the water swirled around them, unfastening the halter of her bathing suit, caressing her breasts made slippery by the water. Oh, Christ, what if someone comes? And then she didn't care anymore, and later, riding up in the elevator, the halter stuffed in a pocket of the robe, with Harry's hands roaming over her body while he kissed her again and again, she could hardly wait until they were back in their room, giving herself to him like a whore, but receiving a pleasure the whore never knew.

"I went there last year," Tracie said. "I even looked at houses. There was this one place in Scottsdale, on Pinnacle Peak? The backyard was the desert. It was so beautiful."

Kate smiled. "It sounds like the place for you."

"It's my dream," Tracie replied wistfully. "I'll make it come true, somehow. Soon."

"Why did you change the calendar so soon?"

Tracie smiled. "Sometimes I get impatient."

"Would you like a cat?" Kate asked.

Tracie smiled for the first time that day.

He sat on a bench on the courthouse lawn, drinking orange juice and eating a second jelly doughnut. His sister didn't like him to eat jelly doughnuts, but she wouldn't know. He wasn't mad at her anymore, though. She had called Kathryn Anne and invited her to dinner. Kathryn Anne would come and he would show her the stamps. I'll show her the first-day issue of the Elvis Presley stamps. Postmarked in Memphis and everything. She'll be impressed with those.

With the glare of the sun, it was hard to see into the small office across the street. But he could see the two women as shadows, moving back and forth past the window. He couldn't tell which shadow belonged to his beloved Kathryn

Anne and which was the whore. He had decided that he would always call her Kathryn Anne. It was such a lovely name, much better than Kate. It matched her grace and beauty. He didn't like it when his sister called her Kate. When they were together, he would always call her Kathryn Anne. And when they were together, Kathryn Anne wouldn't have to associate with whores anymore. He would see to that.

He was sticky from the doughnuts. He carefully wiped his lips and fingers with the napkin and reluctantly stood up to return. There was work to be done. A young woman, killed in a car accident, had been brought in overnight. He wondered if the victim would have nice breasts like Kathryn Anne.

"What's going on here, Tracie?"

"What do you mean?"

"Back home, if the cops brought me this case, I wouldn't file it. Not with what they have. I'd say we didn't have enough evidence. I'd tell them to go back and get me some hard evidence that would put the perp at the scene. Something more than circumstantial."

"Kate, I agree with you. I read the file very carefully last night. There's reasonable doubt all over the place. It jumps out at you from damn near every page. I don't think they have much of a case. I think we'll tear them up at the prelim. There's no way they're going to hold Drew to answer for Billie Rae's murder."

"Tell me about Wilson Cowles: why would he file something as flimsy as this and even prosecute it himself? He should know he's going to lose. Damage his reputation. Everything is circumstantial. There's no hard evidence that puts Drew anywhere near his cabin that night."

"Wilson's ambitious. Maybe all this Delta Ripper publicity got to him."

"When I was in the library, I looked up Jack the Ripper.

All of the books on the subject have been checked out by the newspaper reporter, except for one that was on the reference shelf. Wilson has that one. So maybe it's a high-profile case that he'd better win if he wants to go places."

"Perhaps. Wilson suffers from the same thing that any black American in Mississippi does—he has to be twice as good as a white man in order to get any respect. But he's an honorable man. I don't think he'd hide anything from us."

"Maybe not," Kate said, "but I think we'd better file the formal motions for discovery. I want everything on the record."

"I drew them up last night. We'll see the judge this morning. Hearing's at eleven."

"Did you ask for the investigating officer's notes?"

"Yes. I want to know why no mention was made of Billie Rae's gun."

"Good. Let's see what we can find. It may be that we'll go after their personnel files. One of them might have a history of suppressing evidence." It was the shotgun approach to criminal defense. George Devers had taught her that: fire blindly into the morass of criminal law and hope like hell one of the pellets hits something.

"If the defendant happened to be black," Tracie said, "that might be true. I doubt it with a white man, but you never know."

"After the discovery hearing, I want to look at Billie Rae's apartment. Drew gave me a key. We'll have to get permission, I suppose."

Tracie nodded. "Did Billie Rae have a key to his place as well?"

"He said she didn't. I don't know, though. Drew's been acting strange."

"With good reason."

"I suppose, but I keep having this nagging feeling that he's holding back something." Kate shook her head. "I just don't know. What about the judge? Tell me about him." That was something else Devers had taught her. If you're weak on the facts, attack the law. If you're weak on the law, attack the facts. If you're weak on both, attack the prosecutor . . . or the judge . . . or the cops . . . or everyone and everything.

"Old money. Old family. Served several terms in the state legislature. When he lost a campaign, the governor appointed him to the bench. He's been a good judge. Always treated me fairly, although his heart is with the prosecution. He's tough in sentencing. He's given a couple of my clients the max when they didn't deserve it."

"Why did he lose his campaign?"

"I don't know. It was before my time. He's been on the bench since way before I got here. A long time."

"I think I'd like to find out why he lost. I don't think it has any bearing on the case, but it won't hurt to know everything there is going in. There might be a reason to lay some paper on him."

"He won't like it if you try to disqualify him."

"Too bad."

The discovery hearing lasted ten minutes. Girardeau granted each of the defense motions and permission to visit Billie Rae Scott's apartment.

Afterward, Wilson Cowles said, "There was no reason for that. My policy is to give the defense everything we have."

"We appreciate that, Mr. Cowles. We'd just like to have everything on the record."

"What about Billie Rae's gun?" Tracie asked.

"What gun?"

Crime scene tapes crisscrossed the door of Billie Rae Scott's apartment even though she had been killed elsewhere. Inside, the apartment was hot and stale. The air conditioner had been turned off; Kate turned it on full blast. She didn't think Billie Rae would mind. She wouldn't have to pay the bill now.

The police had not desecrated Billie's place as they had the hunting cabin. Kate wondered whether it was out of respect for the dead, or just plain laziness on their part. To their minds, they had arrested and charged the murderer. Presumably, they didn't expect to find anything. With that attitude, they wouldn't come up with anything.

"Where do you want to start?" Tracie asked.

"The bedroom, I guess."

"Everything always comes down to the bedroom, doesn't it?"

"Usually. It's where I keep everything important."

"That's not what I meant," Tracie said.

"It's not what I meant, either."

They started their search slowly, gingerly, each feeling as though she was invading Billie Rae's privacy. It was Tracie who found her birth control pills. Kate discovered a drawer of bikini panties and matching black and red lace brassieres with openings for Billie Rae's nipples. Idly, Kate looked at the tag. Thirty-six C. It was her own size. Kate discarded the brassiere. She closed the dresser drawer carefully.

Tracie uncovered a batch of what appeared to be letters between Billie and a former lover. "She dotted the Is in her name with little circles," Tracie said.

It was Kate who found the nude photos of Billie, modeling in a variety of seductive poses. They reminded Kate of the young women from the magazines she'd found in Drew's cabin. In each photo, Billie worked too hard, too self-consciously to be sexy, appearing pathetic in her effort to please whoever took the pictures. In one, Billie stood with her back to the camera a red devil tattooed on her left buttock grinned evilly at the camera.

"Look at these," Kate said, passing the amateur photos to Tracie.

"She must have thought she was being very sexy."

"Jesus, I feel sorry for her."

"Drew was right."

"About what?"

"She *did* have a birthmark on her breast."

"He didn't say anything about the tattoo."

"One of those you paste on, probably. They only last a week or so."

Kate slipped the photos in her purse. "I'm taking these. She must have a family. They don't need to see them."

"I wonder why the cops didn't take them. It's the kind of thing they'd do. Sit around laughing at her."

"They didn't even take her address book." Kate opened the book to the beginning of the alphabet. Drew's name and telephone number were written in. His was the fifth or sixth name on the page. All men. "They didn't take anything. Christ, this is sloppy police work. Why?"

"I haven't seen anything like this before," Tracie said. "They're smalltown cops, but they're usually pretty good. Better than this, at least."

"What the hell is going on?"

"It's as if they don't care."

Kate and Tracie were sitting on the living room couch leafing through Billie Rae's high school yearbook when the door pushed open and a man asked, "Who are you?"

Tracie rose quickly. "I'm Tracie Sanders. This is Kathryn Gallagher."

"Don't answer the question none. What're you doing in my sister's place?" He was a tall, gangling man in his early forties. He wore faded jeans and a Budweiser T-shirt. A cigarette package was rolled into the sleeve of the shirt. His face and arms were dark from spending his days in the sun. Behind him, a woman asked, "Who is it, George?"

"Be quiet, Mama," he said over his shoulder. "Well?"

"We're representing Drew Anderson," Kate said.

"That asshole."

Kate's temper flared. "Don't call my brother an asshole."

"You got no right to be here."

"We have court permission to go through Miss Scott's possessions."

"Miss Scott," he said contemptuously. "Miss Tramp be more like it."

"Don't talk about your sister that way, George." A small, birdlike woman pushed past him into the apartment. "I'm Mrs. Leonard, Billie Rae's mother?"

"I'm sorry to meet you under such dreadful circumstances," Kate said. "Please, come in out of the heat. I turned the air conditioner on. I hope you don't mind."

"I guess it don't matter much anymore. We just came to see what needed to be done about collecting Billie Rae's things. I reckon there's no hurry. Rent's paid till the end of the month." She looked around the small apartment. "My, she had it fixed up real nice, didn't she?"

"Yes, she did," Kate lied. The apartment was filled with cheap furnishings and prints on the walls.

"Billie Rae was always good about things like that. Had a real gift for decorating, being a beautician and all?" She took another look around the apartment. Satisfied, she turned back to Kate. "Who'd you say you were?"

"I'm Drew Anderson's sister. Drew didn't kill your daughter, Mrs. Leonard."

"Police say he did."

"You hush, George. Let the lady speak her piece."

"I'm a lawyer, Mrs. Leonard. Drew asked me to represent him. He's broken up over what's happened. He told me he loved your daughter. He didn't do it."

"Billie Rae told me about him. Said she'd found a real man at last. That's the way she put it—a real man. Maybe he didn't do it and maybe he did. But all's I know was, Billie Rae was real excited about him."

"We want to know who really killed Billie Rae just as much as you do," Kate said. "Make sure he pays for his crime."

"I reckon so," Mrs. Leonard said. "Billie Rae was a good girl, a little wild sometimes."

"Ha."

"George, you just shut up, or go sit in the car."

George unrolled the pack of cigarettes from his sleeve in an elaborate ritual, taking one out, pulling a lighter from his pocket, lighting it, blowing smoke toward the three women, before carefully replacing the pack in his sleeve.

"Billie Rae was a good girl," Mrs. Leonard repeated. She picked up the yearbook and sat with it in her lap. "She was real popular in high school. Got good grades. Went on dates. Real popular—everyone liked her."

Kate and Tracie had found only a few photos of Billie Rae in the annual. There were a lot of autographs, but few from other girls. Most were from athletes. Billie Rae had been popular among the members of the football team. Kate could guess why.

"Couldn't wait to graduate from high school and leave the farm," Mrs. Leonard continued. "Didn't see much of her after that cause she'd rather be in the city. Always liked the bright lights, even as a little girl when we'd drive into town. But she never did nobody no harm."

"I know," Kate said soothingly.

"Funeral's on Sunday. She looks real nice. Peaceful now."

Kate made a mental note in her mind to change her return reservation from Sunday morning to Sunday night. "I'd like to come," Kate said. "Pay my respects."

"Did you know my daughter?"

"No, ma'am. But Drew talked about her a lot," Kate lied for a second time. "As I said, Drew loved Billie Rae." That much was true, at least.

"Strange way of showing it," George said.

Eight

The cat was on the porch when Kate and Tracie arrived. He stretched languidly, arching his back, extending one front leg and then the other, never taking his eyes off the two women. By the time Kate and Tracie climbed the steps, he was ready to greet them, going first to Kate as though to thank her for the hospitality of the night before, allowing her to scratch behind his ears. Then, making his choice, he turned to Tracie, rubbing against her leg.

"He's darling," Tracie said, kneeling to scoop him up. The kitten settled docilely into her arms.

"He likes you," Kate said. "He's yours."

"Oh, Lord, what am I going to do with a cat?"

"Name him, for starters."

"I'll have to think about that. We'll have a christening after lunch."

In the kitchen, Kate unpacked the bag of groceries from Kroger's. Cans of tuna fish, light mayonnaise, chili peppers, rye bread, a red onion, celery, curry powder. "Why don't you put some coffee on, or make a pitcher of iced tea? That's about all Drew has in the house except for beer and Scotch."

"He needs a good woman," Tracie said. "Billie Rae wasn't for him."

"He needs a keeper," Kate said, turning to the electric can

opener. I don't want to talk about Billie Rae yet, she thought. Not after this morning.

"How about iced coffee?" Tracie asked.

"Perfect."

While Tracie put the coffee on, Kate opened the tuna and began making lunch. The kitten leaped on the counter and followed their movements with interest.

"You know," Tracie said, "this place isn't what I thought it would be. It's light and airy. I expected something different. Big, gloomy and . . ."

"Haunted?"

"Well, yes, I've heard all the stories about the house."

"Drew's done a lot of work on it. It's been his passion for years. But drive up here at night sometime when no one's home. It's gloomy then. The trees make it even more forbidding. Throw in a lightning storm and you have the original lair of the wicked witch. When we were kids, we came here at Halloween. I couldn't sleep for weeks afterward."

"I'll try to stay away at night. I don't like dark and scary places."

"The world is filled with scary places," Kate said. "Did you ever read Joseph Conrad's *Heart of Darkness?*"

Tracie shook her head. "I read *Lord Jim* in college."

"You get a little feeling for his concept of the world in that. But in the beginning of *Heart of Darkness,* Marlow says, 'And this too has been one of the dark places of the earth.' He's referring to London and England. One of the centers of our Western civilization." Kate shook her head. "Lord, I'm feeling literary today." She told Tracie about her nightmare and going to the library that morning.

"So death is a woman," Tracie said, when Kate paused in the telling.

"That's exactly what I said. Or thought, rather. I still whisper in libraries."

"What does it mean?"

"Nothing, except that I have an overactive imagination and I misspent my youth as a literature major."

"Are you married, Kate?"

"Divorced." Kate started chopping the onion. "After Christopher's umpteenth affair, I couldn't take it any longer. I used to think it was my fault—that I wasn't attractive enough anymore, good enough in bed, something. Afterward, it took me a long time to realize that it wasn't my problem. I have two wonderful daughters, though. They're the only good things to come out of my marriage."

"I don't know how anyone could find you unattractive," Tracie said.

"Thank you, but I feel like an old hag next to you."

Tracie blushed. "Are you involved with anyone now?" she asked. "That sounds so old-fashioned. I mean, anyone special?"

"Yes. There's someone special. His name's Harry. Someday, we might get married. He wants to. He proposed the night before all this started. I don't know, though."

"That's nice."

"Yes, it is." Kate put some of the tuna on a saucer for the kitten. "You give it to him," Kate said, handing the saucer to Tracie.

Tracie put the food on the floor. "Here, kitty."

The kitten leaped from the counter, landing agilely. He purred and growled as he attacked the flaky chunks.

"My God," Tracie exclaimed, "he's got a loud motor."

"He's saying he approves of you." Kate started mixing the tuna salad. "He's also hungry. I didn't have anything to give him last night or this morning except milk."

"Poor, lonely kitty."

"Are you so lonely, Tracie?"

"Sometimes. Mostly I work. I read. When I can't stand it anymore, I spend a weekend in Memphis, going to movies. If you plan it right, you can see three or four films in a day.

Live on popcorn and diet Coke and fantasies. Sometimes, I'll just get in my car and drive. West, always west, never east. Once I got as far as the Texas border before I turned back. I won't be able to do that with a cat."

"Take him with you."

"Why not?" Tracie said wistfully. "He'll be better than the men I've known."

"I take that to mean you're not involved with anyone special?" Kate smiled. "In the old-fashioned sense?"

"No," Tracie replied. She shook her head sadly, looking out into the big backyard. "I keep waiting to meet someone, but I haven't found him yet. Once, I thought . . ."

"Who hurt you so badly, Tracie?"

Tracie looked at Kate, started to speak, turned back to the window. "It was in law school," Tracie said finally, still staring into the yard. "We were going to get married and set up practice together. That was before I told him . . ." Tracie went abruptly to the refrigerator and started to take out ice trays. Then she put them back and closed the door, leaning against it, slumping.

"Told him what, Tracie?"

Agitated, Tracie circled the kitchen table once. The kitten looked up from his food.

"Tracie, what's wrong?"

Tracie looked at Kate, turned away, her eyes empty of emotion. "When I was fifteen, my brother raped me."

"Oh, Jesus, I'm sorry."

"When I told him about it, my fiancé couldn't handle it. I wanted his help, his understanding, and he ran away." Tracie cried then, silently, without sobs, tears the only evidence of a long-suppressed suffering.

With the tears streaming down her cheeks, Tracie told Kate how her brother had terrorized her. She spoke in a cold and distant voice. "And then he laughed at me, said I was no good in bed, that no real man would ever want me."

"Oh, Tracie," Kate said. Despite all the training that told her a rape victim did not want to be touched, Kate took the young woman into her arms. Was there a statute of limitations on the pain that lingered long after the physical violation?

Tracie returned the embrace, sobbing then, burying her face on Kate's shoulder, clinging to her.

Kate held her tightly, seeing the cat leap to the counter, watching and mewing softly as though he understood the woman's anguish.

"It doesn't matter anymore," Tracie said at last. "It was all such a long time ago."

Kate knew how much Tracie lied and hugged her even more, as she would hug one of her daughters who might be in pain, trying to provide long overdue comfort.

"I don't know why I told you," Tracie said, pulling away to wipe at her tears, looking down at the black mascara streaks on her fingers.

"I'm glad you did."

"It only happened once. I carried a knife and swore if he came after me again, I'd cut his balls off." Tracie sighed deeply and then laughed bitterly. "I should have done it anyway and saved everyone a lot of grief and trouble."

It's never too late, Kate thought.

During lunch, Kate decided Tracie possessed both strength and resiliency. The young woman quickly reclaimed control, returning from the bathroom with her makeup repaired, the only evidence of her previous distress her slightly reddened eyes. Perhaps the telling of that distant ordeal had been cathartic for Tracie, a cleansing of emotions.

For the moment.

"This is wonderful tuna salad," Tracie said matter-of-factly.

"Thank you," Kate replied. "I think it's the chili peppers that add a certain tang."

And what had Tracie thought when she'd first looked on the photographs of Billie Rae, bound so grotesquely, and killed in such a horrible fashion? Did it awaken memories of her own ordeal? Christ, I couldn't help but think of it.

As she ate her sandwich, Kate remembered her own scars, that terrible night when Nelson had waited for her in the dark parking lot, attacking her, ripping her clothing, forcing a gag into her mouth, until the specter of Clarence—dear, wonderful not-all-there Clarence—had appeared from the bushes, giving her an opportunity to break away, to draw the pistol from her purse, to feel her finger tightening on the trigger while the bastard begged and pleaded for his life.

God, I came so close to killing him.

"You also put just the right amount of mayonnaise in the tuna," Tracie said. "I hate it when there's too much mayonnaise."

"So do I," Kate said.

You should have shot the motherfucker, the policewoman told her afterward.

The stuff they'd found in Nelson's car . . . Kate made Rainey tell her about the ropes and the handcuffs and worse. She could only imagine what Nelson had planned for her. I should have pulled the trigger. Let it go, Kate. He didn't make you cry, not then, not later in court, when Priscilla Waverly took you ever so gently through your testimony. You had so much help to get you through it. Who was there for Tracie? No one. She had only the strength of her own character to sustain her. Ah, Tracie, you should have cut his balls off.

"Would you like some more?" Kate asked.

"Could we split a sandwich?" Tracie asked shyly.

"Of course." Kate went to the counter and began making another.

Behind her, Tracie said, "he's purring again."

"I told you, he's one happy kitty." He's not like us, Kate thought. Why wouldn't he be happy?

After lunch, Kate said, "Let's get our nails done."

Tracie held her fingers up for inspection. "Lord knows I need it," she said, "but why?"

"I want to know who's got the vapors."

When Kate was growing up, her mother always returned from the beauty parlor filled to overflowing with both news and gossip of the intricate labyrinth of smalltown relationships, the complex interweaving of friends, relations, neighbors, enemies. So-and-so was sick. Again. Someone else was pregnant and being sent away to have the baby. Jane somebody was seeing Tom somebody secretly. Someone else was drinking . . . again. Somebody's uncle was in an auto accident down in Jackson. Somebody's cousin over in Oxford cut his big toe off with a chainsaw. Someone else's brother-in-law was out of work again. Missus so-and-so had the vapors, that archaic smalltown euphemism for nervous depression and hysteria.

Kate had been forced to turn to the dictionary to find out what it meant to have the vapors. Kate had thought it would be nice to take to her bed with the vapors and do nothing but read all day instead of going to school. Her mother had been characteristically unsympathetic to Kate's announcement of the vapors. I'll vapor you, young lady, if you don't get out of that bed right now. I'll tell you when you can be nervous and high-strung.

Kate laughed. "I've always wanted to be able to say that."

"I'll call and get us an appointment," Tracie said. "Late afternoon all right?"

* * *

They took the still unnamed kitten to Tracie's apartment after stopping at the pet store to buy the essentials—a traveling cage, litterbox and litter, food, and dishes for food and water. Kate threw in a variety of toys—rubber balls, a fuzzy toy mouse, another filled with catnip.

"This is going to be the most pampered cat in history," Kate said, as she helped Tracie carry everything in.

Tracie's apartment was furnished in a Southwestern style. Two large oil paintings of desert scenes hung in the living room and in the bedroom, above the twin bed covered with a brightly patterned spread that might have been Indian in design, and there was another painting, a portrait of an old and wizened Navajo woman pounding corn in front of a hogan.

"I figure I might as well be ready for the move to Arizona," Tracie explained. "I had the paintings shipped home from a Scottsdale gallery. They were my extravagance for last year."

"They're very nice," Kate said, noticing the lack of any personal touches or family photos as Tracie showed her through the apartment.

"This is my other extravagance," Tracie said, showing Kate into the second bedroom, which had been set up as a home office, complete with a computer work center in oak and a matching bookcase and file cabinet. "I feel like an attorney here. Sometimes, in the office, I feel like an ambulance chaser."

The kitten, which had been taking its own tour of the apartment, leaped to the computer.

"Whoa, kitty," Tracie cried, scooping him up.

Kate laughed. "Just like a cat—find the most expensive thing in the place and claim it for his own."

"That laser printer would be the most expensive cat toy in history."

The telephone rang. Tracie went to the desk and put the cat on the chair before answering. "Hello."

Kate went into the living room, not wanting to eavesdrop on a personal call. She was looking at one of the Arizona paintings when Tracie returned carrying the cat.

"I've just been called a whore again," Tracie said.

"Did he say anything else?"

"I hung up. I guess I should have tried to get him to talk."

"You did the right thing."

"It was probably my brother, or somebody he put up to it. I didn't tell you this morning . . . but, well, you know everything else about me now. He's done this kind of thing before. It was probably him with the car, too."

"You'd better change your telephone number. And don't park your car on the street."

"He won't hurt me again," Tracie said, "not this time. I'm not afraid of him."

At the local bookstore, the true-crime section was filled with an amazing array of paperback books on the crimes of America. Confronted with crime every day of her professional life, Kate did not bother to read nonfiction accounts of sensational, headline-grabbing crimes. But Kate realized she should not be shocked at the popularity of true crime. After all, mysteries were enormously popular. Her daughters devoured them, and particularly liked those that placed women or girls in great jeopardy. Allison and Melissa both enjoyed being scared to death while they read. It would be a natural transition to accounts of true crimes for those fascinated with what one human being is willing and capable of doing to another.

Kate was initially surprised at how many dealt with sex. Husband murders wife to get mistress. Mistress murders wife to get husband. Wife murders mistress to get husband back. Wife hires killer to murder husband to get teenage boy from next door. Teenage girl imprisoned as sex slave. Woman sold into prostitution by boyfriend kills boyfriend in revenge. And then, Kate also realized that it was the sexual nature of the crimes that would appeal to the reader. Who wanted to read about some punk who worked up the nerve to rob a convenience store?

But there was nothing about Jack the Ripper.

"We had a couple of books," the clerk said, "but we sold those as soon as people started hearing about the Delta Ripper. I could order something for you, though."

"Thanks anyway."

Kate tried to envision what would be written about Billie Rae Scott. Unknown killer murders woman for unknown reason? Why? Why? Why? If we can only figure out why, will we find who?

Marian Rogers was more than willing to talk about her former assistant. "Billie was a good worker, and the ladies liked her. Always joking with them. Teasing them. Always had the latest dumb man joke, you know. Gonna miss Billie Rae. But it's sure been good for business. Like you and Tracie—everybody wants to come in and see where she worked. I think it's kinda morbid myself, you know?"

Tracie had arranged the last appointments of the day. In fact, Marian Rogers had closed her shop for the day, drawing the curtains down, before starting on Kate's nails.

Tracie sat next to Kate, a legal pad on her lap. "Did Billie ever talk about any problems she had? Did she mention anyone who might be bothering her?"

"Nothing like that. We'd talk sometimes when things was slow, but she wasn't real outgoing when it came to her personal life. Oh, she'd say she was dating somebody new—things like that. But she never went into details much. I know she was real pleased when she started seeing your brother. Happier than I'd seen her in a long time. Billie had a kinda hard life, you know? I think she felt things would be different with Dr. Anderson."

"Did you ever meet any of her friends?" Kate asked.

"You mean her boyfriends?"

"Yes. Or any women friends she might have had."

"Well, there was this guy last year. Came into the shop and started yelling at her. I remember Ms. Mullins like to have jumped right out of the chair at the things he was saying. Billie Rae—now, she was cool as a cucumber. She just went right to the phone and called the police."

"What happened then?"

"That ole boy just took off. Said he'd be back, though. When he backed out, he scraped his car against another one out there. Screeched off. When the police got here, they was real nice, but said there was nothing they could do."

It was a familiar story to Kate. Tracie, too, probably. There was very little a woman could do to protect herself from an irate husband or a jealous boyfriend or a stranger, even with the new stalking laws. Get a restraining order. But until the physical violence occurred . . . and then it was too late, usually. If someone really wanted to get you . . .

"But when they found out about the car, they said they'd take care of it. And that dumb ole boy called back and started haranguing Billing Rae on the phone. She hung up and told the cops he was at home. Gave him the address. Found out later they towed his car. Cost him a pretty little bundle to get it back. Billie Rae didn't have no more trouble after that."

Kate nodded approvingly. A good cop could dispense street justice within the bounds of the law. Impounding a car would cause the perp a little pain of his own, especially if it cost him money.

"What was his name, do you know?"

"Oh, Lordy, it was so long ago. I don't know."

"There'll be a police report on it," Tracie said. "I'll track it down."

* * *

After another tension-marred dinner with Margaret Anderson, Kate and Drew left as quickly as they could. Kate knew her mother would blame Drew for their early departure along with everything else, but she was as relieved as her brother to be away from Margaret's disapproving silence.

"Let's sit on the porch awhile," Drew said.

"Okay."

"Want a beer?"

"I bought some wine today. I'll have a glass of that."

Kate sat in the swing and rocked gently back and forth. Crickets sang in the night. Moths fluttered around the halo of light above the door. With her sweat-dampened clothes sticking to her, Kate wondered again how people could stand the humid Delta summer days and the lingering heat that lasted through the night. In the distance, a truck roared laboriously through its gears. The sound of trucks in the night had been the siren call of her youth, a seductive cry that beckoned to her, promising the allure of distant places. No more.

"Heard you and Tracie got your nails done today," Drew said, handing her the glass of wine. He perched on the porch railing with his bottle of beer.

Kate frowned. The smalltown gossips were buzzing. "I'm trying to learn as much about Billie Rae as I can."

"Seems like a waste of time."

Kate shrugged. "I don't tell you how to doctor."

"This keeps up, I won't have a practice anymore. Had six more patients who didn't show up today. Didn't even call to cancel."

"They'll come back when this is over. You know what it's like here. They'll come back like nothing ever happened."

"Well, maybe I won't be here. I've been thinking of buying into a practice along the Gulf Coast, somewhere close to my place down there. Been here too long. I should have left long ago . . . like you."

"It would kill Mama if you were to leave."

"She hasn't exactly been on my side through this."

"That's not true. She's upset."

"So am I, Kate, so am I."

Kate went to bed feeling too tired to sleep and praying that Billie Rae Scott wouldn't haunt her dreams again. She didn't want to see the flesh dripping from Billie Rae Scott's face again. She wondered what a psychiatrist would make of her nightmare and decided there was no deep meaning. I'm disturbed by what's happened and it surfaced in a dream. There's an explanation for everything. It's the stress of what's happened. At least, I found a home for a stray kitten. But what about the other stray? What about Tracie?

Poor Tracie, carrying the ugly, unhealed scars of incest and rape beneath her beautiful appearance. Allison and Melissa were so lucky in their sheltered existence, worrying only about who would call and invite them to the prom, their scores on college admission tests and essays on application forms, learning to drive, girlhood crushes on a favorite English teacher. Tracie's brother had stolen her youth. Add grand theft of innocence to his other horrible crimes—and fear. I'll kill you if you ever tell, he'd threatened.

God, I'd like to get that bastard brother in my courtroom back home. Max him out on the sentence. Send him to Pelican Bay. If he resembled Tracie in any way, they'd love to see him. His asshole would be a lot bigger coming out than going in. Just like Nelson. Without remorse, she hoped someone was sticking it up Nelson's ass right now, making him scream with pain.

Sleep still eluded Kate. An evening shower had washed away the sweat and grime collected during the day, but it had been unable to cleanse her of sordidness. Those forlorn and pitiful photographs of Billie trying to please some unknown lover, fulfilling some cheap fantasy, bothered her. The more Kate learned of Billie Rae Scott, the more she agreed with her mother. She couldn't decipher what attracted Drew to the dead woman. From the suggestive inscriptions in her senior year book, Billie Rae had been the class slut, servicing half the football team. Christ, I've only slept with six men in my entire life, and one was my husband and another will probably be my next husband. Billie Rae probably notched that many in her freshman year in high school alone.

Perhaps Drew was just trying to save a stray kitten. That would be just like him. What had Billie Rae done for Drew to entice him so? Christ, if she was going to adorn her body with a tattoo, why not a butterfly or a bird, or something attractive and sexy? What a nice title for a story . . . the girl with the butterfly tattoo.

I wonder if Harry wants me tattooed, parading around in trashy lingerie, nipples sticking out all over the place, while he takes pictures of me. Do I really know Harry and his secrets? Would I do it?

I did it for Rainey. I let him handcuff me to the bed when he thought he was impotent. It helped him and it cost me nothing, because I trusted him. I gave him power over me. It wasn't taken from me, and that's the difference. I even grew to like the sense of helplessness, because it took away my responsibility, my control. It stripped away all the charade. I was a willing participant, but I didn't have to pretend it was wonderful when it wasn't, like with Christopher, always having to feign pleasure over the years. All I ever had to do with Rainey was enjoy the delights he gave me, and there were many. He could reduce me to tears with the love he showered on me. Perhaps I should buy a pair of handcuffs for Harry. Would it shock him? Would he like a submissive female? Am I submissive? No.

What strange fantasies control our lives, prowling through our hidden thoughts, dictating our pleasures. Ah, Billie Rae, I'm no better than you. Harry likes my breasts, so I take every opportunity to display them for him, letting him watch as I apply my makeup, sitting there brazenly for his enjoyment.

But if I *did* have a tattoo, it wouldn't be a devil. It would be a butterfly, a delicate little butterfly spreading its wings on my breast. The girl with the butterfly tattoo. That would be the first line of the story. The girl with the butterfly tattoo on her breast danced for her lover. What happens next? Does she dance for all eternity like Billie Rae dances in my mind now?

Please, Kate prayed, fill my mind with sweet oblivion.

Oh, Lord, I forgot to call Sally Roberts. I really should try to see her before I leave. Tomorrow. Sally will understand.

Please, come darkness, let me sleep now.

Nine

He didn't understand.

Why didn't she call? Kathryn Anne said she would call, said she would come to dinner. But she didn't. It wasn't fair. She promised. It was that whore. The whore kept Kathryn Anne from him. He had seen them together. In the office, and later, at the beauty shop.

He stared down at the pages of his album. Each stamp was in its precise place, telling its own little story, row after row, page after page, album after album. These were the individual stamps, of course, not the blocks of four with serial numbers, nor the sheets of a hundred. Those were special, too, and he maintained them just as painstakingly.

Stamp collecting was orderly and exact, like death. Once he set a stamp in his collection, it remained for all time, just as he set the features of the girl who'd been killed in the auto accident, removing the pain and outrage at sudden traumatic death from her face, putting her at rest. Sharon Wilts had been her name. Nineteen-year-old Sharon Wilts, frozen in time, like a stamp in his collection.

He wanted to tell Kathryn Anne the story of each stamp, how he came to find it, the thrill of the discovery at an estate sale or an auction when he came across an old shoebox filled with postcards and letters from a long ago time. He wanted to tell her of waiting all night in the rain to get the first-day issues of the Elvis Presley stamps. He would impress Kathryn Anne with his knowledge as she sat next to him, slowly turning the pages. Her breasts would brush against him as she leaned over, rapt in her attention as he explained each stamp, like that dental assistant so long ago when he was twelve, pressing her pussy against his arm as she helped the dentist. She hadn't even noticed, but he had felt the warmth from her secret place flow onto his arm, into his own secret place as he sat unmoving, wanting her to stay there. She would be old now, not like Kathryn Anne. The thought of Kathryn Anne's soft body against his gave him an erection.

But she didn't come. She didn't call. Why, Kathryn Anne, why?

"Jimmy—dinner's ready."

"I'm not hungry."

"Stop pouting and come eat. We're having chili dogs."

"It's too hot for chili dogs," he complained. Sally wouldn't make chili dogs if Kathryn Anne were coming.

"I made them for you. I'm having a salad."

"Why can't I have a salad?"

"Do you want a salad?"

"No."

His sister shrugged. "What's the matter with you today?"

"Nothing," he said. "I thought Kathryn Anne was coming for dinner."

"She's probably busy. It's a terrible thing for her, I'm sure."

"Yes, it probably is," Jimmy agreed.

"Maybe she'll call tomorrow. Or the next time she's in town. When she has more time."

"Yes, next time," he said, closing the album carefully. He waited until he could stand without the bulge in his pants showing. Then he followed Sally to the kitchen.

* * *

After dinner, he went to his bedroom, locking the door after himself. He liked it better when he had the old house to himself, but most of the time it wasn't too bad, having Sally at home again after her divorce. Except when she nagged him. He wondered if she had nagged Robert that way. Was that the reason she had appeared suddenly one night wearing dark glasses to hide the black eyes? No . . . most of the time Sally was okay. Except when he wanted to watch one of the videos he'd ordered by mail and had delivered to his post office box. Then he had to turn the sound way down, which made it difficult to hear the women cry and moan. He liked to listen to the sounds of their suffering.

Tonight, he knew which video he wanted to watch. It was the one where the blonde was tormented. He didn't think they really hurt the woman in the video. It was just make-believe, but she had long hair just like the whore, and he could pretend it was Tracie Sanders writhing in pain. There were lots of whores in the videos who looked like Tracie Sanders. But not Kathryn Anne. His Kathryn Anne would never do anything like that. The whore deserved it. The whore deserved real pain for taking Kathryn Anne away from him. He knew exactly what he would do to her when the time came.

Kathryn Anne would belong to him then and he would never have to worry about going back to that other place ever again.

Ten

The trappings of death always upset Kate.

For Kate, funerals were poorly written and poorly performed plays, charades with hollow words to comfort the living. Only the grief and sorrow of the living were momentarily real. Kate didn't really believe that, either. Probably they were tears of joy because the mourners were each happy not to be the one lying exposed in the casket. Only the dead, with no words to speak, played their roles to perfection. And afterward, there was always the reception with overflowing platters of food and a table crowded with bottles, strong drink to ease the painful reminder of mortality.

Billie Rae Scott's funeral was sparsely attended. Kate, Drew, and Tracie sat in the last row of the chapel. The immediate family was sequestered behind a curtained enclave. Marion Harper was present, the only person Kate recognized. There were a few other people, perhaps cousins or acquaintances. None of them looked like a murderer.

In front of them, people twisted and turned in their seats to stare at Drew and then whisper among themselves.

Kate could imagine their conversations. They say he's the one who done it, the one who kilt Billie Rae. Some nerve, showing up here this way. Maybe he didn't do it. Hah! That's what he wants people to think.

Drew stared stoically above their heads.

Perhaps he's looking at Billie Rae, Kate thought. She could just see Billie Rae's face and hair and the swell of her bosom in the open casket.

The service was mercifully brief. Kate knew the minister who presided did so by rote, pausing each time it was necessary to fill in the name of the deceased in his canned sermon.

Drew took Kate's hand and squeezed. She turned to look at him. There were tears in his eyes.

"Let us pray." The minister sounded relieved to arrive at the generic portion of the service.

At the end of the brief service, a funeral attendant said, "You may now come forward."

Kate forced herself to the open casket. Drew and Tracie did not follow her up the aisle. Kate had seen Billie Rae Scott only in the photographs of her death and the amateur pornography. She tried to tell herself that more than morbid curiosity drove her steps forward through the cloying sickly sweet smell of the flowers. Without knowing Billie Rae, she could not feign a sorrow she did not feel. She did regret that the woman had died so young and so brutally. Finally, Kate admitted that it was curiosity that had brought her to look at the dead woman. She still wondered what power Billie Rae had possessed to so infatuate Drew.

Sally's brother, Jimmy, stood at the head of the casket. He wore the black suit and white shirt that was his uniform for funerals. Kate nodded to him gravely. He smiled in recognition. Had Jimmy been the one who'd dressed Billie Rae, applied her last makeup? How obscene to have a man, a stranger, prepare a woman's corpse for burial! It was the last indignity. What had he thought of the devil tattoo?

Billie Rae was at peace in death. The gaping eyes of the crime scene were closed and peaceful. The hardness that had been apparent in the lewd and suggestive poses was softened. Kate didn't know whether it was death or the mortician's makeup that gave the young woman the appearance of calm. Kate turned away from Billie Rae. Even the nude photos were a better memory of a woman she had never known than the still figure in the casket.

Drew and Tracie were waiting for her outside. The air was thick and still. It was thunderstorm and tornado weather, although the skies were clear.

"Do you want to go to the grave?" Kate asked Drew.

"Yes."

They followed the hearse through the flat cemetery until it parked. They followed again as the pallbearers carried the casket across the grass to the newly dug grave.

On the way to the grave, Kate read names and dates on the headstones in a passing blur. *Beloved Husband. A Loving Wife. Ruth Foster. James Foster:* she had outlived her husband by thirty years. A child's grave: *B. 8-15-77 D. 8-17-77.* At each grave, people had gathered in sorrow during rain and bright sunshine, in the cold of winter and the humidity of summer. How many were remembered still? How were they remembered? A trio of tiny American flags fluttered bravely on one grave above a bouquet of flowers. Someone remembered a loved one. Kate stopped and read the inscription.

L/Cpl Harold Millerton
United States Marine Corps
July 17, 1949—April 21, 1969
Quang Nam Province
Republic of Vietnam

My God, he hadn't even reached his twentieth birthday. He would have celebrated his forty-fourth birthday only a few days ago. If I'd died so young, I'd have missed nearly a quarter of a century of my life, Kate thought. I wouldn't have graduated from college, nor married Christopher, nor gone to law school. Allison and Melissa would never have been born. I'd never have met Harry or Rainey. How much pain and sorrow I'd have missed . . . but I'd have missed the moments of love and joy, too. I wouldn't be here today. Would anyone remember? Rest in peace, Harold Millerton, rest in peace . . .

She hurried to catch up with Drew and Tracie.

They stood apart from the other mourners as the last rituals were carried out.

Only Mrs. Leonard sobbed as she sat in a folding chair at her daughter's grave. George Leonard, uncomfortable in an unaccustomed suit, sat next to her.

When it was over, Drew went to Billie Rae's mother.

Kate held her breath, hoping that George would not create a scene, start a fight. But as Drew knelt in front of Mrs. Leonard and took her hands, George only turned away to light a cigarette.

The moment passed and Drew returned. "Let's get out of here," he said.

"What did you tell her?" Kate asked.

"That I loved her daughter."

"What did she say?"

"Said she knew that. Said she'd pray for me."

"Kate."

She turned to see Jimmy walking between the graves. "You all go ahead," she said. "I'll be along in a minute." She turned to greet Jimmy.

He took her outstretched hand and shook it shyly. "I didn't expect to see you here."

"No one did, I guess," Kate replied, releasing his hand. It was cold, like his profession. How can it be so cold in this heat?

"It's a terrible thing about your brother. I've been reading about it. They shouldn't be saying those bad things about him."

"Thank you," Kate said. "How have you been? I talked to Sally yesterday."

"I know. She told me. She was real disappointed that you couldn't get by to see her. But she understands how busy you are."

"I know. I'd like to see her, too. I'm going home tonight, but tell Sally, we'll get together next time I'm here."

"I'll tell her that. She'll be real pleased."

"I have to go now. It's been nice to see you, Jimmy."

"When you come back, I'll show you my stamp collection. I got all the Elvis Presley stamps."

"I'll look forward to it, Jimmy." Oh, Lord, Sally said he was still doing that. We'll have to go through the whole collection, stamp by stamp.

Kate looked back as she neared the car. Jimmy was still there, watching. She waved to him.

Jimmy waved to her. "Goodbye," he whispered. "Come back real soon."

Tracie refused their dinner invitation. "It's a family affair and I don't want to intrude. It's your last afternoon here. You just go ahead."

"You're welcome to come. You know that."

"I know, but . . . I just don't feel right about it."

"Are you okay?"

Tracie smiled. "A little depressed, but I'm fine. I'll just go play with the cat."

"I'll stop by on my way out of town. Is that all right?"

"Sure. We probably need to talk anyway. I'll be waiting for you. I've got lots of stuff to do. Besides, I need to spend some quality time with the cat."

* * *

Betsy greeted Kate at the door, squealing happily as they hugged. "Hey, Kate, how you doing?"

"Fine, Betsy, fine."

Betsy's husband, Jack, came out of the kitchen with a bottle of beer in his hand. "Hey, Kate, how are y'all?"

"It's good to see you, Jack." Kate turned back to Betsy. "Where are the kids?"

"Oh, we got a sitter. They're getting to be too much for Mama, all that screaming and hollering all the time."

"That's not true, Betsy, I told you to bring them along."

"Truth is, Kate, they're getting to be too much of a handful for me. Mama's right—I'm the one who can't stand the hollering and carrying on." She hugged Kate again. "God, it's good to see you."

"You, too, Betsy. It's been too long."

"Whose fault is that?"

"I know," Kate said, "I know."

"How are Allison and Melissa?"

"Fine. Allison loves college. I think she's just glad to get away from me. She's even going to summer school."

"Melissa still want to be a rock star?"

"I'm afraid so. I'll be glad when purple hair goes out of style."

"You better be careful, big sister, Melissa might just fool you and get to be a big rock star, purple hair and all."

"Hey, Kate, you want a beer?"

"Sure, Drew."

"Betsy? What you want?"

"I'm fine, Drew. Still got half a bottle around here somewhere."

"No, you don't, honey," Jack said. "It was getting warm, so I polished it off."

"What if I like warm beer?"

"Ain't nobody likes warm beer."

"Maybe I do."

"Well, you want me to put a couple of bottles out in the sun for you?"

"Drew, I reckon I better have another bottle of my own. You just keep your hands off this one, Jack. It's mine." Betsy turned back to Kate. "After dinner," she whispered, "let's me and you sneak off for a while. I got something I wanna tell you."

"So," Margaret asked. "Was it a nice funeral?"

"Don't start, Mama."

"Drew Anderson, I just asked if it was a nice funeral."

"It was very nice, Mama," Kate said quickly. She didn't want to hear a repeat of the argument on whether or not Drew should attend the services.

"That's all I wanted to know."

"God, Mama can be such a bitch sometimes," Betsy said quietly. "All this trouble Drew's got, and she just keeps nagging at him. I know he's hurtin' real bad right now."

"Mama's upset. She doesn't know how to handle it. She's hurting, too, Betsy."

"I know. We're all upset. I'm real glad you came down here. She needed you. She's been crying her eyes out on the phone to me all the time."

"Lord, it's sure a mess, isn't it?"

"Drew don't deserve none of this. I think Mama's right. I don't mean to speak ill of the dead, but that woman was nothing but trouble from the minute Drew first laid eyes on her."

"Me and Kate's going out for a while. We'll be back in a little bit, Mama."

"Where y'all going?" Jack asked.

"Out for a little sister talk. Go to the bar at the Holiday Inn and have a drink, just like you guys do all the time."

"Oh, Lordy, Ms. Anderson, your youngest daughter's becoming a woman of the world."

"That's right, Jack." Betsy leaned over and kissed his cheek. "We'll be back soon. Ain't there a ballgame for you and Drew to watch?"

"I reckon there is, Ms. Anderson."

In the car, Kate asked, "You really want to go to the Holiday Inn?"

"Sure. It's quiet there on a Sunday afternoon. We'll have a chance to talk." Betsy pulled a package of cigarettes from her purse.

"When'd you start smoking?"

"Oh, these, they're just for social occasions. Like for having a drink with my big sister." Betsy paused to light a cigarette. "Or my boyfriend," she added.

"What!"

"I don't know how it happened, but I'm just so glad it did. Oh, I ain't going to leave Jack or nothing like that. I love Jack. You know that. It's just that . . . just that . . . Ken is so nice to me. He's kind and gentle and makes me feel so good. Not that Jack isn't good to me—he is—but I'm not hardly there anymore for him. I might as well be a piece of livestock, some old cow he's got to service once a month whether I need it or not. Do I shock you?"

"No. Yes. I don't know." Kate was confused. She felt like there was a stranger sitting across from her, smoking cigarettes and drinking manhattans. Betsy, her little sister, who'd dropped out of high school, who'd married when she was barely seventeen and spent the next twenty years as the dutiful housewife.

Betsy laughed delightedly. "Yes, I do. I shock you."

"I guess you do. You certainly surprised me."

"It surprised me. I didn't know I had feelings like that any-more. Scared me, too, the whole time he was undressing me the first time. I was shaking so bad, I thought I was gonna faint. But I never wanted him to stop, not once. I ain't never been with no one but Jack—before this, at least. I can't even remember what it was like with him the first time. Not like this. It was never like this."

Kate watched as Betsy took a sip of her manhattan. There, in the dimness of the Holiday Inn bar, Betsy seemed to draw the light to her. She was radiant—in her smile, in the sparkle of her eyes, in the lilt of her voice. Kate had never seen Betsy so animated, so . . . so . . . *happy*.

"Do you disapprove, Kate?"

"No." Who am I to disapprove, to judge? I love Harry, but I love Rainey, too. Sometimes I want to be with Rainey.

"I want you to be happy for me, Kate."

"I am. You deserve all the happiness in the world, Bets."

"You haven't called me that for a long time. Ken calls me Bets, too."

Kate smiled. "Do you love him?"

"Yes, I think so. I'm not sure what love is, sometimes."

Who does? Kate thought. "And does he love you?"

"Yes."

"Well, then . . ."

"There's something else, Kate."

Oh, God, what now?

"I'm going to get a job. It's all set. I'm going to be a waitress at the truck stop. Jack don't like it none, but I can't help that. I want to work. I know being a waitress ain't much, but it's something I want to do."

"There's nothing wrong with that. You'll be a great waitress. I'm surprised you haven't done something like that before."

"I'm not like you, Kate. I wish I'd done all the things

you've done. Read books, traveled . . . I should've listened to you and gone to college, like you did. You know, I never had a manhattan until I met Ken. I've never done anything except get married and have kids. Oh, I don't regret the kids. I don't regret anything, and I guess I'd probably do it all over again if I had the chance. But I'm thirty-seven years old. I want to have a little fun before it's too late."

Billie Rae had been thirty-seven. Suddenly, Kate reached across the table and took Betsy's hand. "I love you, you know."

"I know that, Kate, and I love you, too."

"I'd like to meet this Ken of yours, make sure he knows he'd better treat you right."

"I'd like that, too. Maybe when you come back?"

"Sure, Bets. When I come back."

"Yeah, you have to come back. I'm just sick about what's happened to Drew. You don't think he did it, do you?"

"Of course not."

"I still can't believe it. When Mama called and told me, I almost fell over. I guess it's not right."

"What's not right?"

"Me being so happy when Drew's in trouble."

"We're going to get him out of it. He's innocent, that's all there is to it. We just have to stick together until we find out who really killed Billie Rae."

"How are you going to do it, Kate?"

"I don't know."

"Mama couldn't take it if Drew had to go to jail. I couldn't, either, I guess."

"I don't think there's much of a case against Drew. I believe that I can convince a jury of reasonable doubt. That's all it takes—reasonable doubt."

"I don't know. Drew's been acting awful strange the past few months. Mama's right. Ever since he met that woman, there's been something wrong. It ain't the old Drew. It ain't the old Drew at all."

"We'd better get back."

"It's been good to see you, Kate. Just like when we were little girls."

"Except now you drink manhattans."

Betsy laughed. "Ain't it grand?"

Outside, the sluggish air hit them like a wall. To the west and south, the sky was dark and ominous.

"Storm's coming," Betsy said. "It's going to be a bad one."

Kate was relieved to get away. She used Tracie and the impending thunderstorm as her excuse for an early departure.

"I don't know why she didn't come here," Margaret Anderson complained. "She was welcome. You could have done your business here. You shouldn't have to leave so early. Your plane isn't for hours yet."

"It's not the same, Mama. We can't work here. Besides, I have to return the car, and I don't want to get caught in the storm."

"I suppose."

"I'll be back soon, anyway."

"You take care, Kate."

"You, too, Bets." The sisters embraced.

"Hey, Kate."

"Hey, Drew. We'll be talking soon." Kate pulled him aside for a moment. "Don't worry," she said. "Everything's going to be fine."

As she pulled out, Kate waved to her family clustered on the porch. Jack had his arm around Betsy's waist. Her mother had the handkerchief to her eyes again. Drew waved. Kate even thought he might have smiled, but she couldn't be sure. She sighed as she headed for Tracie's apartment. She loved her family, but she was glad to be away from them. My God,

Betsy, having an affair. Kate shook her head in disbelief. My little sister, committing adultery. What other surprises do we have in store? Kate wondered.

"His name's Sam."

"Why Sam?"

Tracie smiled and shrugged. "He just looks like a Sam to me. I always wanted to be named Samantha. I thought it would be nice to be called Sam. If I can't be Sam, well, I might as well have a Sam around."

Sam was perched on the back of the sofa, listening to their conversation with great interest. His ears swiveled back and forth from Tracie to Kate.

"It's as good a reason as any for naming a cat. At least you didn't call him Fluffy."

"Please. What kind of woman do you think I am?"

"I'm not prepared to answer that question anymore," Kate said, "not after the afternoon I've just spent with my sister."

"What happened?"

"Oh, nothing. She just surprised me, that's all. You think you know someone . . ." Kate's voice trailed off.

"Most of the time, I don't even know myself. I've given up trying to figure out anyone else."

"Yeah, I wonder about me, too. So, how'd you spend the afternoon?"

"Working. I put everyone who was at the funeral into the computer. I'll add them to my list of people to contact while you're gone."

"How did you do that? You couldn't have known everyone there."

"While you were viewing the body, Drew and I copied the guest book. There weren't that many people there. It was easy."

Kate took a card from her purse and wrote her home telephone number on the back. "We should talk every night."

"I'll keep you posted. I plan to spend the week tracking down every potential witness. I'll also find out why the gun wasn't mentioned."

"And the research on Girardeau and Cowles."

Tracie nodded. "If you think of anything else, just let me know."

"Christ, this is going to get expensive." Kate slapped her forehead in exasperation. "Damn, I forgot your retainer."

Tracie shrugged. "It doesn't matter."

"I'll call Drew tomorrow and ask him to drop a check off at your office."

"That's fine, but there's no hurry. Really."

"It's okay. And Tracie . . ."

"Yes?"

"If Drew gives you any trouble, let me know."

"We talked a little bit while we waited for you today. He'll be fine. He said he was glad to have me working with you."

"Good. He can be stubborn sometimes."

"He's been broken by this," Tracie said. "It's almost like he's given up, like he doesn't care what happens anymore."

"I know." Kate scratched Sam behind his ears. "There's one other thing before I go, Tracie."

"What's that?"

"I want you to tell me if you get any more telephone calls or messages on your car. Don't play heroine. Okay?"

"I'll be fine."

Kate nodded. "I'll talk to my boss tomorrow and see what I can arrange. I've got a lot of vacation coming. I can use that, and I'm pretty sure he'll give me a leave of absence if I need it."

"Let's hope we can settle this sooner than that."

"I'll get back as soon as I can, or as soon as it's necessary."

"You know, I'm going to miss you, Kate. I've gotten used to having a friend around."

"It *has* been nice, although I wish we'd met under better circumstances." Kate turned back to the cat. "You take care of her, Sam, you hear?"

As Kate drove out of town, she felt empty, drained of life and emotion. She felt like a minor player in some surreal medieval masque, condemned to stand aside helplessly while the tragedy unfolded before her. How long had she been here? Only a few days. Just a few short days. If she closed her eyes, she could pretend it had never happened, that it was only a bad dream. She would wake up in her own bed at home with Harry beside her. That would prove it was only a dream.

The early evening was filled with bizarre contrasts. Behind her, lightning danced through the black clouds, bringing the dark night before its time. To the north, the sun was still shining brightly. Kate drove toward the light. She was leaving the darkness behind.

Wasn't she?

Kate glanced in the rearview mirror. The darkness filled the mirror, invaded the car. Kate pressed the accelerator, but she could not escape. The darkness would follow until she was enveloped in its suffocating shroud.

Part II

Eleven

Old Abe was at the lake fishing for his dinner, dozing in the last glare of that hot evening sun. It was peaceful and still there at the end of the dock, a quiet time near the end of a day, near the end of a life.

There was a time when he would have gone across the levee to the big river and cast his hooks for catfish in a backwater eddy, waiting patiently for the strike as he smoked his briar pipe. Too hot now to make the effort, even if he stood out at the side of the road waiting for some young nigger to come by in a clanking old pickup. Plenty of young niggers around to do a courtesy for an old man, if only they would. There were a few yet who might respect the wisdom painfully acquired during a lifetime of hard work and travail and sorrow. Not many, but a few.

Lake catfish would do. River catfish were too big, anyway. Too big for a lonely old man who'd buried three wives already and a passel of kids. There were a few kids left—he couldn't rightly remember how many—but they didn't come round no more, not after heading north to Chicago or Dee-troit or south to New Orleans or Atlanta and catching that disease spread by bright lights. They'd seen too many juke joints and painted young women to remember an old man. Women like that took a man's memory away. Maybe there ain't none of them left no-how. Didn't matter, not so long as he could get to the store on the first of each month, pick up that government check, buy salt and tobacco and a bottle of that good juice that eased the aches for another thirty days. Problem was remembering when the first of the month came. Lost track of time at the lake. Lost track of time decades ago.

The bobber on his line swayed gently in the slight ripples that marred the placid surface of the lake. A cottonmouth swam by, near to the shore, a graceful dark shape undulating through the water. It passed under the dock. Old Abe took no mind; the snake was going about his business. No need to bother ole Mistuh Snake. No need atall.

He dozed off again, dreaming of the old days. He'd gone off to Dee-troit himself as a young man, but didn't like it none. White folks hated niggers there just as bad as they did to home. Maybe worse. Couldn't never leave a man alone. No, sir. Always had to be messin' with a man, out on a Saturday night. Wasn't right. Wasn't right atall.

A slight pressure on the line awakened him. When he pulled the line in, Abe saw that the worm had been nibbled away. He still used worms. Worms had caught him a mess of fish over the years. He saw no reason to change now, get something fancy. Ole Mistuh Fish didn't want to be Abe's dinner. Smart ole Mistuh Fish. Got his dinner clever-like. Et the worm and didn't disturb ole Abe. That was considerate-like. Let the old man get his rest. Didn't matter. Don't catch ole Mistuh Fish, cook up a mess of greens instead.

He baited the hook again and dropped it in the water, watching the ripples flow away from the splash. He packed his old pipe with one hand, scooping the tobacco from the pouch with the ease of long practice. He flicked the kitchen match into flame with his thumbnail. When the pipe was going, he waved the match out and placed it carefully on the dock beside him. No use tossing it in the water, distracting Mistuh Fish.

The summer heat lulled him to sleep. When the strike on his hook awakened him, it was near dark. He pulled the line in. The fish was silvery and glistening in the last light as it struggled against the biting metal that pierced its mouth. Too small . . . As gently as he could, Abe disengaged the hook and released the fish. It disappeared with a *plop*.

The red glow at the horizon was fading quickly. The old man sighed and got to his feet. It would be dark soon.

The woods at night didn't scare him none. The woods was where he lived, long time now. Longer than he could remember, and the woods was good to him. They was always a rabbit or a squirrel or a possum, if he had a mind. In the fall, he could talk to the wild turkeys better than anyone, better than any of them turkey calls that was supposed to be so good. Ole Mistuh Turkey stick his head right up, looking round for that female talking so good. Say, here I am, honey pie. Wisht he'd kept his pecker in his pocket then. Male of the species sure didn't have much sense, always lettin' his pecker do his thinkin'.

Everything was peaceful and still at night. Orderly, too. Everything was in its proper place, from the smallest ant to the biggest black bear.

As the old man walked through the woods, he made a little noise, although he could walk as silently as any of nature's creatures, if he wanted to. But during the hot summer nights, he always made a little noise, a warning for snakes that he was coming. He wasn't concerned with snakebite so much—he'd been bit before—as he was with showing a consideration for the snake. Ole Mistuh Snake had better things to do than bite ole Abe. No use disturbing Mistuh Snake when there warn't no call for it.

He had crossed over the road when he heard the car. The old man faded into the woods again. There was no use taking chances. An old man didn't get to be born with the century and die with the century by taking chances. No, siree. He stood motionless as the headlights swept around a bend on the road. Abe saw the black shape slithering across the road and watched as the car swerved and crushed the snake.

Warn't no car atall.

It was ole Mistuh Death hisself, driving right along in his chariot.

Somebody gonna die tonight, just like before.

The old man stayed in the woods. Mistuh Death couldn't find him in the woods.

After the sound of Mistuh Death's chariot faded, Abe heard the chilling sound of the rattler's last throes. It was dead, but didn't know it yet. The snake's rattles whirred in the night, protesting fate. The sound followed old Abe.

And then the night was still where ole Mistuh Death had passed.

Twelve

Kate was disoriented.

Her body was at home, but her mind remained in the Mississippi Delta. The once familiar surroundings of home and office now seemed alien to her. Her own place was tiny and cramped after Drew's big, rambling house, her bedroom was foreign, as though someone lese lived there. The clothes in the closet and the dresser belonged to a stranger. The barren guest bedroom in the old Randall place was where Kate Gallagher should be.

Even the accustomed route to the office appeared drastically altered. The streets were clogged with traffic. Buildings had apparently been built overnight, billboards had been changed in her absence, detours for road work were set up, new strip malls and fast food joints installed.

Christ, I was only gone for a few days, not even a week.

At the office, too, Kate felt like an outsider. Her friends and colleagues were strangers, acquaintances of the strange woman who inhabited her house. Case files had multiplied on her desk. There was a new deputy district attorney, a young woman, a transfer from Long Beach, in the staff meeting. Dr. Death introduced her around. "This is Jennifer Mills, everybody," he said.

I should be the one introduced.

"Jennifer's going to be working with Kate for a while."

What?

After the staff meeting, Kate followed Dr. Death to his office. His nickname reminded Kate of the wizened old black man at Drew's cabin. Old Mister Death. Who had Abe seen?

"It's good to see you, Kate. How did it go in Mississippi?"

He listened patiently as Kate explained the situation. "It looks like I'm going to have to take some time off," Kate concluded.

"I figured that. I checked into your vacation time. You've got a lot of time coming, and if you need more, well, I'll just arrange a leave of absence for you."

"I hope it won't come to that, Phil."

"Well, if it does . . . Why do you think Jennifer Mills is here?"

"Thanks, Phil. I appreciate that." It was good to have friends like Phil Moore, Kate thought, even if he *does* seem like a stranger.

"Bring her up to speed, and when you have to leave, she can just take over until you get back. Let's go down to her office. I've put her next to you temporarily. I'll introduce you formally and then you two can get to work."

"By the way," Kate said, as they went down the hall together, "how did you come out on my case?"

"Kate, is there any doubt in your mind?"

Kate smiled. "Not really."

"The little prick got the max."

"Good."

"You did a good job of preparation, Kate. I'd have to be a real incompetent to screw up what you did."

Kate liked Jennifer Mills. The young attorney was about the same age as Tracie, not nearly so beautiful, of course, but few could match Tracie in the beauty department.

"We call them career criminals," Kate said, "but it's nothing so grandiose as the big time they deal with downtown. Basically, we're after repeat offenders here, the three- and four- and five-time losers. They're mostly punks, and if they're convicted, we want to send them away for the max. We've been pretty successful, but for each one who goes away there seem to be a half-dozen ready to take their place. Sometimes, I think there's a training school for punks out there somewhere."

"I think it's called the public school system," Jennifer said, twisting the wedding rings on her finger.

"And the shitty home environment."

"And the streets."

"I just had a baby," Jennifer said. "I just came off maternity leave. That's why I was available to come over here. I'm already worried about her having to go to a public school."

"Congratulations," Kate said. "What's her name?"

"Allison Leigh," Jennifer said.

"My oldest daughter is named Allison. She just started at UCLA."

"In the summer?"

Kate smiled. "Allison was impatient to get going. She went to public schools all the way through. Some of them aren't so bad. Both Allison and Melissa have done all right. But they grow up so fast in high school now. Not like when I went." Kate's mind drifted back to Mississippi. Suddenly she wanted to look at her high school yearbooks.

"Things change."

Kate forced herself back to the Los Angeles County DA's South Bay office. "Look, why don't you go through some of the files? Get familiar with them. Then we'll go over and I'll introduce you around. Meet the judges and their clerks, that sort of thing."

"That'll be fine, Kate."

"Normally, I'd take you to lunch today, but there's something I have to do. But how about tomorrow?"

"Sure, I'd like that." Jennifer hesitated, then made a decision. "Phil told me why I'm here, Kate. About your brother, I mean. I'm sorry."

"Thank you." Now Kate realized why she felt like such an interloper in the office. Everyone knew about Drew and they wondered if their colleague was related to a killer. "He didn't do it," Kate said.

But what if he did? she thought.

And then she called Rainey to invite him to lunch.

"Aw, that's bullshit," Rainey said, when Kate had finished telling her story for the second time that day. "Delta Ripper. Where do they get this stuff?"

"It sells newspapers," Kate said, "even in Mississippi. The Nightstalker. Hillside Strangler. Freeway Killer." Kate shrugged. "What can I say?"

"Tell me how I can help, Kate. I'll do anything I can."

Kate looked at Rainey and smiled. "I like the beard," she said. Rainey was very nearly handsome, but there was more gray in his thinning brown hair, particularly around the temples, than she remembered. The beard, which was new for Rainey, was full, but neatly trimmed. It, too, was streaked with gray. "It goes with your tweedy appearance."

Rainey wore slacks and a tweed sports coat with a pale blue shirt opened a fashionable two buttons at the collar. "It goes with the bookstore," he said. "I'm the literary type now."

"You'll always look like a cop, Rainey."

He smiled. "I'm probably the only bookstore owner with a permit to carry."

"You still carry a gun?"

"Kate, I wouldn't go to Disneyland without my gun."

She remembered when she had called Rainey in a panic. I want a gun and I want it now. No waiting period, nothing. He had delivered the revolver that evening. It had saved her when Nelson attacked her in the parking lot. It was duly registered in her name now, and Kate had no intention of giving it up. Every once in a while, she took it to the range and shot a box of shells. You never could tell . . .

"Same old Rainey," Kate said.

"You still haven't told me how I can help."

Kate looked around the bustling coffee shop. Young waiters and waitresses scurried by, juggling trays and menus. The buzz of conversations rose and fell. "I'm not really sure, Rainey," Kate said finally. "I brought a copy of the file for you. Maybe you'll see something . . ."

He nodded. "I'll be glad to look at it, but I don't know what I'll see if you don't. You're good, Kate."

Kate shrugged the compliment off. "So, how have you been?" she asked.

"Same old stuff. Running a bookstore is a lot harder than I thought it would be. All I really wanted was an excuse to sit around and read. The customers interfere with that."

"Seeing anyone?" Kate asked casually.

Rainey shook his head. "No, not really. I go out occasionally. Nothing serious."

Kate felt a pang of jealousy that he went out and relief that he wasn't seriously involved in a relationship. Christ. What are you doing, Kate? Leave it alone. "You deserve a good woman."

"We're soulmates, Kate."

"Star-crossed lovers?"

"Everything will work out the way the universe intends," Rainey said seriously. "If not in this life, why, then, in another."

Kate knew he really believed that. Rainey had found peace for himself in the metaphysical foundations of the New Age.

He no longer banged futilely against the things that were out of his control. Instead, he waited patiently for the mysteries of his universe to unfold.

"You're a strange guy, Rainey, but I love you."

"Oh, and I love you, too, Kate." He took her hand and traced the lines in her palm as though committing them to memory.

At his touch, a thrill raced through her. She closed her eyes, remembering the hypnotic trance of the moment as she'd finally allowed herself to be seduced by him.

They stopped for a drink at an elegant bar, dark and wooded, sitting in luxurious black leather chairs. The others in the quiet room were distant and apart when he shared his secret. He took her hand then, too, and felt the weakness in her body and the strength of her desire. Trembling, she said, yes, oh, yes.

He prolonged their agony, ordering another drink, while they talked quietly of other things. She pitied the others in the room for the routine of their mundane existences and tried not to think of the promises he made, the pleasures he would provide her. When they finally rose, she took his arm and together they went into the night, where he kissed her for the first time.

His voice awakened her from the hypnotic trance. "Do you still have the scarf?" he asked.

Go shopping one day, he said, and choose a black scarf, knowing as you make your selection it will be used as a blindfold to intensify your beauty. Smile as you make your purchase, knowing that the clerk does not share your secret. But if she did, know also that she would be envious and wish that she could take your place. And when I arrive, we will exchange the symbolic tokens of friendship and devotion to one another.

Smiling, Kate opened her eyes. No dark and elegant room

appeared. It was only a coffee shop, sterile and gleaming. "Of course," she said. "I have everything you gave me."

"I think of you often," he said.

"I know," Kate replied. "Oh, Rainey, what happened?"

"The time wasn't right," he said.

After work, Kate sat at the dining room table, going through the file on Billie Rae Scott once again, reading the crime reports and the notes she had made in Mississippi. There had to be something there, something she was missing, something that Tracie was missing. Perhaps Rainey would find it.

Kate turned to the photos of the murdered woman, studying each for something. She didn't know what she was looking for. "Ah, Billie Rae, who are you?" Kate caught her mistake. "Who *were* you, Billie Rae? Who wanted to do this to you?" Kate looked at Billie Rae's lifeless eyes, as though hoping she would see the image of the killer there.

Shaking her head finally, Kate closed the file and went to the refrigerator. She poured a glass of white wine and went outside, into the backyard.

The evening was pleasantly warm, not like the stifling humidity of Mississippi. A cooling breeze off the ocean ruffled the leaves of the avocado tree. The flowerbeds had weeds that hadn't been there when she left. I'll take care of them this weekend, she thought. The six tomato plants along the fence had grown taller, and the tomatoes were beginning to ripen. She had planted them a week apart.

Kate wandered around the yard. It was one of her pleasures, and it was a rare night that she didn't take a glass of wine out to enjoy her tiny estate, even in the winter, when darkness came early and the nights were chill. For Kate, the yard was a refuge in the metropolis of concrete and glitter and flashing neon. The quiet residential neighborhood filtered sounds, muting them until only the occasional distant whine of a siren reminded Kate of the outside world.

Tonight, though, a restless Kate found little solace in her sanctuary. Memories of Mississippi intruded as they had throughout the day. She brushed an inquisitive bee away from her wineglass and wondered what Drew and Betsy and Tracie were doing. It would be almost dark in Mississippi.

Had more of Drew's patients deserted him, a smalltown punishment for real or imagined transgressions against their perception of order? Had Betsy seen her lover today? My God, Bets, do you know what you're doing? At least she wasn't lonely like Tracie. Kate sighed. It was time to call Tracie.

When Kate went back into the house, she found Melissa leafing through the file.

"Oh, gross," she said, looking at one of the photographs of Billie Rae in death.

"Melissa!" Kate snapped. "You shouldn't be looking at that."

"Oh, Mom."

"Melissa, please."

Melissa sighed. "It's no worse than biology."

Kate gathered the file, shuffling papers and photos together before closing it. "I don't know what kind of biology they're teaching today, then."

"Is Uncle Drew going to jail?"

"No, honey, he's not going to jail." God, I'm beginning to sound like my mother. Kate, honey, it's so good to have you home.

"That's good. Of course, he's still got the best lawyer in town."

"Well, that's nice to hear."

"It's true."

"Harry and I are going out for dinner. Would you like to come?"

"Janie's coming over later. She'll probably spend the night. We're going to watch MTV."

"Don't want to hang out with the old folks?"

"Don't take it personally, Mom. It's nothing against you and Harry, but . . ."

"You don't want to hang out with the old folks—right?"

Melissa smiled sheepishly. "Yeah. Besides, Janie's got a new boyfriend. I want to hear all about her date Saturday night."

"How about you?" A steady stream of boys passed through the house in pursuit of Melissa. "Did you have a date?"

"God, how embarrassing not to have a date. Of course, I went out. Frank took me to the movies."

"Frank. He's been around a long time."

"We celebrated our fourth anniversary Saturday night."'

"Fourth?"

"Four weeks, of course. I really like him—everything except his name. Sounds like some old hot dog or something. Why would anyone name their kid Frank? That's not what I call him, of course."

"Dare I ask?"

"Lover boy."

"What?"

"I call him Lover boy, 'cause he's so good in bed."

"Melissa!"

"Gotcha!" Melissa cried. "You know I'm kidding." She put her arm across her eyes. "I still have my honor," she said, sighing deeply. "I practically had to force him to kiss me the first time. He's *such* a gentleman."

"Try to match him. You could at least try to be a lady."

"Oh, Mom, that's so boring." Melissa skipped away down the hall. "Gotcha. Gotcha. Gotcha."

Kate shook her head. What am I going to do with her? She wouldn't be surprised to learn that Melissa had made love with someone she cared about. Or would soon. She was sixteen, ready to start her junior year in high school. Allison, too. Shy, pretty, studious Allison, who had never dated much while she was in high school because she was a formidable challenge and therefore too intimidating to boys of her own age, had started going out with a senior she'd met in the library, an English major and an aspiring writer who'd read even more than Allison. They were reading *Paradise Lost* to each other, for God's sake. Kate was happy for her. How much trouble could you get into reading *Paradise Lost?* A lot, probably. Let's experiment with original sin.

Kate remembered her conversation with Jennifer earlier that day. My God, they grow up so fast, and there's nothing I can do about it, except be there for them when they fall down. Help them get up again and send them on their way into adulthood. Oh, Christ, why is it so hard to let them go?

Tracie answered on the first ring.

"Don't you know you're supposed to let the phone ring for a while? You don't want people thinking you're just sitting around waiting for it to ring."

"I knew it was you, Kate. I can always tell who's calling. Almost always, anyway. Some sort of ESP."

"Did you get another of those phone calls?" Kate asked. She couldn't hide the concern in her voice.

"No. Everything's been quiet here."

"That's good." Kate was relieved—more than she wanted to admit.

Tracie had little to report. She had interviewed more witnesses. For their purposes in Drew's defense, however, the interviews were all dead-ends. "I'll keep trying, though. Something will turn up."

"Let's hope so. Did Drew drop a check off?"

"Yes. Thank you."

"How was Drew?"

"Worried. Distracted. He didn't stay long."

"I won't have any trouble getting time off," Kate said. "I'll be back as soon as it's necessary. At least a week before the prelim."

"Okay."

"Well, I guess I'll talk to you tomorrow."

"I wish I had more to report."

"We'll find it." Kate was tempted to tell Tracie about Rainey, but decided to wait and see if he came up with anything. "Goodnight, Tracie."

Kate was glad she hadn't brought up Rainey when Harry had come in moments after she'd hung up. She didn't want to argue with him again.

"Hi," Harry said.

Kate went to him and kissed him.

"I missed you," Harry said.

"I missed you, too," Kate said, knowing that it was the truth. She had missed Harry despite Rainey.

"How about someplace new?" Harry said. He named the restaurant adjoining the bar where Kate had begun her affair with Rainey.

Jesus, this is getting too close to home, Kate thought. "I feel like something lighter," she said. "I've been eating my mother's cooking. I must have gained ten pounds."

"You look find to me," Harry said.

"I'm just in the mood for fish." Kate knew that the restaurant Harry suggested specialized in steaks and prime rib. Rainey had taken her to dinner there. "How about someplace overlooking the water?"

"Tonight, you can have anything you want."

They were lucky and got a window table over the water that splashed and swirled around the restaurant's pilings. Kate was grateful that she didn't have to repeat the story for Harry.

He'd heard it after picking her up at the airport. So they were free to enjoy a quiet evening together, watching the sunset as it slowly changed colors from pale to deep red.

It almost seemed as though their relationship had returned to that untroubled place it had been—before their argument over marriage had upset Kate's comfortable world and before her mother's telephone call had sent it spinning wildly in another direction.

"Jack the Ripper!" Kate exclaimed.

"What does Jack the Ripper have to do with anything?"

"I'm sorry. I can't seem to get my mind off Mississippi." She explained the reference to Harry. "I wanted to get a book on Jack the Ripper. I don't want some Mississippi DA knowing more than me about the subject."

"We could stop on the way home."

Kate shook her head. "It doesn't matter. I'll try to find something tomorrow."

On the way home, Kate said, "I'm kind of sorry Melissa is home tonight. It's been a nice evening, but we'll have tomorrow night."

Harry smiled and said, "Any evening with you is nice."

He parked in the driveway and walked her to the door.

"You could come in for a drink . . ."

"You're tired. I'll see you tomorrow night."

She reached in and turned off the porch lamp before turning to face him. "No use letting the neighbors watch."

"And what would they see?"

"Well, I would hope they would see that handsome Harry fellow kissing that pretty southern belle, Kathryn Anne."

He put his arms around her waist, drawing her close, crushing her breasts against his chest.

"Oh, Harry, I do love you," she said. "I really do."

She responded to his kiss almost desperately, as though trying to convince him—or herself—of her love.

Kate heard Melissa and Janie giggling behind the closed bedroom door. She knocked and waited for Melissa to call, "Come on in, Mom."

They were in their pajamas, sitting cross-legged on the twin beds. Melissa's television was still tuned to MTV, although the sound was turned low.

The neighbors will appreciate that, Kate thought. "I just wanted to say goodnight. Don't stay up too late."

"We won't, Mom. Goodnight."

"Goodnight, Mrs. Gallagher," Janie said politely.

Alone in her bedroom, Kate went to the dresser and took the black scarf from where it was hidden. It was long and soft and silken and cool against her skin.

Kate undressed slowly and went to bed with the scarf wrapped around her waist.

And when they reached his apartment, she offered her hands, trembling, and he was breathing heavily as he placed the handcuffs on her wrists. He kissed her then for the second time, before going to pour a glass of wine for her.

She raised the glass to her lips with both hands. The metal that imprisoned her wrists had warmed to her flesh. Was she frightened, knowing that she had placed herself within the power of another? There was no need for fear. In her bonds, she knew she was beautiful and enslaved the man who would shortly be her lover. She turned and faced him as he told her of the pleasures to come.

This is for you, my darling Kate. You will be fastened to the bed, naked, of course, arms stretched above your head. But your bonds are not so tight that you are denied all movement. No, you have freedom enough to writhe as your plea-

sures begin with my gentle kisses on your lips, your cheeks, your eyelids. As excitement slowly grows, you raise your head to return the kisses. I take your tongue in my mouth, and together . . .

But there is more. Your breasts are impatient for their attention. Your nipples are erect, tingling with anticipation, and they grow even larger with my caresses and kiss after kiss.

I wonder what sounds you will make. Will you groan or whimper? I wonder what expression your face will assume. Will you remain placid and accepting, or will you bite your lip or contort with the pleasure and pain that provides sexual excitement? I only know there will be transformations from the Kate I know. Perhaps you will struggle to embrace me. But it is not time for that, not yet . . .

The smooth flesh of your thighs crawls with more anticipation, but they must wait, for again I kiss your lips. You grow frantic, wanting release. Not yet, for your pleasure must be long, lingering. I explore your body, kissing and caressing each part, savoring your reaction. Once again, the kisses continue down the length of your body. I tease you with my tongue even as my hands caress your breasts. Finally, I relent and part the hair between your legs with my lips, my tongue. I seek and find that tiny repository of all your pleasure, teasing, caressing, licking, entering you with my tongue, savoring your sweet taste, exploring, teasing, caressing until . . . you explode with the urgency of your climax . . . again and again, until you beg me to stop. You can take no more. Then I will kiss the sweat from your face, your brow, and your heavy-lidded eyes, bringing you down gently, with love. Will I then submit to your wish for release, or will I take you to another explosive climax, one you do not think possible?

In another fantasy—this is for me—you are again naked and restrained. But this time your wrists are handcuffed behind your back. You kneel before me and we kiss. Your breasts fill my hands as you take me in the warmth of your mouth. It would be easier for you if your hands were free, but that is my pleasure. You tease and caress me with our lips and your tongue until I can stand it no more. It will not take so long, as with you, for I will be impatient I know. And my greater pleasure is always found in carrying you to the wild, exhilarating heights of sexual delights and bliss.

All that he promised was true. And more.

Rainey, what happened between us?

Thirteen

Mary Jane Kelly, aged 24, three months pregnant, a sometime prostitute who was thirty-five shillings behind on her rent, went out on the night of November 8, 1888, picked up a man, and took him back to her room in Miller's Court, a drab and depressing hovel in London's Whitechapel section, arriving shortly before midnight. Her body was discovered the next morning. She was the youngest, the prettiest, the best educated, and the last victim of Jack the Ripper.

The grainy black-and-white photograph was gruesome. It showed Mary Jane Kelly, horribly mutilated, lying in her bloodied bed, the only one of his victims to be killed indoors.

The murders of Mary Jane Kelly and four earlier women, all prostitutes, were never solved.

The legend of Jack the Ripper spawned a spate of books, novels, and movies over the years. Theories and speculation abounded over Jack's identity. He was alternately a member of the royal family, a doctor, a mentally depressed barrister. Each suspect had advocates, but no conclusive evidence pointed to any one man as the chief candidate. Those fascinated by the mystery of the century-old killings called themselves "Ripperologists."

Kate found no fascination in the case or curiosity about the killer's identity. He was a serial murderer, no more, no less, a sociopathic killer of women. Given the opportunity, Kate would have undertaken his prosecution dispassionately, asking for the maximum penalty of life imprisonment without the possibility of parole or death in the gas chamber. Which was the worse fate? Kate could not imagine the horrors of spending the rest of her natural life in a penal institution. Nor could she bring herself to believe in capital punishment, an unusual stance for a prosecutor. It made the state as barbaric as the most violent criminal. If and when the time came for her to prosecute a special circumstances case—one that called for the maximum sentence society could impose—she would do it. That was her job. But . . .

Would she be able to sleep without nightmares ever again?

As always, Kate was drawn to the victims.

Who cared about the women so brutally murdered by the unknown assailant? Who remembered Mary Jane Kelly, except as a freak of history? Had the desperate young woman taken a different turn that fateful night as she'd wandered through the poverty-stricken warren of the East End, she might have passed into history unnoticed. But her steps took her inexorably to the man who would kill her. And, Mary Jane Kelly became a footnote for all time.

The Delta Ripper was only the latest sobriquet applied to a killer in journalistic fancy. There were others—Jack the Stripper, the Yorkshire Ripper. Some had been caught; others, like their namesake, had disappeared in the deepening shadows of time.

But not the Delta Ripper. Was he out there somewhere right now, Mr. Death, stalking another victim in the hot and steaming delta night?

Who are you, Mr. Death?

Where are you?

Do you know I'm coming for you?

Catch me if you can, Jack the Ripper mocked.

* * *

The two scruffy-looking undercover deputies from the Burglary Apprehension Team were pleased with themselves. With good reason, Kate thought. After months of painstaking work in trying to solve a long series of residential burglaries, they had found the perps by staking out pawn shops in the unincorporated area covered by the sheriff's substation they used as a headquarters.

Sergeant Pete O'Bannon, in charge of the detail, couldn't help laughing occasionally as he went through the details of the hunt and subsequent arrests. "These two guys are a real piece of work, Kate. And just wait until you hear about Lucy."

Kate already knew about Lucy. She'd skimmed through the report quickly while O'Bannon and his partner, Hap McGuire, were getting coffee, but she didn't want to spoil their moment. It *was* pretty funny.

"So anyway," O'Bannon continued, "we finally got the lead when Lucy pawned the stereo while the two guys waited in the van. It matched the loot from a burglary months ago. After that, it was easy. We picked them up yesterday morning and followed them up the hill. I was disappointed Lucy wasn't with them, but you can't have everything, right? Figured we'd get her later, so I could live with it. Anyway, it was obvious they were out shopping and when they came to the house, the garage door was open. No cars in it."

People never learn, Kate thought. Might as well leave the front door open with a blinking neon sign saying, we're not home, burglars welcome.

"They were a ballsy pair. Drove the van right into the garage and started loading up. Got some good pictures of them, too. Hap's getting pretty good with the camera."

Kate looked down at the photos and then over at Jennifer Mills. One of the shots had the perps struggling to carry what looked to be a 32-inch television set to the van. They were looking right at the telephoto lens. Did everything but say cheese. Jennifer smiled and shook her head in mock amazement. They weren't the smartest perps in the world.

"When they took off, we followed them until we got to a place where we could make the stop without putting any civilians in the line of fire."

"Any problem?" Kate asked.

"We scared the shit out of them," McGuire said.

Kate could imagine the scene. There they were, driving along on a nice sunny morning, the day's work already behind them, probably gloating over how easy it had been, when the stop went down, unmarked cars suddenly growing red lights and sirens, the loudspeaker blaring orders to put their hands on their heads or the dashboard, shotguns pointed menacingly from in front and back.

"No resistance. There might have been a slight hesitation when the driver thought about taking off. We did everything by the book after that. Read them their rights, transported them to the station, had the van towed in. And here's the best part, Kate. We had some guys out that afternoon looking for Lucy when she walks right into the station and asks for the keys to the van. Arrested her right there at the counter. It was beautiful."

"Pretty dumb," Jennifer said with another smile. It was the first time she'd spoken. "My baby's only three months old and she's smarter than that."

Slick, Kate thought. McGuire had been looking sideways at her the whole time. Jennifer sent the message that she was unavailable without hurting anyone's feelings. It might not stop him, but cops were like that. At least he knew. But McGuire was a good guy. They were both good guys. And good at their jobs.

Kate looked down at the mug shots and the rap sheets. The perps were in their late thirties, and both had done time before. "It's a good bust, guys. I think we can classify them as repeat offenders." Lucy was clean, however. Only twenty-one, it was her first arrest. "What's Lucy's story?" Kate asked.

The mug shot showed a pretty and frightened young woman, trying and failing to look tough. Too bad, Kate thought. The dykes out at the women's prison were going to enjoy having her around. Maybe they already were.

"True love, what else?" O'Bannon said.

"Creeps like that ought to come with a warning label."

"Arraignment's set for ten tomorrow morning. Jennifer will handle it."

"You leaving us, Kate?"

"Going on vacation for a few weeks. Jennifer's taking over for me."

"Have a good time," O'Bannon said.

"Yeah, relax. Have some fun," McGuire echoed.

Some vacation.

Kate was surprised that she hadn't heard from Rainey yet. She reached for the phone to call him and then changed her mind. If she knew Rainey, he was brooding over the file, seeking what had eluded Kate and Tracie. So far. He would call when he was ready to talk about it.

Mycroft, Allison, and Richard McLaughlin were sitting on the front porch when Kate pulled into the driveway. The cat was in Allison's lap. She'd been the one to name him Mycroft, after Sherlock Holmes's older and smarter brother.

"What a surprise, Allison. Why didn't you tell me you were coming?"

Allison shrugged. "It was kind of a last-minute thing. Dad invited us down for dinner."

Kate felt jealous for a moment and then pushed the unkind thought about Christopher away. She was angry more at herself than at her former husband. It wasn't his fault he'd done what she should have, and he was the father of her children, after all.

"Good evening, Mrs. Gallagher," Richard said shyly. His hair was long and he wore a full beard. He was tall and slender, taller than Allison. Her height had caused her so much trouble growing up. She nearly always towered over the boys in high school.

He looks like a romantic poet, like Keats or Shelley might look if they were alive today, Kate thought. "It's nice to see you, Richard. Come on in. Can I offer you something? A soft drink or a glass of wine, perhaps?"

Allison dislodged Mycroft with difficulty. He didn't want to leave her lap. "How about we split a glass of wine?" Allison said, looking at Richard.

Another surprise . . . Allison drinking. Don't make a scene and embarrass her by pointing out that she's underage. Probably they did sit around drinking wine and reading poetry to each other by candlelight. What else were they doing by candlelight? Kate decided she'd rather not know.

"Sure," Richard said.

"Don't I get a kiss first?"

"Sure, Mom."

Allison leaned over and kissed Kate's cheek. "So, how was Mississippi? How's Uncle Drew? And Grandma?"

"He's all right, considering the circumstances." Kate led the way into the house. "And your grandmother's as feisty as ever."

"That's so ridiculous, treating him like he's some kind of ax murderer or something." Mycroft rubbed against Allison's leg.

"We are not a family of ax murderers, Richard. I can assure you of that."

Again the young man smiled shyly. "Allison told me about it. It sounds like a very bizarre set of circumstances."

"It is," Kate said. "Like something out of a southern gothic novel. With Drew's house, we even have a substitute for the gloomy old castle." And murder, rape, incest, a faithless wife. Christ, it *was* gothic.

"I like Uncle Drew's house. It's so . . . so . . ."

"Gloomy?"

Allison smiled sheepishly. "Well, yeah." She turned to Richard. "You'd like it, hon, it's just like Faulkner's old place."

Hon? Kate had never heard Allison address a boy—a man—with an endearing term. But I've never heard Melissa joke about a boy being good in bed. God, I hope she's joking. Nor have I ever defended Drew against a murder charge. This Year of Our Lord has certainly brought plenty of firsts.

"I'd like to visit Faulkner's home one day," Richard said.

"I'll take you on the tour," Allison said. "It's pretty impressive."

"I'll pour the wine," Kate said, going into the kitchen. She overheard Allison say, "She's not so bad . . . for a mother."

"I heard that. I'll *get* you for it, too."

"Oops."

Allison and Richard were side-by-side on the couch when she returned. They were holding hands. "And just when did you start drinking?" Kate asked.

"Oh, Mother—ages ago. In Mississippi, in fact. Uncle Drew always slipped us a beer when you weren't looking."

That was just like Drew, Kate thought. The old Drew, before all this mess happened. "It figures," Kate said.

"Okay. Get the lecture over."

"No lecture," Kate said, watching Allison sip from the glass and hand it to Richard. My God, she's grown up drop-dead gorgeous. Tall and blond, just like Tracie. A real California girl. "How's school?"

"Lots of work. It seems like I have to read all of English literature in one quarter."

"Still working your way through *Paradise Lost?"*

"Just the good parts," Richard said.

"He's got a great voice, Mom. You should hear him read."

Richard blushed.

"I'd like that sometime, Richard. I'll have you guys over for dinner soon."

"When do you have to go back to Mississippi, Mom?"

"I'm not really sure. It depends on what happens. I'll have to be there for the prelim, though."

"Uncle Drew's innocent. You have to prove that, Mom."

Yes, but how?

Waiting for Harry, Kate sat quietly in the living room, leafing through the yearbook from her senior year in high school. All of the fresh, young faces beamed at her from the pages. There was Tommy Harper, with his graduation cap askew on [illegible] head, the puckish grin on his face, frozen for all time now. There were Sally Roberts and Harriet Martin, grim and unsmiling. She turned to the freshman class portraits and [illegible] Cory Martin, hometown cop, and Sally's little brother, Jimmy, now a mortician in town. And Betsy Anderson, her little sister, smiling wickedly for the camera. She had been such an imp. She still was.

Oh, Kate, who are you to judge?

Her own pictures seemed to be of someone else, a distant relation, perhaps, someone long since disappeared. She read the inscriptions from friends, some dead now, some long gone, moved away, like the girl she'd once been. Kate shook her head sadly. She felt like she was intruding on another's past, just as she and Tracie had intruded—were intruding—on Billie Rae's forlorn and tormented past. She closed the yearbook and replaced it on the shelf before going to the phone to call Tracie and Drew.

Drew was in a depressed funk.

Tracie had spent the day tracking down more dead-ends.

The brief conversations left Kate in a depression of her own.

They walked down to the pier after dinner and stood at the edge of the continent to watch the last glows of the summer sunset slowly disappear.

"You've been awfully quiet tonight," Harry said.

"I'm kind of down. This whole situation with Drew . . ."

"It's going to turn out all right . . . you know that."

"Do I please you, Harry?" she asked suddenly.

"What kind of question is that?" he asked, putting his arm around her waist, drawing her close. "I'm always happy to be with you."

"Sometimes I wonder . . ." She snuggled in his arms, finding warmth there. And strength. "It's not you. It's me."

"I love you in strange and wondrous ways," he said.

"Let's go home, darling."

"How would you like me to fuck your ears off?"

"I think that would be pretty peachy keen."

"Pretty peachy keen?"

"That's what we always used to say when we were going to get our ears fucked off. Isn't that what you used to say? Or were you just making a promise you can't keep?"

"Just wait."

"Race you home."

Her melancholy mood was gone now, like the sunset.

* * *

"Help me find my ears, darling. They're here somewhere."

"I take that as an expression of approval?"

"Oh, yes."

"That'll teach you to doubt."

"You can teach me anytime.'"

"Be glad to."

"Harry?"

"Mmm?"

"Would you like me to get a tattoo?"

Kate awakened once during the night when Harry stirred beside her, reaching out to embrace her, knowing then, even in his sleep, that he was not alone. It was enough to dispel the fears that come with the darkness.

Kate lay quietly, loving him and enjoying the soft caress as her breast filled and overflowed his hand. Her own fears and despondency had dissipated, driven away when he'd made love to her slowly and deliberately, taking her to that other world where there was only the pain of a pleasure so intense that nothing could co-exist with it. She had cried out, begging him to stop and begging him never to stop, and when he took her from behind, mounting her like a bitch in heat, she writhed and squirmed against him shamelessly, alternately demanding and pleading, fuck me, darling, fuck me.

In the darkness, the usually ever-so-proper Kathryn Anne Gallagher blushed at the memory, but refused shame and guilt. Harry had been too good to her for that. Instead, she placed her hand over his and awaited sleep, knowing that she was not alone, either—at least for tonight.

The next morning, however, reality flooded in with the early morning rays of sunshine. Kate fought consciousness, struggling to remain in the Lethean world engendered by blessed sleep.

* * *

The arraignment went smoothly, quickly. The two perps had been around the block enough to know they were going bye-bye and entered guilty pleas, hoping for a plea bargain. They were held in lieu of $25,000 bail..

Lucy cried as she entered her guilty plea. Her bail was set at $10,000.

Sentencing would be in two weeks.

Kate listened as Jennifer and Lucy's public defender bargained.

"She'll testify against both of them," the PD said.

"Who needs her testimony? They're going away, with or without her testimony. So is she. We've got her name on a dozen pawn slips."

"She needs a break."

"She's going to CIW," Jennifer said. The California Institute for Women was in Corona. There was another CIW in Northern California.

"At least wait until we get the probation report."

"Okay," Jennifer conceded. "We'll wait. Maybe we can work something out."

"How did I do?" Jennifer asked at lunch.

"Fine," Kate replied.

"Was I too hard on Lucy's PD?"

"You played it just right," Kate said, "letting him know that she wasn't going to skate entirely free."

"I feel kind of sorry for her. I hope the probation report is good. No use sending her to finishing school if she can still be saved."

"She might be acting."

"It's possible, but I think it's also possible that she was just sucked into it by her boyfriend. Haven't you ever been fooled by a man?"

Kate laughed. "Yeah, my ex-husband. He still knows how to get to me."

"That's too bad."

Kate shrugged. "It took me a long time to get over it, but it doesn't matter anymore. I don't let him bother me most of the time."

"Well, one way or another, Lucy's going to have a long time to find a better boyfriend."

"How about you?' Kate asked. "Have you ever been suckered by a man?"

Jennifer shook her head. "I've been lucky. Jim's my high school sweetheart. We've been together forever."

"You're lucky. What's he do?"

"Teaches high school math and science. He was always kind of nerdy. But he's a special nerd."

Jennifer seemed content, even happy, with the routine of her life and family. Kate envied her. It was the quiet, normal existence that Kate had so painfully developed over the years after the bitter divorce, sharing Allison and Melissa with Christopher on alternate nights and alternate weekends, meeting Harry and falling in love with him, becoming good at her work, carving out a new career, only to have it disrupted so badly by Nelson and Thompson. It had taken time to put her life in order again. I almost made it, Kate thought. And then Dr. Death walked into my courtroom.

"I'd like to meet Jim," Kate said.

"I want you to," Jennifer said eagerly. "Perhaps when you get back from Mississippi . . ."

"Yes," Kate agreed. "When I get back." Everything has to wait until I get back from Mississippi. Hello, this is Kate Gallagher. I'm sorry I can't come to the phone right now. My life is on hold. Please leave a message and I'll return your call when . . . if . . . order returns.

"Oh, hell."

"What?"

"Nothing." Kate smiled at the younger woman. "My mind wandered. I was composing a new message for my answering machine."

After lunch, Kate picked up her message slips. Still no call from Rainey. Tracie?

She was drawn back to Jack the Ripper. She knew what Cowles planned. The comparison between the original and the Delta Ripper would play nicely in an opening statement. The prosecutor would be able to horrify the jurors if it came to a trial. Would Girardeau be impressed by the comparison during the preliminary hearing?

And Kate was forced to admit there were comparisons between the two cases. Mary Jane Kelly was the only one of the Ripper's victims to be killed indoors, away from the possibility of discovery. The other women had been killed in streets and alleys, their murderer striking quickly. On one occasion, he'd escaped discovery by only minutes. But with Mary Jane Kelly, he had the whole of the night to satisfy the blood lust.

Jack's Mississippi counterpart, too, had the whole of the night to torment Billie Rae, even though she'd been strung up and killed outdoors. Her killer had chosen his remote spot carefully, a place where there was no one to interfere, no one to hear her tortured moans, no one to witness the terrible final moment, except for the possibility of one old, addled black man. He had seen something that night, but what? Maybe Tracie should try and find Old Abe, see if she could learn something.

Kate glanced at her watch. It was nearly five P.M. in Mississippi. Tracie might still be in the office. Kate looked up the number and pressed the buttons, adding her own long calling card code from memory.

"Hello," Tracie's soft Southern accent said, "you have reached the law office of Tracie Sanders. Please leave your name and number and I'll return your call as soon as possible."

At the tone, Kate said, "Hi, Tracie, it's Kate. Please call me as soon as you can. I'll be in the office for another couple of hours. It's three o'clock, California time. I'll try you at home, too."

Kate tried Tracie's home number. Another answering machine clicked on. Kate left the same message.

Kate was nearly ready to leave the office when Rainey finally called.

"How are you, Rainey?"

"Fine, Kate. It was good to see you the other day."

"Yeah, I enjoyed it, too."

"I'll be honest with you, Kate—this thing with your brother is a real mess. It's random, that's all I can figure. I don't like this Delta Ripper stuff, though. Something like that might get to him, make him think he's the incarnation of the great Jack the Ripper who screwed the London police, laughed at them. Who knows? Maybe he *is* Jack the Ripper. There a lot of whores in Mississippi, Kate?"

"Hell, I don't know, Rainey. I suppose. There are prostitutes everywhere. I've been away a long time now. I guess you could make the case that Billie Rae was at least an amateur prostitute, a tramp, anyway."

"Maybe he thinks he's an avenging angel, just like his namesake, on a vendetta against prostitutes."

Oh, Lord, Kate thought. And maybe he goes one step further and decides just who is a prostitute and who isn't. "Rainey, there's something you ought to know."

WHORE.

Kate told him about the message written on Tracie's windshield.

"I don't like it, Kate."

"I don't either, Rainey."

"Tell her to watch her six." Translated from cop vernacular, it meant, watch your ass, keep looking over your shoulder.

"I will."

"Anything else I should know, Kate?"

TELL YOUR SISTER TO COME HOME.

OR ELSE.

Kate sighed. It can't be connected. It was delivered months ago. It's too farfetched. "Maybe," Kate replied. "My brother received an anonymous note."

"What did it say, Kate?"

" 'Tell your sister to come home. Or else.' "

"Jesus Christ, Kate, why didn't you tell me? He wants *you!*"

Fourteen

Kate reached deep into the desk drawer and took the .38-caliber revolver. She opened the cylinder and removed the cartridges, arranging them in a line on her desk. The six deadly projectiles gleamed in a ray of late afternoon sunshine. The empty revolver was still heavy in her hand.

Rainey had frightened Kate, more than she would admit. It was absurd. He couldn't be right. It's nonsense, Kate told herself. Who would go to such elaborate lengths to kill me? Why not just fly to Los Angeles and find me? It wouldn't be that difficult. Not if he knows me, knows my family. I'm always sending short notes and cards home, each one of them with a neatly printed return address.

Kate called Tracie again, leaving messages on both answering machines. "Call me, it's important."

Damn it, where is she?

Kate reloaded the revolver carefully. It was time to go to the range. Get in some serious practice, even if Rainey wasn't right. He couldn't be right.

Wait for me, Rainey said. I'm leaving now. We'll have a drink. Talk it over. Kate agreed to meet him—reluctantly. It just didn't make sense. The precisely lettered anonymous note didn't even specify which sister. Maybe the note was meant for Betsy. Maybe Jack had found out about the affair and the note was his way of telling Betsy to break it off.

TELL YOUR SISTER TO COME HOME. OR ELSE. I LOVE HER.

Of course. *I LOVE HER.* Jack prepared the anonymous note in the hopes that Betsy would stop seeing her lover. And when the affair continued, he decided to wait it out, hoping that the affair would end of its own accord. That had to be it. At least, the explanation offered a rationale. Otherwise, it just didn't make sense.

Unless someone was crazy. Kate's fingers drummed against the desk. The Delta Ripper was crazy.

Kate called home. Melissa was out, too. She left a message. "I'll be a little late." She stared at the telephone after hanging up, willing it to ring, wanting Tracie to call.

After the initial shock of Rainey's statement, Kate still couldn't be concerned about herself. Her mind told her that it made no sense whatsoever to fear something that had happened months ago. It was such a tenuous connection. But what about Tracie? She had received two messages in the last week alone.

WHORE.

Christ, why didn't I do something about it when I was there? God damn it, Tracie, call me.

Kate called Drew. Maybe he's seen Tracie. There was no answer at Drew's office. Why didn't he leave his answering machine on? No answer at the house, either. God damn it, where is everyone?

This can't be happening. If I don't meet Rainey, if I just go home and go to sleep, I'll wake up in the morning and none of this will be true. Harry will not send my emotions into turmoil with proposals of marriage. Dr. Death will not come into my courtroom and tell me I have a phone call from home. Drew will not be in jail. Billie Rae will not be dead. The last ten days will be gone, cut from my life entirely. Everything will be just as it was before.

No.

They were all minor players now in some still unfolding, yet incomprehensible form of classical tragedy. Once the inexorable machinery of the gods began its ponderous turning, their human pawns could not escape the destiny decreed for them. Like Oedipus, each must play out the appointed role. They might flee, but ultimately they must rush headlong into the violent conclusion of their small drama. Fate demanded it.

Kate went to meet Rainey.

It was happy hour. Kate always thought it was a poor name for a period of forced gaiety, stimulated by a series of drinks. On Friday afternoons and into the evening, the bar had a reputation as a meat market, a gathering place for the singles and the not-so-single to meet and appraise each other. During the week, however, the bar was the domain of a few regulars and people who dropped in casually. Kate wondered if the Friday crowd came equipped with test results, proof that they were HIV-negative. Christ, what a world.

A table in the bar was covered with hot and cold hors d'oeuvres. Kate passed it, uncaring, and took a booth near the back to wait for Rainey.

Again Kate wished for escape. An exit sign across the room glowed red, beckoning flight to a nightmarish asylum of old where electrodes applied to the temples removed all trace of the hated days with sudden jolts of electric shocks. Must you go willingly? Or, once committed, was the treatment forced upon you? Knowing human frailties and weaknesses, did they escort you to the chamber with arms tightly laced into a straitjacket and restrain you on the table with straps at wrists and ankles and waist. Did it hurt? How much?

No more than the travails and pain of daily existence and the memories that never went away, even with the passage of time.

A waitress came and asked, "Were you at the services?"

Kate looked at her, not understanding the question.

"Were you at the services?" the waitress repeated. "For Mike? Big guy. Came in here all the time?"

"No, I didn't know him."

The waitress took Kate's order. People were entering now, gathering at the other end of the room, sitting at the bar, standing behind it. The bartender hurried to fill their orders. Snatches of conversation drifted across the room to Kate.

"There were people there I've never seen in the daylight."

"Very nice services."

"Here's to big Mike."

Finally, Kate understood. A patron, a regular, had died, and the other regulars had just returned from his funeral. We've walked into a wake. Death follows me. Death follows Kate Gallagher.

The waitress returned with her glass of wine. Drink enough wine and the memories would vanish.

Memories caused pain. The memories of slights and hurts and a thousand cruelties, a careless remark, a thoughtless act, all accumulated over a lifetime, remained to dance and shimmer in the shadowy recesses of the brain, always there, always awaiting their moment to surface once more to the accompaniment of renewed tears.

How many times did Tracie remember that fateful night when she was stripped of innocence and youth forever?

How many times must I remember Christopher's announcements of yet another affair with a younger, more desirable woman?

The sign invited flights. Blessed oblivion.

Kate waited.

Rainey would be there soon now.

* * *

Across half a continent, a young woman drove through the gathering darkness in uneasy flight from herself. The mood had been building throughout the day. Tracie had trained herself to function asexually, forcing her normal desires and cravings away. Often she could go weeks, even months, without thinking of the sexual act. At times, however, her body and mind rebelled, betraying her until she could think of nothing else but the tender caresses of some unknown lover. Hard work might drive the mood away again by focusing intense concentration on a case or a problem in the law. Or again, the mood persisted until Tracie feared she would never be able to satisfy the lust within her belly.

She passed the River Inn, knowing that she could enter the bar and take her pick of men, satisfy her appetite. They would fight to possess her, even once. But at what price to her self-respect? She wanted more than just a man; she wanted love.

When Tracie neared the Mississippi, she found the old, unused trail and drove slowly over the ruts toward the river. She stopped the car and went to stand at water's edge, listening as the current lapped gently at the bank.

Alone, she slowly stripped her clothes away until she stood naked in the moonlight, a goddess with long hair streaming down her back in golden strands, awaiting purification. She waded into the water, feeling the cleansing warmth of the river tug at her ankles and her knees. Again and again, she scooped water with cupped hands and let it trickle over naked breasts and belly, forming tiny rivulets on her pale flesh.

Then she dived, parting the water sharply with outstretched arms. She was a strong swimmer and drove against the current with powerful strokes—one hundred yards, two hundred, three, four, five, and more. When she was finally winded, Tracie stopped to tread water with only her head above the surface. Around her face, the blond hair spread in a decorative lace.

Tracie touched her breasts, lifting them. They seemed weightless in the water, as though belonging to another, but the nipples were hard and certainly belonged to her as she felt the water's caress that sent pleasurable sensations coursing through her body.

Tracie wanted to be loved.

But the river was her only lover tonight.

Effortlessly, she turned to float on her back, looking up at the stars in the night sky, allowing the current to carry her, kicking only for direction.

When the river brought her even with her car, she sighed and turned, swimming ashore with the same powerful strokes. She waded the last steps and padded across the soft white sand to her clothes, stopping once to stretch her arms to the heavens.

The night was so peaceful and quiet, with only the sound of her river lover calling to her from the bank.

But she was no longer alone.

When Rainey came into the bar, Kate waved to attract his attention.

"What's going on?" Rainey asked, nodding over his shoulder at the assemblage behind him.

"Someone died," Kate said, moving over to make room for him beside her. "Apparently this is the appointed spot for refreshments after the funeral. He was a regular here."

"God, what a sad commentary. Didn't he have a family?"

Kate shrugged. "I don't know."

"Do you want to go someplace else?"

"We're here now," Kate said. "I have to get home soon, anyway."

When Rainey ordered Scotch, Kate raised her eyebrows.

She knew he only drank Scotch when he was deeply concerned about something. The whole time they were together he drank only beer and wine—until near the end.

He saw the gesture and said, "I'm worried about you, Kate."

"Don't be. I'm fifteen hundred, two thousand miles, from whoever did that note. I'm in no danger."

"Listen to me, Kate. There are only a few possibilities. One, your brother did it and he's one of the dumbest murderers in history. Two, someone has a vendetta against your brother and is trying to frame him, but it's pretty crude and won't stand up in court—you know that. Three, someone in that bar picked up the woman and something went wrong. Maybe she was the target all along; I don't know. Maybe it's just another random and senseless killing and Billie Rae was the target of opportunity, but taking her to your brother's hunting cabin is just a little too coincidental for me. But if you add the note into the equation, it begins to make sense. This guy, whoever he is, wants you, Kate."

"Why does it have to be me? Why couldn't the note be meant for my sister?"

"It's you, Kate."

"You're scaring me again, Rainey."

"Some nut case wants you, thinks he loves you. Gets the note to your brother. When you don't show up, he takes the most natural course to get you back to Mississippi. You're an attorney. Your brother is arrested. Who's he going to call? Who's going to show up the next day in good old Butt Fuck, Mississippi?"

Kate shook her head. "Why didn't anything happen when I was there? I mean, there was no contact of any kind."

"What about Tracie? Maybe he thinks she's some kind of threat."

"That's crazy."

"So is he."

* * *

Tracie dried herself with a big yellow towel and dressed slowly, secure in the knowledge that she was alone in her secluded and isolated spot. She stepped into the panties and then the jeans, buckling the belt around her slim waist. She slipped into her loafers and then bent to retrieve her blouse, leaving her bra on the sand. Wet strands of hair brushed over her breasts. Slowly, she buttoned the blouse. In her loneliness, Tracie crossed her arms over her breasts, hugging herself tightly, wishing for someone to love her.

A silver path of moonlight crossed the river. She could follow the moonbeams to paradise . . . to beyond, if she wished. Downstream, the river parted around a sandbank. It hadn't been there before, but the river was always changing, always mysterious.

Across the river in Arkansas, lights twinkled like lost stars, fallen from their accustomed place in the sky.

Reluctant to leave, Tracie looked around one more time. It was still her secret place, her special place. In all the time she'd been coming here, she'd never encountered anyone. But she longed to share her private spot with someone. She dreamed of lying on a sandbar, tight in the arms of another as he slowly made love to her.

The wake had grown raucous with the flow of alcohol easing sorrow and the fear of mortality.

"When are you going back?" Rainey asked quietly.

"I don't know. Soon, I guess." Yes, it would be soon, Kate realized . . . perhaps as early as the weekend. It was starting to happen now.

He took her hand, covering it with his own. "I'll go with you, if you'd like."

"I'll be fine. There's no need to disrupt your life, too."

He stroked her forearm. "Be careful."

"I will. Don't worry about me."

"I always worry about you."

Kate was suddenly afraid, not for herself, but for him. A fear that she would never see him again darted through her. "Hold me, Rainey, I'm cold."

He put his arm around her shoulders and drew her close. She looked up at him, waiting for his kiss, wanting it, returning it eagerly when it came.

"Oh, Christ, I want to make love to you again."

"We will, Rainey."

"Is that a promise?"

"Oh, yes," Kate said. "We'll make love again someday. When I know. Be patient with me." She didn't tell him that it would be either the end or the beginning.

Hidden in the shadowy recesses of the room, he kissed her again.

"I have to go now," she said.

"Don't leave without telling me, Kate."

"I won't."

He watched as she dried herself. When she leaned over to dry her legs, her breasts hung down like the teats on a milk cow. A man wouldn't mind milking her twice a day. He watched as she dressed, not bothering with the brassiere like a decent woman. The slut. But a decent woman wouldn't be swimming buck-naked in the river, either. It was one more transgression to punish her for. He watched as she folded her bra and stuffed it into her purse.

"How was dinner last night?" Kate asked.

"Oh, it was okay, you know."

"I like Allison's boyfriend," Kate said.

"Yeah, he's okay. Not my type, though. He's kind of a wimpy hunk, you know."

Wimpy hunk? Kate supposed that to mean that Richard was a hunk, but a literary hunk rather than an athletic one. Melissa went for athletes. "What about Kevin Costner, then?" Kate asked. Melissa's room was decorated with pictures of the actor.

"He can put his shoes under my bed anytime he wants."

Oh, Lord, adolescence is raging tonight—again. When does it end? Never, if last night is any indication.

"Why are you blushing, Mom?" Melissa laughed wickedly. "I'll bet you wouldn't toss Kevin Costner out, either, if he came calling."

"Melissa," Kate stammered. Well, what do you expect? You started it.

Tracie drove home remembering her phantom lover's soft caress washing over her body, still wishing for someone to give herself to, someone who would appreciate all she could offer. I'd be so good to him, God, if only he were good to me in return. Please, God, let me meet someone who will love me. I don't want to be hurt anymore.

Kate waited restlessly for the telephone to ring. She browsed through the bookcase looking for something to read, but nothing appealed to her. The books, mostly novels, reflected the eclectic tastes of three different women. Kate had to admit it—her daughters were young women now, not girls.

Kate picked up the latest issue of the *New Yorker.* In all the time since Tina Brown had taken over as editor and installed a new and gaudier format, Kate still could not get used to it. There were some things that should never change and the *New Yorker* was one of them. Again she considered letting her subscription lapse, and again she decided against it. It wasn't *that* bad.

Kate jumped when Melissa's telephone rang. In her bedroom, Melissa picked up after the second ring. Damn it . . . Tracie, where are you? Why don't you call? Kate glanced at her watch. It was after nine in Mississippi.

She tossed the magazine on the coffee table with the others. There was never enough time to read them all. Maybe I should let the subscription run out, but what would life without the *New Yorker* be like? It would be like life without Harry. Or Rainey.

Oh, Lord, what am I going to do? How did I fall in love with two men so different? Harry was sound and practical, always quietly logical. Rainey lived in a mystical world of his own creation, a buffer against the horrors of too many years investigating the cruelties of man. And yet they were so alike. Both were kind and gentle. Both loved her. Christ, I'm lucky, Kate thought, but what am I going to do?

Mycroft jumped on the couch beside her and began kneading the cushion to meet his satisfaction before twisting and turning to find the proper position. Once he was settled, he looked up at Kate with big yellow eyes and mewed once. She stroked his fur gently. He purred and closed his eyes. Kate envied him.

When the telephone rang finally, Kate stared at it for a moment, willing the caller to be Tracie, visualizing her in the small apartment, perhaps taking an earring out and shaking her hair aside before lifting the receiver.

"Hello."

"Kate, it's Tracie. I just got in and found your message. Messages."

"Are you all right?"

"I'm fine," Tracie said. "I went for a drive after work."

"I was worried when I didn't hear from you."

"I'm sorry. I didn't expect to be this late. I should have stopped and called earlier."

"It's all right. I'm just glad to hear from you."

"You said it was important."

Kate hesitated. Secure in the warmth and familiar surroundings of her home, with Melissa giggling on the telephone, it all sounded so crazy again, not like when Rainey was telling it. "Have you had any more of those phone calls?" she asked. "Or messages?"

"No. It was just some crank. My brother, or high school kids, maybe."

"Rainey doesn't think so."

Tracie listened as Kate went through Rainey's theory again and then said, "Your friend can't be right. Why me? Why you? It's crazy."

There was that word again. It was the word of the day. Crazy. Crazy. Crazy. "I think so, too, but I want you to be careful. Like Rainey says, cover your six."

"I will."

"Good." Kate paused. "I'm coming back on Saturday."

"Why so early?"

"I feel out of it here," Kate said. "I want to get it over with." Whatever *it* is.

"Let me know when you're going to get into Memphis. I'll drive up and get you."

"You don't have to do that."

"It doesn't make sense for you to spend money on a rental car. You can use mine. We can work something out."

"That would be nice," Kate said. "I'll make the reservations tomorrow and let you know."

"Goodnight, Kate. It'll be good to see you."

"You take care, Tracie." Kate hung up. Thank God she's all right, but why don't I feel better?

* * *

For the second time that night, Tracie slowly undressed until she stood naked in the darkness of her bedroom. This time, however, she imagined the teasing fingers of a mystery lover as he unfastened the buttons of her blouse. She shuddered as he slipped the blouse from her shoulders, revealing her breasts, and shuddered again when she lifted their soft weight for his kiss.

The hands that unfastened her skirt and let it drop to the floor were not her own. The hands belonged to another now.

She held his head as he knelt before her, showering her with kisses. She moaned softly, helpless in his embrace. Her tongue flicked over full and red lips, aching to feel the strength of his kiss. When finally he would kiss her, he would take her tongue, drawing it into his mouth, holding it prisoner, while she rubbed against him eagerly, desperate for his piercing.

Perhaps, though, they would prolong the sweet agony and she would kneel in her turn to caress him with her lips, her tongue, finally taking him in her mouth, deeper and deeper, tasting the first of his seed and then his explosion. He would beg to be released then, but she would not let him go until she had drained him, enduring his frantic lunges willingly as the expression of her love.

Tracie moaned and cried out at the thought of the pleasures she would give and take from him.

They would begin anew then. She would take him willingly in her bed, spreading her legs wide. It would be his fingers and not her own that caused her to cry out softly in her passion. It would be his tongue, his lips, that burrowed through the silky blond hair, torturing her to pleasure while she whipped her head back and forth against the satin pillows.

"Oh, yes," Tracie cried from the loneliness of her bed. "Oh, yes, my darling, oh, God, yes."

Now, please now, it's time.

He would mount her, penetrate her, fill her with the evidence of his love, thrusting deep while she arched her back and forced her hips to meet him until . . .

Her orgasm burst against her fingers, rocking her with delightful spasms. She pinched her nipples as her lover might, hurting herself and not caring, wishing for his bite.

When it was over, Tracie fell back and took one of the pillows in a lover's tight embrace. The tears came then; they always did. Tracie cried until she finally fell into an uneasy and restless sleep.

Kate tossed and turned, sleeping fitfully, but not because she was lonely, although she missed Harry's warm and comforting presence. Kate's mind worked overtime. She could not stop the thoughts that raced through the darkness. Rainey. His concern. His kiss. Harry, sharing her bed and much of her life. Betsy. Anonymous notes and messages streaked on a windshield. Drew. Damn, I never called Drew again. Where was he? How was he holding up? The revolver in her purse. Can't take it on the plane. Drew has guns if I need one. Oh, Rainey, are you right?

Kate turned over and looked at the numerals on the alarm, glowing a bright blue in the darkness. After midnight. She closed her eyes again. Where was sleep?

He dreamed of the many ways he would punish the whore. He would teach her not to strut around and flaunt her filthy nakedness. It wasn't right that he suffered because of her. He would make her pay for that. She would beg to be allowed to please him and he would let her, but it would be too late. She would die knowing the enormity of her sins.

He hoped he wouldn't have to do the same to his beloved Kathryn Anne.

* * *

Oh, Christ, who are you? Why are you doing this to me? What do you want with me? The endless questions tortured Kate.

Fifteen

The dawn began sluggishly, with a faint glow forcing itself above the horizon, growing brighter, sending tiny streaks into the black sky, the first harbingers of the new day. And when the first burning crescent of the sun peeked over the Mississippi Delta to fill windows with light, Tracie turned over in her bed, still clutching the pillow tightly, both for the comforting caress of a lover and to shut out the day. The tears had dried during the night, but the memory of her loneliness lingered into her awakening. She longed to sleep the day away, but nagging memories, like the dawn, crept into her bed.

At least the sexual tension was gone, but still she was unloved. Even when Rodney had made love to her awkwardly and selfishly, taking more from her than he could give in return, she had known she was a woman and desirable. And she had never awakened still empty. Rodney gave her that much, at least. But Rodney was gone. Tracie wondered if he missed her, ever thought of her, if he was happy with the woman he had married in her place. Claire—that was her name. Did she love him? Rodney, you bastard, why didn't you understand? Forget him. Don't start that mood again. Think of something else.

Anything.

Even the dream.

She was crying in the dream. And all the time she scrubbed furiously at the word on her windshield, the neighbors called her names, laughing and pointing fingers at her. Each time she finished, red-faced and humiliated at the cruel taunts of her neighbors, the word reappeared.

WHORE.

Over and over, she washed the word away, only to see it come back.

Jesus.

Who are you? Kate had warned her to be careful. Maybe she was right. But it couldn't be. It had to be some crank, someone like Willie who enjoyed being cruel to a young and unattainable woman. Or maybe I am a whore, and I'm the only one who doesn't see it. Last night I would have fucked anyone.

Oh, Christ, don't start. Not again. Not so soon. Please let me spend my day in peace.

A mound beneath the sheet at her feet stirred, wriggled forward until Sam's whiskered face peered up at her with wide, unblinking eyes. She stroked his chin until he purred contentedly.

"Oh, Sam, you don't think I'm a whore, a slut, a bitch, a cunt, a pussy, do you?" Willie had called her all those names. Tracie punished herself with the words. Her moans and cries of the night before had frightened Sam, sending him into the living room. She didn't know when he had come to bed, burrowing beneath the sheet to sleep next to her feet.

Tracie threw off the sheet and slipped into her robe, drawing the belt tight, knotting it against her waist. Barefoot, she went into the kitchen, the sun-washed tiles already warm against her soles.

Sam followed her, leaping gracefully to the back of a chair and then to the counter, padding silently across the stove to the coffeepot.

It was empty. She'd forgotten to make the coffee and set

the timer. Tracie sighed and prepared a new pot and turned it on. She stood there listening as the machine sighed and wheezed the first drops of water through the coffee grounds. Deftly she removed the pot and replaced it with a cup, holding it there as it slowly filled. When the cup was half full, she replaced the pot, missing only a few drops that sizzled on the warming plate.

She took the first sip and then put the cup on the table. At the door, she peeked through the peephole, seeing only a distorted door across the hallway. Tracie never used the peephole. Be careful, Kate had said. She opened the door. The hall was empty. When she bent to retrieve the paper, she held the top of her robe tightly closed. Be careful.

Of what? Of who, or was it whom?

Tracie locked the door again.

Who was out there?

How do you defend yourself when it could be anyone—the fresh-faced paperboy, the staid and sober mailman, a smiling convenience store clerk, a dignified instructor at the community college, even a cop sworn to protect? There was no program to provide the names and faces of murderers, rapists, burglars, child molesters, wife beaters, until after the fact, when it was too late. It had been too late for Billie Rae. Someone who seemed innocuous had approached Billie Rae after she left the River Inn, someone nonthreatening. She had allowed her killer to approach, perhaps even smiled at him, and then . . . Whatever happened then had been too late for Billie Rae.

How do you protect yourself when the threat comes from within, from someone you know and trust, from someone you love? It had been too late for Tracie, too. She forced the memory of her brother and his brutal attack into the deep recesses of her mind. He no longer existed for her. Willie Sanders was dead, as far as she was concerned. He always would be.

Who was out there, waiting?

Tracie told herself once again that she was merely the target of a cruel prank. By the time she finished her second cup of coffee, she almost believed it.

Almost.

The day brightened with the cleansing hot water of the shower, which washed away memory . . . until Tracie thought of Janet Leigh in *Psycho* and the swirling bloodied water sucked into the void of eternity. There were so many ways to die.

But later, the dull, steady roar of the hair dryer drowned the sounds of the outside world and Tracie felt secure until she realized that someone could enter the apartment, creep into her bedroom, and lurk there until she left the bathroom, and she would never hear him.

She snapped the dryer off and listened. Nothing. The apartment was quiet except for the soft music from the clock radio. Sam sat on the edge of the bed, watching her warily. He hated the sound of the hair dryer.

Christ, I'm going to be paranoid before this is over.

What was the old saying? Just because you're paranoid doesn't mean that someone's not out to get you.

God, I'll be glad when Kate gets back.

Tracie hurried then, eager to leave the quiet apartment, to be with people. But outside, he would be able to find her. Perhaps he had already found her. If he was the one who had soaped the message on her windshield . . . If he was the one who'd called . . . If . . .

When she was dressed, Tracie filled Sam's bowls with water and dry food, glanced around to make sure that everything was in order, double-checked to make sure that the answering machine was on and the coffee maker was off. When Tracie was halfway down the hall, dreading what she might find at her car, she couldn't remember locking the door, and retraced her steps. When she tried the door, it was locked. Shaking her head, Tracie went out into the already sweltering day.

Her car was untouched.

Thank God for that.

Tracie parked in front of her office. Across the street, courthouse workers hurried past the Confederate memorial to climb the steps into the building. The regulars were scattered around the park benches. Waiting. Chewing. Spitting. Waiting some more. One man was eating a doughnut and drinking coffee. He was a regular, too; Tracie had seen him before. She wondered if it was a jelly doughnut. She could almost taste a big, thick jelly doughnut. It would be so good, Tracie thought, and so bad for my figure.

Inside, she switched on lights and air conditioner and listened to messages from the answering machine. They were all from Kate. "Call me, Tracie, it's important." Tracie erased them, but left the machine on to screen calls.

She looked at the checklist on her desk. The remaining witness interviews had all been checked off. Four remained.

Girardeau
Cowles
Abraham?
Gun???

Doing the background research on Cowles and Girardeau would be easy. It simply meant spending an hour or two in the library.

Billie Rae's gun was an enigma. Tracie had gone back to the waitress at the River Inn. Linda was adamant that she had told the police about the gun. The investigating officers were equally adamant that it had never been mentioned. Tracie added a fourth question mark behind the notation.

Abraham?

Kate wondered if they might learn something with another interview with the old man. Kate felt he might have seen something, someone, that night. Kate also thought he would be a marginal witness, vulnerable to cross-examination. Cowles would be able to devastate his memory on the stand, confuse him. But it was worth another try.

Library first, and then Abraham.

The drawers of the metal storage cabinet were labeled with typed dates—a hundred years and more of newspapers stored on microfilm. The local newspaper was there, of course, along with the Memphis and Jackson papers. Tracie went back ten years.

Tracie threaded the microfilm into the viewing machine. With a turn of the handle, days, weeks, months flashed before her eyes in a whirring blur of black newsprint streaks on the screen, denoting births, deaths, happiness, agony. An entire football seasons passed over the screen faster than the fleetest halfback returning a kickoff for a touchdown. The rise and fall of cotton, rice, and soybean prices flashed past in a dizzying swirl of economic fortune and misfortune. Political fortunes, too, were inexorably recorded in final vote tallies. Tracie stopped at that long-ago election day. She had been twenty-three years old, in her first year of law school, dating Rodney, making plans. She had been filled with hope for the future. Where did it all go?

Girardeau had been gracious in defeat, congratulating his opponent, perhaps already knowing that he would be taken care of. And he had been, receiving his appointment to the bench a few weeks later. The local pundit at the time had credited the winner with running a more energetic campaign, spending huge amounts of his own money to win the legislative seat. There had been a second element to Girardeau's defeat, the political reporter wrote. The people desired a change.

Tracie turned back the pages, occasionally dropping a quarter into the slot and pressing a print button. She copied the account of the election, an in-depth profile of Girardeau, occasional features on the campaign.

Then, she went back four years to Wilson Cowles's first campaign for District Attorney. It was more of the same. The people wanted a change, a different reporter wrote. Just as she had done for Girardeau, Tracie made copies of what she thought Kate might find interesting. But it was all old history. There was nothing useful there.

Tracie took her copies back to the office. The jelly doughnut man was gone.

Tracie drove out to the woods, but she could not find the old man. Wherever he lived, old Abe's shack was well hidden. She drove up and down the old road twice, hoping to run into the old man. Each time, she passed the turnoff to Drew's hunting cabin. Before leaving town, she had stopped by Drew's office to ask him for the key. "As long as I'm out there . . ." But he hadn't bothered to fix the lock.

On her third pass down the road, Tracie turned in. Maybe old Abe will find me. He found Kate.

Tracie followed around a curve in the path and there it was. Even though Tracie had prepared herself to view the murder scene dispassionately and with a professional attitude, she was still shocked by the sight of the frame.

It stood exactly as it had been that night. Christ, how did he get her up there? Of course, she was unconscious. The bruise on her face where she had been struck by a fist or a blunt instrument told them that. But still . . .

How did it feel to awaken slowly, confused and disoriented, to find yourself bound and gagged, to finally realize that you were staring down at the man who was doing to kill you slowly and painfully?

Tracie turned away from the drying frame. Her imagination

was already running away with her. What if it was me up there? Or Kate?

The woods were eerily quiet.

Tracie listened for any sound of man. Nothing. Tracie walked to the cabin. The steps creaked beneath her feet. When she pushed the door open, the hot, musty air swept over her. The killer had been here, too. Tracie forced a growing fear back and entered the cabin. It was just as Kate had described it.

Tracie heard the creak on the steps and whirled to face the doorway.

There was no one there.

Jesus. She was sweating and breathing heavily. Warily, she crept to the door. No one. Beyond, her car was embraced by the shadow of the frame. It was waiting for her. If she went near, it would embrace her, too.

Tracie closed the cabin door with trembling fingers and turned to face her fear.

It waited patiently for her.

Tracie fled.

The hideous instrument beckoned grotesquely in the rearview mirror, shimmering in the fluttering heat waves. I want you, it called to her. Come and let me hold you, it seemed to say.

Back at the highway, Tracie stopped. She knew she had reacted irrationally, but she couldn't help herself. In the stillness of the woods, it had seemed real enough. There's nothing to be afraid of, Tracie told herself, but when this is over, I'm coming back to burn that God damned thing.

A vehicle, black and distorted, appeared in the heat waves that danced over the blacktop. Tracie waited for the vehicle to pass. It was a hearse.

Jesus, that's all I need now. Mr. Death.

Tracie found the nine-by-twelve manila envelope when she returned to the office. It had been dropped through the mail slot in the door. She picked it up and turned it over. The precisely aligned letters screamed at her.

TO THE WHORE.

Tracie dropped the envelope as though it had burned her hand. She turned and left the office, not bothering to shut the door. She went next door to the travel agency. A man and a woman were seated at desks.

"Did you see anyone deliver an envelope next door?" Tracie asked.

"Sure didn't," the woman said.

The man shrugged and shook his head.

"Is something wrong?' the woman asked. "You look upset."

"No," Tracie said. "Just curious. Thanks anyway."

"I wonder what that was all about?" the woman asked, when Tracie was gone.

"Beats me," the man said.

Tracie went to the florist shop which had the space on the other side of her office. A bell rang as she pushed through the door. A high school girl smiled at Tracie. "May I help you?"

"I have the office next door," Tracie said.

"Sure. I recognize you."

"Did you see anyone drop an envelope through my mail slot this afternoon?"

"No. I've been working in the back, mostly. Had this big arrangement to do. I just this minute finished."

"Thanks." Tracie lingered a moment, not wanting to go back and look at the envelope again. It was cool in the shop, but it smelled like death. Florists shops always reminded her of death.

"Is there something else I can help you with?" the girl asked.

Tracie didn't reply. Mr. Death was waiting for her next door.

"Miss, are you okay?"

Tracie started. "I'm sorry. My mind was someplace else. Thanks again."

Back in her office, Tracie locked the door and picked up the envelope again, carefully this time, by the edges, and carried it to her desk. She sat staring at it for a long time.

TO THE WHORE.

Tears of angry frustration came to her eyes. Why are you doing this to me? Who are you? What have I ever done to you? Tracie found it odd that she wasn't afraid. I should be, but I'm not.

At a rap at the door, Tracie looked up. It was the woman from the travel agency. She tried the door and rapped again when it wouldn't open.

Tracie covered the envelope and brushed at her eyes before going to let the woman in.

"I was worried about you—with good reason, I see. Can I help?"

Tracie tried to smile. "No. It's nothing, really." Tracie fumbled for a story to tell the woman. She meant well. "My boyfriend and I had a fight."

"Oh, is that all? Men aren't worth crying over, honey. You take it from me. They're just like buses. There'll be another one along in fifteen minutes, specially for a pretty thing like you. Well, I'm glad it wasn't nothing worse than that. You looked a fright when you came in."

"I'll be all right. I guess we'll patch it up."

"That's right, honey, patch it up. But if'n you don't, you just remember what I said. Just like buses."

"Thanks. I appreciate your concern."

"You take care, now."

Tracie locked the door again and went back to her desk.

TO THE WHORE.

You son-of-a-bitch.

Tracie opened the clasp. There wouldn't be any fingerprints. Whoever he was, the bastard would be too smart to leave prints. The flap wasn't sealed, either. Probably worried about leaving saliva traces.

There were three sheets of paper inside. The first was similar to the lettering on the envelope.

TELL KATHRYN ANNE TO COME BACK. I LOVE HER, MISS HER.

The newspaper columns looked as though they came from a scrapbook. They had been cut out and aligned just as precisely as the lettering on the outside of the envelope. They were dated a week apart, seven years ago. Tracie began to read.

"A modern-day Jack the Ripper struck the Gulf Coast again last night . . ."

Tracie turned quickly to the second article.

"A Biloxi woman was discovered brutally murdered Wednesday night . . ."

Why would he send this to me? Who is he?

Tracie read through the accounts carefully. The two women had been killed in the same way as Billie Rae. After reading the two newspaper accounts, Tracie was ready to bet that the police reports would show that each of the victims had the same little square carved into the flesh between their breasts.

For the second time that day, Tracie was in the library's microfilm section. The library didn't have the Gulf Coast papers on file, but the Jackson newspapers carried accounts of both murders. Tracie made copies of every reference she could find. The cases had received less and less attention as days built into weeks and months. The murderer had never been caught.

Carrying the stack of copies, Tracie went back to the office to call Kate.

* * *

"Oh, God," Kate said when Tracie told her of the double murders in Biloxi.

A chill swept through Tracie. "Kate, what's wrong.?"

"Drew has a place down there," Kate said. Her voice was tired and resigned, even frightened. "He's had it for years."

Sixteen

"Tracie, hold a minute. I'll be right back."

Kate went to close the door of her office. Christ, what's happening? It can't be Drew. How's he going to have an alibi for seven years ago? What was I doing seven years ago? How can anyone remember?

"I'm back, Tracie."

"Kate, there's more."

Oh, God, now what? Don't let it be Drew. Please. "What is it, Tracie?"

"It was addressed to the whore. And inside there was another message for you."

"What did it say?"

" 'Tell Kathryn Anne to come back. I love her, miss her.' "

"Dear God. What's going on, Tracie?"

"I don't know."

"Look, I want you to get out of town."

"I'm not afraid. I'm angry, but I'm not afraid."

No, but I am, Kate thought. "It's not that," she said. "I just think it's better for you to get away until we figure out what's going on. Drive up to Memphis tonight. Make sure you're not followed. Check into an airport hotel, a big one with lots of people, not a motel. Call me when you get there and let me know which one. By then, I'll have reservations and I can tell you what flight I'm arriving on. You can meet me. I'll get out as early as I can in the morning. Okay, Tracie? I'll just feel better knowing that you're safe."

"All right, Kate."

"Tracie?"

"Yes."

"Be careful. I don't want you taking any chances. We need time to figure this one out."

But how? Kate stared at the telephone for a long time after hanging up. Why? That was the essential question. If we know why, then everything else will fall in place. Kate finally admitted she knew why. "Someone wants me," she told the office walls. It all started with me. Billie Rae might be alive if Drew had paid attention to that anonymous note. No one bothered Tracie before I walked into her office. It begins and ends with me. Who wants me? Why?

Unless Drew is a murderer. She still couldn't believe that about her brother. Never. Drew was not a killer. Tomorrow, she would confront Drew, and together they would reconstruct his past. There would be some way to reconstruct his whereabouts on the dates in question seven years ago. There would be an alibi. There just had to be.

Therefore someone else had killed the two women in Biloxi. Someone else, probably the same person, had murdered Billie Rae, threatened Tracie, and claimed a perverse attraction for her. *I LOVE HER, MISS HER.* He called her "Kathryn Anne." No one did that except her mother, when she was angry. It's someone who knows me? Who? Why? Someone from high school? Someone from college? God damn it! Why?

At least I'll be able to ask for a dismissal after we connect the two cases. If Drew has an alibi, and if he can prove he was not in Biloxi when the two women were murdered. It'll be over then.

Kate shook her head sadly. It wouldn't be over, though. It wouldn't end until they found the real killer.

Kate picked up the telephone again to call for airline reservations. Then she went to Dr. Death's office and asked Margie, "Is he in?"

The secretary nodded. "He's just going over some case loads. Go on in."

Kate rapped lightly on the open door. "It's happening, Phil," she said.

Going to the range always reminded Kate of Rainey. She had first met Rainey at the police academy range. And when he had given her the gun, he had told her what she would have to do. His instructions remained deeply ingrained. "Just point it like you were pointing your finger and pull the trigger," he had told her. "And keep pulling the trigger until it stops shooting. None of that 'Hands up' shit, no 'Up against the wall, motherfucker.' Just pull the trigger and keep shooting. Kill the son-of-a-bitch. You understand?"

Kate understood. She didn't like it then, and she didn't care much for it now. But the gun had saved her life once. She hoped she wouldn't have to follow Rainey's instructions, but if it came down to that . . .

She aimed and squeezed the trigger. The revolver jumped in her hand. That was six. She opened and emptied the cylinder. The brass was hot in her hand. She dropped it on the table with the rest that she'd fired, before pulling the target back to her. There were six holes in the black of the bull's-eye.

Someone wanted her. Someone who had very probably killed Billie Rae after torturing her and mutilating her body. Whoever it was professed love. Bullshit! Kate reloaded the revolver and raised it again, steadying the butt in her left hand. She took a deep breath, exhaled. Slowly, slowly, she squeezed the trigger. The blast was deadened by the earmuffs she wore to protect her hearing. Slowly . . .

She was one with the revolver and the target. Another hole appeared magically in the target.

But it wasn't the same as shooting a man. Targets didn't beg and plead for their lives.

Targets didn't bleed.

Tracie had lied to Kate. She was afraid and wished for someone to turn to for comfort and protection, someone like her dream lover, who was strong and understanding. He would be able to tell her what to do. But he wasn't there. He appeared only when the mood struck and when she was alone in the safety of her bedroom. She longed for his caress now. Despite the chill that had settled in the pit of her belly, Tracie had to smile. Danger makes me horny, she thought. Tonight, darling. Come to me tonight and I'll be a willing whore to your embrace.

As she drove through town on her way back to the apartment, she looked at the pedestrians on the street, the man who pulled up next to her at a light, the two men sitting on the hood of a truck at the gas station, drinking from cans of beer. One of them was the killer. Who?

Screw you, whoever you are.

Tracie followed Kate's instructions, looking in her rearview mirror always expecting to see a monstrous image, but it was empty of all but the innocuous when she turned on her street and parked. She remained in the car for five minutes, watching and working up her nerve to enter the empty apartment. It was broad daylight. No one will bother me in the daylight. He comes with the darkness.

Inside, Tracie locked and chained the door, leaning against it for a moment as Sam scampered down the hallway to greet her.

"Hey, babe, how was your day?" Tracie asked. Sam replied by rubbing against her leg and purring. He followed her into the bedroom and watched as she changed clothes, brought an overnight bag from the closet, and hurriedly threw items of clothing in it. Twice, she had to pull Sam from the bag. "You have to stay here, but it's just overnight. And then I won't leave you alone again. I promise."

Tracie distracted the kitten by filling his bowls with food and water. When he was eating, Tracie left the apartment and carried her bag to the car. It's just another business trip, Tracie thought, as she placed her bag in the passenger seat. It's nothing but a business trip.

Tracie drove out of town, heading north on the two-lane highway to Memphis. Again, she kept an eye on the mirror. When a car or a pickup appeared, she slowed enough to cause irritation in the driver behind, making him swing out and pass with a blare of the horn. They quickly disappeared in the heat waves ahead and Tracie resumed her speed until the next vehicle roared up behind her.

For long stretches she was alone on the highway, except when she came upon a slow-moving tractor on the shoulder. Then she swung into the other lane to pass. On both sides of the highway now, there were cotton fields or the swirling patterns of the rice paddies.

Some daredevil duster was flying late, diving his small airplane low over the neat rows of cotton, releasing the spray even as his wheels appeared to touch the plants. At the last second, he roared into the sky in an abrupt and steep climb to avoid the high power wires. At the conclusion of a short turn he dived again, dipping low after he passed over the wires, the fine mist already spreading over the next rows of cotton.

Tracie relaxed finally. Away from town and the confines of her office and apartment, the threat seemed distant, and she began to anticipate a long, hot shower and a relaxing meal in the hotel restaurant. Afterward she would buy a paperback to read while she waited to see if her dream lover cared enough to make another appearance tonight.

Kate's mind raced as she cleaned the revolver behind her closed bedroom door. She didn't want to alarm Melissa. Both Allison and Melissa knew of her occasional forays to the indoor shooting range, but neither new why she did it. Kate had never told them of Nelson's attack on her. She'd kept that part of her job away from them. They would only worry.

Her mind stayed in high gear as she wondered why the killer was providing his press clippings. Were there more to come? Maybe he's been reading about Jack the Ripper, too. *Catch me if you can . . .*

Why didn't VICAP reveal the Gulf Coast murders? VICAP was the Violent Criminal Apprehension Program run out of the FBI Academy in Quantico, Virginia. Kate knew the fifteen-page VICAP report should have been submitted even if they thought Billie Rae's murder had been solved with Drew's arrest. It was standard operating procedure for any law enforcement agency confronted with a murder of this type. The files would be compared, and similar murders would appear on the computers. Were they lazy, incompetent, lost in the bureaucratic maze, what?

For that matter, why didn't the detectives investigating the Gulf Coast murders step forward? Billie Rae's murder had received attention, probably statewide. Didn't cops read the newspapers? Did they retire? Were they dead? Didn't they care?

Kate inspected the revolver after running a patch stained with bore cleaner through the barrel. She wouldn't take the pistol to Mississippi with her. It wasn't worth the trouble of explaining the presence of a gun in her luggage to the airline personnel. Drew would have a gun she could borrow.

Was it nickel-plated?

She shook that thought off and ran another patch through the barrel to leave a thin film of oil. With a cloth, she wiped her smudged fingerprints from the bluing of the revolver. When she replaced it in the small red carrying case, it was unloaded. She hid it in a dresser drawer beneath her lingerie. Melissa was always borrowing her clothes, a blouse or a sweater, but she wouldn't look in that particular drawer. Even so, Kate left the revolver unloaded and stood on tiptoe, straining to put the unfired cartridges deep on the shelf of her closet.

Then she opened the bedroom door and put her suitcase on the bed to pack.

"Have you been shooting again?" Melissa asked.

Kate looked up to see her daughter in the doorway, leaning casually against the wall.

"How did you know?"

"It smells like gun in here. You now, that cleaning oil. Besides, the only time you ever shut your door is at night, or when you're cleaning your gun."

"So much for my secret life," Kate said.

"Is it fun?"

"What? Shooting?"

"Yeah."

"I like to do it occasionally. I find it relaxing."

"Even with all that noise and everything."

"Yes," Kate said nodding. It was strange, but shooting did relax her. She had been surprised to discover that fact. She had grown up around guns. Drew had taken her squirrel hunting in the woods when she was a girl and taught her to shoot his air rifle and then his .22 rifle. And one or another of her uncles always brought venison over when they killed a deer during the season. The meat did not come without a price, however. In return, the women were expected to listen as the hunt was recounted in detail. So Kate was accustomed to guns and still she had been shocked to find she liked shooting and was good at it. Except she never wanted to kill anything. Never again.

"What's it like?" Melissa persisted.

"It's kind of like shutting out the world. When I aim, all I see is the target. Everything else is gone. There's just me, the gun, and the target. It's like Zen."

"You mean meditating?"

"It's hard to explain."

"Will you take me sometime?"

Dismayed, Kate looked at her youngest daughter. She was too young to learn the world was not a very pleasant place, that it was populated by too many who swam against the tide of society, but perhaps it was time to teach her to shoot. It might save her life someday. It saved mine, Kate thought, as she remembered the encounter with Nelson. Again. "Maybe when I get back," she said.

"How long are you going to be gone?"

"I don't know. A week or two, at least."

"I'll miss you. I don't like staying with Daddy all the time."

Kate was startled. Melissa rarely made reference to the alternating nights and weekends spent with her father and his wife. It had been such an established routine for so long now. Kate had grown accustomed to the arrangement. She supposed her daughters had also fallen into the familiar habit as well. "I'll miss you, too, Melissa. It won't be long, though. I'll get back as soon as I can, and then we'll have the rest of the summer together."

"It's all right," Melissa said. "How come you're going back so soon? I thought the prelim was still a couple of weeks off."

"Something's come up." Kate hesitated. She didn't want to tell Melissa the truth. *WHORE. I LOVE YOU. OR ELSE.* Kate put a folded blouse in the suitcase and went to the closet for another. "The police found some similar murders that were committed a few years ago. With luck, we'll be able to prove that Drew is innocent." Kate was a little ashamed of the lie, but there was no reason for Melissa to worry.

"The police down there must be stupid. They should know that Uncle Drew wouldn't hurt anyone."

"I know. It's just a bad nightmare."

"Tell Uncle Drew I love him."

"I will, hon."

"I love you too, Mom." Suddenly Melissa was crying.

Kate took her in her arms. "What's wrong, hon? What's wrong?"

"I don't want you to go," Melissa sobbed. "Please, don't go!"

"It won't be that long. I'll call you every day."

"That's not it! He's going to hurt you!" Melissa broke away and ran to her bedroom.

Kate followed and watched with concern as Melissa reached beneath her pillow to pull out two envelopes. She knew what they were immediately, even before the chill went through her body. Kate held her hand out, trying to be dispassionate, but her hands shook as she looked at the envelopes. The first was addressed to Melissa Gallagher, the second to Allison Gallagher. They were postmarked in Mississippi and both had been opened. Kate removed the single sheet of paper inside the envelope addressed to Melissa. "When did they come?" Kate asked, attempting to hide the tremor in her voice.

"Yesterday."

Kate read the note. *MELISSA. I LOVE YOUR MOTHER. TELL KATHRYN ANNE TO COME HOME. OR ELSE. ARE YOU AS BEAUTIFUL AS YOUR MOTHER? DO YOU LIKE TO FUCK?* Oh, dear God. Except for her name, Allison's note was exactly the same. God damn you, whoever you are. Leave my children alone, you son-of-a-bitch!

* * *

Tracie checked into the hotel and went directly to her room and placed the call to Kate. "I'm safe," she said, when Kate answered the phone. "No one followed me. I feel a little silly.'

"Don't take any chances," Kate said harshly. "This is serious."

"What's wrong?"

"I can't talk right now. Give me an hour and I'll call you back."

Tracie recited the telephone number. "I'm in room 9-1-1," she added.

"Let's hope that not too symbolic," Kate said. "I'll call you in an hour."

The phone went dead. It took a moment for Tracie to recognize Kate's reference to the emergency number. What's happened out there? Kate's not like that.

Tracie glanced around the room, looking for something to occupy an hour. There were pay-per-view movies on the hotel's cable system, but nothing of interest to her. She picked up and discarded the room service menu. It was too early to eat. Tracie took her purse and the electronic card that functioned as a room key and went down the hall to the elevator.

She rode to the lobby alone and went directly to the gift shop. The paperback racks held the usual assortment of novels best suited for traveling—Danielle Steel, Jackie Collins, Tom Clancy, Elmore Leonard, John Grisham. Again, nothing appealed to her. Instead of a book, she selected several magazines and *The New York Times.* She had already read the Memphis paper. As an afterthought, she added two miniature bottles of Scotch and a bag of mixed nuts. There goes my figure, she thought, but no one cares anyway. Tracie paid and went back to the room with her purchases.

An hour later, Tracie had changed into jeans and a T-shirt

and sat cross-legged on the king-sized bed surrounded by the rumpled newspaper and scattered magazines. She sipped the second Scotch and nibbled at the last of the mixed nuts while leafing through *Harper's Bazaar,* looking at the latest fashions and lingerie in the full-page color advertisements. She had followed the instructions to release the scent from a perfume ad and the pleasant smell persisted as she turned the pages, stopping occasionally to admire a suit or a dress.

The first drink had calmed the restlessness that came with being in a strange hotel room with nothing to do but wait. But as Kate's promised hour grew to two, the uncertainty returned, and she felt the tension and the first dull throb of a headache. Tracie leaned back against the plumped pillows, the magazine open on her lap, and looked at the telephone, wondering what was wrong in California and whether she should call Kate again. She took another sip of the Scotch and decided against it. Kate would call.

Tracie brushed her hair aside and held the glass to her temple. It was cold against her skin, and the condensation dampened a wisp of her blond hair. She closed her eyes and put the glass against her other temple, sighing as the cold deadened the pain.

Momentarily.

Harry waited while Kate drove Melissa through the familiar streets to her father's home. Christopher lived only ten blocks away, but for Kate he was in another world. They saw each other rarely, usually a wave through the window as one or another of them picked up or dropped off the girls. Occasionally, they talked on the phone when one of them—usually Christopher—wanted to change the schedule. Tonight, Kate had called and said simply, "I need to see you." She could tell by his reaction that he expected an argument over child support payments or something like that. She didn't need his help, but made him pay anyway, just because he'd been such a prick during the divorce, wanting to keep everything for himself.

Kate shook her head. She was looking forward to the confrontation. She glanced over at Melissa, who sat glumly holding the big white teddy bear. She never takes the teddy bear, Kate thought. "Feeling better?" Kate asked.

"Yeah, I guess."

"Everything is going to be fine. I'll call you every night. I promise."

"Okay. Just don't let him hurt you."

"Don't worry, I won't."

Patti met them at the door, greeting Kate coolly. Patti was the new model Christopher had finally traded Kate in for. Fifteen years younger than Kate and Christopher, Patti had seduced—or been seduced by—Christopher when she was a student in one of his graduate architecture courses. Allison and Melissa both disliked Patti, thinking her stupid and vapid. But she was attractive and probably fucked like a rabbit to keep Christopher's mind off the next generation of graduate students. Kate wondered how long she would last.

"Hello, Patti."

"Christopher's waiting for you in his office."

"Thanks."

Christopher went on the offensive immediately. "Look, Kate, the agreement was that child support ended when the girls went to college. Isn't it enough that I'm paying for college . . ."

"It's not about that," Kate said, hating the look of relief that swept across his face. He was so damned stingy.

"What, then? You sounded upset."

She told him everything and then waited for the explosion.

"God damn it, Kate, what have you gotten the girls into this time?"

"It's not about the girls. It's about me."

"And what? You're going to go down there like some kind of superwoman and put the bad guy in jail? That's the trouble with you, Kate, you always think you're better than anyone else."

"Don't start on me. I'm just asking you to take care of Melissa while I'm gone. She's in no danger. This guy, whoever he is, wants me."

"I ought to see my lawyer. This could be construed as child endangerment."

Kate lost her temper and borrowed Dr. Death's line. "Don't fuck with me, little man. You bring a lawyer into this and I'll have your head swimming. I'm sure a private detective would just love to take some pictures of you and your latest student."

"Now, Kate . . ." He held his hands up in a conciliatory pose.

Kate knew she had struck home then. He *was* having an affair . . . again. She wondered if Patti knew yet. "Just keep an extra eye on Melissa. It's only a precaution. Whatever's happening down there concerns *me.* Period."

"Don't worry. We'll look after her."

"I'll let you know when I get back."

Kate left his office then, noting bitterly that he had expressed no concern for her safety. He probably wishes somebody would kill me. Simplify his life for him.

Melissa walked Kate back to the car. "Don't pay any attention to him. Daddy can be a real jerk sometimes. He's just feeling guilty about what he did to you. I mean, marrying Patti and all."

"It's okay, Melissa. He just makes me mad, but he always did. Give me a hug."

When the telephone finally rang, it startled her, even though she had been willing it to ring. She grabbed the receiver. "Hello?"

Silence.

Oh, Christ, he's found me. "Hello."

"It's me, Tracie." Kate's voice was tired, strained.

Thank God. "When you didn't answer right away," Tracie said, "I thought . . ."

"I'm sorry. I've been a little distracted here."

"What's wrong?"

"He sent notes to my children. The bastard sent notes to my children."

"What? How?"

"They came to the house. One for Melissa and one for Allison. Melissa was pretty upset. I had to tell Allison."

"What did the notes say? Did he threaten them?"

Kate quoted the notes. "They still focus on me, but he asked them if they liked to fuck. The sick son-of-a-bitch asked them if they liked to fuck!"

"Oh, God. What are you going to do?"

"I'll be in tomorrow.' Kate paused. "Can you change the message on your answering machine from there?"

"Yes."

"Do it, then. Just say that Kate will be back tomorrow. No, use Kathryn Anne. He calls me Kathryn Anne. Say Kathryn Anne will be back tomorrow."

"How do you know he'll call me?"

"You're the only other person he contacts."

"If it's the same man."

"Yes. If it's the same man."

"Do you think you should leave your girls?"

"He wants me. One way or another, he'll know I'm back tomorrow. He knows everything else."

"I don't think you should come. You should be with your daughters."

"He doesn't know Allison is away at school and Melissa will be with her father. Christopher's being an asshole about it, but he'll take care of her. Harry's going to take the cat to his place. This house will be deserted. Besides . . . he wants me. I'm going to give him his chance."

"Oh, Kate . . ."

"It's the only way to end it."

Kate hung up and turned to Harry.

"I don't like it," he said.

"We've been through all that. It's not just me. I have to help Drew. This is our chance to end this nonsense. What else can I do?"

"You can let me go with you."

That's what Rainey had said. They were both so God damned macho at times. "I have to do it myself." Kate smiled then. "Besides, who would feed Mycroft while I'm gone?"

Tracie's curiosity overwhelmed her. She had done as Kate asked, calling home to leave the new message on her answering machine, wondering at the time if Sam could hear her and what he thought of the disembodied voice. Now she stared at the phone for a moment and then pressed eight for the long distance line. Quickly she pressed the numbers. When her voice came on the line, she pressed the code that played her messages. An answering tone told her that one message had been received. She knew who it would be before his voice came on the line.

"Where are you, whore? Tell Kathryn Anne I love her. I'll be seeing both of you soon. Goodnight, whore. Sleep well."

His words echoed in her mind.

Goodnight whore goodnight whore goodnight whore . . .

Seventeen

Women were so stupid. Like the whore. He knew she was there when he called, listening in fear, but pretending he would go away if she didn't answer the phone. And the dumb cow waiting in the trunk of the car, thinking he would believe her when she promised not to tell anyone, begging and pleading and promising to be nice before the tape shut up her whining. They all think I'm stupid, but I'm not . . . *They're* the stupid ones.

Kathryn Anne wouldn't be like that, though, not his beloved Kathryn Anne. Look how smart she was, even knowing how to send a message to him. The others would never think of something like that. He was proud of her and pleased with himself for choosing so well. Kathryn Anne. Soon now. We'll be together soon.

He finished the glass of milk and rinsed the glass.

It was nearly dark, and time to go. April was waiting. He would take her to the river, to the place where he had watched the whore strip off her clothes shamelessly and play with herself beneath the moon like a witch waiting for her demon lover. Maybe she was a witch. The witch-whore would be frantic when they found April, knowing that she had led him to that secret place. The whore would know he had seen her. She would know then that there was no escape. But that was later. Everything was ready for April now.

Then . . . the whore would be next. The bitch, the slut. Strutting around the way she did, flaunting her body for all the men to see and lust after. She would not be so beautiful when he was finished with her. Kathryn Anne wouldn't like her when she was ugly. No one would like her ever again.

And then we'll be together, Kathryn Anne.

He went to the car.

April. It was a ridiculous name. It didn't have the beautiful poetic ring of a name like Kathryn Anne. Beautiful Kathryn Anne. Be patient, darling. I love you and I know you love me. That's why you sent me the message. Beautiful, clever Kathryn Anne.

She blinked against the glare of the flashlight when he opened the trunk, looking up at him still dazed and disoriented from the sleeping pills he had forced her to take. By the time they got to the river, though, she would be fully awake. She was alert enough, however, to cringe and moan when he put his hand on her white nurse's uniform. He saw the revulsion in her dulled eyes and it saddened him. "Go back to sleep, April," he whispered. "I'll let you out soon now." He closed the trunk gently. There was no use in slamming the lid and hurting her ears. Hurting her would come later. He had all night to hurt her.

He was glad she was a nurse. April would play the part of other nurses, the ones at that terrible place who laughed at him and thought he was crazy. When they released him, he wanted to kill them, but that wouldn't do. The police would just come and take him back there, and he didn't want to go back. He would just pretend that April was one of them. She would have to do for now.

It would be different with the whore. He was going to take her on a vacation, a long respite where she would learn the cost of coming between him and Kathryn Anne. She would beg for mercy, to be allowed to please him. He wouldn't grant her wish, of course. He had to save himself for Kathryn Anne.

He drove slowly out of town and turned toward the river.

Even in the hot and sultry Delta night, old Abe felt the chill of Mr. Death passing by. It was like walking in the woods, scrambling down a hollow into an abrupt change in temperature that chilled the bones. When a body stumbled into the chill air, there was nothing that could be done except whistle forlornly in the night and hope that ole Mistuh Death wasn't looking for you.

In his ramshackle cabin, the flame in his lantern fluttered and old Abe felt the chill and knew that ole Mistuh Death was out prowling, gathering those who had come to the end of their allotted lifespan. The old man tried to whistle, but his mouth was dry with fear. But then the cold air was gone and it was just another hot Delta night.

Old Abe grinned. He had eluded ole Mistuh Death once again, but he knew that someone else had not been so lucky.

Part III

Eighteen

As the aircraft descended, Kate looked out at the long, meandering course of the stately river curving away to the south, where it disappeared into a distant haze. The length of the great river was uncertain as it twisted and turned through the massive flood basin, all too often flowing over land of its own creation, ever changing as it nibbled away at both halves of the continent. Each time she flew home, Kate waited impatiently for the first sight of the river and was thrilled at its appearance. She always thought of the river as the dividing line of the continent and the dividing line of her life. But today, the usual excitement and anticipation was missing and she looked down at the river with a sense of dread and uncertainty, wondering morbidly if this would be the last time for her to view the great Mississippi River.

Kate had pampered herself, using an accumulation of old frequent flyer miles to upgrade her ticket to first class when she saw that the flight would be full. But even the relative luxury of the first class cabin and the constant attention of a pretty young flight attendant could not dissipate the uneasiness Kate felt. And then the river was behind them as the plane curved down into its final approach and roared over a chain-link fence to bump down on the runway.

When the plane swayed to a halt at the gate only fifteen

minutes late, panic seized her and Kate remained in her seat even though she could have been one of the first passengers to disembark. It was one-thirty local time. She and Tracie would be home by three-thirty, time enough to start what had to be done, if only she had the courage to get off the plane when all she wanted to do was remain in her seat until the airplane took off again, heading anywhere that would take her away from the Delta and whatever awaited there.

Finally, she could delay no longer. The flight attendant and the captain waited at the door to thank her for flying their airline. Kate sighed and got up.

The hot humid air hit Kate as she stepped into the runway, and then she was in the air-conditioned terminal, looking over the people clustered around the gate who had greeted relatives and friends. Kate saw Tracie waiting alone, standing against the far wall away from the crowd. Tracie smiled and waved. Kate was struck again, as she was each time she saw Tracie anew, by the young woman's haunting beauty. It was enough to make a man's heart ache. I wouldn't want to take my chances if Harry or Rainey ever met her. Men were so stupid, Kate thought. The man Tracie finally accepted should get down on his knees each morning and night to thank God for his great good fortune.

"Hi, Kate," Tracie said, reaching for the carry-on bag. "Good flight?"

Kate allowed her to take it. "A little bumpy over the mountains, but otherwise it was fine." The earlier anxiety disappeared with the sound of her voice, although Kate felt foolish for her irrational thoughts.

"While I was waiting, I kept hearing all the announcements and decided once this is over I'm going to take a vacation."

"Arizona?"

"Where else?" Tracie smiled. "Your bag's light."

"I left things at Drew's last time. This is going to be my

last trip down for a while. Figured I'd better leave room to take everything home."

"I'll miss working with you, but I hope you're right. I'm going to miss you generally."

"Have you ever thought of coming to Los Angeles? The PD's office would love to have someone like you. I'd give you a glowing reference. You'd have to pass the California bar, of course, but you wouldn't have any trouble. I made it the first time. You could, too. And if you wanted to join the DA's office . . . well, I think that could be arranged."

"I appreciate it, Kate, but I don't know. Los Angeles is so big, and I've got my heart set on Arizona."

"You'll never run out of work in LA on either side. We've got a full employment act for criminal lawyers."

Tracie laughed. "There's always going to be enough work for us, no matter where we work."

"How are you holding up?" Kate asked, as they went through the double doors to the street.

"I'm okay. My car's over this way."

"Did you leave the message?"

Tracie nodded. "Kate, he called again. He got the message. He knows you're back. I'm worried about you."

"What did he say?" Kate asked, trying to ignore the nagging fear that had built through the night and all during the flight.

Tracie had memorized his words and repeated them exactly for Kate: "Where are you, whore? Tell Kathryn Anne I love her. I'll be seeing both of you soon. Good night, whore. Sleep well."

"Polite bastard, isn't he?" Kate said. "Could you tell anything about his voice?"

"No. He was trying to disguise it. He sounded like Marlon Brando in *The Godfather.*"

They were at the car then. Tracie opened the trunk and put

Kate's bag on top of her own. There was barely enough room.

"I should have remembered how small the trunk is," Kate said.

"That is the one drawback to a little sports car," Tracie said, "but it's worth it."

Kate looked around the parking lot. Arriving and departing passengers lugged bags to and from the terminal. Those leaving were subdued, while those who had so recently flirted with the dangers of hurtling through the skies at six hundred miles an hour thirty-six thousand feet above the earth were animated.

Around them, everything seemed normal, but none of the other people in the parking lot had a madman who loved them. "Jesus Christ," Kate muttered.

"Kate?"

"Yes."

"I lied to you yesterday. I *am* afraid."

Kate took Tracie's hand and squeezed. It was easy to show bravado for Melissa, Harry, even Rainey. In the glare of the hot sun beating down on the parking lot, Kate felt very vulnerable. "I know," she said. "I am, too."

"What are we going to do?"

"The first stop is Drew's. I'm going to get one of his guns. I want you to have one as well. I also want you to stay with us."

"Okay. I'll feel better knowing I'm not alone."

"After that . . ." Kate shrugged. "I guess I'll just have to wait for this asshole to propose to me."

"That's funny," Kate said, when Tracie pulled into the circular drive fronting the big, ominous house and parked behind Drew's car. "Drew shouldn't be home yet."

He was in the living room and stood up quickly when Kate

and Tracie entered. "Kate, what are you doing here? You didn't tell me you were coming."

"Things are happening," Kate replied. "What are you doing home so early?"

Drew shrugged and picked up a bottle of beer, finishing what was left before answering. "No patients. April didn't even show up. I guess the pressure got to her finally. What good is a doctor without a nurse or patients?"

"It's almost over, Drew," Kate said. "I think."

"What's going on?" he asked, groaning.

"What's wrong with you?"

"Hangover. Betsy and Jack had me over for dinner last night. I guess they felt sorry for me. I drank too much. Spent the night there. Christ, Kate, I'm falling apart."

"Where were you in July seven years ago?"

"Oh, fuck, what is this, twenty questions? How would I know?"

"It's important, Drew."

"I want another beer. You guys want one?"

"I'll get it," Tracie said. "Kate?"

Kate nodded. "Drew?"

"Christ, my head hurts. I'm never going to drink again."

Kate smiled. "After this beer?"

"After this six-pack." Drew grinned. "Or maybe the next six-pack."

"You need a chili dog. They're great for hangovers."

"Bad for fat, though."

Tracie returned with three bottles.

"Thanks, Tracie," Drew said. "My sister won't tell me what's going on. Will you?"

"I defer to lead counsel," Tracie said.

"It's a fucking conspiracy against me."

"Think, Drew. We may have a break, something that will prove your innocence."

"Seven years ago . . ."

Kate and Tracie waited.

Drew snapped his fingers. "I'll be right back," he said. He took his beer upstairs.

Kate took the old newspaper clippings from her purse and checked the dates again, although she remembered them clearly enough. Please, God, let him remember an alibi.

Drew came downstairs again, holding a blue-covered passport out to Kate. "I was in Central America on a missionary trip."

Each year Drew went on missionary trips to Mexico, Central America, Haiti. He had been doing it for as long as Kate could remember. "The whole month?"

"I left on June twenty-ninth and returned on July thirty-first. The dates are here. Now, are you going to tell me what this is all about?"

Kate gave him the clips to read.

When he finished, he looked up at Kate. "You think it's the same guy?" There was hope in his voice for the first time.

"We're going to have to check with the police down there, but I'm betting on it. There are just too many similarities for it to be a coincidence."

"Where did you get these?"

Kate told him then of the notes and the telephone calls to Tracie.

"Jesus, Kate. This guy's crazy and he wants you. He wants *both* of you."

"That's why Tracie's going to stay here until it's over. I want to borrow a gun, two guns. One for each of us."

"Shotgun, rifle, or pistol?"

"Pistols," Kate said. "after all, we're ladies."

"Billie Rae's gun didn't do *her* any good," Drew said soberly.

"Billy Rae didn't have a warning. We do." Again Kate wondered why the killer had provided a warning. Probably he had the arrogant superiority common to serial killers. *Catch me if you can.*

Tracie drove Kate into town. They stopped at Tracie's office first. "I should have called for messages while I was waiting for you, but I didn't think of it."

"We'll check now, and then let's call Wilson Cowles. We need to get in and see him today."

"We'll track him down."

Tracie hit the play button on the answering machine and raised her eyebrows at Kate when the district attorney's voice filled the room. "Tracie, this is Wilson. I need to speak with you as soon as you get in. It's important. I'm going to try and reach Mrs. Gallagher also."

"He sounds tired," Kate said.

"Defeated is more like it," Tracie said.

"I wonder what it is?"

"Let's go find out." Tracie pushed the numbers on the dial pad from memory. "This is Tracie Sanders. Is Wilson available?" Tracie nodded at Kate. He's getting on, she mouthed for Kate. "Wilson, I'm in my office. Kate's here, too." She listened for a moment. "We'll be there in ten minutes."

He watched as they jaywalked across the street. Deep in conversation, they paid no attention to him, probably didn't even notice him. Still, he kept his face hidden behind the newspaper. He was elated that she'd come back, just as she'd promised. God, Kathryn Anne was so beautiful. He got an erection just watching her walk. Her thighs beneath the summer dress beckoned provocatively. Oh, God—soon, now, she'd stand before him, trembling with eagerness. There would be no need for the knife, not with Kathryn Anne. She would beg him to unbutton her blouse. He hoped her bra fastened in front, between the cups. He wanted to watch as her pale breasts spilled free from their covering that first time for him, only for him.

The whore blocked his view of Kathryn Anne as they passed. The bitch. She was always getting in the way. The interfering bitch. It was all her fault that April had been such a disappointment. The whore was to blame, the memory of her naked body seducing him into going someplace that was wrong, all wrong, throwing his schedule off, forcing him to drive around, looking for alternatives. She would pay for that, too.

After they walked by, Kathryn Anne's heels clicking on the sidewalk, he turned and watched again. Her skirt swirled around her legs. Beneath it, her buttocks moved rhythmically, enticing him. He forced himself to turn away, fearing an accident that would stain his trousers for all to see. Oh, God, she's so beautiful.

Wilson Cowles waited for them in a conference room adjoining his office. He rose as his secretary ushered Kate and Tracie into the room and greeted them formally. "Mrs. Gallagher, Miss Sanders. Thank you for coming."

"Wilson," Kate said. "It's good to see you again."

"Please, be seated. Would either of you like coffee, a soft drink?"

"Thank you, no."

"Well, there have been developments. I hardly know where to begin. Perhaps chronological order would be best. This morning I received documents from the Federal Bureau of Investigation which detail two murders committed seven years ago, down on the Gulf Coast."

"In July of that year," Kate said.

"You know?"

Kate nodded. "Tracie received copies of press clippings on

the murders. A person or persons unknown dropped them through the mail slot at her office yesterday. The details were sketchy, however . . ."

"It was the same person," Cowles said.

"The square was carved between their breasts?" Tracie asked.

Cowles nodded.

"I knew it," Tracie said triumphantly.

"I have an old passport belonging to my brother which verifies that he was out of the country that entire month."

"That would seem to eliminate him from that set of murders," Cowles said, "but do you know where your brother was last night?"

"There's been another?" Tracie asked.

"I'm afraid so."

"Drew spent the night at my sister's."

Again Cowles nodded.

"I believe the judge would consider a motion for dismissal of the charges against my brother."

"His presence at your sister's will have to be verified, of course, but I will present the motion myself. Still, it would seem that your brother is somehow involved . . ." Cowles threw up his hands hastily to cut off Kate's protest. "Not as a killer, but perhaps as a victim himself."

"What do you mean?"

"The woman who was murdered last night was his nurse. April Stuart."

"Dear God!" Kate cried. "He said she hadn't come to work today." Poor Drew. He would be shattered. First Billie Rae, and now April. And then . . . ? *TELL KATHRYN ANNE TO COME HOME HOME HOME HOME HOME* . . . The words built to a crescendo in her mind. "I believe we have some information for you," Kate said with a calmness she did not feel inside.

* * *

"Go home," Cowles said, after listening to both Kate and Tracie tell of the anonymous notes and the telephone calls.

"I can't do that," Kate said.

"You're in danger here."

"My daughters will be in danger if I leave. He knows where I live. His obsession is with me. Who knows what he'll do if I leave?"

"What if we don't catch him immediately? After all, he's eluded the authorities for seven years now. How long are you prepared to stay here?"

"I don't know," Kate said. "We just have to find him. I'm not going to live my life in fear."

"What about Tracie?"

Tracie answered for herself. "Kate's right. We're not going to live in fear."

Kate and Tracie repeated the story for detectives before finally leaving the courthouse. It was after six when Kate paused at the top of the courthouse steps to look over the empty square and the town's main business section. Here I am, you bastard, come and get me.

Below her, Tracie stopped and looked back. "What's wrong, Kate?"

"Nothing. I just wanted him to see me if he's out there."

"What are we going to do, Kate?"

Kate looked beyond the town then, out to where the sun was sinking toward the horizon, leaving fear and apprehension behind in its wake. Kate turned back to smile down at Tracie. "Wait. He's out there somewhere, and I'm going to find him."

* * *

"Oh, Lordy, Kathryn Anne, you gave me such a fright. Why didn't you let me know you were coming? You like to give me a heart attack when I saw you coming up the walk." Margaret Anderson hugged Kate and then turned to Tracie and hugged her, too. "I'll bet you have better manners than this scalawag daughter of mine."

"Hello, Mrs. Anderson."

"I didn't know I was coming until last night, and then everything was in such a hurry," Kate said.

"Oh, Lord, there's more trouble, ain't there?"

"No, Mama, everything's all right for Drew now. They're dropping the charges."

"Oh, praise the Lord," Margaret cried. "Praise the Lord. That boy's been such a mess since all this started. I just knew you'd find a way to make them think clear. Did they catch the man who really did it?"

Kate shook her head. "No, Mama, and I'm afraid I have some bad news."

"Drew's okay, ain't he?"

"Drew's fine, Mama. But there was another killing last night. It was Drew's nurse, April."

Margaret Anderson sagged. "Oh, that poor child. She's so sweet, and been a real godsend to Drew during his trouble. She was the only one who stuck by him. I know her mama, too. Saw her over at the Kroger's just the other day. I've got to call her."

"No, Mama, she doesn't know yet. The police are looking for her."

"How awful. Does Drew know? I don't think he can stand another shock like this."

"I'll tell him, Mama."

"You girls come in and sit a spell. I've got dinner all ready. There's plenty to go around. I was expecting Drew anyway. Shoulda been here by now."

"I'll give him a call."

"Never you mind," Margaret said, pointing to the window. "Here he comes now. Tracie, you just stay with me and I'll get you something nice and cold to drink."

"Yes, ma'am."

"Kate, you go on and tell Drew, now. Make it as easy as you can. That boy sure don't need no more hurt."

Kate walked back down the sidewalk to meet Drew.

"Hey, Kate. Did everything go all right?"

"They're dismissing the charges in the morning."

"Thank God."

Kate took his hand. "There's bad news, Drew. He killed April last night."

"Aw, Kate, no. That can't be true. Not April, too. No, God, no."

The telephone interrupted a dinner no one felt like eating. Kate and Tracie had not known April, so neither felt a personal loss, but both felt the terror of death's presence touching so close once again. Kate was thankful when her mother called. "It's for you, Kate. It's Sally."

"Hey, Sally, how'd you know I was back?"

"You know us. No secrets in a small town like this. Jimmy was driving by the courthouse and saw you. Thought I'd call and see if we could get together for that dinner I promised you. I sure would like to see you before I leave for Europe. Don't know when we'll have another chance."

"I want to see you, too."

"How about tomorrow night?"

"Okay. What time?"

"Oh, come about six. We'll have a drink or two. Talk over old times."

"Sally, is it okay if I bring a friend?"

"You got a gentleman caller down here I don't know about?"

Kate laughed. "No, it's a woman. An attorney friend who's been helping me. I don't have any gentlemen callers down here anymore." Except one, Kate thought, and he was definitely not a gentleman.

"I sure was sorry to hear about Drew's nurse, but I guess the police know what fools they were thinking Drew could kill anybody."

"News sure does get around," Kate said.

"Like I said, Kate, no secrets in this town. Sometimes I think there must be a toll-free number where folks can call just for the latest gossip. See you tomorrow?"

"I'm looking forward to it. Give Jimmy my best."

"Be prepared. He's going to bore the pants right off you with that ole stamp collection of his."

"I'll bet it's kind of interesting."

"You won't think so after a while. 'Night, Kate. You have a good evening, hear?"

"You, too, Sally. Goodnight."

"That was nice of Sally to call," Margaret said, when Kate returned to the table.

"Yes. Tracie and I are having dinner with her tomorrow." Kate glanced over at Tracie expecting a protest, but she simply nodded. They had an agreement not to discuss any of the other ramifications of the situation. Margaret Anderson knew nothing of the anonymous notes, and Kate wanted to keep it that way.

"I suppose that oaf of a brother will be there."

"Oh, Jimmy's okay. He's just a little different."

It was dark when Kate and Tracie arrived at the apartment complex to pick up Sam and get some additional clothes for Tracie.

"I'm glad you invited me. I sure didn't like the idea of being alone right now," Tracie said.

"Don't worry. We're going to be inseparable until this is over."

The cat greeted them enthusiastically, going from one to the other, rubbing against their legs, purring, generally getting underfoot. When Tracie opened a suitcase on the bed, Sam climbed in and waited.

Kate laughed. "Mycroft does that when I pack. He hates traveling, but he hates the thought of being left behind even more."

"I'll get his carrying case. It's hard to pack around a cat in your suitcase."

"I'll get it," Kate said. "You get your things together."

Kate went down the hallway to the closet and pulled the case out. When she returned to the bedroom, Tracie stood over an opened nightstand drawer, staring down in horror.

"Tracie, what's wrong?"

"Kate, look."

Kate went to stand beside Tracie. There was a nickel-plated revolver in the drawer.

Tracie turned to Kate with eyes rounded by fear. "It's not mine, Kate. I didn't put it there."

The detectives found no sign of forced entry. The manager had let no one into Tracie's apartment, nor had any of the neighbors noticed a stranger lurking about. No one knew if the revolver was the one belonging to Billie Rae Scott, either. The police would run the serial number later, but Kate was convinced that it was Billie Rae's missing gun and that it had been put in Tracie's apartment by the killer.

Tracie?

No one thought Tracie was a killer. There was an explanation—logical or illogical—for how the gun came to be in her nightstand. But what?

Kate had been in bed for an hour. Tracie was asleep in the

next room. At least, Kate hoped she was sleeping. Tracie had been horrified at the violation of her privacy and the sense of helplessness it engendered. The killer had demonstrated how easily he could take away her control, and it shattered Tracie.

But . . .

Multiple personality syndrome.

The words had been nagging at Kate all evening and into the sleepless night.

Was there another person—a killer—lurking in Tracie's mind?

Christ, it happened. It was possible. Whole criminal defenses had been built around multiple personality syndrome.

Its etiology was frequently terrible with repeated acts of abuse in childhood. An incestuous rape was certainly traumatic enough for Tracie's mind to create multiple personalities for protection. Was one of those personalities killing women? But why women? Why not strike out against men, the brother who had committed the horrendous act?

Kate got out of bed and put on her robe. She knew Drew had a variety of texts. Kate was sure there was an old abnormal psychology text somewhere on the shelves of his office. She went downstairs quietly, found the book exactly where she had remembered it, and took it into the kitchen to read.

"I couldn't sleep, either," Tracie said from the doorway.

Kate jumped and closed the book quickly. "You startled me."

"I didn't mean to. I'm sorry."

"Come on, sit down."

"What are you reading?"

"I looked up serial killer in one of Drew's old books," Kate lied. "I wanted to see if it would trigger anything."

"Did it?"

"Not really."

"I'm glad you're still up. I've just been lying there, thinking and thinking."

"Any answers?"

"I'm afraid, Kate. This is just too strange."

"I'm afraid, too, Tracie, but everything is going to be all right."

"It's never going to be all right, not the way it was before. Too much has happened. I keep thinking of those poor women, Billie Rae and April . . . Jesus, I can't imagine what it must be like."

Kate took Tracie's hands in her own, squeezing gently to comfort the young woman, wondering if there had been blood on those hands twenty-four hours ago. But she was in Memphis at the hotel.

Wasn't she?

Nineteen

There had been a time when Kate had tried desperately to please Christopher, to identify and overcome the flaws in herself that drove him to the arms of other women, a long succession of younger and prettier women. It was only after the final separation and months of counseling with Francis, dear, gentle Fran, that Kate had come to realize the fault belonged with Christopher and not herself. The realization had come suddenly, unexpectedly, a bright epiphany that explained the dead relationship and allowed Kate to put it behind her.

With knowledge came power—until now. She had taken charge of her life and restored order—until now. There had been disruptions, of course, the sexual dysfunction that came of prosecuting too many sexual crimes, identifying with too many helpless victims, enraged at what had been done to them. There was the uncertainty that came with Harry's proposal of marriage, the doubts, the fears, the conflicting loves raging within. But all that was normal, easily explained, if not so easily solved.

Until now.

The old sense of weakness and helplessness had returned. Some malignant and unknown force governed now, manipulating her movements, disrupting her life, the lives of her children, and the two men she loved. Kate no longer controlled events, only reacted. It wasn't right.

All she had to do was call Harry or Rainey—or both—and they would be on the next flight to Memphis. But what could they accomplish? It was not their problem. It belonged to her and her alone.

Now, lying awake as the first light brightened the curtains of the bedroom window, Kate searched for the strength necessary to go in harm's way. The old naval expression came from some dimly remembered history course. In harm's way . . . I'm going in harm's way, Kate thought, and I don't care, because it is the only way I can bring this to an end and regain command. I will not be orchestrated like a sacrificial pawn. I will not allow myself or Tracie to become a victim of a sick and demented mind.

Kate was surprised to find that she'd exonerated Tracie sometime during the night. She did not believe Tracie could be a killer anymore than she could believe it of Drew. Standing in the kitchen doorway last night, Tracie had been soft and vulnerable, looking to Kate with trusting eyes. And she had entered the fray unsuspecting of the twisted developments that came. What would have happened if Wilson Cowles had recommended a man? Would April be dead now?

Kate pushed aside the sheet and went to the bedroom window. In California, it was still dark and would be for another two hours yet. On the regular schedule, Harry would have spent the night with her. Perhaps she would be awake there, too, reaching out for Harry in the darkness, drawing strength from his presence. But she was in Mississippi, looking down at the wall surrounding Drew's property. They could barricade themselves behind the wall, block entry to the house by pushing furniture against doorways, guard the windows, wait. But that was surrender, giving in to the fear, acknowledging the killer's power. Kate could not do that.

She returned to the bed.

But not to sleep.

Despite her resolve to go in harm's way, Kate could not shake off the sense of helplessness. Turning in the strange bed, she felt like a small fish, hooked and struggling futilely to escape to the depths of dark waters, fighting the line that drew her inexorably toward death. Old Mr. Death.

Abraham.

Tracie had been unable to find the old man. Was he still alive? April's body had been discovered near Drew's cabin. Had old Abe heard Mr. Death in his chariot that night?

One sign, one little indication, Kate thought, that's all we need. Something to start with, anything. They would see the police reports later today. Perhaps the killer screwed up this time. If not, we'll go out there. If he wants me, thinks he loves me . . . Would he leave a message for me, something only I would understand? Unlikely. But what else do we have?

Kate answered her own question.

Nothing.

Kate went downstairs to put the coffee on.

Drew was already in the kitchen. His hair was unkempt and tousled from sleep. "Morning. Coffee's ready."

"You're up early."

"Couldn't sleep for thinking about April and Billie Rae."

"That makes three of us," Kate said, pouring a cup of coffee and taking it to the table to sit across from her brother.

"Something else I've been thinking about."

"What's that?"

"I think you'd best go home."

"Somebody wants me to stay. You and Cowles want me out of here. Someone better make up their mind."

"Kate, that somebody wants you. He's sick. God damn it, do you want to wind up like April and Billie Rae?"

"I'm not going. I don't like it much, but this whole thing revolves around me."

"It's somebody you know."

Kate shrugged.

"Somebody from high school. College, maybe."

"I don't know, Drew. It could be somebody who saw me walking down the street once. It could be anyone."

"I still think you should go home. And take Tracie with you."

Kate stood. "I'm taking a cup of coffee to Tracie. That's it."

"You're bullheaded."

"I guess."

"Tracie? Are you awake?"

"Come in, Kate."

"I brought some coffee."

"Thanks." Tracie sat up in bed. Sam meowed at the disturbance.

Kate sat on the bed. "Nobody seems to be able to sleep around here. I thought you'd like some coffee."

"I was awake half the night. I feel so violated just thinking that he was in my apartment. I haven't felt like this since . . . since . . . "

"I know, Tracie."

"I'm making the move, Kate. I decided that this morning."

"Arizona?"

Tracie nodded. "As soon as this is over. I'll get a job doing legal research or something until I can take the bar."

"You don't have to wait. This doesn't concern you. Go today."

"It does concern me. I've been included in his sick plans, whatever they are. Besides, I can't leave you while this is going on."

"I appreciate the thought, but it might be better."

"I'm angry, Kate. He had no right. I can't live knowing he might be out there somewhere, waiting. I wish I could disappear entirely. Just wake up tomorrow morning in Arizona and be someone else. But it's hard to disappear completely. I can't erase the memories. God knows I've tried."

The media had been alerted.

Carole Vaughn was there, along with her cameraman. The newswoman waved. Kate walked over to her. "Hello, Carole," Kate said, smiling.

"You look much better today," Carole said.

"I was a little upset the last time we met."

"You were right. I'm happy for you."

"I'm glad for my brother, of course, but it's still a terrible thing."

"Is there anything you can tell me?"

"You probably know as much as I do."

"Off the record?"

Kate shrugged. "I just don't know anything that isn't public knowledge already." Kate wondered what Carole Vaughn would say if she could tell her of the notes. It would be a bizarre twist: *Defense attorney loved by madman.*

"Are you going back to California now?"

"Not immediately."

Carole raised her eyebrows in an unspoken question.

"Nothing like that," Kate said hastily. "I have some vacation coming, and I thought I'd spend it with my family. It wasn't very relaxing the last time I was here."

"If anything comes up, will you call me?"

"Of course."

"Your Honor, the People move for dismissal."

"New evidence, Your Honor . . . the court concurs . . . dismissed . . ." Girardeau rapped the gavel sharply. It echoed through the courtroom with finality. "Call the next case . . ."

It was as simple as that.

After the temporary disruption in Drew Anderson's life, he walked out of the county courthouse to resume a normal life—if he could. If Andy Warhol was right, if everyone had his fifteen minutes of fame, Drew Anderson's came with being a temporary suspect in the Delta Ripper murders.

The prosecutor in Kate hoped that a mistake had not been made, but the blood of her family told her that justice had been served for her brother. She watched him leave the courtroom, shoulders slumped. He should have been elated, but he had not finished mourning the death of Billie Rae and now April . . . Kate wondered if he would ever have a normal life again. Will any of us?

Kate and Tracie watched outside the courtroom as the reporters swarming around Drew rushed to confront Wilson Cowles.

"What new evidence . . . Why did you release . . . Delta Ripper . . . arrest soon . . . suspects?"

Cowles held up his hands to silence the shouted questions. "We have reason to believe that the person responsible for the two murders here also committed similar murders seven years ago on the Gulf Coast. The police are vigorously pursuing every lead in this case. Additional information will be released as it becomes available. I have no other comment at this time." He turned abruptly and pushed through the crowd of reporters.

Kate and Tracie followed Wilson Cowles to his office, trailing behind the still clamoring herd that swarmed around the district attorney.

Inside his office, Wilson Cowles retained his formality of the day before, showing no concern at dismissing charges in the biggest case of his career to date.

"The gun belonged to the victim," Cowles said. "Of course, the question remains, How did it get into Tracie's apartment?"

"The killer put it there."

"Agreed. But *how?* Does anyone else have a key to your apartment?"

"No, Wilson. I told the police over and over. No one has *ever* had a key."

"But how?"

"I don't know."

"Very well."

"Do you have the reports on April, Mr. Cowles?"

"There is a copy for you. I made it as a professional courtesy, although . . ."

"Yes, Mr. Cowles?"

Cowles repeated his advice. "Go home, Mrs. Gallagher. Let the police do their work here. We will find this person and bring him to justice."

"I can't," Kate replied. "I won't. Not yet."

Cowles nodded in reluctant acceptance of her decision.

Kate thought it was obvious from the look on his face that Wilson Cowles considered her an interfering fool, now more than ever.

Kate and Tracie glanced once at the photographs of April Stuart in death and quickly turned them facedown. Neither had the stomach to examine them in detail. Except for the way the young nurse had been bound, the characteristics of the crime were all too similar. They had seen it all before in the photos of Billie Rae.

The police and coroner's reports revealed little, except that the body had been reported by an anonymous telephone call. The officer who had taken the call said the voice was that of a black man. The call came in from a pay phone at the old country store by the turnoff to the cabin. No one had been there when a deputy arrived.

Abraham? Kate asked herself. It was possible.

The police report described the scene in the labored and

stilted language common to police everywhere. Subject was this, subject was that, subject . . .

God damn it, she wasn't a subject. April Stuart had been a living, breathing, laughing, crying woman. She wasn't a fucking subject.

She wasn't anything now.

The reports were incomplete. The police had not had time to trace April's movements. They didn't know who had seen her last—except for the killer. They didn't know where he had abducted her.

The didn't know shit.

The cause of death was evident from the photographs. April Stuart had been gutted, just like Billie Rae, just like a hunter's trophy. Kate read the results of the autopsy anyway and passed it on to Tracie.

"Well?" Kate asked, after Tracie had read through the reports.

"Everything's the same, except for the weapon. They didn't find the knife this time. I don't know, Kate, but it sure seems like he wants you. Drew's arrest forced you to come home. Just like he wanted. And here you are again. Maybe Wilson is right—maybe you should go home."

"No," Kate said. "Let's go out there."

"Is that wise? I'm not sure you should be out wandering around the woods alone."

"I won't be alone. You'll be with me. And with our guns, there'll be four of us. We'll be a two-woman riot waiting to happen."

Tracie laughed uneasily. "Why not?"

It was easy to find the spot where April Stuart had died. Some zealous cop had strung the yellow crime scene tape from tree to tree, encircling the tree where the killer had suspended the young nurse. Left behind, the tape was a flimsy border marking a rustic temple, a shrine of death. Kate wondered idly if the tape was biodegradable and then was instantly ashamed of her thought. It seemed a mockery of the young woman she had never met and a violation of her shrine.

The woods smelled sickly sweet. The air was still, and as thick and heavy as the surrounding foliage. Thunderstorm's coming, Kate thought. She was glad they had locked their purses in the trunk of Tracie's car, bringing only their guns into the isolation of the woods.

Tracie's voice disturbed the quiet solitude. "It's just like last time, Kate. I stood there looking up and wondering how Billie Rae must have felt. It's horrible."

The bark on the trunk of the tree was scarred where the killer had secured the rope after hauling April aloft, to leave her dangling and twisting above the ground, awaiting her fate.

Kate could only nod. She could not banish the same disturbing thoughts from her mind. Even the cursory glance at the photographs of the dead woman had burned horrific images in Kate's memory.

The old man watched the two women. The older woman, the one he had talked with before, looked like she knew how to handle that gun she carried. Nobody want to mess with a woman like that. No sirree. Young buck might lose sumpin he wouldn't wanna lose, go messing with that woman.

She had the right idea, though. Next time ole Mistuh Death came calling in his chariot, gonna take a shotgun, not like last time when all he could do was slip away quietly until he was far enough away to retch his guts out right there on the ground. Wasn't nothing to do 'cept hike on up to the store and call them three funny little numbers and disappear into the woods again before them white policemen got there.

White folks was strange that way. Wouldn't think nothing of blaming some poor ole nigger for what a white man went and done. Ain't gonna let em get this ole nigger, lessen he starts acting like some ole fool. No sirree.

Still, wouldn't hurt to step out and pay respects to the lady. She was real nice, treated people kindly. He seen the other one, too, that time she was up poking round the other place. Admiring that fine young body, even if he couldn't get it up for thirty, forty years, and she was white, anyway. She'd be a heart-breakin' handful for some young buck. Legs like a skittish colt, that one. Wrap them long ole legs round a man and he could die, thinking he was in paradise the whole time. No, wouldn't hurt to pay respects, get a close look at them fine old titties. An ole man could remember, couldn't he?

Kate circled the tree, skirting around the yellow tape, examining the ground carefully, kneeling to stare into the shadows beneath the thick brush, using the barrel of the revolver to part the branches. It was useless. They weren't going to find anything the police hadn't come across. A snake, maybe. A big old thick timber rattler. It wasn't wet enough for a cottonmouth. Kate rose hastily and brushed dirt and twigs from her knees.

"There's nothing here, Kate."

"I just thought . . ." She turned to look at Tracie, carefully holding the gun pointed up. "I just thought the bastard might have left a message for me."

"You know, I didn't check my answering machine this morning. Do you think . . ."

"I don't know, but how long a message can you record?"

"I'm not sure. Thirty seconds, maybe."

"Let's go back to your place. I think I'll leave a message for him. Record it myself."

"What are you going to say?"

“I don’t know. I’ll think of something.”

Old Abraham walked out of the thicket then and stared ole Mistuh Death right in the eyes. Lordy, that woman moved fast. The hole in that muzzle looked like a big ole train tunnel with that engine fixing to clatter on down them tracks right between his eyeballs. “Oh, Lordy,” he cried, “don’t shoot. Please, don’t shoot. Ain’t nobody but ole Abe.” He raised his hands slowly, looking up at the lady all the time. Lordy, she had cold eyes. White folk’s eyes. The skittish colt, too, ’cept she warn’t so skittish now. These ladies would kill.

Kate lowered the revolver.

Thank the Lord, she was smiling now.

“Mister Abraham. You scared me half to death. Just like last time.” She shifted the revolver and offered her hand to the old man.

“Ceptin’ you didn’t have no gun last time.” He took off his old slouch hat and wiped his hand on the faded coveralls before shaking her hand.

“This is Tracie Sanders,” Kate said.

Ain’t no figuring white folks, sometimes. That young colt steps right up and shakes my hand like she’s real pleased to meet me, like I was somebody. “I’se pleased to meetcha, missy.”

“I came out looking for you last week,” Tracie said.

“Know that, missy. Ain’t nothin’ I don’t know about these here woods,” he said proudly, even though the good book warned about getting too much pride. Warn’t good for the soul, no-how.

“Why wouldn’t you talk to me?”

“Don’t do no good messing in white folks’ business.”

“Do you know anything about what happened here the other night?” Kate asked.

Thas what comes of pride, the old man told himself. Gettin’ yourself in a place where you got no business messin’. “Nossum. Surely don’t know nothing.”

"You must have seen the police."

Sly one, this lady, sly like ole Mistuh Fox. "Oh, yassum. I saw the polices all right. Surely did. But ole Abe, he just kept right on walkin' down the road. Well, warn't the road, exactly. Ole Abe thought it best just keep to hisself. Mindin' your own business never got nobody in no trouble."

"Mr. Abraham," Kate said, "would you walk back to the car with us?"

"Yassum. Don't mind atall."

"I'd like to give you my telephone number."

The first distant peal of thunder rolled ponderously through the woods.

"What a sweet old man," Tracie said. "Do you think he knows something?"

"Yes, I think he does. I think he's the one who called to report April's body."

"Why wouldn't he say something?"

"Like he said, he's learned not to mess with white folks."

Kate had given him ten dollars. At first, the old man refused the money with dignity: "Ole Abe, he gets everything he needs from the woods. And I alwuz keep two shiny dimes in case I wanna make a telephone call. But ain't nobody to call no more. I thank you, though. It's right kind, missy."

Kate said then, "It's for a job, Mr. Abraham. I need you to keep an eye out for me. I'm just paying you in advance, that's all. You'll earn the money. You see Mr. Death in his chariot again, all you have to do is call me."

Kate recorded the message—several times, finally deciding to say: "This is Kathryn Anne. You say you love me. If that is true, meet me on the courthouse steps at noon. I will be there every day. I want to help you. I *will* help you."

Kate pressed the button to replay it.

"What do you think?"

"We're not even sure he's the killer. Not really."

"One thing is true, anyway."

"What's that?"

"If any of your friends call, they're going to get a very strange message."

"I don't have any friends. Except you."

As they drove back to Drew's house, the first fat drops of rain splattered on the windshield.

Sally was right. Jimmy bored everyone to death with his stamp collection. They sat on a comfortable old couch across from a gun cabinet. Jimmy was in the center with the stamp album on his knees. Kate and Tracie flanked him, looking down with increasingly feigned interest as he slowly turned the pages, explaining each acquisition and its collector interest.

"You must have hundreds of stamps," Kate said.

"Thousands," Jimmy replied.

"And he'll show you every one of them, if you let him," Sally said, laughing. "I'm lucky. I see them as they come in, not all at once."

'Aw, Sis."

"Keep going, Jimmy. I find this very interesting."

"I do, too," Tracie said.

"Now, I really like this stamp . . ."

Page after page of neatly and meticulously arranged stamps. They were all new and attached to the page with hinges and protected by plastic coverings.

"This must take you hours," Tracie said.

"It's fun."

"He can play with them for days, an entire weekend," Sally said.

"I believe it," Kate said. "Everything's so orderly."

He was trembling with excitement as he closed one album and set it aside on the coffee table only to take up another.

"This is the last one," Sally said. "We have to feed these girls sometime."

"Okay, Sis." He turned to Kate. "I saved the best for last," he said shyly. He opened the album to blocks of four with the serial numbers and the first-day issues of the Elvis Presley stamps.

"They're beautiful," Kate said.

"They certainly are," Tracie agreed. "He's still the best after all these years."

Jimmy smiled shyly, pleased that the Elvis collection was popular. He knew it would be. He was very happy when he followed the three women into dinner.

At the table, Kate and Sally talked over old times—boyfriends, escapades, former teachers, friends and enemies—while Jimmy and Tracie listened.

"I know we're boring you," Sally apologized, "but we see each other so seldom now."

"I don't mind at all," Tracie said.

"It's your turn, Sis." He grinned at Tracie.

Once, when Jimmy went into the kitchen for another bottle of wine, Sally turned to Tracie and said, "I think he's smitten with you, but who wouldn't be?" She turned back to Kate. "We used to look like that, Kate, but now we're a couple of old hags in comparison."

"Over the hill," Kate agreed.

Tracie blushed helplessly.

When Jimmy returned, he filled Tracie's glass first.

"See?" Sally said.

"How long are you going to be in Europe?" Tracie asked.

"Three weeks. I'm really looking forward to it. I've been saving for two years. I just don't know how Jimmy's going to get along without me, though."

"I'll be just fine, Sis."

Afterward, Jimmy brought out a Polaroid camera and snapped pictures—Kate alone and with Tracie, Tracie alone, Kate and Sally, Kate, Sally, and Tracie. Then Sally took the camera and took a picture of Jimmy with Kate, and Jimmy with Tracie, and finally of Jimmy standing between Kate and Tracie, his arms around their shoulders, smiling foolishly for the camera.

It was Jimmy who distributed the prints, one for each of the women. "Souvenirs," he said, "for while we're apart." The rest he kept. "So's I can remember you," he explained.

Twenty

When the power failed, he was in his room leafing through his private scrapbook, adding the new photographs of Kathryn Anne to the others collected over the years. They were arranged chronologically, some cut from her high school yearbook and then some from her college yearbook. He had driven down to Cleveland, to the college library, and cut out every page that had her picture. He had her photograph from the newspaper when her engagement was announced and again when she had married, looking so sweet and virginal in her wedding dress. The newspaper photographer charged him twenty dollars each for eight-by-ten glossy prints. The man she married hadn't deserved her then; he didn't deserve her now. He was glad she had divorced him. Neither did the other guy she talked about at dinner—Harry somebody—even though she called him sweet and good. Nobody would be as sweet and good to her as he would.

The power failure was a sign, an abrupt punctuation to his love for Kathryn Anne. He went downstairs, his path lighted by flashes of lightning. The house was quiet. Sally had gone to bed early. The candlesticks were still on the table, but he had to fumble through a kitchen drawer for the matches and burned his finger using one to guide his path to the dining room table. He lit both candles and went to replace the matches, sucking on his burned finger, but it was only a nuisance. It did not stop the swelling of love he felt in his heart for Kathryn Anne.

Back in his room, he carefully arranged the candlesticks on each side of the photographs. The light flickered over Kathryn Anne and Tracie. Tentatively, he reached out and caressed Tracie's image, remembering how she had looked at dinner. He could see right through the blouse she wore. He thought again about how bad it was that she had to die and wondered if there were another solution. His flesh still burned where her breast had touched him. It had been hard and firm against his side as they'd posed for the camera. He wondered if Tracie's tits would jut out against her chest like the women in the videos. But they had operations for that. They were nothing but whores. Tracie acted like a whore, dressed like a whore, didn't mind when he stared. Maybe Tracie had an operation, too.

Kathryn Anne wasn't like that. He could still smell her perfume. Kathryn Anne's breast was soft and warm as he drew her close for the photograph. She had not resisted when he'd put his arm around her for the picture. She had welcomed his touch, his embrace. That's what it will be like all the time when we're together, he told her image. He brought the photograph—the one he had taken of Kate alone—slowly to his lips and kissed her, hearing all the while the enticing call of the whore.

He took Tracie's photograph and studied it by candlelight. Tracie smiled at him and he wanted to kiss those lips, the whore forcing him to be unfaithful to Kathryn Anne. She would pay for that. He lowered the photograph to his erection, rubbing it against himself, imagining those blood red lips closing around him.

She had to die. It was the only way he could remain true to his love for Kathryn Anne.

The whore lips caressed him as he thought of sweet, beautiful Kathryn Anne.

The bolt of lightning streaked down through the black skies and struck the tree. The crash of the falling trunk and the instant clap of thunder shook the old cabin, frightening the old man. "Lordy, thas too close," he muttered, wanting to snuggle up against one of his wives, all dead so many years now. Thas the best thing about a woman. Make everything all right in the night when a man wasn't so brave. Like your mama, when you jus a little tyke. Man needed a good woman for the scary parts a life. Lotsa things to scare a man in this world. All time comin' up on a man when nobody was specting nothing.

The good Lord could be sneaky like that. Lettin' a man just cruise right along, thinkin' everything was jus fine and then slap you up alongside the head. Jus lettin' you know who's the boss in charge and don't you go gettin' so cocky. Sometimes God act mighty like a white man. Outta my way, nigger. Like that ole water fountain down to the store. Them letters still on it even though somebody take the time to scrape 'em off. Still know what it said: Whites Only. Them young bucks don't pay it no mind no more. Ole Abe, though, he ain't drinkin' outta no white man's fountain, no matter what they says is the law now. Might catch sumpin bad. Yessiree. Catch white man's trouble.

Thunder shook the old cabin again.

Don't you be actin' like that with ole Abe. You jus leave an old man to peace here. Ole Abe, he be good. Ain't no call to torment ole Abe, jus cause ever once in a while, he liked to look at a woman's titties. Jus rememberin' the way things usta be. No harm in that. And Lordy, why you send them women to me if you don't want me lookin' none. Both them ladies got a fine pair. You gotta admit that, Lord. You's the one gave 'em to 'em and ain't ole Abe suffered nuf torment for one day, lettin' me step outta the bushes like that without singin' out to let 'em know I's comin'. Ole Abe like to pee his pants, embarrass hisself in fronta them ladies like that.

Lordy, they was quick with them guns. Don' wanna get them mad at me. And then just as quick, be so nice to ole Abe. Mistuh Abraham this and Mistuh Abraham that. Almos make me cry, they's so nice.

The ten-dollar bill was pinned inside the breast pocket of his coveralls with a safety pin, jus like his mama taught him to do. The card she gave him was pinned in another pocket. She so nice and all. Almos' told her all 'bout Mistuh Death. It was sure nuf worrisome. "It's for a job," she said. Ole Abe never went back on no job yet. Alwuz give a good day's work for a day's pay, even when the pay warn't all that good. Oh, Lordy, you keep that ole Mistuh Death and his chariot way from ole Abe. Don't wanna be messin' in no white folks' business. But you gotta be tellin' ole Abe what to do now. You listenin' now, Lord? You jus help out an ole man who's always tried to do right.

Twenty-one

Kate worried about Drew.

When they got home, he had been in the living room in front of the TV set, a nearly empty bottle of Scotch next to his chair. He was drinking too much. She knew it and he knew it. "Christ, Kate, first Billie Rae, and now April. It's too much. It ain't right. I'm going to bed. Maybe I'll be able to sleep now."

Kate watched him carry the bottle up the stairs.

"He's hurting," Tracie said. "He's hurting real bad."

"I know."

They watched the late news together. Carole Vaughn reported the dismissal of charges. "Authorities remain baffled in the so-called Delta Ripper case," she concluded.

The weatherman told them to expect thunderstorms throughout the night.

The sports reporter talked about the first round of a PGA event.

The last piece was about a woman who had thirty-one cats.

Sam, who was sitting in Tracie's lap, perked his ears up at the sound of the mewing from the television set.

"It's good to know there's a nice home waiting for Sam if anything happens to me."

"Nothing's going to happen to you, Tracie."

"I just hate this waiting, not knowing. I don't know how you stand it."

"I can't." Kate switched off the television set.

They went through the house together, ensuring that the doors and windows were locked against intruders—the intruder.

"Sleep well, Tracie."

"You, too, Kate."

Kate went through the evening ritual of telephone calls, reaching Melissa, reassuring her once again that everything was fine and that she would be home soon. She said nothing of April Stuart's murder.

Kate had no luck when she called Allison. She was at the library studying, according to her roommate.

She reported the events of the day—again eliminating mention of April Stuart—to Rainey, and listened patiently when he said, "I wish you'd get your sweet little ass out of that town." She replied as she had to Melissa. "I'll be home soon. Don't worry."

"Your job's done. Your brother walked. It's over, Kate."

"You don't believe that any more than I do, Rainey." A case ended when the interests of justice were served—with a plea bargain, or a trial and a conviction, a sentence. The guilty went to jail while the victims picked up the threads of their shattered lives.

"I still wish you'd get out of that fucking town."

"Soon, Rainey. A few more days."

"You're a stubborn woman, Kate."

"Yes."

"Obstinate."

"Yes."

"Pig-headed."

"Yes."

"Beautiful."

Kate laughed. "I don't know about that last one."

"I do. Take care of yourself, Kate. I love you."

"Love you, too."

"Call me tomorrow."

"I will. Good night."

She leaned back against the pillows. The telephone was in her lap. She had saved the other man she loved for last, wanting his voice to be in her head when she fell asleep. She lifted the telephone receiver to place the call when the lights went out suddenly. She replaced it and swung her legs out of bed, taking the revolver from the nightstand.

"Kate?"

"I'm here, Tracie." Kate stumbled through the darkness to the door. A flash of lightning illuminated the hallway. Tracie was in her doorway. She had her gun out too. Drew had not awakened.

"It's just the storm," Kate said.

"What if it's not?"

"We'll check the house together."

"Drew has candles in the kitchen. I saw them the other day."

Kate led, feeling her way along the wall to the staircase. "Watch your step."

The old house creaked in protest against the storm's onslaught. Rain pounded against the windows. Another streak of lightning provided momentary light. The answering thunderclap shook the house, rattling windows.

Tracie found the candles and struck a match, lighting one. "Does Drew have any candlesticks?"

"If he does, I don't know where they are. Use a saucer."

Tracie held the candle sideways, letting the hot wax drip into a molten pile. She stuck the candle in, holding it while the wax hardened. She repeated the process for Kate.

They went through the house for the second time that

night, holding the candles aloft. Both doors were locked and bolted. The windows were shut tight and latched. Everything was just as they had left it earlier.

"I feel like Lady MacBeth," Kate said, when they were sure the house was secure, "creeping through the gloomy castle."

"Lady MacBeth didn't have a gun," Tracie pointed out. "I feel just a little foolish now, but I hate thunderstorms. I always did. They're frightening, like nature has gone berserk."

"I've always thought it was God's way of showing displeasure with us."

"Maybe lightning will strike the killer dead."

"Then we'd never know," Kate said. "We would always be waiting, looking over our shoulders, expecting something bad to happen, wondering. No, I want it over. One way or another, I want it to end. And soon."

"You're right."

"Would you like to come in for a while? Just talk."

Tracie smiled then. "No. I'm okay. If it gets bad, I'll just pull the covers over my head. That's what I did when I was little."

Kate hugged her.

"Kate, do you have a dream lover, someone who comes to visit at night?"

"Yes, all the time."

"I hope mine comes tonight."

"He will."

Tracie lay in the darkness, listening to the steady fall of the rain, and waiting for her lover, but he would not come. Only her demons would visit tonight. As the storm passed on, her lonely room filled with the monsters from her past.

* * *

Kate used the glow of the candlelight to press Harry's telephone number and then blew the flame out, settling back in the darkness to await his reassuring voice. When he answered, Kate said, "I'm lonely and afraid and I miss you. I love you and I wish we were together and I want you to tell me what you'd do if I were there right now."

"Go to sleep."

"You bastard. Tell me."

He did.

Kate and Tracie waited on the courthouse steps as the workers and civil servants and the participants in criminal and civil justice streamed past them in search of lunch.

Kate's skin crawled with chills despite the muggy heat that had returned so quickly after the thunderstorm of the night before. She knew he was out there somewhere, watching, waiting. She was positive he had received the message. Someone had called Tracie. There was no message, only a long pause, and the sound of the caller hanging up finally.

A few men and women scattered around the benches on the lawn to open brown bag lunches. Most passed the square by, however, preferring the air conditioning of coffee shops or the cool darkness of taverns.

"Maybe he doesn't have a watch," Tracie said.

"He doesn't need one," Kate replied, as the bell in the clock tower chimed twelve times. It was a mournful sound, a heralding of death. They would bury April Stuart this afternoon, but Kate had decided there would be no more funerals for her. Drew and Mama would be there, of course. Kate had promised to make dinner for them afterward.

Kate had also vowed there would be no more searching through a dead woman's apartment, violating her even after death. Let the police do it this time. Let them find the nude photos. Let them paw through trashy lingerie. The memories of Billie Rae's funeral and her sordid belongings remained too strong and depressing for Kate. Wilson Cowles had promised to share anything the police found. It was a reluctant promise, but one Kate felt he would keep. The police reports would have to do this time. And she would be there for Drew after the funeral, provide support and sympathy, drink with him, if necessary, but she would be damned if she'd attend another funeral.

"How long shall we wait?" Tracie asked.

"Let's give him half an hour and then I'll buy you lunch."

He didn't show, of course.

What did you expect? Kate asked, berating herself. Did you really think he'd walk right up to you at high noon to apologize and surrender, saying, Help me? Please help me, Kathryn Anne. Why would he? He might be sick, but he hadn't been stupid. At least, not so far. You son-of-a-bitch, where are you?

She glanced over the square again. There was no one out there who resembled a killer. They were all normal people, eating a normal lunch, waiting, probably dreading the imminent return to another afternoon of drudgery.

"Let's go eat," Kate said.

"Where would you like to go?"

"How about the Holiday Inn?"

"Sure."

Wilson Cowles was there, sitting alone at the end of the bar, looking over the menu. He had a glass of iced tea in front of him.

"Would you like to join us?" Kate asked.

"That would be very nice," he said, swiveling on the bar stool to face them. "Are you sure I won't be intruding?"

"Not at all."

"Then I would be delighted." He picked up his glass and followed them to an empty table near the back.

When they were seated, Kate looked around the room. Some of the people were looking at them with disapproval in their eyes, but they turned away at Kate's glance.

Cowles smiled sadly. "Some things never change," he said.

"What they think doesn't matter," Kate said.

"I agree," Tracie said.

"But you have a well-known reputation. Mrs. Gallagher has not yet been so tainted."

"My brother was a captain when Ole Miss was integrated. He said then that it was the law and people were going to accept it or else. It's been a long time, but I believe his exact words were, 'It's the law, God damn it, and that man is going to go to school.' He integrated his waiting room by the simple expedient of telling the whites who objected that they were free to wait in the hall and that he would call them when their turn came. I admired him for those actions. I still do. I've tried to follow his example."

"I apologize. I meant no disrespect."

"I took no offense. I just wanted you to know that no one tells me who to eat with."

"Obviously, your reputation was sullied long before you sat down with me."

Kate smiled then. "I believe it was. There are even some in my family who do not approve of Drew or me."

A waitress brought menus for Kate and Tracie. "Can I get you folks something to drink? Coffee, or iced tea?"

"I'd like iced coffee," Kate said.

"That sounds good," Tracie agreed. "I didn't sleep all that well last night. Maybe it'll keep me awake."

They talked about the Delta Ripper then. Cowles kept his promise and related everything that had developed in the past twenty-four hours. There was nothing of substance in April Stuart's apartment, nothing that would provide a link to her killer. Little else had happened. "It's not much," Cowles said bitterly. "It's less than that. We need a break."

"Something is going to happen," Kate said.

"A woman's intuition, or a prosecutor's?"

"Both."

"I hope you're right. I would not like to be the prosecutor who presided over a long string of serial killings."

They ordered—salads for Kate and Tracie, a sandwich for Cowles. When the waitress left, Cowles said, "I hear you visited the latest crime scene. I don't think it's wise for you to be wandering around alone."

"How did you know? Are we being followed?"

"Observed," Cowles said. "I thought it a prudent course. We do not need another dead woman," he said staring at Kate. "Or two," he added, shifting his gaze to Tracie.

"We were armed."

"So was Billie Rae Scott."

"As people keep reminding us."

After lunch, Kate and Tracie went back to the small law office. As they entered, the clock tower chimed two. The funeral services for April Stuart were at three. Kate dismissed the thought and turned to the telephone. More often than not, Dr. Death ate lunch at his desk. Kate took the chance that he would do so today and called California, listening to the clicks on the wire as the call went through.

He answered the phone himself. "Moore."

"Phil, it's Kate."

"Kate, how are you?"

"Mostly good. They dismissed the charges against Drew, but there's been another murder. This time, Drew has alibis all over the place."

"I'm glad, Kate. I know this has been a strain for you. Are you coming back now?"

"That's what I wanted to talk about, Phil. The murdered woman was Drew's nurse. It's still too close to home. I'd like to give it another week. If nothing turns up . . ."

"Take the time you need, Kate."

"I appreciate it, Phil."

"But you cover your ass, hear now? Isn't that what they say down there—y'all hear now?"

Kate smiled. "That's what they say, Phil."

"Well, you listen to me. I want you back here in one piece. I don't intend to lose one of my best prosecutors."

"I don't want you to lose me either, believe me."

"Good."

Kate was looking at the *Arizona Highways* calendar—it was turned to October now—when she said, "Say, Phil, do you know anyone in Arizona . . ."

After hanging up, Kate told Tracie, "He has a friend in Phoenix. A prosecutor, but he'll have contacts with the PD's office. I'll talk to Dr. Death more when I get home. With an introduction, maybe we can arrange an internship or something until you pass the bar."

"Thanks, Kate, but you didn't have to do that."

"What are friends for if they can't help out a little?"

"I appreciate it," Tracie said.

"I'm happy to do it."

"Why do you call him Dr. Death?"

"He's very good at prosecuting cases with special circumstances. He's sent a lot of people to death row."

"The Delta Ripper will get the death penalty."

"Would you defend him?"

"He's entitled to the best defense possible, no matter what he's done, but no, I don't think I'd care to defend him."

"We'll make a prosecutor out of you yet."

"Would you like to prosecute him?"

"Yes," Kate replied simply. "I would."

* * *

In the supermarket, Tracie pushed the cart as Kate shopped for dinner. "Aren't you getting tired of me?" she asked. "I feel like the little sister tagging along everywhere."

"No one's tired of you," Kate said. She dropped a head of lettuce in the cart. "I don't like my salads. Never did. Just can't seem to get them right."

"I'll make the salad. I don't mind. Pay for my keep a little bit."

"I'll let you. Gladly. I noticed Drew has some ripe tomatoes in the backyard. Do you put cucumbers and carrots in your salads?"

"Radishes, too, and we'll need a package of crumbled blue cheese. But really, Kate, I just feel like I'm in the way, what with moving into Drew's place and all. And your mother would probably like you to herself once in a while."

"Don't be silly. Besides, I like a little sister tagging along. Betsy always did when we were kids. At least, until she discovered boys. She was a hell raiser. Still is. Drove Mama crazy. By the way, she's invited us down for dinner over the weekend. You, too," Kate added before Tracie could deliver another protest. "You're stuck with us, I'm afraid. One of the family now, whether you like it or not."

"I could do worse," Tracie said. "I did do worse, with my own family."

He watched as Kathryn Anne and the whore went into the backyard. The whore was barefoot. His Kathryn Anne picked tomatoes and handed them to the whore. Then she pulled green onions from the earth, shaking and brushing them free of dirt. Kathryn Anne spoke. He couldn't hear what she said, but the whore laughed. He could hear that. She laughed and reached out to touch Kathryn Anne. Maybe she was a lesbian and wanted Kathryn Anne for herself. Probably why she didn't have herself a husband to keep her straight. The whore was happy now. That wouldn't last much longer. Unless . . . unless she was good.

The headache was building just like before, when they'd made him go away to that place. He knew it came from indecision and confusion. He wanted to kill her, but he wanted her to be good, too. He didn't want her to be a lesbian. Perhaps if he scrubbed her face free of the whore's makeup and if she promised never to use it again . . .

He pressed his fingers to his temples, watching as the whore led beautiful Kathryn Anne inside again. He wanted to cry out, Don't leave. Love turned to anger as the whore led Kathryn Anne from his sight.

The bitch. The nigger-loving bitch.

Kate found it pleasant to work together with Tracie in the kitchen. It was like spending a rainy Saturday afternoon with Harry when the two of them lazed around and then made dinner together or like being with Melissa and Allison on the increasingly rare occasions when they were alone together.

And it was like having a little sister again.

Kate poured a glass of white wine for each of them. Kate held her glass up. "To Arizona," she said.

Tracie raised her glass to Kate's. "To a good friend," she replied.

The idea came to the old man slowly while he fished for his dinner, waiting for the bobber to disappear beneath the placid surface of the lake. He was thinking about it while he baited the hook again after catching the first fish. The idea was still there when the second strike on his line awakened him from the doze.

It stayed with him while he trudged through the woods, the cold pipe stuck in a corner of his mouth. It was still there when he stopped to pay his respects to Mr. Squirrel, sitting there on the branch watching him, unafraid. Mr. Squirrel chatted excitedly for a moment and then scampered away up the trunk of the tree, stopping once to glance back at the old man before disappearing in the higher reaches of the tree. Mr. Squirrel seemed to approve.

That was the trouble with an idea like that. Once it got ahold of you, it wouldn't let go. It grew while he gutted and cleaned the fish and became stronger as he watched the slabs of white meat cooking over the fire, using his finger to probe the meat of the fish, testing its readiness to turn.

He mulled the idea, working it over methodically, deciding finally, and then changing his mind, only to change it back again ten minutes later. He worked the idea to death, but he couldn't shake it. It stuck with him as he sat in the old rocker, smoking a pipe after dinner, watching the darkness creep through the trees.

He couldn't escape it. He had to do it.

Ain't no use lying to yourself, ole man. You ain't never turned your back on no job of work. 'Sides, you wanna see that lady again and that skittish young colt. He grinned foolishly in the growing darkness and tried to remember what it was like to be with a woman like that. Given a druther or two, a course, he'd take Miss Kate. She'd be kind to an old man, take pity on an old man. That youngun, though, Miss Tracie, she'd be a handful for any man. He remembered Dick Tracy and wondered why somebody'd name a beauty of a girl after some comic strip character with a square jaw. She had wild eyes, just like a colt seeing sumpin for the first time. It'd kill a man, trying to ride a woman like that. Just roll over and die after. Powerful pleasant way to go meet the Maker. How do, Lord, sure do wanna thank you for that last ride. Good Lord gonna crack you a good one, thinkin' like that. Keep your crazy ole head straight. Don' be thinkin' about them ladies like no bitches in heat. They's been nice to you.

He reached up to his breast pocket and touched the safety pin. That ten-dollar bill was still there, burning away just like it usta be on Saturday night, just itching and burning away, wantin' to be down at the juke joint, chasing them sweet young things. He wondered what day it was. Maybe it was Saturday night passing him by. Might be Wednesday, too, or Sunday. Wouldn't be right, thinking 'bout them ladies like that on the Sabbath. Oughta get to church. Put that ten-dollar bill in the collection plate, where it'll do some good.

That's where that idea came from. It's sittin' right there in that pocket, reminding you of what's got to be done. Ain't no way to get around it. You owes that lady a job of work. He touched the other pocket. Safety pin right there, holdin' that card with the numbers on it. Colt's name was Tracie Sanders, Esq. He wondered what and Es-que was. Funny kinda name. Just like Dick Tracy. Es-que. Never heard a that family. Maybe from Texas. They's some strange ones come from Texas. Knew an old boy from Texas once. Wild one, too. Warn't so wild after Henry took that knife to him. Took all them stitches and hotfooted it right back to Texas, lookin' like his mama been sewin' on him. Ole Henry, he was a pistol. Took off up north after messin' with some lady he shouldn't been messin' with. You jus keep on thinkin' you gonna hafta go north, too. Ain't no business thinking like you doing. Jus keep your mind on that piece a work you gotta do.

"Mama," Kate said. "I think you ought to come visit when this is all over. You haven't been to California in a long time. The girls would love to see you."

"Maybe I will, hon, but it *is* over, ain't it? I thought it was all done with, now that them old fools at the police don't think Drew's done nothing wrong."

"They still have to catch the real killer, Mama."

"What's that got to do with you?"

Everything, Kate thought. She glanced quickly at Tracie and Drew. It was a mistake. "Nothing, Mama," she lied.

"Don't you be spoofing me none, young lady. I may not be educated, like you and Drew and Tracie, but I'm nobody's fool. What's going on here, anyway?"

"Nothing, Mama. Really."

"Kate just meant that this whole thing can't be over until the police find the killer," Drew said. "That's all. There's no reason for you getting upset."

"Well . . ."

"Mama, all I said was that you should visit California."

Margaret Anderson was slightly mollified. "It would be nice to get away, I reckon. All this has been a real strain. That poor girl, April. Even Billie Rae. I know I didn't like that woman much, but she didn't deserve nothing like what happened."

"Come on, Mama," Drew said. "It's getting late. I'll drive you home."

Margaret Anderson hugged Kate. "I'll see you tomorrow, darling." She turned to Tracie and hugged her, too. "You talk some sense into these children of mine. You seem to be the only one around here with any brains."

Moths fluttered around the light as Kate and Tracie waved goodbye from the porch. Back inside, Kate locked the door and leaned against it. "I love my mother dearly, but she sure does wear me out."

"You should go home. You're in danger here. She's right—let the police handle it."

Kate sighed, shaking her head. "*Et tu,* Tracie?"

"I just don't want anything to happen to you. I care about you. I'm worried about you."

"And what about you? You're in no danger?"

"I don't have a madman sending me notes, telling me he loves me. I'm just a whore."

"I don't know which is worse," Kate said.

Twenty-two

"Saw your nigger-loving sister on TV the other night."

It was just enough to throw Willie's shot off. He missed putting the eight ball in the corner pocket. It rattled in the pocket, but wouldn't drop. God damn it. It was a fucking duck. His last five dollars, too. That was another one he owed his bitch of a sister.

"Right there, Willie Boy." The cue tapped the corner pocket, right where the eight ball waited. All he had to do was kiss it. But he didn't. He punctuated winning the game by slamming it home. "Easy money, Willie Boy."

"Don't call me Willie Boy, you asshole."

"No offense, Willie—just kidding. You know me."

"Yeah, I know you suck. Always have, always will. Rack 'em up."

"Whatcha gonna use for money?"

"Just rack the fucking balls, okay?" Willie Sanders turned to the big man sitting in the high chair against the wall. "Hey, Jimmy, loan me twenty bucks till payday."

"Sure, Willie." He pulled his wallet out and took a twenty-dollar bill out. When Willie took it, the big man whispered, "You shouldn't let 'im talk to you like that. You're better than he is."

"Thanks, Jimmy, but watch this. I'm gonna clean his ass this time."

"Okay," Jimmy said.

"Why don't you get us a couple a beers, Jimmy?"

"Sure, Willie."

Willie Sanders turned back and took the chalk from the rail of the table, watching as the asshole broke the rack with a flourish. Nothing dropped.

"You think your sister sleeps with them niggers she's always defending? You oughta do something about that bitch. Gives your family a bad name."

Willie took the stripes, dropping three in a row before missing. He turned to the asshole. "At least she gets paid for it. Not like your old lady, chasing down to the truck stop with a mattress on her back, giving it away to any bald-headed old trucker rolling through."

Jimmy returned with the beers. He heard what Willie said about his sister. She was a whore. Getting paid to do it with niggers. Wasn't right. Wasn't right at all. "Here, Willie."

"Thanks, Jimmy." He watched the asshole miss.

"Don't be thinking bout your old lady flapping them big tits a hers around. Bet she's down at the truck stop right now. Probly in the toilet, sucking some good ole boy off. I don't know how you can stand to kiss the bitch. Lips that touch dirty dicks will never touch mine." Willie bent to line up his shot.

"Look out, Willie."

Willie jumped just in time to avoid the cue stick that slammed hard against the table where his head had been. Before he could react, though, the bartender was there, waving that old double barrel around. God damn, that fucker was fast

"Take it outside, boys," Billy the bartender said.

"You wanna go outside, asshole?"

"Damn straight."

The bar emptied out behind them, the crowd whooping and hollering, eager for a little entertainment. It had been a dull Friday night so far. Willie noticed none of 'em left their beer behind.

Willie faced off with the asshole. "Fore we start, I wanna get one thing straight. I ain't doin' this cause I care none about my sister. I don't give a good goddam about her. She ain't no sister a mine. No, sir, what pisses me off is the way you tried to mess with me. You win my money fair and square, well, thas all right with me. But you fucking around, playing head games. That ain't right. And I'm going to beat the shit out of you for it." He bowed to the whoops and hollers and applause.

"You gonna fight or make another speech?"

Willie Sanders did exactly what he promised. He beat the shit out of him, damn near breaking his right hand in the process. When it was over, he bent over and pulled the roll of bills from the man's shirt pocket and extracted the thirty bucks he had lost and threw the rest back. "I figure you cheated and don't deserve the winnings. Thas the way I see it."

"You right, Willie," someone shouted. "Fuck him."

"Here, Jimmy, thanks for the loan."

"I brought your beer," Jimmy said, holding out the bottle.

"Good thing. Otherwise, one of these assholes woulda grabbed it for sure." He drank it down and then sailed the empty bottle across the parking lot and into the bushes. "Let's go have another."

After washing his face and letting his right hand soak in cold water, Willie went back to the bar and sat alone, brooding. He was still pissed. He didn't want anyone thinking he was defending that bitch of a sister. Maybe it was time to pay her a little visit, lay down the fucking law. He hadn't seen her in what, two, three years? Alwuz was too big for her britches, swishing and strutting down the road, waving her ass around like a bitch in heat. Then you give her what she wants and she gets all uppity about it. No-good bitch. Maybe it was time to pay her a little visit. Just say howdy, real friendly-like. Willie smiled into the mirror behind the bar. "How do, Sis," he said.

Twenty-three

The weekend would pass slowly, drifting by in the lazy hot summer days and the freedom of the languid warm nights. It was like the freedom of long ago summers when there was nothing to mar the days and nights, no thought of school, no nagging homework, no cares, only swimming and playing and picnics with fried chicken and potato salad and chilled watermelon.

There was never enough money to go to the big state fair down at Jackson or the circus that stopped in Memphis each year, but there was always the excitement and the unbearable anticipation that built when the first billboards went up to announce the carnival was coming to town with its ferris wheel and merry-go-round and the persistent cry of the barkers and the games where a quarter and three baseballs might be enough to knock over the pyramid of milk bottles and win a big white teddy bear and the sideshows with the world's smallest human and the fat lady and the two-headed snake and cotton candy and candied apples and scuffling through the sawdust, pleading, please, Mama, just one more ride.

And when the holy rollers came to town for the revival meeting and the big tent went up and Kate and Sally snuck under the tent flaps to sit in the back and watch and giggle and punch each other in the shoulder, sometimes we'd fall down with them and hit each other some more, and going home we'd roll in the grass and Sally would shout, I've got Jesus and I'd shout back. I've got more Jesus than you've got. Oh, God, we were terrors. And sometimes they threw us out, but if you kept going back, maybe they'd let you stay. Otherwise, we'd watch their shadows through the tent. For some reason, the shadows were always a kind of orangy-brown.

But when the dog days came, everything turned dreamy and the nights were filled with the sound of crickets and it was never quite the same again because school loomed and the summer that seemed so endless in June was nearly over and the next June was a lifetime away.

Kate sat on the courthouse steps, basking in the hot summer sun, remembering and thinking, Oh, God, those were good days. They were gone forever now. The dog days were upon them now and Kate was always reminded of *To Kill a Mockingbird* and the part where Atticus came home from work to kill the mad dog. It had to be done, but that part of Harper Lee's novel always made her sad. God, what a good book that was. The South had all the best writers—Faulkner, Carson McCullers, Eudora Welty. Maybe I should just go back to teaching English. Lord, I'm getting nostalgic.

Tracie waited with Kate, again counting to twelve along with the chimes. Around the square, there was the hustle of a Saturday afternoon in town as farmers from miles around brought their families in to do the shopping for another week and pick up feed or tools or otherwise replenish supplies.

Sitting next to Kate on the steps, Tracie felt exposed and vulnerable, despite knowing that they were secure in the midst of the Saturday activity. Still, though Tracie knew it wasn't the killer's style to strike from afar in daylight, she felt defenseless anyway, even with the heavy revolver that weighed down her purse. Billie Rae had been armed, too, as Wilson Cowles was so quick to point out yesterday. But

Tracie kept telling herself that Billie Rae had no warning. That would make all the difference. We know he might be coming. Billie Rae didn't; neither did April Stuart. We do.

Tracie looked over at Kate, feeling the inevitability of it all, knowing that her friend would be the next target. It was the only thing that made any sense whatsoever. She was determined to be with Kate when it went down.

Kate smiled. "I don't think he's coming, either," she said, "but let's wait the half hour. Give him a chance." Kate turned away and looked over the square. "He might be out there, working up his nerve."

He was calling Tracie more often. Every time she checked the answering machine, there was the unnerving silence, growing longer, and then the ominous click as the telephone was replaced. Kate wondered what he thought during the pause. Was he about to speak? Each time, Kate shuddered when she realized he was thinking about her, perhaps relishing the thought of what he wanted to do to her.

Still, after each call, Kate recorded a new message. The last had been, "Please come talk with me. The courthouse steps at noon." After leaving the message, Kate had turned to Tracie and said, "He's listening anyway. Maybe . . . just maybe . . . we'll wear him down."

Their observer—as Wilson Cowles described him—was still with them. He was sitting in a car parked diagonally at the curb. What they didn't know was that the officers were fighting over the duty. Everybody wanted to spend a shift or two on boob patrol, tailing the two women, especially Tracie. There was even talk of starting a pool to see who would be the first to get into her pants.

The thirty minutes crept by in silence.

Finally, Kate stood and looked over the square one last time. "Let's go have a picnic," she said.

They nodded to the young cop before crossing the street to Tracie's car.

* * *

Betsy and Jack lived thirty miles out of town, where they rented a big old frame house across a dirt road from a cotton field. In the old days, the plantation manager or the field boss probably lived there.

Betsy squealed when she ran into the yard to greet them. She was barefoot and wearing a bathing suit. "I knew you'd do it," she cried. "I saw you on television the other night. Just imagine, my big sister, on TV."

"I didn't do anything. Things just worked out for Drew."

"Well, if you'd had to, I just know you'd've got him off. They wouldn't have a chance against you and Tracie. Come on in, everybody's out in the backyard, sitting around the pool."

"I didn't know you had a pool."

"Oh, shoot, didn't Mama tell you to bring bathing suits?"

"She didn't say anything."

"Well, it don't matter none. I got some extras. Bought 'em when we moved in, in case people came over. Except everybody's all the time bringing their own, so these are still brand new. I betcha they'll fit, too."

"I hope they're modest," Kate said. "I'm not exposing myself for the world to see."

" 'Course they're modest, Kate. Can't have nothing racy with Mama around alla time."

Drew was in a lawn chair. He had taken his shirt off to sun himself. The hair on his chest was gray. Unconsciously, Kate's hand went to her own streaks of gray. He's getting old, she thought. We're all getting old.

There were hugs and greetings all around. Jack passed out cold bottles of beer from an ice chest and then went back to listening to the Cardinals' broadcast from St. Louis. They were playing the Dodgers. "What's the score?" Kate asked, leaning over to kiss him.

"Four to one Dodgers, but the Cards got the bases loaded with nobody out."

The boys—Jack's and Betsy's children—stared shyly at Tracie.

Tracie approached them. "You guys want a beer?"

They shook their heads.

"Want me to push you on the swing?"

They nodded.

Tracie had a wonderful time with the children, pushing them on the swing set. When it was her own turn, they pushed her higher and higher. She pointed her feet to the sky and leaned back in the swing, letting her hair fall.

"They love you," Betsy said. "They don't get so much attention from me, I'm sorry to say. It's the one bad thing about living out in the country like this. The nearest kids is a mile or so down the road."

"They're great kids."

"Yeah, they are."

Kate, sitting with her back to the picnic table and drinking a beer, felt homesick while watching Tracie play with the boys. It hadn't been so long since she'd been able to take the girls to the park and romp like that. They grew up so fast. Kate missed them. In another two years, Melissa would be off to college, too. And I'll be alone, unless I marry Harry. Is that what you want, Kate, to live alone until no one wants you anymore?

Restless, Kate finished the beer and dug into the ice chest for another. "Hey, Bets, where's that swimsuit you promised?"

"I'll show you, Sis. You wanna come too, Tracie?"

"Sure. A dip will be just the thing."

Upstairs in her bedroom, Betsy went to her knees to rummage through a bottom dresser drawer. She came up with a black one-piece suit for Kate and a flowered bikini for Tracie.

"You can change in the kids' room," Betsy said, sitting on the bed. "Right across the hall."

"Go ahead, Tracie," Kate said. She sat on the bed beside Betsy.

Betsy jumped up again. "I wanna show you something." Again she pawed through to the bottom of a dresser drawer and returned with a snapshot.

"Is this the guy?" Kate asked.

"That's him."

He looked to be about mid-forties. His hair was graying, too. He had stood facing the camera, smiling and holding a bottle of beer up in a toast.

"He's good-looking," Kate said.

"He's sweet," Betsy said, taking the picture and returning it to the drawer.

"Aren't you afraid Jack will see it?"

"Not unless I hang it on the TV set while he's trying to watch a ballgame."

They heard a faint whoop from Jack just then. "Cardinals must have scored," Betsy said. "What about you, Kate? You made up your mind to marry Harry yet?"

"Not yet. I get so confused sometimes. I want to be with him, but I don't want things to change. Sometimes, I like being alone. You know?"

"What I know is, if you love him, you oughta marry him."

"What if he changes after we're married? What if he's just like Christopher?"

Tracie returned to the bedroom.

"Forget it," Kate said. "I'm not going out there and let everyone compare me with you."

"Me neither," Betsy said. "This was one bad idea. They'd sure like you on wet T-shirt night over to the Palace, though." Betsy looked down at her own breasts. Winking at Kate, she said, "Jack's sure gonna see what he's been missing all these years."

Tracie blushed. "Oh, come on now. Don't be picking on me like that. I can't help it. Sometimes I wish I were ugly."

"Ugly on you would sure be mighty pretty on anybody else."

"Go on, Kate, change. Or else I'm not going downstairs." Tracie stamped her foot in frustration.

"We're just teasing," Kate said. "I'll be back in a minute."

"I ain't teasing," Betsy said. "And don't you be moving none. When you get downstairs just stand real still, so nothing jiggles. Oh, Lordy, but you're just one pretty lady. How come nobody's snapped you up?"

Drew whistled when they went out to the pool again. It was the first time Kate had seen him smile since they'd learned of April's death. "I hope that whistle was for me," Kate said.

"It's for three lovely ladies. And the first one to bring me a beer can have my heart."

"Let's go, girls," Betsy said. They jumped into the pool together.

"Aw, shit," Drew said. "Hey, buddy, you gonna get me a beer?"

"Sure, Uncle Drew." The oldest boy hurried to the ice chest and took him the beer. Then he jumped into the pool, too, sending a wave of water over Drew. "Aw, shit," he repeated. "Hey, Jack, what's the score now?"

And afterward, after they left the pool and dried off and changed clothes again, they crowded around the picnic table, and it was just like Kate remembered.

Jack said Grace. "Thank you, Lord, for all the food on our

table, and thank you, Lord, for our families and friends. Amen."

"Amen," they chorused.

"They's more hamburgers on the grill," Jack said, "so don't be shy."

When her mother went into the house to lie down for an hour, Kate fixed a plate and carried it out to the policeman sitting in his car down the road. "I'm sorry, I can't invite you in, but my mother doesn't know anything is happening. I don't want to alarm her."

"I understand, ma'am. I appreciate this."

"Take care."

He was disappointed that Tracie hadn't come out.

As the evening enveloped them, Kate and Tracie and Betsy slipped away to walk down the dirt road. It reminded Kate of the years when they'd lived in the country, when going into town had been a dress-up-in-their-finest-jeans-and-tennis-shoes affair. Kate kicked up dust as she walked and imagined walking down the road with Harry, holding hands, watching the sun set.

"I did it once, you know," Betsy said.

"Did what?"

"Had a little too much to drink one night over to the Palace. Jack, too—otherwise he'd a-been mortified to death when I got up there during the wet T-shirt competition."

"You didn't!" Kate cried.

"I surely did. None of the other girls showed too much, and I figured I had just as much chance to win as anybody, so I just closed my eyes and sucked up my breath and got up there. Shoot, that water was cold. They couldn't see much anyway. Most of them ole boys was drunk, anyhow. Woulda won, too, except they save this one girl till last, you know. She had some real bombers on her, she did. Anyways, I was real disappointed when I didn't win."

"What would you win?"

"Free dinner for four. Food's pretty good at the Palace, if'n you don't mind grease. Tracie would win hands down."

"Boobs down, don't you mean?"

"Hey, Tracie, let's us go over to the Palace. Wouldn't you like to win a free dinner for your friends?"

"No, thanks. I might get to liking it. Have to go on the wet T-shirt professional circuit."

"Tracie, I don't know this woman. She looks like my little sister, but I think someone must have snuck in and changed places with her when no one was looking."

"How about you, Kate? Bet you could win, too."

They turned around when they reached the church. It was old and weatherbeaten and needed a good coat of white paint, but the worshippers would come in the morning anyway and put their hard-earned dollar bills in the collection plate. God wouldn't care about a fresh coat of paint.

"I teach Sunday School now," Betsy said.

"Not in your T-shirt, I hope."

The long day drew to a close. They gathered up the last of the things scattered around the picnic table and the yard. Kate was pleasantly tired for a change. God, it's peaceful out here, Kate thought, but suddenly she remembered a movie scene from *Bonnie and Clyde,* the part where the gang got together with Bonnie's family and they picnicked out in the country. The sun was setting peacefully then, too, and Warren Beatty and Faye Dunaway drove off into eternity.

Drew led off. He was taking their mother home first. Tracie and Kate followed. The young policeman took up station behind them.

"This has been a great day," Tracie said. "It's almost like I had a family again."

"I'm glad you enjoyed it."

"Oh, I did. Very much."

But Kate couldn't shake the sadness of the movie scene, and she could almost hear the bluegrass of the soundtrack playing for her own ride into eternity.

It was Sunday morning—although the old man didn't know it yet—when he got up with the dawn as always and pulled out the nearly new pair of coveralls, the pair that hadn't faded with repeated hand-washings, and dressed, carefully transferring the ten-dollar bill and the card to the new pockets, pinning them down once again for safekeeping. He debated which shoes to wear—the comfortable everyday pair, or the nearly new pair that boy gave him last fall after skinning out his buck for him. They was for good, but they was a little mite tight. Wouldn't do to wear the old shoes, though, not when you was earning your keep. Gotta show the lady respect for the way she's nice to you.

It was a good five miles into the little river town. Take him three hours to make the trek, unlessn he got lucky and some ole boy happened by to give him a ride. He started out, occasionally stopping to wipe the sweat from his brow with the big red handkerchief and look back hopefully down the dirt road for the trail of dust that would signal a car or pickup. But the only pickup he saw was coming toward him. The three white boys crowded in the seat hooted at him as they passed. The driver gave him the finger. The old man trudged on with dignity.

He reached the little town right next to the river at midmorning and realized it was Sunday when he heard the chorus at the little frame church beltin' out one of the old spirituals. He was glad then he had put on the new tennis shoes. After he did what he had to do, he might just sit a spell in church with the other folks. Never did no harm to let God know you still appreciated all He done for you.

Had to do the job first.

He put the two shiny dimes in the pay phone outside and dialed the first number. A voice came on the telephone and said, "Please deposit fifty-five cents for three minutes." He hung the telephone up and waited for the two dimes to drop back into the slot. When he took them out, he found a quarter there as well. Well, howdy do.

The old man climbed the steps to the general store, carefully removing the old slouch hat before he went in. White folks might take your money and let you shop with them these days, but they sure did want their respect. Wouldn't do to keep a hat on in the store. Some white folks was still funny that way, not like Missy Kate and Missy Tracie.

"Morning, Abe, what brings you into town?" the white man behind the counter asked.

"Mawning, suh. I'se got to make a telephone call, but I needs some change." He offered the ten-dollar bill that he had unpinned.

"Where'd you get all this money, Abe?"

"A nice lady gave it to me."

"You got a girlfriend, Abe?"

"Yassuh, I reckon that's right."

"Well, don't that beat all?"

"And could I have one of them Dr Peppers, too. In the bottle, if you please, suh. Don't like them new cans. Powerful hot and a man works up a mighty thirst."

"Sure thing, Abe. Gotta charge a nickel for the bottle, though. You bring it back and I'll give you the nickel back."

Them voices was mighty sweet, singing like that. Almost like they's in the phone booth here. Old Abe carefully dialed the number again, squinting a little to make sure he got it right. Again the voice told him to deposit fifty-five cents.

When the coins clicked in, he heard the telephone ringing. And then he heard her voice saying, "Please come talk with me. The courthouse steps at noon . . ." A sharp *beep* rang in his ears.

He held the telephone out away and looked at it. He jumped at the sharp warning blast from the river barge behind him. The screech of the horn drowned out the hymn for a moment. He put the telephone back to his ear. "Howdy," he hollered into the receiver. "Anybody to home?"

There was no response. He looked at the phone again. Ain't nobody there. Thas strange. Hear her talkin' but ain't nobody to home. He hung the telephone up and heard the coins drop, but when he tried to retrieve them, they weren't there. Feeling cheated, old Abraham walked down the street and went into the church, still sipping from the bottle of Dr Pepper. He settled in a back pew and got himself ready to worship. They was plenty of time. Black folks knew how to go to church. They didn't hurry it through none. They wasn't impatient, like white folks was. He could rest his feet for a good spell. He would go back home then to wait for her. She'd be back. He'd let her know he'd tried to do the job for her. He'd tell her then all about ole Mistuh Death.

They went to church in the morning.

Tracie had stopped going years ago, right after blaming God for letting Willie rape her, but she accompanied Kate and the others anyway, unwilling to lose the sense of family yet.

The members of the congregation, dressed in their Sunday finest, gathered on the lawn of the church. The men were freshly scrubbed and their hair was slicked down, but if you looked closely they had the dirt of a lifetime of hard work beneath their fingernails. Their women wore cotton print dresses, plain and somber for the services, and shushed their children who were not yet in Sunday school. Most carried their Bibles. It was just as Kate remembered from a child's lifetime of Sunday mornings. It was a scene being repeated all over Mississippi at that very moment.

A number of well-wishers greeted Drew, rushing to shake his hand, bid him good morning, and tell him, "Terrible thing, but we knew right along that was just all trumped up."

Drew shook their hands and smiled and shook more hands, but he whispered sardonically to Kate, "All my friends have returned to the fold."

Kate greeted a few old acquaintances, but she was surprised at how few people she knew anymore. Kate knew, however, that she was not there to see old friends; she was there for her mother to show off. The implication was always to say to her friends, Look how well Kate is doing.

During the service, Kate enjoyed singing the old hymns with the congregation. The sermon was less to her liking as old Reverend Brubaker droned on and on, warning his flock about the impending apocalyptic doom to a chorus of "Amens." Brubaker had been the pastor for as long as Kate could remember, and she wondered if he was getting too old. Still, she filed out with the congregation to shake his hand and say, "Very inspiring, Reverend Brubaker."

Back on the lawn, standing in the hot sun, Kate said, "We have something to do, Mama. We'll be over in a little bit."

"Well, don't you girls be late. Dinner's at one."

"Okay, Mama."

At noon, they were back at the town square, waiting on the steps. The town was eerily quiet on a Sunday. As the old courthouse bell tolled the hour, the sound echoed in the empty streets. There were only two cars parked on the street—Tracie's, and the one with the new cop, sitting there bored and smoking a long black cigar while he waited for them. Kate and Tracie waited the thirty minutes anyway, even though both knew it was useless.

* * *

Back at her mother's, Kate called Tracie's telephone number. She knew it as well as her own number now. At first, she thought he had called again, but then she heard the blast of the horn. It was faint, but unmistakable. The call had been placed from near the river. Then she heard Abraham's voice and realized the answering machine had confused the old man. Damn.

She handed the phone to Tracie. "Call your machine and listen to the message."

"Was it him?"

"No. Abraham."

Tracie called and listened. When she hung up, she turned to Kate and said, "He called from that little store out at the point. Near a church. You could hear a hymn in the background. At least, until the horn drowned it out."

Kate nodded. "Let's drive out after dinner and see if we can find him."

But they were too late.

If they had left right after checking the message, they might have been in time to find Old Abe, trekking back down the dusty road. As it was, when Kate and Tracie drove into the little town on the river, they could find the telephone booth he had probably called from. The church was right down the street.

When they went into the general store, Kate asked the clerk if he knew an old black man named Abraham.

"Sure nough, ma'am. Everybody knows old Abe around here."

"Do you know how we can find him?"

"Sure don't, ma'am. Can't nobody find ole Abe most of the time. He finds you."

"If he returns, would you ask him to call me again? And please, explain to him about how an answering machine works."

"I'll surely do that, ma'am," he said, accepting the card she offered and wondering what two fine-looking ladies like them wanted with an old nigger, anyway.

They told the cop what they were doing and tried to find the old man, driving slowly down the dirt road to Drew's hunting cabin, stopping at an occasional path along the way, even walking into the woods for a bit.

The cop trailed along behind, thinking they were both crazy.

At Drew's cabin, they turned around and retraced their path without success.

Kate would realize only later that finding the old man might have made all the difference. By then, of course, it was too late.

Twenty-four

He was going on vacation in the morning. Technically, he had been on vacation since Friday night, he supposed, but it wasn't the same. Vacation didn't start until Monday morning when the alarm went off and there was no reason to get out of bed, unless, of course, he wanted to. And he did. He surely did.

The headaches had gone away as soon as he'd made his decision.

Everything was ready, but he spent Sunday night going over everything one more time. It was all there—a brand new roll of tape, the soft white coil of rope, the thick dowels, and the gun.

He had sharpened the knife, spending hours spitting on the Arkansas stone and rubbing the shiny blade back and forth. It wouldn't split a hair, but pretty near. Maybe it wouldn't be necessary—not if she was good. It all depended on her. If she acted right, it wouldn't be necessary at all. And if she didn't, well, couldn't blame that on him.

He would give her the choice, though—to live or to die. She would make the decision this time, not like with them other ones. What happened to them had been inevitable, no matter what he told them. It was their time, simple as that.

He was surprised at the pity he felt, and hoped she would

make the right decision. If she did, why then, we just disappear when the time comes. People went away all the time and never came back. That's what we'll do. Just go away and never come back.

Satisfied that everything was ready, he took one last look around the basement, and climbed the stairs. He was shivering with anticipation when he switched the light off at the top of the stairs, plunging her prison into darkness. It was all so perfect. Nobody ever went down there. He could keep her there forever, if he wanted, and nobody would ever know, even when Sally got back. But it didn't have to be a prison. It could be a love nest if she did right by him. Just temporary, of course, until later, when they all went away together.

He wandered through the rooms aimlessly, still thinking about his vacation. It was nice being alone in the big old house with two weeks of freedom stretching out endlessly before him and nobody to tell him what to do. That was the nicest thing about it all. He'd have someone to spend the time with. He'd be giving the orders, whether she acted like a fool or not. All she's got to do is be nice to me. That's not so much to ask, is it? And if she followed orders, did what she was told, why, it wouldn't be so bad at all when they were together.

He went upstairs after turning out all the lights and making sure the house was locked up for the night. Wouldn't do for some thief to sneak in and see the preparations he had made. Wouldn't do at all.

In his bedroom, he didn't have to close the door. It wasn't like there was anyone around to see what he was doing. He could sit there all night and watch one video after another if he wanted. And once he brought her here, why, maybe if she was real good, he'd bring her upstairs and let her sleep with him. Show her how nice he could be if he wanted. He could do anything he pleased. He was free.

He carefully set the alarm for the regular time. He wanted

to be up early and ready to take advantage of the first opportunity. He would have to be fast. He didn't want to waste his vacation.

And then he took out her photograph and stroked those nice Polaroid titties until he fell asleep.

Twenty-five

The bluejay's angry cries awakened Kate at first light Monday morning. The bird chattered loudly, insistently, rebuking her for . . . for what? Everything. A failed marriage, two murders, a messy and disordered life, loving two men, unable to choose between them, unable to decide what she wanted. The noisy reprimand went on and on, pausing momentarily as though to ask, Well, young lady, what do you have to say for yourself?

Nothing, Kate replied. It's all my fault.

The scolding resumed.

Kate had slept fitfully. She was restless and uneasy, still blaming herself for not leaving immediately after receiving Abraham's message. It was a mistake. Maybe it wasn't a bad mistake. The dinner could have—should have—waited. Her mother would have been disappointed, but they could have returned immediately, had dinner then. Now . . . well, they would just have to try and find him this afternoon. Kate hoped it wasn't too late.

Outside, the jay screamed in outrage.

The long-suppressed memory returned with the same old rush of guilt. She was ten years old again, walking a country path, carrying Drew's Red Ryder air rifle. The jay was on a fence post, watching her placidly. When she raised the rifle to her shoulder, she never expected to shoot, and if she did, the bird would fly away unharmed. But the air rifle went off unexpectedly and the bird dropped to the ground. Her elation quickly turned to sorrow as she approached the dying bird. A single splash of red dotted its throbbing breast. Glazed eyes stared up at her in reproach. It blinked once and died. Horrified at her deed, she burst into tears. For weeks after, she felt the remorse and lay awake at night, begging God to forgive her. Perhaps He had. Kate didn't know. She had never forgiven herself, though.

The blue jay raged on.

"I'm sorry," Kate said. "For everything."

When they arrived at Tracie's office, Kate called Wilson Cowles immediately, eagerly, only to be disappointed when he reported there had been no developments over the weekend.

"You've had an interesting weekend. I hope you're not finding your 'observer' intrusive?" Cowles asked.

"It's rather comforting to know he's there," Kate replied. "Did they report everything to you?"

"Your movements, at least. The man on Saturday appreciated the plate of food. That was thoughtful."

"It was the least I could do."

"Why did you go to the river yesterday?"

"Abraham left a message." Kate paused. "Or rather, he didn't leave a message. He didn't know what to do with the answering machine. I should have anticipated that. I fought getting an answering machine for years. Anyway, we tried to find him."

"Without success, apparently."

"You already know that."

"Yes. What do you think this elusive old man wanted to tell you?"

"I don't know. We're going to try again this afternoon."

"You'll call me immediately, if you find him, and if he has anything to say."

"Of course."

"Kate, I wish you would reconsider. There's nothing you can accomplish here."

So it was "Kate" again. "I'll be leaving soon."

"When?"

"I don't know."

Kate heard him sigh.

"Keep me posted," he said before hanging up.

Kate watched as Tracie turned the *Arizona Highways* calendar again, this time to a photograph of a mountain of red rock awaiting an onslaught by dark and brooding thunderclouds. "I wish I could control time the way you do," she said.

"It's beautiful isn't it?" Tracie said, looking over her shoulder at Kate, "but the trouble with my system is that I run out of time. Pretty soon, I won't have any months left."

"When you get to the end of the year, you can always start over."

"It's not the same. I'll have to wait for the new calendar then."

It was driving Kate crazy. She had to know what Harper Lee had written in *To Kill a Mockingbird,* the thought obsessed her just as it had with *Appointment in Samarra.* This is what it's like to get old. More and more, your mind returns to the past, to the old familiar things that provide comfort in an increasingly hostile and alien world. Is this what it's like for Abraham? Did the old man's mind wander through his youth and young manhood, when he was strong and virile, possessing the strength to do anything he wanted? Or was it simply a refuge, infinitely more pleasing, to wander the corridors of distant and dusty decades, rather than confront the harsh realities of the present?

All weekend—ever since she'd come home—Kate had been able to think of little else but the past. The dog days of those long ago lazy summers were more tangible to her now than the world that passed by the window of Tracie's office.

"I want to run down to the library," Kate said. "Why don't you come along?"

"You go on, Kate. I need to make a couple of calls. With everything else that's been going on, I've forgotten about some cases that are pending. I better get back to paying attention."

"You sure you'll be okay?"

Tracie smiled. "Nothing's going to happen here. Look at all the people running around. I'll scream loud and clear if anything does happen."

"Promise?"

"Absolutely. They'll hear me in Memphis. I can guarantee it."

"If Abraham calls . . ."

"I'll find out where he is and come get you."

Still, Kate hesitated.

"Go on, now," Tracie said. "I'll be fine."

"You sound like my mother," Kate said. " 'Go on, now. You kids go out in the yard and play, get outta my hair for a spell, hear?' "

Another young cop in plain clothes had the assignment this morning. When Kate left the office, his eyes flicked back and forth between the looker in the office and the older woman—still in mighty fine shape—and made his decision. He got out of the car and swaggered after Kate, feeling mighty good in his new cowboy boots and the loose-fitting blue cotton pullover that concealed his weapon. Nothing was going to happen in the courthouse square, not in broad daylight with cops going in and out of the courthouse all day long. Besides, the older babe had a mighty fine ass. Follow that ass all day long. Sure better than driving around in a hot uniform and even hotter squad car, trying to keep the niggers from killing each other. It'd be a shame going back on the four-to-midnight, answering one fight call after another in one juke joint after another. Crazy fucking niggers anyway. Heat's what did it. Wasn't just the niggers. Made everybody crazy.

Across the street, he watched Kate leave the office and walk down the street. He could just make out Tracie's shadow in the office. It looked like she was just sitting there, waiting. Well, he could wait, too. He had plenty of time. He was on vacation. He brushed a gnat away from his eyes and with it the impatience he felt. It would do to hurry things along. If it didn't happen today, there was always tonight. Or tomorrow. He hoped he wouldn't have to wait that long. Everything was ready and waiting for her.

At the library, Kate quickly found Harper Lee's novel and took it to a reading table. An old man sat across from her, reading a newspaper, wetting his finger when he turned a page.

Kate leafed through the pages, looking for the place where the rabid dog wandered down the street. She couldn't find the passage. Did I imagine it? Was it some other novel? Am I making it up? She went through the pages again, slower, reading a paragraph or two, glancing over a page here, skipping on when she saw a reference to winter.

Suddenly, there it was. The old dog slowly making its way down the street, weaving and lumbering along, already caught in the throes of its madness. It was February in the novel, though. That wasn't right. It should have happened in the dog days of August. But that was the brilliance of the novel. Things happened when they shouldn't. Just like in real life.

The old man sat in the shade of a big tree, just whittling on a stick with his old jackknife. He'd got it out to cut the blister on his foot and then it had felt so good just sittin' there with his shoes off, kinda cool-like, and he'd just picked up that ole stick and started whittling. It wasn't so good, though, 'cause the branch was fresh, and when he cut through the bark, the wood was still slippery with green sap.

He'd thought he might make a whistle like he done when he was just a kid, but while he was sawing away, he forgot what it was he started out to do. Warn't nobody to give it to no-how. Usta make whistles for the kids when they was younguns. So when he forgot what he was doing, he ended up just whittling, passing the heat of the day away. Waitin' patient-like to see what the day would bring. Sumpin would happen. Alwuz did. Alwuz would, if'n a man was real patient and didn't try to hurry things along none.

Tracie looked up at the sound of the door and there he was, standing over her, grinning down at her with that arrogant smirking twist to his mouth.

"Hey, Sis," he said.

"What do you want?"

"Hey, what's with the attitude? Just stopped by to say hello to my little sister. What's wrong with that?"

"I'm not your sister."

"Everybody says you've been on the *TV* lately." He drawled the two letters out, making them sound somehow disreputable, as though she'd been found dancing in a topless bar or had committed some other unsavory crime. "Didn't see it myself, but everybody said you was looking good. I guess they was right."

"Get out. Leave me alone."

He sat on the corner of the desk, still grinning down at her.

Tracie took a deep breath, trying to still the panic, the revulsion.

He reached out and touched a strand of her hair that had fallen loose.

Tracie froze. It was happening again. She wanted to scream, jump up, flee, but she was unable to move.

He laughed and brushed the strand of hair back into place.

She slapped his hand away. "Don't touch me," she cried.

"Hey, Sis, no big deal. You must be doing right well, being on *TV* and all."

Tracie didn't respond. She didn't know what to say. She wanted him to get out and leave her alone. But he wouldn't do that, not Willie Sanders. Not asshole Willie Sanders. He wouldn't leave until he had tormented her to death.

"So, I'm a little short this week. Figured since you was doing so good, you might see your way clear to a little loan. Maybe forty bucks to tide me over till payday. That's what a good sister would do."

"I'm not a good sister."

"Oh, fuck, girl. Just give me the forty bucks and stop whining. If you ain't got it in cash, just say so. I'll take a check."

"You son-of-a-bitch." His smile was maddening. Tracie wanted to slap it off his face. Or better yet, shoot it off. "Will forty dollars get you out of my life?"

"Sure, Sis—for a time, anyway. We're blood kin. Got to check in occasionally, make sure you're all right. Wouldn't want anything to happen to my little sister."

Tracie went into her purse, not taking her eyes off that sarcastic smile on his face. Her fingers touched the wallet and then moved to close around the butt of the revolver. "Fuck you," she said, pulling the gun out, pointing at him. "I'm not giving you forty cents."

He laughed then. "Well, shit. What you gonna do, shoot your brother? How's that gonna look? Big fucking deal lawyer kills brother."

"Oh, I'm not going to kill you," she said coldly, lowering the revolver from his chest. "I'm going to shoot your balls off. I should have done that a long time ago. Probably would have saved a lot of women a lot of grief."

"You stupid no-good bitch."

Tracie cocked the revolver. "He came in here, Officer, and attacked me. Threatened to kill me if I didn't give him money. He always was the black sheep of the family. No good. It was self-defense, Officer, pure and simple. Who do you think the cops are going to believe, me or a scumbag white supremacist?"

"Girl, you sure are a crackerjack." He laughed again, holding his hands up. "Careful with that trigger now. I reckon I gotta be going, but you better watch your back, Sis, or something bad might happen to you."

"The next time I see you, Willie, I'm going to shoot your balls right off. That's a promise. Believe me."

"Okay, I'm going, but I'll be back."

The windowpanes rattled when he slammed the door. Tracie waited until she heard the grinding of gears on his old pickup and the screech of tires as he pulled out before she lowered the revolver, using both hands to carefully uncock it.

Then she put her head on the desk and cried.

He had touched her—again. His hand left years of dirt on her face, her body. She had to get clean, erase the trace of his hand. If she could. If she could ever be clean again.

"God damn him," she sobbed. "Why did he have to come here?"

Get hold of yourself. Don't let him do this to you. That's what he wants. You're letting him fuck with your head.

Don't. Just go and take a hot shower. Let the steaming hot water rinse away any trace of him. Let his touch wash off into the drain and the sewer. That's where he belongs—in the sewer.

Tracie wiped the tears away and quickly wrote the note on a legal pad, ripped the sheet off, and taped it to the office door, facing out. Then she locked the door, got in her car, and drove off. Kate would understand.

She had to get clean again.

It was a burden to the old man. All the time he sat in the shade, wasting his time away whittling on that little ole green stick, he knew he hadn't kept his word to that fine young woman. His ole feet hurt, but he finally decided there weren't no way round it. He had to make another journey. Just no other way.

He crossed the street and read the note as he passed the storefront. It had been hurriedly scribbled in block letters. It wasn't at all neat and precise the way he liked it: *K. GONE TO DREW'S. BACK SOON. T.*

He went down to the corner and waited for the light to change before crossing the street and going back to his car. He was smiling as he turned the key in the ignition.

Tracie wheeled her little sports car through the streets, careening around corners, glancing in her rearview mirror expecting to see Willie's pickup truck filling the glass. She swerved and braked when a cat ran across the road in front of her. It dashed out from between parked cars. Tracie caught a glimpse of the cat racing across a lawn and up the stairs to a porch. Thank God. Christ, that was close. She forced herself to drive more slowly then. God, what if it had been a child?

Still panic-stricken, she pulled through the gate of Drew's home and slid to a stop on the gravel.

Tracie ran into the house and slammed the door shut, locking it, leaning against it with the full weight of her body, as though he might come crashing through after her. When her breathing quieted, Tracie went upstairs to the bathroom and turned the shower water on.

The doorbell rang.

Oh, God, he followed me.

She took the gun from her purse again and went to the hallway window that overlooked the front yard. It was Kate's friend, Jimmy—only Jimmy. He had stepped back from the door and seemed to be trying to see through the curtains. What was he doing here? Why was the trunk of his car open? That was funny. He had something in his hand. Maybe he was delivering something to Kate, something from Sally, but Sally was in Europe now.

The bell rang again.

Tracie went back to the bathroom and replaced the gun in her purse before going downstairs to answer the bell. She took a deep breath and pulled the door open. It was an effort to smile, but Tracie did. It wasn't Jimmy's fault. He hadn't done anything. "Hi, Jimmy," she said.

It was pleasant sitting in the coolness of the library, surrounded by books. Libraries were pleasant places. Kate missed the cramped old library of her youth, though. But when the tornado ripped through town a few years back, one of the casualties was the old library. The black funnel had ripped the roof right off and strewn books across six city blocks. The new library was an improvement, but Kate still missed the musty smell of the old building and the dark stacks where you had to get down on your hands and knees to read the titles on the lower shelves.

And old Miss Bailey, the stereotype of the spinster librarian who had kept Kate out of the adult section until she was fifteen, succumbing only when Miss Bailey had asked Kate's mother how she'd liked *Peyton Place*. "Oh, I didn't read it myself. I been checking all these books out for Kate."

Horrified, Miss Bailey had given in and allowed Kate to check out any book she wanted after that. Within reason, of course.

Old Miss Bailey, dead all these years now. Kate's mother had sent the librarian's obituary to Kate. It was probably still in a box somewhere in one of the closets.

Kate looked at her watch and sighed. There was plenty of time until noon. He wasn't going to show up today, either, but Kate got up and returned the book to its proper place on the shelf. I'm going to read it again, though, when I get home, she vowed. Maybe I'll just read everything again. She smiled at the librarian.

"Did you find what you needed?" the librarian asked.

"Yes, thanks."

"You know the district attorney returned that book you were asking for. The one on Jack the Ripper, you know? I could let you have it now."

"I was able to find another copy," Kate said, "but thanks anyway."

"I'm glad you were able to find it. I really shouldn't let a reference work circulate."

Kate stopped in the lobby to examine some old grainy black-and-white photos of the Delta taken at the beginning of the last century. One showed an old riverboat docked at Friar's Point when it had still been a bustling stop for the steamers. Black men were rolling bales of cotton up the gangway. There was another photo of the old Randall Place—Kate found it hard to believe Drew owned it now and she was sleeping there. In the photo, the Randall clan had gathered for a Sunday afternoon reunion. The women posed with parasols twirling over their shoulders. The men were all stiff and proper in their Sunday suits, slicked back hair, and beards and waxed handlebar mustaches. Yet another photo showed the hands—men, women, and children—picking cotton, the long sacks trailing behind as they made their way through the low rows. As a child, Kate had ridden along on the sacks. It had been a game then. She now realized what a burden she must have been to the old black woman who pulled her along cheerfully, never complaining. There were contrasting photos of two sharecroppers' cabins. Except for the color of the families gathered on the ramshackle porches—one was white, the other black—they were indistinguishable from one another in the stark poverty and hopelessness etched on their faces.

There were fewer sharecropper cabins like that, but they still existed. There were still far too many of them left. One was too many.

Kate went back to the reference desk. "Those photographs in the display case, where did you get them?" she asked.

"They're from our local history room. We have a collection of old photos. Do you like them?"

"They're wonderful and terrible at the same time."

"Yes, that's how they always strike me," the librarian said. "We should never forget how far we've come and how far we must go yet. If you like them, you can go through our collection. They're available for circulation and you can have them reproduced. I can show you, if you like."

Kate looked at her watch. She was tempted. "I have an appointment now," she said. "Perhaps tomorrow."

"Anytime."

Kate left the library and stepped into the hot air shaking her head, still wondering about a state, a nation, that could not eradicate such symbols of dire poverty and provide hope for its people, all people.

It's time to go home, she thought.

But it was no better there with the growing number of homeless, displaced people. They were on all the street corners. God damn it, we're marching to the twenty-first century and the banner says, *Will Work for Food*. What happened to all the promises?

Kate strolled back toward the office. It was still only eleven-thirty. When she stopped to admire a dress in a shop window, she saw the reflection of the police officer. What's he doing here? He should have stayed with Tracie.

Kate turned and walked quickly down the street, not really alarmed. Concerned. That's all, Kate said. A slight concern.

But when she turned the corner and saw that Tracie's car was no longer parked in front of the office, a cold fear set in. She hurried and then broke into a run.

Kate read the note taped to the glass and then tried the door. Locked. God damn it. What was Tracie thinking about, going off alone like that? Kate turned and ran over to the young police officer leaning against the fender of his car, looking at her with amusement. "Do you know the old Randall place?" Kate cried.

"Sure. Everybody does. Usta go there when . . ."

Kate cut him off. "Get me there. Right now!"

"But . . ."

"I mean it. Right now, God damn it!"

"Yes, ma'am."

It was irrational. Kate admitted that, but . . .

"What's going on, ma'am?"

"You should have stayed with Tracie."

"I figured she'd be all right there. I mean, with all the people coming and going. You shoulda said something. I didn't know."

"You're right. I'm sorry. It's probably nothing. I'll buy you a beer after."

"You don't hafta do that, ma'am." He was beginning to

think she was crazier than the niggers. They were all crazy. And he'd entered the pool, too.

"I'll buy you two beers if you stop calling me ma'am."

Tracie's car looked abandoned rather than parked. The driver's door was open, and Tracie's white chiffon scarf trailed across the seat on to the ground.

Kate sighed with relief. At least she's here.

"I'll be right back," she told the young officer.

"Yes, ma'am."

Kate ran up the stairs and opened the door. There was a faint but bitter and acrid smell in the hot, still air. Inside, she heard the shower running upstairs. Kate climbed the stairs slowly, suddenly tired. Christ, Tracie, you scared me.

The shower was louder at the top of the stairs and Kate could see the bathroom door was open. Steam billowed out. "Tracie," Kate called.

There was no answer. Tracie couldn't hear her. It would be hard to hear over the sound of the running water.

Kate looked through the door. The shower curtain was pulled across the tub.

Psycho. She could see Anthony Perkins raising the knife.

The bathroom was filled with steam.

"Tracie!"

Psycho!

Kate jerked the shower curtain open, expecting to find Tracie's slashed and mutilated body and her blood swirling down the drain. A blast of hot air and scalding steam hit her face.

The bathtub was empty.

Behind her, Sam mewed piteously.

Twenty-six

He made a fresh pitcher of lemonade. He did not like the concentrate from the supermarket. It never tasted as good as lemonade made the way his mother had taught him. He had boiled the water and sugar together and put it in the refrigerator to chill before leaving that morning. Now he cut and squeezed the lemons in the juicer, pouring the juice into the pitcher after removing the seeds. He left the pulp. He thought it provided substance and he liked getting just a little of the pulp in his mouth to suck and chew. After adding the ice cubes and stirring the big pitcher of liquid, he poured just a tiny bit into a glass. He held it to the light and examined it critically before taking just a taste and rolling it around in his mouth. It was just fine, a good batch.

He poured half a glass of lemonade for himself and sat at the kitchen table, feeling very pleased. Everything had gone just the way he had planned it, the way he had practiced it. One. Two. Three. Precise and exact. She had struggled ineffectively. The burning Mace in her eyes disabled her and took the fight right out of her. The tape slapped across her mouth silenced her. Three turns of the tape around her wrists, another three turns around her ankles. And it was done, just like a cowboy in a rodeo. He wished now he had timed it. He would bet that from the time she'd opened the door until he'd slammed the trunk closed, it had taken less than a minute.

He had gone back and closed the door, picked up the can of Mace and retrieved one of her loafers that had slipped off when he carried her to the car. It was probably no more than three minutes after he drove in that he was driving away again. Maybe more. It had taken her a long time to answer the door.

He wondered what she had said to Willie to make him so steamed. He surely was angry when he left her office, red-faced and muttering to himself. Didn't matter now. Willie wouldn't have to worry about his sister anymore.

The first thing he did after he got Tracie fixed up in the basement, moaning and crying from behind the tape, was wash the burning away, flooding her eyes with the cool cleansing water and adding the eyedrops. She hadn't liked it when he'd cut her blouse off, but after he told her to hush and lie still, she acquiesced, blinking against the water and the drops, but she had done what she was told. He was pleased with her so far. The eyes would burn some for a while and be red for a while longer, but he had been careful not to use too much, just a quick squirt. He had practiced that, too.

Got most of that makeup off as well. Not the lipstick, of course, but most of the rest of it. She looked a lot better now. Clean-like.

Oh, dear, sweet Jesus, what am I going to do?

The fierce burning had eased a little, but the tears still flowed. Tracie didn't try to stop them. They helped wash the pain away. But the tears could not erase the fear.

She sat on a stool, already cramped and aching from the ropes tied around her ankles, her knees, her arms.

He had used the thick dowel as a yoke across her shoulders, stretching and tying her arms to the wood at wrist, elbow, and shoulder. The ropes at either wrist were anchored to ring bolts he had imbedded into both ends of the rod that pressed harshly against her back. A thicker rope was tied to the center of the yoke, right between her shoulder blades. He had run that through another, much larger ring bolt, in the ceiling, and tied it off against the wall. If she struggled, she would fall off the stool and just hang there—like Billie Rae, like April.

Oh God, please God, no.

She looked down at her breasts and the white bra she had chosen that morning. At least he'd left her jeans. She could see her torn blouse where he had tossed it.

Oh God, what am I going to do?

She waited for him to return, to take the tape from her mouth, so she could reason with him. We'll help you, Jimmy. Please.

Please, God, oh please, God . . .

He finished his lemonade, rinsed the glass carefully, and placed it in the sink. Then he took two clean glasses and placed them on a tray, along with the pitcher and two straws. He carried the tray downstairs. The ring of the ice cubes against the pitcher was a pleasant chime.

Tracie waited just where he had left her. She hadn't tried to struggle or do anything foolish. That was good. She sure looked pretty, sitting there on the stool in that lacy white brassiere all plumped out and full of her pale breasts. He could see the dark of her nipples against the fine material. Her long hair was tangled, though. He'd have to take a comb or a brush to it later. He hadn't thought of that. Couldn't think of everything.

"Bet you'd like some lemonade," he said. "It's really good. I made it myself."

She watched him with teary, red-rimmed eyes as he placed the tray on a small table.

He took a fresh tissue from the box and dabbed at the tears. Black streaks came away. He must have missed some of that mascara.

She cringed when he took the knife from the table. He liked that. Showed she was ready to do whatever he said. At least, she would be soon. "Don't worry," he said. "I ain't gonna hurt you none. Just wanna make a little hole in the tape so you can have some lemonade, that's all. Okay?"

She nodded.

He placed his hand behind her head to steady it and raised the point of the knife to the tape, piercing it just slightly. "Okay?"

She nodded again.

He put the knife away and poured the glasses of lemonade, putting a straw in hers. He poked the straw through the hole in the tape, wiggling it around until she could drink.

Tracie sipped the lemonade greedily. Drops of icy water fell between her breasts. She drank half the glass.

"More?"

Tracie shook her head.

"Maybe later."

He pulled the straw from her mouth and took the glass away. He was smiling when he turned back to her. "Don't worry," he said, "I ain't gonna hurt you none if you're nice."

Tracie shuddered when he brushed a strand of hair away from her eyes. Willie had done that. Oh, God, it's starting. She wanted to scream, but she could only moan helplessly and shake her head as he reached for her breast.

Twenty-seven

The police were maddeningly slow. They responded quickly enough when the young cop—Kate had learned his name was Andy—had called in to report Tracie Sanders was missing. He had barely made the report before Kate heard the first siren. Wilson Cowles arrived hard on the heels of the detectives. But after they arrived, everything took place in slow motion, as they began the painstaking investigation.

Kate described what Tracie had been wearing. Her description was immediately broadcast. Officers went through her bedroom upstairs. Others were dispatched to Tracie's own apartment and her office. Yet another was ordered to track down Willie Sanders. The neighborhood was canvassed for possible witnesses. Laboratory personnel arrived.

No one assumed that Tracie Sanders had disappeared voluntarily.

Kate repeated her story three times, the last time to Captain Lew Martins. She established the timetable as exactly as she could. "I was gone less than an hour. She was fine when I left. She was going to make a few phone calls. When I got back, there was a note on the office door saying she'd come here."

"She didn't say anything before you left?"

"No. I was just going to meet her back at the office. That's all. We were going to drive out to the river after lunch."

"Was she impulsive, likely to change her mind suddenly, do something crazy?"

"Like suddenly decide to take a shower?"

"Yeah."

Kate shrugged. "No. Something happened at the office during the forty-five minutes I was gone, something that made her come out here. That's the only explanation."

"What?"

"I don't know."

Kate also pointed out that Tracie's purse was still on the bathroom counter, the pistol inside. "It didn't happen upstairs. There are no signs of a struggle. She wasn't afraid."

"The shower's running. She hears the doorbell over the sound of the water." Martins paused. "Could she? Hear the doorbell over the sound of the water, I mean?"

"It's loud, but I don't know."

"Ralph, go upstairs and turn the shower on. Full blast. And tell me if you can hear the doorbell."

The bell rang out downstairs.

The detective appeared at the head of the stairs. "It's faint, but I heard it."

"Thanks, Ralph." He turned back to Kate. "So she heard the doorbell, came downstairs, answered the door. By the way, that smell you mentioned, it's Mace. He used it to incapacitate her."

Kate watched and waited impatiently. "God damn it, she's not hiding in a closet somewhere," Kate muttered. And then Kate did exactly what the police were doing. She went over everything in her mind again.

Andy had been at the foot of the stairs. "Ma'am—what's happening, ma'am?"

Kate had scooped the kitten up and said, calmly and professionally, "I don't know, but call whoever you have to call. Tell them Tracie Sanders is missing."

"Oh, shit. Yes, ma'am."

Kate had gone through each of the bedrooms then, knowing the search was futile.

He had Tracie.

Kate put Sam down and went to call Wilson Cowles.

Once, when Mycroft had been a kitten, they'd been unable to find him anywhere. Kate and Allison and Melissa had searched the house, calling his name. They went into every closet and cupboard and they could find the kitten nowhere. Their search spread outside to the front and back yards, and to their neighbors' yards up and down the street. Allison and Melissa were crying and Kate was near tears when she started through the house again, beginning in her own bedroom. She even opened the drawers of her dresser looking for the damned kitten. Then she went to the bed, which was completely made up and unruffled in any way, and pulled the bedspread back and threw the pillows aside.

Mycroft had blinked and gazed sleepily up at her, as though to say, Oh, were you looking for me?

Kate wanted Tracie to suddenly appear, rubbing sleep from her eyes and say, Oh, were you looking for me?

God damn it. Kate went and stood on the porch, watching as two detectives went over Tracie's car.

The keys were still in it.

"What does that suggest about her state of mind?" a detective asked.

"She was either in a panic and running . . ."

"Why not keep driving, then?"

"Or she wasn't in a panic, felt secure."

"Well, shit."

"Why was the shower running?"

"She wanted to take a shower."

"In the middle of the day?"

"She was hot and sweaty. Wanted to get refreshed?"

"Oh, shit," Kate said. She went back inside to replay the entire day in her mind, just as the police were doing with the house so slowly and methodically. Kate searched for the one detail that would provide an insight, some indication, a place to begin.

She didn't find it.

Neither did the police.

In her review of the day's events, the only thing Kate found was guilt. It was all her fault. If only she had stayed with Tracie, none of this would have happened. They would have been together, and together they could have prevented it. Tracie, why did you come back here? Kate, why did you go to the library? Why didn't you insist that Tracie go with you? Was it so God damned important to find that passage?

Why?

The old man was lucky. First, he caught a ride after walking only ten minutes down the dusty road. He didn't even have to sit in the bed of the pickup because the driver was alone. Then, the bus was waiting for him. It cost him two dollars for the fare into town, and it would be another two dollars back. But he had to do it. Hadn't expected to get that money anyway. Be enough left for whatever an old man wanted to do.

From long habit, old Abraham shuffled to the back of the bus, although it was nearly empty. He knew he could sit right behind the driver if he wanted, but the old ways were too hard to break. Didn't matter anymore, anyway. It was peaceful in the back of the bus. Fifteen minutes after the door hissed shut, the old man was sleeping peacefully, his old and frail body swaying with the movement of the bus.

He did not see the police car streak past in the opposite direction.

* * *

Cowles finally took Kate into the living room and commanded her to sit. He took a chair across from her. As he looked around the room, he told Kate, "You know, my grandparents used to work for the Randalls, the old man, of course, not the one who shot himself. They picked his cotton until they were too old to work anymore. Then they died."

"Tracie's going to die," Kate said. "Tonight, if the pattern holds. He may already be torturing her. Jesus." She put her hands over her eyes, wanting to cry, to scream, to rush out and find Tracie.

"We'll find her, Kate. We've never been so close behind him before. Every cop in town, in the county, has Tracie's description and is looking for her. A lot of them know her. We'll find her."

"How about out at the river? That's where he took Billie Rae and April."

"There are units there already. I understand they're going to use dogs. A unit is on the way out there with Tracie's scarf."

"I want to go out there," Kate said. "That's probably the place he'll take her . . . if the pattern holds."

"The pattern would indicate that he'd be there only at night. The units out there have instructions to be discreet, to watch and wait until nightfall."

"I still want to go."

"What good can you do there, Kate?"

"What good can I do here?"

"I don't know, but I'm not letting you out of my sight again, not until this is over."

"Wilson, why did you arrest my brother?"

The abrupt shift in conversation startled him. He closed his eyes momentarily and then looked around the living room again, not at the furnishings, but at the walls, as though they had once heard an important secret, a revelation that would help him understand.

He turned back to Kate. "We felt the evidence was sufficient to bring charges. The police and my staff urged an arrest. It was my decision, however."

Kate nodded. "It was because he was white."

"Yes. There are elements . . ." He paused. "When a white woman is murdered in the South, there are those who still today immediately believe that only a black man would commit such a heinous crime. Perhaps I feared retribution against the black community. Perhaps . . ." He leaned forward toward Kate. "I found a hangman's noose on the seat of my car. It was not subtle. Oh, I did not fear for myself. But . . ."

"I understand," Kate said.

"Do you?"

Kate reached out and took his hand. She didn't think anyone noticed or cared, but she couldn't be sure.

Tracie held her breath. He was behind her now. She was afraid to turn her head, afraid to see what he was doing. She closed her eyes and waited.

"Does Kathryn Anne wear nice underwear like this?" His hand closed around her breast again.

Tracie cringed and shook her head. I don't know, she wanted to tell him.

"They should open in front, you know." He removed his hand.

Tracie opened her eyes. He was standing in front of her now, holding the knife. "Don't be afraid," he said, as he placed the blade beneath the soft material and cut it open.

Tracie heard his sigh when her breasts fell free to his gaze.

He tugged the bra away.

Please, don't.

He turned away and went to the steps, returning with his camera. "I want to remember this moment forever," he said.

Tracie blinked against the flash.

When the picture slid from the camera, he watched as her image slowly appeared. "You're very beautiful," he said, holding the picture up for her.

Tracie saw a frightened woman, red eyes wide and streaks of mascara and smudged makeup, arms stretched and tied. *I'm not beautiful. I'm hideous.*

"Jesus, Kate, what's going on here?" Drew asked. "I come home for lunch and it looks like a convention."

"Tracie's missing."

"Oh, Christ, no. Not Tracie, too." He slammed his fist into the wall.

Kate went to him. They hugged.

And then they argued.

"God damn it, I want you to go home, right now. Get away from here."

"I won't."

"You'll be next. God damn it, I thought you had cops watching you."

"It's my fault. I went to the library and left Tracie at the office. I wasn't thinking. The policeman followed me."

"Shit."

"She came back here. The shower was running. All we can figure is that whoever he is came to the door and she answered it. He probably used Mace on her."

"Kate, God damn it . . ."

"I know. Damn it, I feel just as helpless."

"We can't just sit here. We've got to do something."

"What?" That was the fucking show-stopping line that always brought down the house. What can we do? Not one fucking thing, except wait.

* * *

Tracie was alone. Her arms and shoulders ached. After cutting away her bra and taking the photograph, he had gone away. He hadn't even touched her again. Please, Kate, come and find me before . . .

Before I die.

I'm going to die.

Her mind filled with regret for all the things she would never do. Never live in Arizona, never see a desert sunset again, never swim in the river, never love, have children, grow old . . .

I'm going to die.

No!

He wants me to be nice to him. He said that. He wants to fuck me. He can't do it like this. He has to untie me.

She twisted her body, swinging her outstretched arms, trying to ease the aching in her muscles. I can hit him, even like this. The next time he comes close, swing your arm. Hit him in the head.

She practiced.

It was hopeless. I can never hit him hard enough. Wait. Wait until he wants to . . . Then. Get the knife. All you have to do is get the knife.

Tracie waited.

She looked down at her breasts. Already she could see herself in other photographs. The photos would be in her file, just like they were in the files of Billie Rae Scott and April Stuart. She could already envision the tiny precise square etched in her flesh. It was just like the stamps in his collection. We should have known, recognized the similarity between the stamps and the notes. They were all so precise. We should have known. Now it's too late.

He's going to add me to his collection.

God damn you. What are you doing up there?

* * *

He was fixing sandwiches, one for himself and one for Tracie. He used the very thin slices of roast beef that came in a package, placing them on top of the non-fat cream cheese substitute. He had purchased them especially for Tracie, figuring that she would want to eat in a healthy fashion so that her figure would not be spoiled. He hoped she liked rye bread. It was his favorite. Instead of chips, he arranged carrot sticks, sliced green pepper, and cherry tomatoes around each plate. It was very attractive.

It had been a long time—two, three years, maybe—since old Abraham had made a visit to town. That was when he had first seen ole Mistuh Death in his chariot. Took his hat off respectful-like when the funeral procession drove slowly by. That was the thing to do when somebody went to the Maker. Pay your respects and rejoice, just like the preacher said. Rejoice cause another sweet little lamb has gone to Jesus. Sorrow was for them left behind, not 'cause somebody died, but 'cause it warn't your time to be with little baby Jesus.

Old Abe couldn't remember why he'd come to town that time. Didn't matter. Here he was again, and nothing much had changed. It was powerful hot with ole Mistuh Sun blazing away down on all that pavement and concrete. Wasn't nice like the woods where a body could alwuz find a cool stream and sit a spell swishing ole Mistuh Feets through the water. Mistuh Toes, too. They alwuz appreciated the consideration. They surely did.

Not like today, when they wuz all crowded in the store-bought shoes, hot and sweaty, with the heat from the sidewalk burning right up into the bottoms of ole Mistuh Feets.

The old man took off the hat and wiped his brow with the

red handkerchief, blinking against the glare of the midday sun. Then, he looked down at the card in his hand. The edges was getting ragged and all pulpy where he had been sweatin' at it. But a body could still see the address there. He reckoned an old man could still find a place when he had to.

He started out down the street, marveling at all the unfamiliar sights and the activity with people scurrying ever' which way.

Lordy, town folks was noisy when they had a mind.

Kate waited, knowing he had been out there the whole time, watching, stalking them, waiting for his opportunity to strike again. They had been the hunted, not the hunters.

And now he had Tracie.

Who did you open the door to? Who did you know well enough to trust? Kate saw a vulnerable and trusting Tracie, like a doe stepping unafraid into a sunny clearing, not knowing that the sights of a rifle were centered on her heart. Did she smile in greeting?

Until the Mace struck.

Kate shook her head violently.

The memories were brutal. Billie Rae spread-eagled to the wooden frame. April hanging from the heavy branch of the tree. What was he doing to Tracie right now? Kate saw Tracie's naked body as she tried to escape the butcher's knife, mouth taped, unable even to scream out the pain of injustice, head twisting frantically.

Oh, Jesus.

"I'm going to take the tape off if you promise not to scream."

Tracie nodded slowly.

He worked a corner of the tape loose. "This won't hurt," he said. He ripped the tape off in one swift motion.

Tracie gasped, but it didn't hurt—not much, anyway.

"Jimmy, please . . ."

"Shh." He put his finger to her lips. "Don't talk yet. First, I'm going to wash your face and comb your hair and then we'll have lunch. Won't that be nice?"

Tracie nodded. She didn't know what else to do.

Yet.

She kept her eyes closed while he washed her face with the soapy washcloth. He rinsed the cloth and then her face, drying it carefully with the towel.

"There, isn't that better?"

Afraid to speak, Tracie nodded again.

"Good. Now I'm going to brush your hair out. It's all tangled."

Tracie closed her eyes. This is just too bizarre. I'm going to scream. She fought the rising panic, biting her lip to stop from crying out, shuddering as he gently stroked her hair with the brush.

Kate was alone with Drew and Wilson Cowles in the living room of the big old house.

Finally, there had been nothing left to do at the house. Or with the car. Or at Tracie's apartment. Officers had taken the keys from her purse and gone there as well, finding nothing to indicate who had kidnapped her, where he had taken his victim.

A command post had been established at the police station where the search for Tracie Sanders would be coordinated.

Still blaming herself, and angry at being so helpless, Kate wanted to scream with frustration. The afternoon was drifting away lazily for everyone but Tracie. For Tracie, time raced all too quickly. If the killer held to his previous patterns,

Tracie had perhaps twelve hours to live, twelve tormented, tortured hours of life remaining. Seven hundred and twenty minutes. Kate watched the second hand of her watch jerk spasmodically around the face, ticking off another minute of her life. And another.

And another.

Like Faustus, Kate wanted to stop time. "Stand still, you ever-moving spheres of Heaven, That time may cease, and midnight never come . . ."

"What?"

"Come not, Lucifer!" Kate cried. "I'll burn my books!"

"Kate, are you all right?"

Kate shook her head, jerking herself away from the mesmerizing sweep of the second hand.

"Christopher Marlowe," Kate said. *"The Tragical History of Doctor Faustus."*

"Jesus!" Drew said. "I thought you were speaking in tongues."

Kate looked at Drew and Wilson Cowles. "Let's go find her, God damn it," she said.

The old man stood outside the office, looking in through the open door. He looked up at the street number above. It was the correct address. But Ms. Kate and Ms. Tracie weren't there. Instead, there were two white men inside, just standing there. "Excuse me, suhs, I needs to speak with the lady who give me this card. Does you know where she is?"

Twenty-eight

It was humiliating to sit half-naked in front of this shambling hulk of a man. It was humiliating to be fed by him, like a child. Tracie didn't want to eat, but neither did she want to anger him, so each time he held the sandwich up for her, she took a small bite. He even wiped her lips with a paper napkin each time. When crumbs fell to her breasts, he brushed them away with his hand. When his hand lingered, Tracie quickly said, "Could I have another bite, please? It's so good."

"Would you like a tomato this time?"

"Yes, please."

Again he put the napkin to her lips.

"What are you going to do to me?" Tracie asked.

Time was her ally, her friend. She had to get him talking, keep him talking, until Kate could find her. Tracie found it strange that she looked upon Kate as her only hope—not the police, not Wilson Cowles. Kate cared. But Kate won't be able to figure it out, either. She'll never find me. She'll never suspect Jimmy. Nobody would. It was hopeless. Unless . . .

"Nothing bad if you like me."

"You know I like you, Jimmy."

"Them others didn't. Nobody's ever liked me, except Kathryn Anne. She was always good to me, talked to me when the others wouldn't. She didn't laugh at me, but she shouldn't have gone and married that fella, either. He wasn't any good for her. Couldn't she tell how much I loved her?"

"Did you ever tell her?"

"Not directly, but she should have known. I don't want to talk about it now."

"Oh, Jimmy, why don't you call Kate and tell her you love her?"

"You're trying to trick me."

"No, Jimmy, I'm not." Please, call Kate, please.

He held the second half of the sandwich for her.

Oh, God, please help me. Tracie took another bite.

"Willie calls you a nigger-loving whore."

"You know him?"

"He wouldn't care if you died."

"I know."

"Please untie me. It hurts so much."

"Not yet."

"When?"

"Soon."

"I have to go to the bathroom."

Jimmy nodded. "I have to undress you the rest of the way."

"Please, Jimmy, can't you just untie me? I won't try to run away; I promise. I want to help you. You could give me something of Sally's to wear."

"I don't trust you. Besides, I saw you naked before. When you went swimming out at the river. You shouldn't do that, you know. It ain't right."

It was another violation of her privacy, her life. God damn

you, what else do you know about me? What else have you seen? "I won't do it again," Tracie said.

"That's right." He untied the ropes that encircled her ankles and knees. Then he went behind her and untied the rope that held her upright. She slumped on the stool when its hold was released. He helped her to stand.

"Please, don't, Jimmy."

"I have to." He released her belt and then unfastened her jeans.

Oh, God, no.

"You're a real blonde," Jimmy said, when she stood naked before him. "I didn't think you were. I thought you were a whore."

"I'm not," Tracie cried, blushing furiously with the added degradation. "I'm not."

He followed her up the steps.

She had to turn sideways to get through the basement door. Upstairs everything looked so normal, despite the fact that the curtains were drawn and the rooms were dim and gloomy. We had dinner here just last week. We sat on that couch looking at his stamp collection, admiring it, praising him.

"Please, won't you at least close the door?" Tracie sighed with relief when he complied with her request. At least, he won't be watching.

She quickly glanced around. There was a small window above the toilet. She might be able to reach the clasp, push it open, scream for help. She turned to the door. Thank God, there was a lock in the doorknob. She knelt and was able to turn it silently with numb fingers.

"How come it's so quiet in there?"

"I'm afraid, Jimmy, please give me a minute."

After, she clambered up on the toilet seat, teetering, almost falling as she turned sideways to push the clamp upward with her numb fingers. It was frozen.

God damn it.

She climbed down and went back to the door, thinking briefly of keeping it locked, but he would only break the flimsy lock. She still was afraid of angering him. Kneeling again, she pushed the lock. God damn it, why wouldn't the window open? It would have given her a chance. Somebody might have heard.

Tracie struggled to her feet and waited. She wasn't going out again until he forced her.

She didn't have to wait long.

When he opened the door, she looked at him with resignation. Tracie went through the bathroom door sideways again and turned to the basement. He was right behind her.

Now.

You have to do it now.

Tracie whirled and struck his face with the dowel tied across her shoulders and her arm, knocking him off balance. She saw the shocked surprise on his face before she turned and ran toward the window. She intended to crash through the window, run into the yard, scream for help.

He caught her easily, spinning her around. She fell heavily to the floor landing on her back, losing her breath momentarily.

He was on her, his face close to hers. "You didn't have to do that. You shouldn't have done that. You promised."

He buried his face between her breasts and cried then. His tears ran over her flesh. If she hadn't been tied, Tracie might have taken him in her arms, to soothe and calm him, offer comfort for a lifetime of pain and ridicule. But she was tied and he was a killer and out of his mind and she didn't know what to say or do. Dear Jesus, help me to know what to do.

"Now I have to punish you," he sobbed.

Twenty-nine

The tragedy of Tracie's disappearance went unnoticed by the vast majority of townspeople. The druggist continued to fill prescriptions, bantering easily with his customers when he delivered their packages to the counter and made out the sales slips. "You feel better, hear?" he counseled each.

Women and a few men pushed shopping carts through the aisles of the supermarket. The loudspeaker at the discount store announced that ice cream cones were on sale for the afternoon. "Choose your flavor," was the message repeated intermittently throughout the afternoon.

Six-packs of beer and single cans of soft drinks were sold at innumerable small grocery stores. Throughout residential neighborhoods, air-conditioning units labored mightily through the afternoon. Babies cried as they awakened from afternoon naps. Workmen started watching the clock as quitting time seemed much closer. A local disk jockey invited listeners to call in and talk about ways to beat the heat.

Of the relatively few people involved in the search for Tracie Sanders, most went about their assignments in a professional manner. Radios hummed as messages were transmitted to the field and others were received. In the corridors, officers laughed and joked. Detectives and police officers passed through the command post. Reports from the roadblocks established on the roads leading to the river were negative. There was no trace of a frightened young woman or her captor.

Kate envied their calm and wished she could mirror their detachment. But that was impossible, of course. She was one of the trio inextricably caught up in the events of the day. Kathryn Anne Gallagher. Tracie Sanders. And a killer. Kate marveled at how fond of Tracie she'd become over a few short weeks and knew that if Tracie died this night, she would blame herself for the rest of her life.

Willie Sanders was brought in and questioned in an adjoining interrogation room. Kate watched and listened as Tracie's brother was questioned.

"Sure, I seen her this morning, but I ain't seen her since. I was only there maybe five minutes."

"We're not accusing you of complicity in your sister's disappearance. We're simply seeking any information that will help find her."

"That's good, cause half a dozen people been watching me shoot pool."

"Did you argue with your sister?" Kate asked.

"Who are you?"

"Mrs. Gallagher is an officer of the court."

"What's that mean?"

"She's a prosecuting attorney."

"You gonna prosecute me?"

I'd love to prosecute you, Kate thought, you creepy little bastard. I know your vile little secret. "Did you argue with your sister?" Kate repeated.

"Yeah, we had words. Same as always. Trace's always too stuck-up to have anything to do with the rest of us. But I don't know where she is. Facta the matter is, I don't much care."

* * *

Outside the command post, life continued on its normal course.

Kate prayed for a miracle.

In darkness and solitude now, Tracie prayed for the strength to withstand the pain and the courage to fight him again if she had another opportunity. No . . . *when* she had another chance. She had to make her own break. Somehow.

Tracie tried to empty her mind of the grim images, but they crowded in—Billie Rae Scott and April Stuart in death. Tracie slowly twisted in the dark and could only think, I'm tied just the way April Stuart was tied when she died.

And the last thing Tracie saw before the cellar went dark was the knife in his hand.

Oh, God, it hurts.

Kate's miracle would have arrived sooner if the two detectives had taken the old man seriously in the beginning. Unable to believe the old man had any real business with either of the names on the card, they had delayed by questioning him at length.

"Which one of these ladies do you want to see?"

"Ms. Kate, or . . ." Without the card to remind him, he had to stop and remember the frisky colt's name. Something out of the funny papers. Dick Tracy that was it. "Ms. Kate or Ms. Tracie."

"What's your business with them?"

"I'm doing a job of work for them," old Abraham said proudly.

"Better take him across the street," one man whispered.

"Shit," the returned whisper came. "You do it if you want. I ain't going over there with this ole fool."

"Well, I will, then."

* * *

He said an hour. Surely an hour has passed. Please, God, have him come back and let me down. It hurts so much. Please. But what will he do when he comes back? Oh, God, why did I try to run? Why did I make him angry?

"There's some old doofer out here wants to see you. Says his name is Abe. Doesn't know his other name. He's older'n dirt."

Kate greeted the old man warmly, to the surprise of the detective. "Mr. Abraham, I'm so glad to see you. We tried to find you yesterday, after you called. We were going to try again today, but . . ."

"Yassum, that was powerful strange. I called jus like you said to do, but you was there and you wasn't."

"It was an answering machine."

"Machine lets you be in two places at the same time?"

Kate smiled wearily. "Something like that." She turned to the detective and asked, "Is there someplace where we can talk?"

"Yes, ma'am. Why don't you use this interrogation room here?"

"Thank you. Would you like something to drink. Mr. Abraham?"

"Yassum, I surely would. It's a mighty hot day out there. If'n a Dr Pepper in a bottle wouldn't be too much to ask."

"I'll get it, ma'am," the detective said. "Would you like something, ma'am?" Might as well be serving the lady lawyer and her old nigger. Ain't nothing else to do. That girl is dead. Plain and simple dead. If she wasn't, she would be soon. No way around that.

"I'll have a Dr Pepper also. Thank you."

* * *

He watched the happy-face clock in the kitchen. The hour was almost up. He had promised it would only last an hour. But she had promised, too. She had promised not to run and she had broken it. He could break his and she would never know the difference. Let her stay like that all night if he wanted and she wouldn't know. Just breeze in tomorrow morning and say, see, that wasn't so long, now, was it? It was all her fault, anyway. He didn't want to do it. She made him do it. Just like the whore Willie said she was.

Trouble was, he got to talking with her. He never talked with the others, just went about his business and done it. Never should have let her talk. She was a lying bitch of a woman, just like the others. Well, he wouldn't believe her lies this time. She had her chance. It was his turn now.

Maybe he should just kill her. Get it over with. It would be better with Kathryn Anne.

The interrogation room smelled of fear. The old wooden table and chairs were burned and scarred from generations of smoldering cigarette butts. Drew might have been in this very room, watching as his life crumpled around him. How many others had sat here—black and white, men and women, the guilty and the innocent? Waiting. Smoking. Praying. Crying. Proclaiming innocence.

He took another picture. While it developed, he went to the rope and loosened it. Tracie fell to the floor in a heap. He tugged at the rope, grunting as he hauled her upright once more.

Please, not again. I can't take any more. It hurts too much.

But he left some slack in the rope attached to the leather

cuffs that held her arms above her head, allowing her to stand, even take a step.

He showed her the picture then. Her eyes were wide and frightened above the hard rubber ball gag protruding from her mouth. The camera had even captured the saliva that dribbled from the corners of her mouth and dripped to her chest.

She used her eyes to plead with him, took an imploring step forward. Please. At least, take the gag out. Don't leave me like this.

He touched her breast. It was wet and slippery with her saliva. She didn't cringe or pull away this time, but he saw the revulsion in her eyes. She couldn't hide that.

He turned away. She was like all the others. She would have to die like all the others.

At the top of the stairs he looked back at her with sadness before flipping the light switch off.

Tracie moaned helplessly as the closing door plunged her into darkness again.

"It come to me sudden-like, in the middle of the night. It's hard to remember sometimes. Time was . . ." His voice drifted off. He took a swallow from his Dr Pepper and put it back on the scarred table. He looked at Kate, waiting.

"And what did you remember, Mr. Abraham?" Kate asked gently.

The old man frowned, brightened. "Membered where I seen ole Mistuh Death before."

"You saw him?"

"Yassum, I did. Shoulda told you before, but I'se afraid. White folks is peculiar-like. Don't do no good for an old black man to go interferin' in they's business. Not when they's a white woman involved."

"You saw him kill a woman?"

"Nossum, she was already dead. Saw ole Mistuh Death again, though. Thought he was come for me next."

"You saw him before?"

"Sometime back, ole Abe, he came into town for sumpin. Don't member why now. But they was a funeral and ole Mistuh Death, he was a drivin' his chariot."

"A hearse?"

"I reckon."

Jesus Christ!

Jimmy. He drove the hearse. Mister Death in his chariot. Jimmy drove the God-damned hearse at Billie Rae's funeral.

The anonymous notes flashed through her mind, each letter exactly aligned. She saw, too, row after row of precisely placed stamps, page after page, album after album.

"Mister Abraham, you wait right here. I'll be right back."

"I ain't done nothin' wrong?"

Kate leaned over and kissed the old man's cheek. "You haven't done anything wrong at all."

Kate hurried across the hall. "I know who he is," she announced. "And I think I know where he took Tracie."

He went out in the backyard and cut a long and willowy branch from the tree, trimming the leaves off right there in the shade. The whore needed a good paddling. That was the trouble with the stuck-up bitch. Needed to lay down the law and let her know who was boss.

He giggled. That was a good one. Lay down the law to a lawyer. He quickly turned serious again.

He didn't want to do it, but there was no getting around it. He had to do it for her own good. Otherwise, he'd have to kill her. If she didn't straighten out after this, he would kill her, by God.

And now he'd have to sharpen the knife again too. Give her a couple of extra for that.

"What's so funny, Jimmy?"

It was the old busybody next door, leaning on the fence.

"Oh, nothing much, Mrs. Cafferty. Just thinking."

"What'cha doing with them sticks?"

"Just whittling, Mrs. Cafferty, just whittling."

"You heard from your sister yet?"

"No, ma'am. Expect I'll get a card soon. Expect you'll get one, too."

"I hope so. It sure must be exciting to travel Europe and all."

"Well, I have to go, Mrs. Cafferty."

"Okay, Jimmy. You take care, hear?"

Kate's announcement stunned the small group of men in the command center. Lew Martins looked at her incredulously. Wilson Cowles finally asked, "How?"

Kate explained.

"Jesus, Kate, Mister Death in his chariot, and you believe him?"

"Yes, I do. And besides, what else do we have?"

"We can't just go busting in there accusing him of kidnap and murder. Maybe you do things different out in Los Angeles, but times have changed in Mississippi. We need probable cause. We need warrants."

"Get them."

"What's the probable cause?"

"Abraham has identified a suspect in Billie Rae Scott's murder. Jesus, that's probable cause in my book."

"He's an old man, for Christ's sake. Pretty near a hundred years old."

"He's still got eyes."

"How good?"

"Good enough to track deer every hunting season. My

brother told me everybody uses him as a guide. If they want to get a deer."

Martins looked at Wilson Cowles. "You're the prosecuting attorney. Do we have probable cause?"

Cowles nodded. "If I were a judge, I'd issue a search warrant."

Martins sighed. "Find me a judge."

He was using the whetstone on the knife when he saw the first police car pull up. It was followed by a second and a third.

He didn't panic, but he went to the gun cabinet and took his father's old double barrel, breaking it, loading it. He knew exactly what he had to do. He had to make them go away. He was on vacation, and if they didn't go away, it would all be spoiled. He couldn't let that happen.

There she was, the old fool from next door, babbling away to them, pointing to the house. Now they'd know he was here for sure. The meddling old bitch. Never did have any use for Old Lady Cafferty. If she wasn't so mean and ugly, he'd have gutted her a long time ago. Shoulda done it anyway.

He opened the front door and stuck the shotgun through. In the street, guns were quickly drawn. "Go away and leave me alone." He punctuated the command by pulling the first trigger on the shotgun. He fired above their heads, but it got their attention anyway. Everyone jumped and ducked behind cars. Sent Mrs. Cafferty scrambling down the street, cawing like the old crow she was. Just had to laugh at that sight.

Jimmy closed the door and went to sit where he could see what was going on through the lace curtains hanging over the big front window. He put the revolver next to the box of shotgun shells, cradled the shotgun across his lap, and settled down to see what they would do next.

There were shotguns out there now, too, pointed at the

house across the hoods of police cars. Didn't matter so long as they went away and didn't bother him.

After the "shots fired" call went out, no one bothered with the quiet approach anymore. Sirens disturbed the quiet evening streets. Blockades were set up at each end of the block. Houses that might be in the line of fire were evacuated. Knots of curious neighbors were pushed away, forced to gather behind barricades, standing on tiptoe and stretching and craning their necks to see what was happening.

Tracie heard the single blast from the shotgun. Jesus, what's happening? And when she heard the faint wail of sirens, she was filled with hope. They've found me. Thank God, Kate's found me. She'll know what to do.

Her elation was quickly replaced by despair. What if he decides to kill me? Now, before Kate can say or do anything. Please, no, I don't want to die.

Tracie swung her legs from the floor and hung by her wrists, hoping to pull the rope free. If she could dislodge the ring bolt from the wall, she would be able to move, hide. But the rope and the bolt were unyielding. All she could do was stand and wait for her fate to be decided.

When Kate and Wilson Cowles arrived, nothing was happening. They joined Captain Martins behind a police car where he was conferring with his subordinates.

"Well, guess you was right," he said, as Kate approached. "Best get ready to duck if the door opens again."

"What's happened?" Kate asked.

"Apparently, the suspect opened the door, told my men to

go away and leave him alone, and fired a single shot from a shotgun."

"Anyone hurt?"

"Naw, he fired over their heads. Killed a couple a birds in the tree across the street. Spoiled their evening. Used the bullhorn to ask him to come out peaceful-like. Didn't say anything to that. House is quiet. No movement. Nothing."

"I want to talk with him," Kate said. "He knows me. Maybe I can talk him out."

"I'd rather talk than send my men in against a shotgun." Martins turned to a uniformed sergeant. "Robbins, take Mrs. Gallagher here to one of them houses we evacuated. Use their telephone."

The telephone rang and rang. Please, Jimmy, answer the phone. Answer the God-damned phone.

Jimmy looked at the telephone when it rang. He smiled, but he didn't answer it. It rang for the longest time and then stopped. Jimmy wasn't worried. He knew she'd call back.

Since the gunshot and the initial whine of sirens grinding down, the house had been silent. Tracie strained to hear the slightest sound, the twisting of the doorknob, anything.

Tracie's tortured breathing was the only sound in the cellar, and it was deafening in her ears. Not knowing what was happening was almost worse than if the door opened and he suddenly appeared, knife in hand. Almost.

Tracie swung her legs off the floor again in another futile effort to pull the rope free.

* * *

Maybe I misdialed the number, Kate thought. She pressed the numbers carefully. It rang. There was no mistake this time.

"Hello."

Thank God. "Hello, Jimmy."

"I knew it would be you, Kathryn Anne."

"Are you okay, Jimmy?"

"Sure, I'm on vacation."

"Is Tracie all right?"

"Yes."

"May I talk with her, Jimmy? Please."

"She can't come to the phone right now." He giggled, a high girlish squeal. "She's all tied up. She's been a bad girl."

Jesus Christ. "I have to know she's all right, Jimmy. I'm very fond of Tracie. She's like one of my own daughters or my little sister. You can understand that, can't you, Jimmy?"

"I guess so."

"Please, let me talk with her then."

"You can come in and see her," he said, "if you want."

"I'm going in there."

"No, you ain't. You surely ain't. That's the kind of trouble we don't need. Let him get two hostages instead of one."

"Do you have a better idea? He'll kill her."

"Maybe he will and maybe he won't. I'm not taking the chance that he'll kill two of you. We got a hostage negotiator coming down from Memphis."

"He could take hours to get here."

"Two, three hours, maybe."

"Tracie could be dead by then. For Christ's sake, he thinks he loves me. He's not going to do anything to the woman he loves."

"That's crazy."

"Yes, it is. I know that, but I'll be all right."

"How many crazy people have you dealt with?"

"I was married, wasn't I?" Kate said. That gives new meaning to *non sequitur,* she thought.

"Well, I reckon you got pluck, even if you ain't got much sense." Martins turned to look at the silent house. "Shit," he whispered before turning back to Kate. "You be careful, hear?"

"If I scream, come get me."

"We'll do that. Right smart."

Kate took a deep breath and turned then, stepping between the police cars to walk up the sidewalk to the big old house where she had played many times as a child. Poor Sally. She's in Europe and doesn't even know this is happening.

The floodlights behind Kate cast her shadow against the porch as she climbed the stairs and knocked formally on the door.

"It's me, Jimmy."

"Come in, Kathryn Anne," he replied pleasantly. "It's not locked."

Thirty

Kate stepped through the door, curiously unafraid. Despite the floodlights, much of the living room was in shadow. The glow of the flickering lights from the police cars outside tinted the room with a devilish red glow.

"Lock the door, please, Kathryn Anne." His voice came from the darkness.

Kate turned and slid the bolt closed. He seemed calm.

"Thank you."

"You're welcome."

"Would you like to sit down?"

"May I see Tracie? She must be frightened."

"Later."

"All right."

"Sit on the couch, where I can see you," Jimmy said. "Please," he added, as though just remembering the manners he had been taught as a child.

"All right," Kate repeated. God, we're being so polite.

"Would you like some coffee or something?" Jimmy asked. "We drank all the lemonade."

"No, thank you, Jimmy, but I'll make some for you, if you like."

"I'm not thirsty right now. Maybe later."

"Whenever you say." He smiled at her. "What are they going to do, Kathryn Anne?"

"Nothing right now. We have lots of time to talk. I want to help you."

"What can you do?"

"I can do a lot. Find you a good lawyer. A doctor. You're troubled, Jimmy."

"No! They'll put me back in that place. I didn't like it there."

"We'll find someplace else for you, then. Someplace nice."

"Why didn't you come, like I asked?"

"The first letter? The one you sent Drew?"

"None of this would have happened if you'd just come back."

"I didn't know, Jimmy. Drew didn't send me the note."

"He should have. I love you," he cried, an anguished voice from the shadows of the room. "Couldn't he tell that? Couldn't you tell?"

"I didn't know," Kate said.

"I always loved you."

"I didn't know," Kate repeated helplessly. Find another topic. Talk about something else—anything. "Have you heard from Sally?"

"You should have come," Jimmy accused. "You made me do it."

"How did it start, Jimmy? If I'm going to help you, I have to know."

"Because they laughed at me. The first one laughed at me. She wasn't nothing but a whore and she laughed. Then she didn't laugh anymore. The second one, too. She had her chance. She ain't laughing anymore, either."

Was there a tremor in his voice? Was he crying? Kate couldn't tell in the eerie flickering light. "I'm sorry," she said. For whom? Jimmy? The murdered women? Everyone?

"It's too late," he said.

"I'll help you as much as I can," Kate said. "That's all I can do now. Everyone wants to help you. Even Tracie, I'll bet."

"I don't believe you."

"Let's go ask her."

"If we go down there, the police will come in."

"I'll go outside and tell them not to do anything. Will that be all right? And then I'll come right back."

"Promise?"

"Of course, Jimmy. I've never lied to you, have I?"

"No," he admitted reluctantly.

"Just wait right here for me and then we'll go see Tracie. Okay?"

"Yes."

Kate went to the door. "I'm coming out," she called, and then stepped outside into the glare of the floodlights. She blinked and held her forearm above her eyes to shield the light.

"What's going on?" Martins asked. "Is Tracie alive?"

"Yes."

"Have you seen her?"

"No, but I believe him. We're talking. I think I can keep him talking. I can bring him out without anyone getting hurt."

"Guns?"

"He has a shotgun and a pistol. There are more in a gun cabinet."

"Christ."

"It won't come to that," Kate said. "Trust me. I'm going back now. He's going to let me see Tracie."

"Where is she?"

"In the basement."

"Christ, Kate, I don't like it. If he gets both of you down there . . . I don't think you should go back. You can talk to him from out here. Use the telephone."

"I promised," Kate said. "He won't hurt me."

* * *

Jimmy waited patiently for Kathryn Anne to return. He trusted her to keep her promise, but if she didn't, well, that would be just too bad for her friend in the basement. And when she returned, he would keep his promise, too. That was only fair. He would take Kathryn Anne to Tracie.

What then?

The headache was returning. All of the sirens and the glaring lights brought it on. It would be better downstairs. They couldn't reach him there and make him go back to that place. Not even Kathryn Anne could make him go back.

"The switch is to your left."

Kate felt for the switch, found it, flipped it upward. The basement was bright in contrast with the gloom of the living room, all of the light focused on Tracie.

Oh, God.

Kate bit her lip to keep from crying out when she looked down at the naked young woman. She averted her eyes and went down the steps carefully, slowly, as in a nightmare, fearing she would trip and fall.

Jimmy followed.

At the bottom of the steps, Kate turned slowly to face him. "I want to take that thing out of her mouth. May I?"

Jimmy nodded.

Kate went to Tracie. "It's all right now."

Tracie nodded.

Kate unbuckled the strap that held the ball in her mouth. She had to help Tracie expel it.

"Oh, God," Tracie gasped, when the ball fell away into Kate's hand. "I was afraid you wouldn't come."

"It's okay, Tracie, it's okay." Kate reached out and touched Tracie's shoulder tentatively. Then she couldn't help herself.

She embraced Tracie, hugging her tightly, smelling the fear and the sweat on her body. It felt strange to embrace a naked woman, but it didn't matter. Tracie was still alive. Thank God, she was alive.

Kate released her and turned to Jimmy. "I'm going to let her down."

"No!" he said sharply. "Leave her. I like to look at her." His tone of voice softened. "She's pretty, not like you, of course, Kathryn Anne. You were always the prettiest girl for me."

"Thank you." She turned back to Tracie, shrugging helplessly as though to say, Just a little longer now.

"I'm all right, Kate."

Kate nodded and stroked Tracie's cheek.

"There are chairs in the corner," Jimmy said. He motioned with the shotgun. "Bring one for me. Please."

They were old plastic chairs that stacked. Kate removed two from the stack and carried them across the basement.

Kate sat where she could see both Tracie and Jimmy. "Tracie's a defense lawyer, Jimmy. She can tell you how we can help. Will you listen to her, Jimmy?"

"She lied before. She said she wouldn't try to run and she did."

"Tracie?"

"I was afraid, Jimmy. I didn't know what to do."

"Will you help Jimmy now?"

"Yes."

"You see, Jimmy? We're your friends. People don't treat their friends like this." Kate nodded in Tracie's direction.

"You can let her down, I guess." Jimmy looked at the floor.

"Thank you," Kate said. "Do you have something of Sally's she can put on?"

"There's an old raincoat in the hall closet."

"Would you get it, please?"

"Okay."

* * *

They were still out there waiting. I won't go back. I'll die first. We'll all die, before you make me go back.

Kate knelt at the ring bolt and fumbled with the knot. Her fingers trembled and she broke a fingernail before the knot loosened.

Tracie's arms fell. "Oh, God, Kate, I was so afraid."

"I know." Kate unfastened the cuffs and massaged Tracie's wrists.

"What are we going to do?"

"Talk."

Jimmy returned with the raincoat and handed it to Kate.

Tracie clutched it tightly around her.

"I'll get you a chair." Kate placed the chair next to her own.

Jimmy was silent.

"Do you want to talk, Jimmy, or should we go upstairs now? No one will hurt you if you give yourself up."

"Do you have a boyfriend now?" Jimmy asked.

"Yes."

"Are you going to marry him?"

"I don't know."

"How come?"

"I don't know that either."

"Isn't he nice to you?"

"It's not that. He's a very good man. I just don't know yet. I don't know if I want to be married again."

"I'd be good to you, Kathryn Anne. You could look at my stamp collection anytime you wanted. I'd even show you how to put them in. We could do it together. I'll teach you everything there is to know about stamps. There's a lot, you know."

"I'm sure there is, Jimmy." Kate watched him disintegrate, regress into a small petulant child. "But I have to be honest with you. I never felt like that about you, but you were always special. You were my friend."

Jimmy looked at her sadly. All he had to do was lift the revolver and pull the trigger. Then, Kathryn Anne would belong to him forever, to love forever. No one would ever have her again. She would be his. Always.

He lifted the revolver slowly.

"Jimmy, please, no," Kate said. "You said you loved me."

Horrified, Tracie watched the gun come up.

"Goodbye, Kathryn Anne. I do love you." He put the barrel of the revolver in his mouth.

"No, Jimmy!" Kate screamed. Too late.

The shot was deafening in the confines of the basement.

Epilogue

The summer would be over soon, another season ended. The year was slowly dying, and the rebirth of spring was distant.

The funeral for the Delta Ripper had been sparsely attended. Sally was there, a few distant relatives, Kate Gallagher. Tracie Sanders did not attend. There was one local reporter. The others had turned to other stories, other crimes. Following the lead of the others at the service, Kate threw a clod of dark, damp earth into the grave and then turned away to embrace Sally briefly. She flew home that night, shunning all publicity, avoiding those who wanted to treat her as a heroine. She didn't feel like a heroine. Not at all.

The sound of earth falling against the casket echoed in Kate's mind, following her as she attempted a return to normalcy and the daily routine of work, and quiet evenings with Melissa and Harry, and then with Tracie when she arrived for a two-week visit.

Tracie had recovered quickly. When she arrived on a Saturday afternoon after a three-day drive with Sam, she jumped out of the car and ran to embrace Kate. "God, it's good to see you," she cried.

"It's good to see you, too. Did you have any trouble finding the house?"

Tracie laughed and said, "I followed your directions exactly. Turn left just before you get to the ocean. It was easy."

While Kate was at work, Tracie explored Los Angeles, driving up the coast to Malibu or down the coast to Laguna Beach to wander alone among the shops and art galleries. She was always back before Kate.

Their evenings were quiet, spent with Melissa or Harry, or sometimes both. Only occasionally did Kate see Tracie's eyes empty. She knew then, Tracie was remembering and waited for her to speak.

"Oh, Kate, sometimes I just want to cry or scream or something."

"I know."

"I wonder if he would really have killed me . . . like the others."

"I wonder, too."

"He could have killed us both."

"But he didn't. We're alive, and we're going to go on. That's what people do."

Kate took Tracie to work one day, introducing her to her friends and colleagues and Philip Moore. Kate could no longer call him by his nickname. Old Mister Death had come too close.

Old Abe had received a $5,000 reward. The authorities had balked at giving it to the old man, but Kate had insisted. The old man had taken the money gratefully. "Ole Abe, he's rich now." The old man wanted to live to be a hundred, wanted to greet the new century. Maybe he would, too. The money would help.

They had lunch with Rainey one day and she felt the pangs of jealousy as she watched her former lover banter easily with Tracie, saying he would visit her in Arizona one day when she was settled. Maybe he would, maybe he wouldn't;

plans went awry. In either case, Kate would wish him well. Tracie could do a lot worse than Rainey. He would love her, be good to her.

Someday, Kate thought, I'll marry Harry, and perhaps Tracie will marry Rainey. And we'll visit each other and be friends. And we'll forget what happened this summer.

Someday.

A single long streak of white marred the sky above the Pacific Ocean, stretching as far as the eye could see, finally disappearing to the south. In its wake, strange celestial lights filled the evening sky. Orange and red and amber and black hues swirled into a majestic vortex, as though the very heavens were opening to allow the hand of God to reach down and finally take evil from the world.

The two women stood at the end of the long pier jutting into the Pacific. Around them, fishermen still hoping for a last strike before the day was done, young couples in love and holding hands, attendants at the bait shop—all were hushed and looking with awe to the shining cathedral window above.

"It's beautiful," Tracie whispered. "It's like God telling us to have hope."

"Yes," Kate agreed.

The mood was broken when a man nearby proclaimed loudly, "It's probably a rocket from Vandenburg."

Relief rippled through the people on the pier. They laughed nervously, the mystery explained. It was not Judgment Day—not yet. There was time enough to beg forgiveness for sins committed and uncommitted.

Kate turned to Tracie. "I still wish you'd reconsider. Phil said he'd hire you in a New York minute, and I'm going to miss you. I've gotten used to having you around the last couple of weeks."

"I'm going to miss you, too, Kate, but I have to go." Tracie turned and leaned against the rail, looking back at the metropolis that stretched as endlessly as the fading contrail above. "Sometimes, when I'm out here, everything is so peaceful and quiet. But when we go back there . . ." She gestured to the city lights.

"I know. It's not a very pleasant place sometimes. We go through our lives with blinders, filtering out the bad and the ugly. It's how we survive, I suppose."

"I want peace and solitude, Kate. And Arizona isn't very far away. A few hours' drive—that's all. We'll be able to visit often."

"Melissa's going to miss you. She adores you. I think she likes having another sister around."

Tracie smiled. "You know, when I was driving out here, after putting everything in storage, I felt so free . . . it was the first time in my life. But at the same time, I was running from everything that happened. You've helped me stop running. Melissa, too. And Harry and Rainey."

"We take care of our stray kittens," Kate said, smiling.

"You do a very good job of it, too. I'm grateful, but I have to go. It's the dream."

They walked back home through quiet neighborhoods.

"It was a missile from Vandenburg," Kate said, going into the living room from the kitchen. "I just heard it on the news."

Tracie looked up from the book she was reading. "I liked it better as a message from God."

"Yes," Kate said. "I did, too."